and Carina Press

*Bad Judgment*
*Loose Cannon* (Woodbury Boys #1)

**Coming soon in the Woodbury Boys series**

*Rough Trade*

To Mom and Rod,
without whom this book wouldn't exist, because
I would've had to quit writing to work at Denny's,
which wouldn't have helped either me or Denny's.
And to Mitch, because all the books are due to you.

# HARD LINE

―――

## SIDNEY BELL

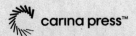

If you purchased this book without a cover you should be aware that this book is stolen property. It was reported as "unsold and destroyed" to the publisher, and neither the author nor the publisher has received any payment for this "stripped book."

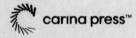 carina press™

ISBN-13: 978-1-335-99684-8

Recycling programs for this product may not exist in your area.

Hard Line

Copyright © 2018 by Miriam Macrae

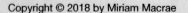

All rights reserved. Except for use in any review, the reproduction or utilization of this work in whole or in part in any form by any electronic, mechanical or other means, now known or hereafter invented, including xerography, photocopying and recording, or in any information storage or retrieval system, is forbidden without the written permission of the publisher, Harlequin Enterprises Limited, 22 Adelaide St. West, 40th Floor, Toronto, Ontario M5H 4E3, Canada.

This is a work of fiction. Names, characters, places and incidents are either the product of the author's imagination or are used fictitiously, and any resemblance to actual persons, living or dead, business establishments, events or locales is entirely coincidental.

This edition published by arrangement with Harlequin Books S.A.

® and TM are trademarks of the publisher. Trademarks indicated with ® are registered in the United States Patent and Trademark Office, the Canadian Intellectual Property Office and in other countries.

www.CarinaPress.com

**Printed in U.S.A.**

# HARD LINE

*Part One*

# Chapter One

*2011*

Later, Tobias Benton would run through the day over and over to figure out what it was that'd set him off. It would take months to nail it down, but once he did, it would be as impossible to miss as a house on fire. *Of course*, he would think later. *Of course that's it.*

But in that moment, sitting in the squeaky chair in his high school guidance counselor's office and holding the blank career quiz with the bright red *see me!* scrawled across the top, he was lost.

"I thought this was voluntary." The page was trembling in his hand; he pushed it onto the desk, neatly aligning the bottom edge of the paper with the edge of the desk. The ominous ticking of the mahogany clock on the mantelpiece was very loud, the ceramic Jesus faintly admonishing from his crucifix on the wall. "I didn't know I could get in trouble."

"You're not in trouble," Mrs. Marry said. She was a squat, horse-faced woman with kind eyes and yellow hair. She was wearing a brown suit and Tobias liked her. She was a good listener, and even after she'd met his parents, she'd never asked what it was like being the white son of a Haitian couple or whether he felt lost in a houseful of Caribbean adoptees or if the Alcides really believed in zombies or spirits. She'd acted as though there was nothing strange about his family, which he appreciated, because there'd been more than a few teachers and school officials over the years who had.

Still, he was less inclined to like her when she called him into her office like this. His stomach ached.

"I'm not in trouble," he repeated doubtfully.

"I have some questions, that's all."

"About my quiz? I can do it now. I didn't know I needed to. I'll do it now."

"I don't want you to take the quiz, Tobias." She leaned forward. "I want you to consider what it means that you didn't write anything down."

"I just didn't do it." He looked over her shoulder and through the window. The parking lot was a congested mess of teenagers in shiny BMWs and Mercedes leaning on their horns and cutting each other off now that school was over. Tobias's parents were big believers that showering children with expensive material goods ran counter to crafting a compassionate, generous human being; unlike most of his friends, he didn't have a car and usually rode the bus. If he didn't get out of here soon, he would have to take the activities bus, which left two hours later. That wouldn't be the end of the world. He liked the halls when they were quiet and he could fill the slow minutes with studying. Either way, though, he needed to get out of Mrs. Marry's office.

"We've talked a lot about medical school." She leaned back in her chair and folded her fingers across her belly. "How much time have we spent discussing science courses, both here and at Denver University? Enough time that I'd think these career questions would be easy to answer."

"I'm not sure why you want me to do the quiz, then." Tobias wished he could loosen his tie but he didn't dare. School rules didn't allow it, and he could imagine the raised eyebrow he'd get from Manman if he tried. It didn't matter that she wasn't here in the room; she would know. She always knew. Mothers were weird like that.

"I don't want you to do the quiz," Mrs. Marry said.

"I can. I will."

"Tobias." She licked her lips, studying him like he was an adorable but obnoxious pet.

He shifted in his chair and the vinyl squeaked. The office seemed suddenly very hot.

"You're not in trouble. You didn't do anything wrong. But I do think it's interesting that a kid who's been in my office for guidance seven times this year about preparing for an eventual career in medicine didn't fill out a simple five-minute quiz about what you want to do when you graduate."

"I didn't think it was necessary." He swallowed. His throat was dry. "You already know what I'm going to be."

"You started it. You wrote your name."

He had. He'd sat at his stupid desk in homeroom the other day and stared at the stupid paper with its litany of ten stupid questions and he hadn't been able to make his hand move. He'd had to concentrate to write his name, and the letters had come out too sharp and aggressive to be his.

"I thought I was supposed to."

"Tobias, you clearly began the quiz. And then you clearly didn't answer the questions. Why not?"

"Because you already know what I'm going to be when

I grow up." *Grow up*, he thought, and mentally rolled his eyes. Like he wouldn't be eighteen in a matter of weeks. Like this—all of this, school, quizzes, meetings—weren't merely a stopgap between him and decades of practicing medicine.

"The quiz isn't about what you're going to be. The quiz is about what you want to be."

"I know that," he snapped, and now she was looking at him with a line of concern between her bushy eyebrows. He shouldn't have snapped at her, but really. All this for a useless quiz. As if the world weren't set in stone. "Look, I'll fill it out now."

"You're willfully misunderstanding me," she said calmly. "And we both know it."

"We're starting on Nixon's gastrointestinal tract tomorrow in Anatomy and Physiology," he said, and she blinked. He thought she probably remembered the name he'd given to the dead cat he was dissecting in his science class because they'd talked about his anxiety attack after that first day of the unit a few weeks ago, as well as his desire to never, ever cut up a once-living thing again. But maybe not. He wouldn't want to think about it anymore if he didn't want to. He'd thought that naming it after a bad guy might help, a little bit of gallows humor, but it really hadn't. He had nightmares about that damn cat.

She came around the desk to sit in the chair next to his, leaning forward and pressing one hand awkwardly on the arm of his chair, like she wanted to reach out to him but the standards and practices of engaging with teenagers in a school forum wouldn't allow her to. Or maybe she didn't actually want to touch him but thought it seemed therapeutic to seem like she did. Or maybe—

"Tobias. It's okay if you don't want to be a doctor."

He jolted to his feet. "I have to go."

"Wait—"

"No, I forgot that I have a, a, um, a thing?" Why wouldn't his backpack move? He yanked and the whole chair skidded, because the strap of his bag was caught on the leg. What had he been talking about? He searched for anything he could possibly be… "Drama Club."

"You're in Drama Club now?" she asked, frowning.

He yanked on his bag again. "It's an interview. Um, a tryout, I mean."

"Tobias, as your guidance counselor, I would prefer—"

"I feel guided." He pushed on the chair so it tipped and the strap came loose. He stumbled toward the door, only realizing he was walking backward when he bumped into the door and the knob tried to take out one of his kidneys. The left kidney was located slightly superior to the right, his brain announced helpfully, and he nodded. He was—nothing in his head made sense.

"Gotta go." Tobias fumbled his way out of the office.

She followed him past the iron-haired secretary typing at the desk, who looked up at him as he blew past her, rustling a couple of papers in his wake. "Sorry," he said.

"Tobias," Mrs. Marry called. "Come back. We need to discuss this."

"Gonna be late." He finally escaped, his shoes and breathing loud in the echoing hallway as he hurried toward the rear exit of the school where the buses were. He'd made it in time; the first one was only now pulling out. He jogged to catch up to his, thinking only about getting home so he could study and read and do all the things he was supposed to be doing, and he could—

Mrs. Marry was going to drag him back into her office tomorrow, he realized.

She might even call his house.

His stomachache got worse.

He wasn't the first one home. All of his siblings were already here: he could hear Ruby's violin wafting down from the second floor, and Mirlande in the kitchen walking Guy through some terms he would need for a class presentation, because Guy's mastery of English pronunciation, though very good after nine years in the US, didn't quite extend to words with multiple Rs in them. Darlin was complaining in *Kreyòl* about America giving him too many states to memorize, and Marie was humming in the background, probably listening to her iPod even though that was against the rules.

Normally, Tobias would join them. As the oldest, it was his responsibility to keep everyone else on task—to make Guy double-check his geometry problems, to tell Marie to put her music away, to ensure that Ruby did something academic in addition to practicing her Mozart. He never had to do much to keep Mirlande working hard—she was only two years younger, and very much like him, devoted to her studies. They would eat papayas and drink *limonade* and work until their parents got home, at which point homework would be checked and dinner begun. Tobias hesitated in the hallway out of sight, just listening, then went upstairs instead.

He unloaded his backpack, putting everything away neatly, getting out what he would need for the next day. He used the handheld dustbuster to clean out the trash from the bottom of the pockets. When that didn't help, he walked around the room, looking into every nook and cranny for any signs of chaos. There was no thought involved in these organizational routines, only habit, only order. He'd taken comfort in it before: his books on their shelves alphabetized by author, his shirts grouped by color in the closet, the fronts all facing to the right, always to the right, his hard copies of his school exams and papers filed by course number and date in the small file cabinet.

There was nothing to be done. Everything was as it should be. He sat on the bed. The sun came in hot through the window, making him sweat despite the air conditioning; he got up, closed the blinds, and sat back down again.

His feet wouldn't stay still on the carpet, his toes following the tracks from the vacuuming he'd given it the day before. It was the oddest thing; his body usually weighed so much more than it should. Usually it was a fight to get up a flight of stairs or to get through his homework without falling asleep. Usually, he could admit, it was hard enough making his way through conversations without losing his train of thought.

This was the most energy he'd had in months. Maybe even a year. There still wasn't color, exactly, but things had definitely sped up. He didn't remember the world feeling this way: overbright, too jagged, his heart hammering—he was probably tachycardic. It was very unpleasant, the way everything was rushing and pulsing inside him.

That stupid quiz. Why hadn't he filled out that stupid quiz? Dream job: doctor. It wasn't hard. He'd written the word a million times, made plans a million times more complicated than a stupid senior-year career quiz. All he'd had to do was fill it out and none of this would be happening. Mrs. Marry wouldn't have looked at him like he was an idiot and she wouldn't be worried about him now, wouldn't call to explain that the Alcide family's oldest son, the young man following in his parents' foot-steps, couldn't manage to answer ten simple questions.

He bent over and tried to breathe into his knees. The temperature had spiked in the room. That was why he was sweating. He couldn't—he had—that stupid, *stupid* quiz. He wasn't sure what he'd expected to happen when he turned it in without filling it out, but he'd hoped…he'd thought…but it was all still *here*.

He got up and went to the bathroom.

He locked the door behind him. It wasn't anything. His younger brothers and sisters always knocked, but you never knew. He sat on the edge of the tub. The porcelain was cool through the denim of his jeans. It might've been nice, given how overheated he was, but it was strangely distant. His legs weren't his, that was the problem. They were very far away.

Somehow, he'd gotten Marie's manicure scissors. She was constantly complaining about her eyebrows, and had several different tweezers, and she would sometimes trim them with these scissors, and she usually kept them in the drawer, but right now they were in his hand.

He tugged up the sleeve on his left arm.

He wondered how much force it would take. He wasn't going to do anything. There wasn't anything to be done about any of it, not really. He was simply wondering.

The next thing he remembered was sitting on the floor in Ruby's room beside her bedroom door. His young-est sister was only six, and while the whole not-spoiling thing meant that the rest of the kids shared bedrooms, no one could stand the repetition of her constant practic-ing, so they'd all agreed as a family that she should have a room to herself.

Her decoration choices leaned toward hot pink and garish purple and extravagant frills of fabric on any object that would stand still, but all frivolity vanished the second she picked up her instrument to practice. Then she became an intent general poring over tactical maps. More driven than any of the adults who fostered her gift.

The family had begun adoption proceedings for Ruby during a brief Catholic missionary trip to Jamaica a few years ago and she'd had trouble adjusting to the States. It had been a twist of fate, Ruby finding the violin. She had literally walked into a street performer playing outside a shop at the 16th Street Mall one weekend while the whole family had gone to lunch for Marie's birthday. Tobias had given Ruby a couple of dollars to put in the woman's case, but Ruby hadn't seemed to realize what the money was for. She'd stood still as a statue, listening; they'd had to drag her away. It was the most interest she'd shown in anything since she arrived from Jamaica, so a few days later, she'd had a cheap practice violin of her own and lessons with a local teacher who'd been throwing around words like *prodigy* and *generational talent* by the end of the first week.

Now, barely two years later, his sister played Mozart and Bach and Beethoven for hours in her bedroom every day.

Tobias loved being in Ruby's room. All right, granted, it was annoying to hear the same bits of music repeated ad nauseum, but by the end of each session she usually gravitated to pieces she knew in their entirety. She so rarely became distracted—a miraculous thing in a six-year-old—and the rest of the household was so respectful of her practicing time, that it was downright peaceful in Ruby's room.

Quiet. It was so quiet here. No noise could possibly reach him past the music.

He listened to her play for what seemed like ages, until it registered that his shirt was soaked, that the half a roll of toilet paper he'd wrapped around his forearm hadn't been able to sop up the mess after all. He'd forgotten about it, and he'd let up on the direct pressure too soon.

He couldn't let Ruby see the blood.

He stood up and let himself out without speaking.

And froze in the hallway. He could smell *diri kole* cooking, the thyme and garlic scents familiar and normally delicious, and hear his other siblings downstairs talking to Papa, and he realized he'd lost a fair bit of time. It was time to eat. It was dinnertime, and Manman was coming upstairs, saying, "There you are. I've been—" Then her gaze went from his face to his shirt, and that was the end of the quiet.

Later he would remember this too, although this memory never made it past his lips to anyone else's ears: his father looming over him, blue nitrile gloves on his hands, which clamped down on the wound in Tobias's arm with thick cushions of gauze, his head jerking up when Marie began shrieking at the sight of her bloody scissors in the sink in the bathroom. Tobias would always remember the way Papa dropped into nearly inaudible, trembling *Kreyòl*. *"Kisa ki rive ou?"*

*What happened to you,* he asked, bewildered, as if he couldn't comprehend that it was Tobias's choice turning the hall carpet red, Tobias who had acted.

When they got back from the hospital hours later, his brothers and sisters were in bed already, and Manman was waiting on the sofa in the light of a single lamp, her bare feet tucked up underneath her, a closed book resting on the arm of the chair—something about water-colors, a recent interest—her reading glasses dangling from the chain around her neck. Nadège Alcide rose and cupped his shoulders, holding him at arm's length long enough to survey his face. Despite the lines of weariness at the corners of her eyes, she was still the most beautiful woman he'd ever seen. When he was little, he'd thought she must be envied even by the great, perfect *loa* Erzulie Freda, Vodou goddess of love—a dangerous idea, for Erzulie could be jealous. It had been years before he'd broken the habit of whispering apologies to her image whenever he passed by the painting of the *Rada loa*—the good spirits—in his papa's study.

For a moment none of them spoke, and the ticking clock on the mantelpiece was the only sound. It reminded him of the guidance counselor's office.

"I'm okay, Manman."

He meant it. He'd lost that manic energy and felt like himself again, if a bit slower and stupider. He could feel Papa watching him, categorizing him, searching for a definition for this. His family often joked that Andre Alcide was half computer, capable of tracking a million bits of data, a million facts and diagnoses, but it had never felt truer than now, when Tobias knew he was a problem to be solved.

Perhaps that wasn't fair.

He was very tired.

"I'm sorry," he said.

*"Non, non,"* she murmured, and pulled him into a hug. Her eyes were damp and red when she finally let him go, and he dropped his gaze to the carpet rather than see her hurt.

"Sit." She gestured at the armchair, sat on the sofa,

and took a deep breath. "Better to do this now." His papa circled the coffee table to sit beside her.

"Do what?" Tobias asked.

"This." She slid a packet of papers toward him.

"Woodbury Residential Treatment Center." He flipped through the pages, catching phrases like *troubled teens* and *housed in cottages* and *intensive, individualized therapy.* "I don't understand."

"It's a facility. They help boys who've been struggling with—"

"You're sending me away?" he whispered.

"We're getting you help," Papa corrected. "The psychologist we met with at the hospital believes, and we agree, that inpatient treatment is called for. This place, Woodbury, it's for teenagers who are struggling. They have psychiatrists there, but it isn't a mental hospital, strictly speaking. No one will know why you're going. This doesn't have to affect your future."

"I don't… I don't need help. I'm sorry about what I did. But I'm not going to do it again. I didn't mean to."

"What you did to your arm is a symptom of a much bigger problem," Papa said. "I believe you that you weren't trying to kill yourself, but that doesn't mean that we can ignore this. We've got to treat the underlying cause."

"I'm not a disease."

"We can't be cavalier about this, Toby," Manman interjected.

"Please don't call me that."

Her lips tightened. "I apologize." She exchanged a look with Papa, who nodded encouragement. "Tobias, you have to understand that the choices you're making aren't good for you."

"The choices *I'm* making," he repeated. "It feels like you're the ones making all the choices."

"Do you know what it felt like to see you bleeding like that, to find your blood in the bathroom after you went to the hospital? After everything that Ruby has been through, can you imagine how upsetting that was for her?" Her voice broke and Papa put a hand on her arm.

"I'm sorry," Tobias whispered.

She cleared her throat. "Your psychological state is very fragile right now, and I will not lose you this way."

Tobias put the packet on the coffee table and dragged his hands through his hair. His skin felt like it was on too tightly. He couldn't breathe. He didn't—he didn't like this, didn't like any of it.

"We love you," she continued. "But this behavior...you need help, and we can't give it to you. You need mental health specialists, and we can't—I don't think it's good for your siblings to witness this. They've already been through so much."

"You're sending me away." He could barely get the words out. He could barely *think* them.

"Only until you've gotten things in hand again. Only until you're better."

"When do I go?" he asked dully.

"Tomorrow morning," Manman replied. "I've already packed your things. Go upstairs and get some sleep and tomorrow...it's a fresh start, Toby."

He opened his mouth to tell her, yet again, not to call him by that childhood nickname, only to stall out. It wouldn't make a difference anyway, and he didn't want them to think he was being combative.

"All right." He didn't say anything else, nothing about

the terrible stillness inside him at leaving. Nothing about the hot tears that he fought back with gritted teeth.

What would be the point of saying any of that? It wouldn't make them keep him.

"All right."

## Chapter Two

"We need to talk," Sullivan Tate told his boss darkly, holding up his coffee-stained white button-down. He was wearing only his slightly less damp tank undershirt now, and while he'd planned to look a little more professional for this conversation, he was out of patience. "If I get one more beverage thrown at me, I'm going to quit. Coffee, Raina. He threw coffee at me."

Raina tapped one long red nail against her color-coordinated crimson mouth as she considered him from where she was seated at her desk in front of the window, paperwork strewn around her. Her glossy black hair was up in its customary chignon, her copper-hued skin was flawless, and her black suit was perfectly tailored to set off her figure to enormous advantage. He sometimes wondered if there was a rule that models should continue to be fashionable after they hung up their stilettos, because her glamour never faltered for a heartbeat. "Did you get burned?"

"No."

"Are you sure? We could sue."

"Your concern is duly noted, but it was cold, and that's beside the point anyway. I want a better job."

She stood up, hitching a hip against the desk. He'd triggered negotiation mode, and in negotiation mode, Raina refused to sit while others stood over her. "You seem very serious this time."

"I am very serious this time. There was enough tequila in his mug that I'm lucky no one lit a cigarette around me or I'd be on fire right now."

"Who puts tequila in coffee?" She wrinkled her nose in disgust.

"Child support-avoiding dirtbags." He dropped the remnants of his nice shirt in the trash before coming to stand beside her at the window. They were in an older part of Denver, full of grand, crumbling red-brick houses and steep crayon-green lawns. Raina had chosen the two-story Colonial they used for office space with the same attention to image that she did everything else, finding the perfect balance between the modern, technologically advanced investigative agencies of the future and the smaller, more affordable and—to be frank—sketchier agencies of the past.

He was pretty sure that drive for balance was why Raina had hired him in the first place. She met with the upper-echelon clients concerned with privacy and status on her own, only pulling Sullivan into meetings when she needed to impress someone expecting a rougher element. On those days, he'd roll into the office wearing big black boots, ratty jeans and a T-shirt that showed off his tat-too sleeves, his dark hair gelled and sprayed into its full, gravity-defying, mohawked glory, and he'd curse every time he opened his mouth.

He'd be lying if he said it wasn't fun to play the brute,

especially since it didn't fit the more upscale image of their firm.

Raina was a monster about money—if it didn't build the client base or contribute to first-rate work, she was a notorious tightwad. Any parts of the first floor that clients might see were exquisitely arranged; the second floor was a cesspool of unfinished renovation. Raina's office was downstairs, her furniture slick and polished, the chairs leather, the windows shining. Sullivan's office, on the other hand, was in a closet near the upstairs bathroom. Because nothing larger than a fifth-grader would fit inside, he didn't have a desk, just a tray that Raina had handed over with such a blank expression that he was certain she'd been laughing wildly at him in her head. Usually he sat in the kitchen next to the constantly complaining fridge, his laptop propped up on his knees because the table wobbled. He spent hours each day violating every rule of ergonomic practice possible, and when he did get out into the world, it was to have assholes throw doctored coffee on him.

Really, everything about his job sucked. He should've stuck with the game plan he'd sketched out when he was six and become Sherlock Holmes. Holmes might've had an opium problem, but the great detective had probably been spared carpal tunnel.

"Talk to me." Raina's eyes, dark and deep, met his. "We'll brainstorm."

He sighed. The air conditioning was up high to combat the August temperatures, and he shivered in his damp undershirt. "I feel like a mouse in an exercise wheel. Running fast and going nowhere."

"Pretty much the definition of serving subpoenas for

a living. But I can't spare you. Cases come and go, but you're the most reliable source of revenue."

He'd been expecting that response. "You could serve some of the subpoenas and I could do some of the actual cases. Split the interesting ones and the boring ones fifty-fifty."

"We could, but I don't want to." She smiled when he gave her a baleful look. "The good part about being the boss is that I can delegate all the shit work to you."

"What if I find an intern? Someone to take over the subpoenas for college credit or something?"

She lifted an exquisitely groomed eyebrow. "What would I need you for then?"

Yeah, he'd walked into that one. He cleared his throat. "Okay, try this out. I do a couple of the more interesting cases on top of my current workload. If it turns out I can balance it, we'll stick with it."

"A raise wouldn't—"

"I don't want a raise," he said in disgust, wondering what the hell went on in her brain sometimes. "You think this is about money? I'm bored. And underutilized, which offends me on a purely theoretical level, but mostly I'm bored."

"And we all know what kind of trouble you'll get into in that state." She thought about it for a moment. "This forces me to babysit you."

"I'm more than capable and you know it."

"You're more than capable when it comes to tracking people down, yes. And the coffee stain on your shirt notwithstanding, you're very capable at interacting with horrible people and getting out in one piece. But the rest of our cases require more discretion and experience than serving subpoenas does." She stared at him like she was trying to see the inside of his skull. "Be honest. How big a problem is this?"

He scrubbed a hand over his jaw. "I'm not going to quit over it today. But if something doesn't change, it'll happen. Sooner rather than later. I've answered all the questions I'm going to find in this work."

She looked out the window, heaving an irritated sigh. "You and your unending quest for complication. You make me so tired sometimes."

He shrugged. He'd long since given up on trying to alter that part of his personality. A few minutes passed while she thought about it, long enough that he was tempted to get up and find something to do. Then Raina made a considering noise and tipped her head closer to the window. He followed her gaze and watched a tan sedan pull into the driveway. The man behind the wheel was barely visible from this angle, but Sullivan recognized the car.

The Devoted Uncle.

Sullivan pursed his lips. "Give me the Devoted Uncle. It's not like I can screw that one up. If I can solve it, you split the subpoenas with me and give me half of the fun cases from now on. If I can't solve it on my own, I'll stop bitching for…six months."

"A year. And that includes the bitching you do about cleaning the kitchen."

"Fine."

They shook on it, and he ran upstairs to change. His heart was already pounding, excitement racing through his veins at the very idea. Excitement and a good deal of relief. He needed this, both for the sake of his sanity and because it was the next step to the dream job.

Opening his own agency. Taking the cases that interested him, working through the riddles no one else could solve. A dozen interns on staff so he'd never have to serve another fucking subpoena again.

Not that he was going to tell Raina any of that. She was a cutthroat sort of dame, and if she knew he was planning to become a competitor someday, he wasn't sure she'd comply with furthering his training at all.

When his phone buzzed, reminding him of the tornado that was his personal life, he hesitated, but eventually decided to ignore the text message for now.

He had a client to meet.

His job involved enough assholes that he'd learned a long time ago to keep spare clothes in the office. When he was wearing a fresh Henley, he checked his hair to make sure it wasn't too messy. Most days he used a little gel to brush the dark strands straight back so they'd stay out of his face, and it'd held out fine against the coffee-throwing bastard. He looked as professional as a guy with the sides of his head buzzed could possibly look.

Back in Raina's office, she was behind her desk and the client was making himself comfortable across from her.

Their longest-standing client, the Devoted Uncle was Nelson Klein, a local insurance adjuster who came in once a year like clockwork. He was solid in that bulky way that was almost as much fat as muscle, and his frizzy, blazing-red hair was going thin on top, something he combated with an unconvincing combover. He was always brisk, occasionally bossy, and frequently bad-tempered—none of which spoke clearly of grief, but then, it had been more than two decades since his sister had been murdered and his young niece had gone missing.

Sullivan wondered if it was habit alone that still had Klein running searches all these years later.

"I assure you, we take the search for Nathalie as seriously now as we did the first time we looked for her," Raina was saying. "Sullivan's appointment is not a sign of lack of interest or effort. On the contrary, he has more time to apply to her cause at the moment, and believe me when I say that he's the best researcher I've ever had on staff."

Sullivan reached out to shake hands with Klein, who got up slowly—he was busy giving Sullivan a sharp up-and-down, gaze lingering on the haircut. "The best, huh?"

"If there's a way to find out what happened to her, Sullivan will find it."

Klein's grip was tight. "If you say so."

Sullivan returned Klein's gaze—the man's eyes were small and brown and bloodshot—until Klein released him. Sullivan tugged out the small moleskin notebook he habitually kept in his back pocket and snagged a pen from Raina's desk before sitting down. "Okay." He thumbed to a fresh page. "Start at the beginning."

"The girl's dead," Raina said, once the Devoted Uncle had gone. She was pulling up the case number in the database so he could look up the files she'd compounded over the years. "You know that, right?"

"Yeah," Sullivan agreed. People didn't go missing in suspicious circumstances for twenty years only to pop up out of nowhere one day, alive and kicking. Almost certainly, her body was in a shallow grave somewhere, and the chances of finding and identifying her at this point were minuscule.

It was, in all likelihood, an impossible puzzle to solve. He could barely stand still, he was so eager to get started.

"If you find anything, it's going to be a corpse." Raina's expression was half concerned, half cold. She probably thought he'd get involved emotionally, only to break down when he realized that this case wouldn't have a miraculous ending where the girl was reunited with her family and lived happily ever after.

Raina might not be wrong about that emotional involvement thing, but it wasn't going to stop him, and he wasn't walking in blind. Sullivan wished he could be shocked by the idea of a ten-year-old girl vanishing, but you couldn't serve subpoenas for as long as he had and not learn that some people didn't give two shits for their own kids, let alone someone else's. Call him a cynic, but just once he'd like to come across a dad who paid *more* child support than he was ordered to by the courts. Just once.

"I'm aware." He reached into his pocket for a piece of nicotine gum. He chewed with purposeful disinterest, trying to project hard-nosed-detective vibes, and she eventually scrawled the case number on a Post-It note.

"Cross your *T*s, Sullivan. If you find evidence of criminal misconduct, you'd better be able to testify with iron-clad precision."

"No problem." He tried to take the Post-It, but she held on to it.

"Be discreet."

"Well, I was planning on shouting Klein's name at anyone who would listen, but…" When she only stared at him balefully, he sighed. "Of course I'll be discreet. He's Bruce Wayne. No word of his secret identity will cross my lips. The facts of the case will only be shared as necessary to meet the needs of my client, and I will present my client with options in the event of a murky, slimy ethical gray area. You know that I know how to do stuff, right?"

"The stakes are higher when you're doing more than shoving a file into someone's face. Deadbeat dads are one thing. If there's foul play here and you fuck it up, someone could get away with murder. And you can forget asking Klein for his opinion on murky, slimy ethical gray areas. He's not with the DA's office. He's not even an attorney, and you can't trust him to uphold the law."

"Right, sure. That's what I meant."

She finally released the Post-It. "I better not be the last one to know if things start to fall apart on you."

"I'm going to be so well behaved you won't believe it," he promised. "Altar boy style."

With Raina's gaze hard on his back, he headed for the kitchen. He grabbed some food—turned out to be a Mountain Dew and a piece of bread—from the gurgling fridge (which he was going to investigate one of these days, and possibly even fix), slid into a chair, and opened his laptop.

Sullivan didn't make a lot of money, and what he did make went primarily to one of three things: his savings, his sex life, or his electronics. As such, his laptop was top of the line, less than a year old, and faster than Usain Bolt. Came in handy, since the first major steps in finding someone all took place online.

He put his earbuds in and got a little BtMI rolling—it was a happy day all of a sudden—and got to work.

First he read over the notes he'd taken during the meeting, then the police reports and witness interviews in the case folder.

On February 2nd, 1992, the home of a midlevel, wan-nabe criminal badass, Lawrence Howard, was invaded by the thugs of an unidentified, actual neighborhood badass, who'd apparently had strong feelings about Howard's at-tempts to infringe on his business. Howard was murdered in his bed, along with two bodyguards and his house-keeper, Margaret Trudeau, who lived on the property with her ten-year-old daughter, Nathalie, who vanished. This was pre-Amber Alert, so the response had been unfor-givably slow, and though the Denver Police Department and the media fanned the flames of the search as high as possible in the following days, she'd never been located.

It was assumed—sadly, if reasonably—that the girl had been taken by one of the killers, probably for horri-fying purposes, and murdered later.

Two years later, with the case largely forgotten in the public consciousness, Nelson Klein, the Devoted Uncle, brother to the murdered Margaret, had gone to a local pri-vate detective agency to fund a search of his own. Eigh-teen years after that, when Raina bought the agency from the retiring owner, the case had fallen into her hands, and she'd worked it solo for the past five. And now, finally, it was Sullivan's.

He looked at the scanned photograph of the girl, clearly taken on a school picture day back in 1991, and studied the blond hair, pale blue eyes, and gap-toothed smile. She looked cheerful and puckish in her pink blouse with the black piping on the collar, her hair curled for the special occasion. Sullivan couldn't help imagining the things she might've witnessed or suffered, and a pulse of pity welled up in his throat.

He tucked the photo out of sight in the file, and blew out a breath.

The obvious steps had been repeated every time Klein had come in, but Sullivan went through them again because you never knew. If he was lucky, he'd find out that her body had already been located in a nearby jurisdiction in the past twelve months, the info kept from her family by some state employee's incompetence.

He started by checking the Social Security Administration's Death Master File with different variations on the girl's name—Natalie Trudeau, Nat Trudeau, Nathalie Martine Trudeau, Nathalie M. Trudeau, and several misspellings of each, just in case.

No joy.

This wasn't proof she was alive, obviously. The records of the Death Master File became scantier the further back you went, and the SSA erred on the side of caution when it came to listing missing people as dead. However, it did give Sullivan a chance to double-check that he had her correct Social Security number and date of birth, which he would need for his other searches. Now it was time to use the process of elimination.

The foundational rule investigators used in cases like this was that living people left marks. If no man was an island, there was always a road you could follow to find him. People needed jobs and places to live and banks and friends and phones, and everything left trails. Sullivan might not be able to prove that Nathalie was dead, but if he checked all the normal places where the living showed up and she wasn't there, then death was the only possibility left.

He started with a simple Google search, using all the same derivatives of her name that he'd used in the Death Master File. He spent an hour combing through results, and came up with squat.

Next he searched the Federal Bureau of Prisons, in case she'd miraculously lived long enough to get arrested as an adult. When that didn't give him anything, he went to each of the local jail and state prison websites, and spent a couple hours searching for her by name and SSN. Some of those sites let him search for parolees and those on probation, too, and he took full advantage.

Nothing. If she'd been incarcerated, he couldn't find it.

He took a break to get Siouxsie started on his iPod and eat a sandwich—accidentally using the last of Raina's peanut butter, whoops—before tackling the long process of checking with the different branches of the armed forces. Nothing. He went through the online court records for alimony, bankruptcy, and the property appraiser's records, and managed to kill another hour finding exactly zip. He would have to actually go to the courthouse to check more deeply, but that was a job for tomorrow.

His phone buzzed, and this time he checked the caller. Caty. And the earlier text message had been her too: don't think I won't sic Lisbeth on you.

After a brief hesitation, he set his phone aside with both the call and the text unanswered. He wasn't in the mood to let her bully him into talking about his damn feelings again. Caty was an excellent friend, and he cared about her a lot, but Jesus, he needed some damn space. It was enough to make him want to go into hiding to avoid the hounding.

Wait. Wait a second. His hands went still over the keyboard.

While the vast majority of the time Sullivan was searching for shitty people hiding from taking responsibility for something they'd fucked up, every now and again, a search would turn up someone hiding for good reason—usually women on the run from abusive exes. Maybe that line of thinking was applicable in some way here.

It was almost certain that Nathalie Trudeau was buried in a field somewhere or resting under a river's worth of water, but what if she hadn't vanished because someone had taken her? What if all these years of silence weren't because she had no voice, but because speaking up would be dangerous?

What if she'd run? What if she'd never stopped running?

She would've needed help. No ten-year-old was going to disappear off the grid without an adult's aid, and Sullivan couldn't begin to imagine who might've played that role for Nathalie, but if the girl was gone by choice, whoever had helped her knew their stuff.

Sullivan tapped his finger on the table as he considered.

He went back to the original police file and reread the section about wannabe badass Lawrence Howard, the unidentified local thugs who'd taken him out, and the poor housekeeper who'd been an innocent bystander, probably killed because she'd seen something she shouldn't have.

Howard had lived in an expensive section of Denver, the kind of neighborhood where cops would respond quickly to reports of gunfire. That didn't leave much time for the murderers to hang around. Maybe they hadn't searched the house thoroughly after taking out Howard.

Maybe they'd missed a ten-year-old hiding in a closet or under a bed.

Maybe he was grasping at straws.

He scrubbed his hands over his face. He needed to keep his head on straight—he was prone to flights of fancy on the best of days because he liked things interesting more than he liked things honest, and that could get him into trouble here. He needed to be ice-cold and by-the-book, not indulging himself in pointless questions about a could've-been that he had zero evidence to support.

He read himself the riot act for several more minutes, nodded definitively to prove that he'd gotten the message, and then promptly ignored all of that and went online to do a search for Nathalie's mother's name.

And okay, on the surface that seemed like a left-field kind of thing to do, but there was method to his madness. It was impossible to hide in modern America without changing your name, and there were different levels of competence when it came to fake IDs. The worst meant you wouldn't be able to buy beer without someone calling you on your bullshit, while the best would carry you through pretty much anything except for a deep background check by a government agency.

The best new identities used names and SSNs stolen directly from the Death Master File, usually those of infants who'd died soon after birth, because there was less of a chance that the deceased's old life would overlap with the thief's new one. All it took was a few forged documents to complete the transfer.

Yes, it would be incautious for someone to help the daughter by using the mother's name, thereby providing a link to the case, but...

But.

What real estate agent or employer or insurance adjuster was going to run a client or applicant's ID against the SSA's Death Master File to make sure that the person breathing in front of them wasn't using a dead child's name? Who looked up family members who had passed to make sure their names weren't being used by thieves?

No one. The chances that someone was going to look were infinitesimal. He was only looking because he was the kind of guy who didn't mind wasting five hours following up a nonsense train of thought for a case from two decades ago because he thought it would be cool if it turned out to be right. If someone had helped hide Nathalie under a new identity, was there really that much risk in using the mother's name? Even the Devoted Uncle wouldn't think to start searching for his dead sister as a way of tracking down his niece.

A memorial, of sorts. A last tribute to a dead mother, maybe.

He double-checked that he had Margaret Trudeau's correct SSN and date of birth, and tooled around a little, fiddling through Google and old websites, running haphazardly through the steps he'd taken with Nathalie, not really expecting anything. He found a marriage license for Margaret Trudeau in the online Denver Courthouse records and her maiden name did match her brother's—Klein. Sullivan did a search for that name too, and found a birth certificate but little else.

He got up to piss, found an old bag of trail mix somewhere, and ate it standing up at the counter. The sun took on the orangey tint of late afternoon while he told himself over and over that nothing would come of this. It was the stupidest waste of time ever.

Then he sat down and typed the name Peggy Klein into the courthouse records database because Peggy was, for some bizarre reason, an old nickname for Margaret.

And got a relatively recent hit.

He sat back in his chair, stunned. He made himself take a deep breath and double-checked the dates and the Social Security number, because there had to be a couple

hundred Peggy Kleins in the world, but Jesus. It was her.
The same Margaret Trudeau who'd been murdered in
her employer's house in 1992 had bought a condo twelve
years ago under the name Peggy Klein and dutifully paid
the taxes on it annually.

Strange behavior for a dead chick, he thought, and
had to force himself to calm the fuck down. He'd stumbled onto something here, and maybe it'd been a flight of
fancy that led him to this spot, but now was the time to
rope everything into some semblance of rationality. He
needed to document every step, make sure he had proof
to support every decision he made. Plus, if he wasn't
careful, he took the risk of driving Nathalie or whoever
it was using the name of Nathalie's dead mother further
underground.

He needed to verify.

He also needed to move. He was climbing out of his
damn skin here. He popped another piece of nicotine
gum into his mouth, looked up Riviera Condominiums
online, and realized he was barely a fifteen-minute drive
away. The clock read 4:28 p.m. There was time, perhaps,
to do a quick drive-by, maybe snap a couple pictures
from the car.

Maybe he'd see a blonde woman in her mid-thirties.

He grabbed his laptop and jacket and headed down
the hall to Raina's office. She was on the phone, making inquisitive noises, and he went to her desk, ignoring
the way she slapped at his hands as he opened the long,
shallow drawer above her knees.

"I'm taking your kit," he mouthed, and she held up a
finger to tell him to wait. Her nonverbal noises into the
phone became impatient. He grabbed the huge lockbox
she stored in the bottom drawer of her file cabinet and

hauled it out, gesturing toward the door. She shook her head and mouthed, "Wait."

He made the universal gesture for "call me," gave her an apologetic grimace, and darted out, hurrying down the sidewalk toward his beat-up black 1974 Buick Regal.

He had a living dead girl to find.

## Chapter Three

The letter rested on the dashboard, the white paper faintly malodorous and stained pink from the rank *salade de betteraves* his manman had thrown out earlier in the week, the torn-open top ragged. The return address, written in a loopy, almost childlike hand, read *Ashley Benton*. Tobias spun the orange plastic lighter in his hand over and over while he stared at it, wondering what the pages inside might say.

The interior of the car was sweltering even with the windows down; the metal spark wheel was hot against his thumb. He imagined, for one satisfying moment, lighting the letter on fire right there so it turned black and curled into itself, watching the flames billow orange, the plastic of the dash scorching and melting, the air filling with smoke. He flicked the lighter several times, testing himself, tempted.

Finally, he sighed and shoved the letter into the front cover of his biochemistry textbook on the passenger seat. The lighter went into his pocket.

He looked out the windshield at the two-story gray building he was parked in front of. Riviera Condominiums was nicer than his friend Ghost's old cramped armpit of an apartment by a mile. Everything there had been worn, from the cracked parking lot to the threadbare carpet to the cheap windows, and the residents had been the same.

This new place was downright shiny. There was a pool with blue water and two tennis courts and the grass was neatly clipped and very green, especially considering it was the first day of August in a semiarid state. Flowerbeds overflowing with geraniums lined the sidewalks leading from the parking lots to the buildings, and interspersed between those buildings were small communal gardens thick with tomatoes and peppers. The patios and balconies were bordered with black wrought iron balustrades.

No way could Ghost afford to live here.

If Ghost even lived here anymore.

Contact between them had been spotty lately, text messages would go hours without a reply, if one came at all, invites ignored, emails answered with a handful of words. It wasn't necessarily personal; sometimes Ghost simply disappeared for days at a time, and he always reappeared with as little fanfare as when he took off. In the past, Tobias had respected those bursts of antisocial behavior and stayed away, letting Ghost come back when he was ready.

But this was different. This was nearly two weeks of complete silence. It was different because of the favor.

Eight months ago, in order to bail their friend Church out of trouble with some local thugs, Ghost had agreed to do a favor for a woman no one should owe. Tobias didn't know the specifics, but he knew enough to worry.

He and Ghost had been friends since that horrible day in Woodbury when Tobias had been jumped by some guys in a badly lit bathroom, and a pale slip of a kid had bailed him out with nothing more than a dangerous rep and a half-mad smile. Tobias still wasn't sure why Ghost—selfish to an extreme, frequently oblivious to the suffering of others—had put himself at risk to save someone he didn't know, but that kindness was one Tobias would never forget.

Not that everything in Woodbury had been bad. That time had been good for Tobias in certain respects. He'd put earnest effort into therapy, and while he hadn't been particularly successful at implementing the changes his therapist had encouraged him to make, he'd come out of it with coping skills that'd kept him stable ever since.

But there'd been a darker side to the facility, a side born of limited funding and political disinterest, where therapists cared but had too many patients, and people slipped through cracks the size of ravines. Ghost lived and breathed that same aura of struggle and poverty and violence, and worst of all was the way he'd never questioned his place there, the way he'd seemed so indifferent to the unhappiness emanating from every brick.

Tobias got out of the car and put his backpack in the trunk before heading down the sidewalk to Ghost's condo. It was on the first floor of Building 18, tucked as far away from the clubhouse as possible, a corner unit abutting the line of trees at the edge of the property that blocked the noise of the traffic from the street beyond. He knocked hard—Ghost was a daytime sleeper—but when there was no answer, he stepped over a low row of bushes to reach the nearest window and put his hands up to block the glare so he could peer inside.

The living room faced north, so it was dim in the late afternoon light, but he could make out the hulking shapes of the couch and the entertainment center. He stared for a long minute, a shiver of unease tracing up his spine. The oddest thing was that nothing was out—no dishes on the coffee table Ghost had gotten from somewhere to replace the board and cinder blocks he'd used at his old place, no sign of Ghost's black hoodie draped over the back of the chair by the door, none of his fashion magazines left open on the arm of a chair, no big black boots in sight. The remote was on top of the TV. Ghost was hardly a slob, but the place looked like one of those model apartments leasing offices put together to tempt would-be renters.

A single house key was resting on the breakfast bar separating the living room from the kitchen. Left in plain view as if to ensure it was found, right next to Ghost's phone.

Tobias stepped back, raking a hand through his hair as he tried to make sense of it.

Had Ghost moved out? Was that why the key had been left? He wouldn't put it past Ghost to move without telling either him or Church, but the phone was a different story. Ghost was very protective of his phone—he kept the numbers of his business contacts there. He wouldn't leave it.

It was possible that Ghost had simply gotten a new phone. There'd been a lot of new upgrades in Ghost's life lately, and this could simply be another one. Tobias pulled his own phone out and called Ghost's number, intending to prove that the phone left on the counter was useless, the number forwarded to whatever new one Ghost had bought.

But a few seconds after Tobias heard the first ring in his ear, the phone on the counter lit up and began vibrating. Tobias let it ring for a minute, hoping maybe Ghost would stumble out from the bedroom to see who was calling him, but there was nothing.

Ghost wouldn't leave his phone. He *wouldn't*.

The small, niggling worry that'd wormed its way into his mind over the past couple of weeks abruptly became full-blown fear. Once again, he thought of the favor.

He thought about texting Church, but it wasn't like Church would keep something from him, so—

Except Church *did* lie sometimes, when he thought Tobias couldn't handle whatever was going on. He'd lied during the whole thing with the Krayev thugs, after all. Church probably didn't realize how upsetting it was to be lied to all the time.

Well, either way, it wasn't like Church would know what was up. He'd been just as frustrated about Ghost's absence as Tobias had been.

He knocked again. Still no answer. He hadn't really expected one.

For a minute, Tobias couldn't help imagining the possibilities: Ghost in his bedroom, too scared to come to the door, Ghost too hurt from getting beaten up or stabbed to get out of bed.

Ghost dead in the tub.

Every fiber in Tobias's body rebelled against that possibility.

Ghost was an inconstant, often absent friend, but Tobias knew in his bones that if someone hurt him, Ghost would move heaven and earth—*or gut a few people*, a small, guilty part of Tobias whispered—to help him.

How could Tobias be willing to do less?

He circled around the building to the rear. Unlike Ghost's neighbors' back patios, his had no chairs or flowerpots or wind chimes to hint at the person who lived inside. After hesitating for a bare second, Tobias grabbed a rock and hopped over the hip-high railing. His hands were sweating; he was pretty sure this was a reasonable step to take, but that didn't mean it didn't feel like a transgression.

He took a glance around to make sure no one would see, and nearly had a heart attack when he saw a guy leaning against a tree about ten feet away, watching him with curiosity.

"Hi." The guy gave him a small wave.

Tobias licked his lips, his heart pounding rabbit-fast. "This isn't what it looks like."

"So you're not breaking in?" the guy asked, not sounding particularly worried about it. "It's okay if you are. I'm not a cop. Feel free to go about your business."

Tobias lowered the hand with the rock to his side. "Why are you watching me?"

"I was hoping that once you've taken care of the window, you wouldn't mind letting me take a look around before you do whatever you're here to do."

The guy was maybe a few years older, in his late twenties, and about the same height, five-eleven. He was rangy in his jeans and brick-red Henley, not quite as solidly built as Tobias, but the sleeves of his shirt were pulled up to the elbows, revealing well-muscled forearms beneath the tattoos that went down to both wrists. He had an iPod shoved halfway into one pocket, and the earbuds were tucked into his collar so they wouldn't get tangled.

His hair was—well, it was cool. It was dark brown, buzzed almost to his skull except for a fat stripe down the center that was gelled messily back in a mohawk that didn't have enough product in it to stay in place. He had a narrow, bony face and interested brown eyes, and he was sort of hot, actually. Not even sort of, now that Tobias took a second look. He was *fully* hot, standing there with his lips twitching like he might be on the verge of smiling, like it was nothing whatsoever to chat with someone about to break in to someone else's place.

"What are you doing here?" Tobias asked.

"Lurking," the guy said pleasantly. "You?"

"I mean why do you want to go inside? Are you here to hurt someone?" Not that Tobias had the first clue what he would do if the guy said yes, but still. Tobias wasn't about to help anyone do anything that might hurt Ghost.

The stranger didn't say anything for a moment, only looked at him as if he were trying to figure out how Tobias's brain worked. "No," he said finally, sort of gently, and for some dumb reason, Tobias felt inclined to believe him. If Ghost were here, he'd slap Tobias for being gullible. Tobias said staunchly, "I'm not going in, and neither are you."

The guy's eyebrows jogged up an inch. "You're very protective of your turf. What if I said I had no interest in fencing anything? I just want to snoop around for a few minutes. Then you can go through the place to your thieving little heart's delight."

"I'm not a robber." Tobias frowned, considering what to say next, while the guy pulled a foil square out of his pocket, opened it, and popped a piece of gum into his mouth.

"Burglar," the guy said, talking around it. "Robbery is when you force someone to give you something in person. Burglary is when you steal from an unattended place."

Tobias had to subdue an urge to roll his eyes. "Fine, whatever, I'm not a burglar. But I at least have a good reason to be here—I'm friends with…and you could be anybody. So."

After chewing thoughtfully for a moment, the guy came toward the railing, pulling his wallet out of his back pocket as he walked. He held out a business card, which Tobias took cautiously, stepping back to put space between them before taking his eyes off the guy to read it.

In large type, it said, *American Secure Investigations.* Underneath, in smaller lettering was printed *Process and Surveillance Specialists.*

"You're a private detective?" Tobias asked.

"Yup."

Tobias eyed him doubtfully. "You don't look like a private detective."

"I left my trench coat in the car." The guy smiled, and Tobias's stomach flipped over at the sight of it. It was earnest and a little cheeky, like they were in on the same secret.

Tobias looked down at the card again, at the name beneath the slogan. "You don't look like a Raina either."

"She's my boss. I ran out of my cards."

Tobias pulled his phone out and dialed the number on the card, noting the bloom of resignation in the guy's expression.

A woman answered. "American Secure Investigations."

"Hi, I'm calling to confirm that this guy works for—"

"Are you a LEO?"

"A…what's a…"

"Are you a law enforcement officer?"

"No. I'm a…concerned citizen and I'm not sure if I should—"

"Concerned citizen," she repeated, and made a noise

that was only slightly too delicate to be called a snort. "What's he look like?"

"He has a mohawk, sort of—"

"Yes, he's mine," the woman said, sounding annoyed. "His name is Sullivan Tate, and he's one of my process servers."

"What's a—"

"It's someone who finds people in order to give them legal papers they'd like to avoid receiving. Why? What did he do?"

"He's—" Tobias broke off. He couldn't exactly say *he's watching me do something illegal so he can do something illegal too.* "I don't, uh—he's snooping?"

"Is that a question?" she asked acerbically.

Tobias gritted his teeth. "No, he's snooping around. If—"

"He's there for a missing person case. It's legit." Impatience rang through the line. "Give him the phone, would you? I need to yell at him."

Tobias held the phone out.

The guy—Sullivan—grimaced. "Hi, Raina. Want a burrito when I come back?"

Tobias couldn't make out what she was saying, but judging from Sullivan's expression, she wasn't happy. After a long minute, Sullivan said, "Yes, I promise. I'll be excruciatingly law-abiding. I'll explain everything later… Well, considering that I'm apparently in the presence of someone who takes all the fun out of things, I think we'll be fine."

Again, Sullivan gave him that friendly, teasing smile, as if he meant it affectionately. Tobias had to work really hard not to make a face. He wasn't going to fall for it. They weren't friends, and Tobias wasn't an idiot.

And he didn't take all the fun out of things. Tobias was fun.

He could be fun if he wanted to, anyway.

When Sullivan hung up, Tobias grabbed his phone back. "Why are you here, Mr. Tate?"

"Oh, God, Sullivan, please." He smiled yet again, charming and handsome, making Tobias's stomach flip again too. *Stop that,* he told his stomach. *Being hot doesn't make him a good guy.* Sullivan added, "My client needs help finding a loved one. My search led me to this address."

Tobias didn't know much about Ghost's personal life or family; he'd talked about them vaguely in the past, but since the details sometimes contradicted each other, Tobias usually assumed they were lies. He did know that Ghost had been homeless as a teenager from time to time. A Woodbury staff member—a more reliable source— had mentioned it during a group therapy session once, so Ghost had likely been a runaway. Could Sullivan's client be someone Ghost was actually related to?

"What's the loved one's name?"

Sullivan paused, studying Tobias as he chewed his gum. "You're friends with the person who lives here?"

"He's my best friend."

"Okay. I'd like to ask him some questions, but I get the impression from your rock antics that he's not here. Can I ask you some questions instead?"

"No." Not until Tobias had found Ghost and talked to him first, anyway.

Sullivan accepted that with good grace. "You don't want to get him in trouble. I get it. I don't want to get him in trouble either."

Tobias narrowed his eyes, and Sullivan lifted his hands

in an *I come in peace* sort of gesture. "Hey, I'm unaffili-
ated, I swear. I'm not turning anyone over to anyone else,
and I'm not planning to make anyone do anything they
don't want to do. I just want my client to stop being terrified that someone he loves is dead."

Tobias swallowed. He got a small taste of that feeling
every time Ghost took off. He glanced around him, hoping against all sense that Ghost would show up and tell
Sullivan to get lost, saving Tobias from making this decision. But of course, Ghost wasn't here. Tobias wished
he could learn to stop expecting otherwise.

"I don't know where he is," Tobias admitted quietly.

Equally quiet, Sullivan asked, "You think he took off?
Or that something happened to him?"

"I—I don't know."

"That sounds frightening. I'll keep my eye out for him
as I work, huh? Maybe we'll get lucky and I'll stumble
across him."

Tobias found himself nodding. Maybe Sullivan could
be useful. Maybe his case had something to do with
Ghost's absence, and talking to him would help Ghost. A
private detective had to be safer than a cop. They couldn't
arrest people, which might be enough to keep Ghost from
killing him when Tobias found him. Maybe.

"I haven't heard from him in a while, but his phone is
inside. He never leaves his phone anywhere, but it's on
the counter—" He could feel his words speeding up; he
clamped his mouth closed.

After a moment, Sullivan asked, "What's your name?"

"Tobias Benton."

"Nice to meet you, Tobias Benton. And your friend's
name?"

"Ghost."

"Okay, Tobias, here's what we're gonna do. I've been given strict orders not to get arrested today, so I'm gonna turn my back in a second. During that time, you can do whatever you think is best for you and Ghost. When I turn back around, you'll either be gone or—to my ever-lasting surprise—I'll find that the window by the door has been broken, and that you're very concerned about the suspicious circumstances. Like you said, he might be hurt, so we'll have to go in to see, and if the cops have to be called, you can say whatever you like about how the window got broken. Since I didn't witness anything, that's on you. Sound cool?"

Tobias exhaled, unable to fight the burgeoning sensation of gratitude welling up inside him. Sullivan knew what to do, and Tobias couldn't begrudge him for removing himself from the *breaking* part of the breaking and entering.

"Okay," Tobias said.

"Please don't hit me with your rock while I'm not looking." Sullivan turned his back. He began whistling, something that sounded familiar—oh, it was the theme song from *Jeopardy*.

"You're hilarious," Tobias muttered, his gratitude vanishing, and broke the window.

## Chapter Four

The sound of shattering glass made Sullivan jump. When he turned around, there was a fist-sized hole in the window pane, and Tobias Benton was staring at it with a conflicted expression.

Sullivan took the opportunity to stare at him a little in turn.

Tobias had sensitive, almost romantic features—a somber brow over big, thoughtful blue eyes; a straight nose; a hard, all-American jaw; and a sweet mouth with a full lower lip. He had nice shoulders—broad and strong under his well-fitted polo shirt, and ridiculously good posture. Paired with those tousled light-brown curls, he resembled an angel from a Renaissance painting. Not the insipid baby cupids, but one of those beautiful, tormented paragons who carried swords on behalf of God and wore silver armor as they led the heavenly host into battle, even while grieving over the necessity of war.

Okay, maybe Sullivan had a streak of the dramatic, but the point was that Tobias gave off a distinct aroma of somber wholesome goodness.

Deadpan, Sullivan said, "Look, a broken window. I do believe a crime has occurred."

Tobias gave him an admonishing look, and Sullivan hopped the railing, flashing a bolstering smile.

"Buck up, Goody Benton. You're not going to jail." Sullivan studied Tobias's handiwork and dislodged a couple more shards with his elbow to make the hole larger. The windows were the solid, insulation-friendly kind with two panels, one of which slid open horizontally and had a screen installed. "As far as these things go, 'I haven't heard from my friend and I thought he might be hurt' is a pretty good excuse for breaking and entering."

"I'm not worried about jail," Tobias said quietly. "Ghost won't like it."

"No one *likes* replacing windows." Sullivan reached through and fumbled with the latch, bitching at the thing under his breath when it proved resistant. "Besides, 'I hadn't heard from you and I thought you might be hurt' isn't a bad excuse to give him either." He tugged the screen out of the way and boosted himself up, concentrating on getting through the open window without crushing his balls on the sill.

He landed on carpet and took a quick glance around. He was in a dining nook, standing beside a small octagonal breakfast table sandwiched between two chairs. From here he could see most of the public space in the condo: nice furniture, upscale appliances in the kitchen, flat screen TV, a key and a phone on the counter. The place smelled musty, but there was no scent of rot or blood.

He heard the soft *thud* of Tobias landing behind him.

"Ghost?" Tobias called, halfhearted, like he already knew he wouldn't get an answer.

Sullivan picked up the key and went to the front door. The tumblers rolled over—it was the right key. He relocked the deadbolt before heading back to the kitchen to return it to the counter. "The fact that he left his key points to the idea that he took off on his own. Better than something happening to him, yeah?"

"Maybe." Tobias set his jaw as he opened the small black flip phone. It immediately gave him a low battery warning, and he rooted through the kitchen until he found Ghost's junk drawer and a power cord so he could plug it in. "But he wouldn't leave this behind."

"Thirty-two missed calls," Sullivan said, looking over Tobias's shoulder. "Your boy's popular, in addition to having ancient taste in technology."

"He's not my—" Instead of completing his thought, Tobias shook his head, finger hesitating over the *check voicemail* option. "He doesn't have a lot of money."

"Present living conditions excluded, I guess. You know his passcode?"

"No." Tobias cleared the missed calls alert, and another alert popped up informing them that Ghost had seventy-six unopened text messages.

Sullivan whistled. "Very popular."

Tobias thumbed the newest one open. It was from a contact named *Piglet* and had been sent about two hours ago.

Please be home. Please.

Sullivan raised his eyebrows. "Whoever Piglet is sounds pretty—"

"That's me," Tobias muttered. "It's—you know. Winnie the Pooh. Ghost thinks he's funny."

"Oh." Sullivan tried to hide his amusement. "Gotcha. Here, go back to the oldest one first. That'll give us an idea of when he left the phone behind."

Tobias obeyed, and found that the earliest unopened text was from July 22nd at 11:00 p.m.—ten days ago. The contact name was *Top Hat Bkpg 7*, and the message read: you still off the market? Wouldn't say no to some hot sexxx. Can do double if that changes your mind.

The next dozen texts were all similar—requests and demands and pleas, some with contact names like *Guns CL 4* or *heels&lace MB on 6th*, some from unknown numbers. The language in the messages ran the gamut from polite and businesslike to lewd and juvenile.

After the fourth or fifth offer to "bang that ass," Sullivan glanced at Tobias, who was keeping his eyes on the phone, his cheeks bright red.

"What does your buddy do for a living exactly?" Sullivan asked.

Stiffly, Tobias replied, "He's in sales."

Yes, Tobias was definitely a Good Boy.

"Not a cop," Sullivan reminded him. "I don't care if he turns tricks. I'm not looking to get him in trouble, remember?"

Tobias didn't respond or look over.

Sullivan studied the strong line of his profile—all that he could see from this angle—a little touched by Tobias's attempt at loyalty in the face of overwhelming evidence. "That's okay. No problem. I'm going to work from that assumption for now, though, because BKPG—that's Backpage. And CL…that's probably Craig's List. Sort of telling in combination."

Sullivan peered around the condo, noting the expensive furnishings. Someone had paid for all of it, and he'd guess it was the same someone who owned the place under the name of a dead woman. "Hard to believe he can afford all this when he's finding customers with personal ads."

Tobias followed his gaze, a crease appearing between his brows. "Yeah."

"Does he work for someone?"

"No way." Tobias gave a short laugh. "Ghost isn't the type to take orders. He wouldn't let someone have that kind of power over him."

Gently, Sullivan said, "Things can get rough in his line of work. Maybe he needed some help, decided to share the profits in the interest of having someone to watch his back."

"You don't understand." Tobias continued flipping through texts, pausing when he got to one sent three days ago from a contact named *K*.

Update.

And yesterday, another text from the same contact with the same message.

"He wouldn't let anyone sell him." But Tobias didn't sound quite as convinced this time.

*He knows who K is.* And judging by the way his fingers had tightened around the phone, Tobias wasn't pleased by K's involvement in whatever was going on. Sullivan was tempted to push, wondering how K might be connected to Nathalie Trudeau, but in the end, he didn't say anything. If Tobias *did* know K's identity, he was hiding it to protect Ghost, and Sullivan didn't want to damage the tentative trust between them.

The only texts not from clients were all from either *Piglet* or someone nicknamed *Rocky*, who sounded equal parts concerned and annoyed by Ghost's silence, and was, according to Tobias, another friend of theirs. When they'd read them all, Tobias closed the phone and put it in his pocket.

They went through the rest of the condo. The refrigerator had been emptied of everything except the ice cube trays—further evidence that Ghost had left willingly—and the trash had been emptied. No new bag had been put in the can.

There was no trash in the can in the bathroom either, and no shampoo, conditioner, or toothbrush.

"Maybe he went out of town, and he'll be back in a few days," Tobias said without much hope in his voice. He'd probably realized that his theory didn't fit the abandoned phone or the key on the counter.

Sullivan said, "Maybe."

There were two bedrooms, the smaller one void even of furniture, and the other occupied by a neatly made queen-size bed. The headboard was bare, as was the top of the dresser where people usually kept loose change or jewelry or the like. The drawers were only half full; Ghost had taken some clothing, but not all of it.

The nightstand drawer held an unopened box of condoms and a bottle of lube still in its plastic casing. As Sullivan closed it, he caught a glimpse of a black synthetic knife grip lodged in a sheath that had been duct-taped to the side of the nightstand nearest the mattress. Sullivan reached down and tugged the knife free—it was short and heavy, the real deal, and when he slid the blade against the edge of the nightstand, it cut into the wood like scissors through paper.

"That's a nasty piece of work." Sullivan glanced at Tobias, who shrugged, looking uncomfortable. Sullivan wondered if it was the blade or the sex supplies that did it. With raised eyebrows, he put the knife back where it was, within easy reach of a sleeper.

"Is your buddy seeing anyone?" Sullivan kept his voice casual.

Tobias didn't look at him. "I doubt it."

"Why?"

"I'm not going to talk about this with you. He wouldn't like it."

"Fair enough."

They went through the closet next, a walk-in with a light that Sullivan flipped on. Against one wall was a basket half-full of dirty laundry, a dusty box fan, and a bucket with detergent and cleaning stuff. The row of shoes included, interestingly, a pair of red stilettos. Sullivan slid a hand through the hanging clothes and came up with a black dress and several miniskirts, one of pink tweed, another of vinyl.

Sullivan nudged Tobias with an elbow and pointed. "Sure there's no lady friend?"

When Tobias didn't answer, Sullivan shrugged and turned to the second wall, where a long, low cabinet had been shoved back under the hanging dresses, a cheap plastic tub on top beside a beat-up shoebox. Sullivan bent to open the shoebox, getting a glimpse of notebook paper, assorted junk, and magazine clippings before it was tugged out of his hands.

"Hey, now," Sullivan protested.

Tobias clutched the box close with visible agitation, and after a long beat of hesitation, he said, "Sorry. But that's his private stuff, okay? It's not related, I promise."

Yeah, that had definitely not been Tobias's instinctive reaction to Sullivan's snooping. Judging from his body language and expression, Sullivan guessed there'd been a far more indignant response forming before Tobias muzzled it.

Intriguing.

Sullivan watched him, curious, as he put the shoebox on the ground, using a foot to nudge it out of the way, the lid falling closed in the process.

"No problem. Sorry. Being nosy is an occupational hazard." Sullivan raised his hands in a compliant gesture. "I'll be good."

"All right. Thanks." Tobias turned back to the bedroom.

"Maybe the lady friend knows where he went, huh?" Sullivan called after him, glancing wistfully at the shoebox. Deciding it wasn't worth getting caught over, he turned his attention to the plastic tubs. After a peek into the main part of the room to check that Tobias was elsewhere—he was sitting on the bed, staring at the floor—Sullivan pulled the lid of the plastic tub off.

Lace and silk and a lot of it. Blinking, Sullivan pulled out a handful that looked like black stockings with a saucy seam up the back, a red bustier, and a couple of demure nightgowns. He checked the labels—unlike everything else in the apartment, the underwear wasn't expensive, though the sizes were larger than he would've expected.

"You might be right about that lady friend," Sullivan muttered. He bent and checked the stilettos, and yup, same size as the other shoes.

The girly stuff was Ghost's.

Maybe Ghost was the one with the appreciation for nice undies, but there was a reason the stuff was here in a bin in the closet instead of in the dresser in the bedroom with the rest of Ghost's regular underwear. Most likely, Ghost catered to a particular type of client with very particular tastes.

He put the silky stuff back and opened the cabinet underneath, where he found a fairly impressive collection of sex toys, and on this at least, Sullivan knew his shit. Dildos, vibrators, cock rings, blindfolds, and even a paddle—extensive, but nothing too uncommon.

"Sales. Yeah, right." Sullivan stepped out, opening his mouth to say that he hadn't found anything useful, only to find that Tobias was still staring pensively at the floor, so grave and lost that Sullivan wondered if Tobias's worry about his pal was based in more than friendship.

The intrigue of trying to figure it out—there was no better puzzle to solve than the motivations of a human being—was undermined by a tiny, unexpected pang of regret. Yup, Sullivan could definitely appreciate the way strain suited Tobias's sensitive features; he looked downright lovely with his eyes solemn and his mouth soft.

*Stop it. You should know better by now. He's a perfectly nice guy, and he doesn't deserve to have you lusting all over his pain.*

He distracted himself by saying, "Anyone else we could talk to about who your buddy's been hanging out with lately?"

"He doesn't have a girlfriend," Tobias murmured. "Or a boyfriend. He doesn't—he doesn't do things like that. He only has me and—"

The sound of a distant thump from the living room made him break off, and they both turned to look at the bedroom door, as if that might somehow tell them what had made the noise.

"Ghost?" Tobias started toward the hallway. A second later Sullivan heard the faint clinking sound that came when someone wasn't careful about letting their keys bang against the door as they unlocked it. Sullivan thought of the key on the counter and his heart leaped into his throat. Shit. *Shit.*

He grabbed Tobias's wrist and wrenched him toward the closet, pulling him almost off his feet.

"Wait—" Tobias said, or tried to say, because Sullivan already had a hand over his mouth.

"That's not Ghost," he hissed as softly as he could. He got them into the closet, slapping the light off in the process, and swung the door half-closed behind them before prodding Tobias to duck behind the hanging rack of dresses and trousers. Fortunately, Tobias was smart enough to realize that silence was called for, because he didn't say anything else when Sullivan pulled his hand away, just let himself be moved around. Sullivan grabbed the hangers they'd set rocking, tried to still them, and reminded himself not to snap his gum out of distracted habit.

He couldn't see much with the light off, so hopefully they were invisible from the bedroom beyond. He could sense Tobias's tension all the same, and that tension seemed to skyrocket when two male voices came into hearing range, speaking…*Russian?*

What the hell?

One of the men entered the bedroom, but he left almost immediately, not even bothering to check the closet, and Sullivan let out a slow breath. That was the nifty trick of the half-open closet. People usually assumed that if someone was going to hide inside, they'd close the door, so they took it for granted that an open closet door meant it was vacant.

They listened as the men moved around in the living room. Judging from the sound of glass crunching, the broken window had caught their attention. After another minute of conversation, the key rattled in the lock all over again.

Tobias started forward, but Sullivan grabbed his arm and held up a finger. *Wait.*

About twenty seconds later, a cough from the living room proved that only one of the men had gone, and a few seconds after that, the TV turned on, switching from one nonsensical burst of sound to another as the viewer channel surfed.

Sullivan leaned in close to whisper. Up close like this, he could smell Tobias's soap, something moody and salty-crisp. "We're gonna go out the window. Fast and quiet."

It wasn't a hard choice, given the information at hand. Sullivan wasn't enthralled with the idea of meeting new people while he was illegally in a condo they might have illegally purchased under a dead woman's name, all while searching for the suspiciously absent tenant who lived there and worked in an illegal field.

Definitely not a time to make new friends.

He stepped out, listening hard. All he got was the canned laughter of a sitcom. He tiptoed to the window and winced as he thumbed the latch, scared it would squeak, but it was satisfyingly quiet.

The window itself was another story. It wasn't stuck, exactly, but he did have to put his back into it, and that had the whole thing making a low *bang* as it finally slid open. He glanced back toward the hallway, but after a good ten seconds, there was no sign that the Russian guy was coming to investigate.

Tobias was hesitating at the threshold of the closet, his eyes big and worried. Sullivan jerked his chin to encourage him to come over, and together they worked quickly to pop the screen out and lower it to the ground outside.

"Go," Sullivan mouthed, and used a hand to steady Tobias as he clambered over the sill and outside. As soon as he was out of the way, Sullivan followed suit, and as a last move, he shut the window again. Most likely, no one would notice the screen lying in the grass until someone from the grounds crew came across it.

Sullivan started walking lazily back toward the parking lot, catching Tobias's forearm when he tried to hurry. "Nope," he said, tugging Tobias back. "Take a breath, we're cool. We're out for an innocent little stroll."

"That was close."

"Yeah, isn't it great?" Sullivan grinned at him, and after a second, Tobias's lips quirked, his nose wrinkling like he was trying not to be amused.

"How did you know it wasn't Ghost at the door?" Tobias asked.

"I heard the keys at the lock, and Ghost's key was on the counter."

"Oh. That's—that's really smart."

"Well, I detect stuff professionally."

The quirk turned into an actual smile, and if Sullivan had thought Tobias looked good when he was strained and nervous, that was nothing to how attractive he was with actual happiness in his grin.

"Okay, so now what?"

"Now it's time to stalk Russians," Sullivan said cheerfully.

Tobias's grin vanished. "I don't know if I'll be any good at stalking. I've never—obviously I've never stalked someone before so—"

"Let me rephrase. I'm going to stalk Russians. You're

going to go home and be a student. If you give me your number, I'll call you if I find anything out about Ghost."

Tobias's expression had been developing storm clouds, but at that last bit, the clouds paused. "You will?"

"Don't let the mohawk confuse you," Sullivan said dryly. "I'm nice. Usually. Frequently." He frowned, considering it. "Sometimes."

"Sorry. I didn't mean—"

"It's fine. Forget it. But seriously, go home."

"How do you stalk Russians?"

"Mostly I sit in cars and take pictures. Go home."

"Wait. How did you know I was a student?"

"When you got out of your car, you put your backpack in the trunk. Detective, remember?"

"Right. Sorry."

As they reached the spot where the sidewalk dead-ended at the parking lot, Sullivan pulled his phone out of his pocket. "You did good back there."

Tobias looked startled. "I did?"

"Yeah. I mean, getting grabbed by someone you barely know isn't awesome, I get that, so lots of people get all offended. You know, 'don't muffle me, don't drag me places,' and under normal circumstances that's the right response, but under these circumstances that could've screwed us. But you went with it."

Sullivan couldn't read the complicated expression that replaced Tobias's surprise. A lot of things about Tobias were unexpectedly hard to read, and even if Tobias hadn't been downright handsome, the puzzle of him would be attractive. A wholesome, all-American boy who was best friends with a missing hustler? How was Sullivan supposed to stay professional in the face of that?

And the icing on the cake was the way Tobias had so

instinctively put himself and his safety squarely in Sullivan's hands. Tobias couldn't know how much that would crawl under Sullivan's skin, how being offered that much trust could easily take Sullivan into an inappropriate mental place that was destructive in all sorts of ways, so he finished up by repeating, "You did good."

Tobias watched him for a long second, like he wasn't having any more luck figuring Sullivan out than Sullivan was having figuring him out. "Thank you."

"Sure."

"And for offering to keep in touch."

"No problem. What's your number?"

Tobias rattled it off. "You'll call, right? Promise?"

"Promise."

With a last, conflicted look in the direction of Ghost's condo, Tobias headed toward his car.

Sullivan followed suit, walking to the far edge of the parking lot where he'd parked the Buick. He grabbed his camera—a Canon 5D Mark III, and worth every penny—from where he'd stashed it in the trunk before following Tobias to Ghost's back door. He climbed behind the wheel.

With a notepad and pen from his glove box, Sullivan started making notes, keeping one eye on the sidewalk so he could catch the Russians if/when they showed themselves. He'd recorded Tobias's tag numbers earlier, so he wasn't worried about not being able to find him if the phone number or address proved to be fake.

He allowed himself exactly one minute to imagine what Tobias would do if Sullivan said more nice things to him, encouraged that trust to go a little further, a little darker, into something closer to obedience and pain. Would Tobias enjoy it? Was he a good boy down to his core, or was this a case of still waters running deep? Sullivan's chest twisted with guilt the whole time, but he liked what his imagination came up with.

He liked it a lot.

Then he tossed his phone onto the passenger seat and slumped in his seat, camera at the ready, and thought about everything that'd happened today.

What was a guy like Tobias doing hanging out with someone like Ghost? What was the point of buying a condo in a dead chick's name?

And what the hell did a young male hooker and a couple of pissed-off Russians have to do with a ten-year-old girl who'd gone missing twenty years before?

## Chapter Five

The foyer was knee-deep in shoes and backpacks when Tobias got home, and he added his own to the pile before heading toward the kitchen and the sound of voices.

All but one of his younger brothers and sisters sat around the table eating papayas and string cheese. Mirlande, now twenty-two and living at home while taking classes in hospitality at DU, was listening as fifteen-year-old Darlin discussed his upcoming soccer game. Sitting beside her, Guy, who was sixteen, had temporarily lost his habitual disaffected teenager sneer in favor of explaining to twelve-year-old Ruby why the kids should pool their Christmas lists to ask for a PlayStation 4 for the family instead asking for individual gifts. Because of their parents' anti-spoiled-kids protocol, Christmas teamwork was the only way Guy would be getting his hands on a console unless he saved up the money on his own, and even then, there was a good chance their parents would demand that the cash go into his college fund.

"But I don't *like* video games," Ruby said, for what was probably not the first time, judging from Guy's groan of frustration. "I want my present to be summer camp. Like on *Bunk'd*."

"Where's Marie?" Tobias bent to steal a bite of Ruby's papaya and got a halfhearted smack on the arm in return.

"Upstairs listening to *Lemonade* for the millionth time." Guy rolled his eyes.

"I know you didn't just roll your eyes at Queen Bey," Mirlande said mildly.

"I'm rolling my eyes at Marie!"

Ruby shot her older brother a dirty look. She put her hands together like she was praying and intoned, "Forgive him, O Queen, for his shortsighted maleness."

"He knows not what he does," Mirlande added, and one of them must've kicked Guy, because he made an outraged noise and turned to Tobias for help.

"Leave me out of this," Tobias said quickly.

Like Tobias, his siblings were all adopted. Unlike Tobias, they were all black. Mirlande, Darlin, and Guy were Haitian, while Ruby was Jamaican. They primarily spoke English at home—Guy and Ruby still needed practice for school and Ruby's grasp of *Kreyòl* wasn't great anyway.

His manman was at the stove, transferring boiled pork shoulder to a baking dish, and the letter tucked inside his textbook in his backpack—forgotten in the drama at Ghost's place—came to mind. His appetite vanished, despite the fact that *griot* was one of his favorite dishes, even when Manman chose to go the healthier route and broil rather than fry the meat.

"Hi." He gave her a kiss hello on the cheek. She smelled like that same rose cream she always wore, and he wanted so badly to not be this angry with her.

"Home late."

"A bit." He tamped down the instinct to bristle at the way she checked up on him as if he were a child, reminding himself that it was only because she loved him and worried. And it wasn't like she was wrong to worry. He *had* spent the afternoon breaking in to Ghost's place. Not that he could say that, so he went with a small lie. "I went to see Church."

She paused, the knife hovering in the air over the cutting board. She didn't entirely approve of Tobias's ongoing friendships with guys he'd met at Woodbury, but neither she nor Papa had pushed him to end the relationships. He was grateful for their circumspection. Church and Ghost were his closest friends, crucial to his happiness, and cutting off contact with either of them would be unbearable. He wasn't sure how he could avoid hurting his parents if they asked him to.

Her tone was politely distant. "Oh? How is he?"

"Good."

Manman nodded and resumed her preparations. The subject was closed.

He considered claiming that he needed to study—it wasn't untrue, because he always needed to study—but it would make her worry. He wasn't antisocial by nature, and if he didn't make at least a token effort to interact with the family, she would notice.

"Want me to start the *pikliz*?" he asked finally. He was the only male in his family allowed to help cook because he was the only one with enough patience to do everything exactly as Manman demanded. She was very particular about her kitchen.

"That would be very helpful, *cheri*, thank you."

He went to the sink to wash his hands. When he'd dried them, he pulled cabbage, carrots, and peppers out of the fridge before ducking his head into the pantry. "We're not out of vinegar, are we? I can go to the store."

"Behind the olive oil," she said, with an air of *why*

*can't men find things* in her voice. It made him smile despite his mood, especially since the vinegar was exactly where she'd said it would be.

"Success." He got out a large bowl and grabbed a cutting board.

She nodded distractedly, focusing on the pork, which he could smell from where he stood—faintly citrus, slightly sour, entirely delicious. "How was your day?"

He wondered what she would say if he told her that he'd broken in to someone's house and hidden in the closet with a tattooed, mohawked private detective. "It was fine. How was yours?"

"Good." She slid the pork into the oven, then stood there staring at the knobs. She'd worked at the clinic today, but she'd changed out of her slacks and white coat into one of the bright dresses she preferred, the rich green a pretty contrast against her obsidian skin as she stood barefoot on the red Spanish tile. She usually put her hair up in a bun while seeing patients, but that was always the first thing to go when she got home, and now her twists elegantly framed her face, though they did nothing to conceal the tension of her pressed-tight lips.

Angry as he was, as much as that letter had him burning on the inside, he loved her, and he couldn't ignore her unhappiness.

"Hey," he said gently, and she startled. *"Ou byen?"*

*"Wi.* I'm fine." She kept her voice too low for his siblings to hear, not that they would've over the raucous conversations taking place. She put the cover back on the pot she'd boiled the pork in, keeping it warm for later, when she would make the sauce. She didn't look up at him. "Dr. Thornton mentioned that you never called him."

Tobias wished that he'd escaped to his room after all.

Or that he'd gotten a place of his own this afternoon. Or vanished from the surface of the planet. Anything but this, where he felt more like a bumbling infant instead of a grown man. "No, I didn't."

"You said you would."

Because it had been the only way to escape that awful lecture last week before he ended up shouting at his parents, not because he needed to be back on meds. And that was what she was getting at—Dr. Thornton was a friend of the family, he knew the history, he knew what Tobias's parents wanted, and he would pull out a script pad, and that would be that. In normal circumstances, it might not even be a bad solution; clinical depression frequently came back, so going unmedicated could be risky for some people who'd been diagnosed with it.

The problem was that Tobias *hadn't* been diagnosed with it. The ER doctor had mentioned depression as a likely cause for his cutting that long-ago day in the hospital, and his parents had accepted it at face value. Tobias had never corrected them, even when the psychiatrist at Woodbury had decided that the cutting hadn't been the result of depression so much as a cry for help from a teenager trapped in an overwhelming set of circumstances that he had no clue how to escape on his own. It had shocked Tobias how fast his mood and thoughts had turned around once he'd gotten away from school and all the expectations and the little voice that said *what you're doing won't be enough*. In fact, once Ghost had come into his life and kept the bullies at bay—seemingly just by breathing—Tobias had been almost happy at Woodbury. The months in treatment had given him better coping skills and a break to bolster himself, and since he'd never felt the need to cut since then, he figured his psychiatrist had been right.

Unfortunately, she'd wanted him to make a lot of big changes in his life to ensure he didn't wander into the same situation twice, something he'd never quite managed to do.

Regardless of that last point, neither Dr. Thornton nor his prescription pad could help Tobias now. Not that he could explain any of that to his manman. So he said, "I've been busy."

"Not with schoolwork."

"Yes, with schoolwork." It chafed that he was expected to explain this. His parents had always been deeply involved in his and his siblings' lives, and it had never occurred to him to mind when he was growing up; his aunts and uncles were the same with their kids. It was normal. But he was much older now, and he couldn't help thinking that the dynamic should've shifted by now. His parents didn't treat Mirlande with such kid gloves. How much longer would he have to pay for a single mistake back in high school?

"Your papa said you haven't taken him up on his offer to arrange an internship at Cancer Care."

He forced his breathing to slow. "That's because I'm not sure that an internship with a parent will look good on my applications, not because I'm not taking care of it."

That was a lie. He hadn't submitted a single internship request anywhere. He had a stack of half-completed ones in his desk, but he couldn't—he hadn't had time.

"It wouldn't be with your papa. It would be with one of the other practitioners. It's not like they won't judge you as strictly as anyone else—"

"Manman." He ground his teeth, trying to choke back

the roughness he'd spoken with, not liking the way her expression twisted when he snapped at her.

"Is it like before? Is it happening again?" Her fingers clamped around the lid of the pot so tightly the beds of her nails went white. "You're so far away."

"I'm right here," he gritted out. *Bondye*, he wanted to walk out.

"I love you. We both love you. We only want to help. We only want you to be happy."

That was the problem. That was the root of all of it, the good and the bad. Their desire to help, to protect, even when it meant taking things that weren't theirs to take. But she was watching him with such awful worry, such…such *fear*, and most of his anger drained in the presence of it. All but the small, hard kernel behind his sternum which remained where it'd been for weeks now.

"I'll call Dr. Thornton." He knew when he'd been beaten. "I'll set up the internship. It's not happening again."

Her shoulders didn't loosen. "Tobias."

"It's not," he insisted. "I've got everything under control. I'm busy, not broken."

"You've never been broken." Her stiffness vanished. She took his hand, squeezed it, and he squeezed back. "You've fought so hard to get your life on track again. You're so close to the next step. We just want to help."

He nodded and pulled away, going back to slicing up cabbage, careful to keep his attention on what he was doing so he wouldn't cut himself.

After a moment, she murmured, "I will do whatever it takes to keep you safe."

He put the knife down and wrapped his arms around her. She leaned into him, and he was tall enough that her face pressed against his collarbone. He could feel her breath, warm against the fabric of his shirt as her fingers pressed hard into his back, as if she meant to hold him so tightly nothing could ever harm him again.

God, he loved her.

God, he wished he could get far, far away from her.

Midnight came and went, and Tobias finally set his books aside. Premed meant a difficult course load, and the expectations of his professors were high. Tobias was smart, but some of his foundational high school courses—those taken at Woodbury, anyway—had been lacking in content and challenge, so he constantly felt like he was playing catch-up. Summer courses were more intensive than regular ones, too, but if he wanted to graduate next spring, it was necessary.

He got into bed. His eyes felt heavy, but his thoughts began whirling again the second he had nothing else to concentrate on. He lay on his back, one hand pressed flat on his belly to remind it to calm down.

His desk was invisible with the light off, but he glanced in its direction anyway as if the letter tucked away in the top drawer might be somehow visible behind the wood. He should read it, shouldn't he? Even if it was twenty-four years too late, he couldn't simply ignore it. And what had been the point of digging it out of the trash where Manman had dumped it if he wasn't going to read it? To do anything else was like admitting she'd been right to keep it from him.

Hell, maybe she had been. Here, in the nighttime dark, it was harder to hide from that old fear, that old certainty of his own weakness. *Broken*, he mouthed into the silence of his bedroom.

*Is it like before*, she'd asked.

No. He remembered that dull, cold flatness too well to mistake it for anything else. A near-constant sense of suffocation, his body leaden and slow, his thoughts as trudging as mud sliding down a drain, when they moved at all, all of him weighed down by the inevitability of his own future, of the expectations he couldn't possibly meet. He'd been as aware as a scarecrow, and about as useful.

This was something else.

These past eight months since the whole thing had gone down with Church and Ghost and the favor, ever since that terrible day when he'd almost lost Church, when he'd been miles away from what was going on and unable to do anything but send a series of stupid texts— it was all sharper and meaner and brighter than before.

Tobias had never told Church about it, not wanting his friend to feel guilty, but he'd had a monster panic attack once everyone was safe. It'd taken his knees out from under him. He'd been on the floor of a dingy bathroom in the Tivoli Student Union, vision narrowing to a pinprick, the voices from the food court a distant buzz in his ears, and all he could think was *I can't do this again. I can't be this powerless again.* It'd started some process that'd only been amplified by finding the letter, amplified further by Ghost's absence, a process that he couldn't define or get a grip on, but which made it increasingly difficult to be polite, to accept only what was offered, to wait and endure and put up with what was left over.

*Before* had been the numbness at the bottom of a gray ocean.

*Now* was red and boiling and—at times—impossible to contain.

His breathing was too fast, and he concentrated on

slowing it. He forced his hands to uncurl out of the fists they'd formed. This creeping electricity buzzed inside him all the time these days, an incessant itch beneath his skin, poised to burst through.

And a small part of him that he didn't want to acknowledge liked how it felt.

Tobias was up at 6:00 the next morning, early enough to sneak into the bathroom before Guy, a necessity if he wanted to get to his 8:00 class on time, because Guy had recently entered a phase in which he had to stare at his zits for ten minutes a day as if he could will them away. Still better than the girls' bathroom, though; between Ruby, Mirlande, and Marie, that one was a nightmare from dawn until dusk.

Manman shoved a bagel in his hand on the way out the door and Papa called after him that they would need to talk internships when Tobias got home. He made the long drive down to the Broadway light-rail station, where he parked and caught the train. He spent the time trying to concentrate on his biochemistry study guide while actually thinking of how to find Ghost.

His classes passed with their usual interminable dullness, the numbers and theories slipping sideways in his head despite his rigorous note-taking. His hours in the writing center went by more quickly; he liked tutoring other students, liked imagining all the fascinating subjects that other people got to study.

On his way back to his car, he got a text message from Church: still no word from ghost?

He paused halfway through the parking lot in the congestive August heat, sweat prickling between his shoulder blades, and considered how to respond. If he explained about Ghost's phone and meeting Sullivan, Church would flip out. He'd tell Tobias to come over and explain everything so that Church would know how to handle it.

At twenty-three, Edgar-Allen Church was almost a year younger than Tobias, and they'd been best friends ever since he'd come to Woodbury on his eighteenth birthday, fresh from a year's stint in juvenile detention for committing assault. He was tall and lanky, black-haired and mahogany-skinned, with a dorky sense of humor, a loyal streak a mile wide, and a temper like a match flame—quick and hot, but short-lived and soon forgotten. Tobias loved Church's fierce goodness, but his friend's impulse to protect the people he cared about meant that he had a tendency to act like Tobias could barely tie his own shoes.

Once armed with an explanation, Church would probably browbeat Sullivan into a meeting, and the two of them would put together how Ghost's absence and the whole debacle with the Krayevs meshed with whatever Sullivan's actual case was, and Tobias would be left on the sidelines, begging for scraps of information.

Because Church was more of a hero than he gave himself credit for being, he'd save the day. But that didn't mean he should have to.

A couple months ago, Church had finally succeeded in getting his abused mother to leave his father, and she was living with Church and his boyfriend—and eventual fiancé, Tobias suspected—Miller. The custom woodworking shop he was starting with Miller was going to have a grand opening soon, so they were working hard to get that set up. Church was taking a couple of carpentry classes, too.

Church had a lot on his plate, was the point.

Plus, Miller hadn't walked away from the Krayevs unscathed, and Church would open a vein before he'd let Miller get hurt again. Even for Ghost. It would shred Church on the inside to make that choice, but Miller would win. It was right that Miller would win, especially considering that Tobias was here to handle the situation and was more competent than a baby rabbit, no matter what Church thought.

He sent back: still no word.

Technically, it wasn't a lie, but he wasn't proud of the hot, shameful rush of vindictive pleasure at being the one with information to withhold this time.

Back at home, Tobias used the relative quiet to catch up on schoolwork. Actually, a more honest way to phrase it would be to say he spent a miserable couple of hours *trying* to catch up. He read the same paragraphs in his textbooks repeatedly before turning to his biochemistry study guide instead, only to stare at the words uselessly for twenty minutes.

His phone rang, but the number wasn't one he knew, and his pulse ticked up a speed. "Hello?"

"Is this Tobias Benton?" Not Ghost. The caller was a woman, her voice tremulous and cautious.

"Yes."

"Really?"

Tobias frowned. "Yes. May I ask who's calling?"

There was the huff of a forceful exhalation in his ear. "Yeah, sorry. It's me. Ashley Benton. Your, ah, your mother. Can we talk?" She paused, but it was tiny, little more than an allusion to manners, not that he could've summoned a response in that time anyway. He couldn't breathe, let alone speak. "I just want to talk. Maybe it's rude to call, but you weren't responding to my letters and I… I didn't know what else to do."

He stared at the wall. Listened to her breathe. Tried to breathe himself. "What do you want?"

"Just this. To talk to you. To…maybe get to know you."

He shook his head, remembered she couldn't see it, and said instead, "Why?"

She didn't respond for a minute. Then, "Because you're my son. Because I… I love you."

"Are you—are you joking?"

"Do you think I would go to all this effort to mess with you?" Ashley—he refused to think of her as his mother, absolutely *refused*—sounded affronted, and he found himself laughing.

"I don't know what you'd do. I don't know *you*. I don't know you because you threw me in the garbage. Your definition of love could use some work, Ms. Benton."

He was getting loud. He swallowed.

It was a while before she spoke again. "I was sixteen," she said quietly. "I was terrified and I'd just given birth alone and I had all these hormones…and I was *sixteen*. I know I did something unforgivable, and I'm sorry, you can't imagine how sorry I am, but…"

She kept going, but he wasn't listening. His imagination had conjured up a picture a frightened teenage girl alone at night, an infant clasped in her arms, maybe still bleeding from giving birth in whatever motel she'd rented for the night so her parents wouldn't find out. He imagined the panic she must've felt.

*Don't think about that.*

"I lost more than half my life so far to prison," she was saying. "And I know it's what I deserve, and I wouldn't blame you if you wanted nothing to do with me, but I can't undo it if you don't give me a chance. That's all I want. A chance to make it up to you. That's all I've wanted for years, it's why I keep making these attempts even though your parents are—"

Leaving aside his bewilderment that she thought she ever could undo what she'd done, that it was possible to make such a thing up to a person, his brain stuttered to a halt as she kept talking.

"Wait, what? What attempts?"

Ashley hesitated. "I've been trying to contact you for years, Tobias. Didn't they—didn't they tell you? No, of course they didn't. Who's the fucking perfect parent now?"

Her words became aggressive, stabbing things in the space of a finger snap, and he tuned her out. It was easy; his heart was pounding so painfully loud that he couldn't hear anything over it. He'd…he'd thought the letter was a one-time thing. That his parents had opened it, read it, and then decided not to share it because the contents would be poisonous for him somehow. It wasn't an excuse, and it was still wrong, but he'd thought it was *once*. A rushed choice born of anger or fear, one perhaps regretted when a cooler head prevailed.

But years?

"I have rights," she was saying, still too hard, still too painful. "Sure, she kept her word, huh, in the literal sense, but we both know she didn't follow it in spirit, damn it, she *knew* why I wanted you to have my name, to keep me informed, and she fucking—"

"I have to go," he managed. It was getting hard to breathe.

She stuttered to a stop, the air shocked between them, and then she rushed forward. "No, no, wait, I didn't mean that, that's not why I called, I just—I've been trying so hard, and this is the first time I've gotten through to you, and I can't—I wanted to do something for you. I want to help or give you something, I want to make something better for you, I don't care what, if you'll let me, I'll— it's your choice, Tobias, not theirs, you can choose to—"

She was right about one thing—it was his choice. Not his parents', not Ashley Benton's. And he chose to stop dealing with this before he had a panic attack.

"If you really want to do something for me, don't call me again. I've got your number, and I'll— Don't call me again."

"Tobias, *please*—"

He hung up on her. He'd never hung up on anyone in his life, but he hit the disconnect button with his thumb with furious satisfaction. The world seemed to swim around him, going too bright and too distant, and every-thing inside him had gone bright and distant too. His fin-gers were trembling.

He had no idea how much later it was when a knock came on his bedroom door and Papa said through it, "Come into my study, Tobias, I'd like to talk with you."

Before the call, Tobias would've had the same reaction he'd always had to one of his papa's directives: the as-sumption that Tobias's schedule didn't warrant so much as a token question as to whether he was available would chafe, but he would say nothing because it was a tiny thing, and it would be ungrateful to raise a stink when his papa was going out of his way to help him.

Now he felt a very strong urge to say words he'd never said to one of his parents before. The panic hummed under his skin, and he thought—still distantly, almost like the words were echoing in his skull—that he was on a precipice, that he was fragile in a way he'd never been before, and that he had to be careful, had to rope this in before he broke down.

With numb fingers, he turned the knob. With shaky legs, he followed his father down the hallway.

Andre Alcide's tastes ran to the practical and meticulous, preferences never more on display than in his home study—the fastidiously organized and polished oak campaign desk, the thick oncology texts with their cloth bindings resewn at the first sign of fraying sitting on the shelves, the framed degrees hung in a line straight enough to satisfy a level. The only personal items in the room were the two paintings on the wall: one of a group of Haitian women in colorful skirts and blouses carrying baskets of fruit on their heads, and another of the *Rada Loa* hanging directly behind Papa's chair. Gorgeous as it was, Tobias hated that painting—he couldn't face it without thinking of countless lectures about school and ambition.

Tobias's father was thin and narrow. His skin was the color of acorns, and he had a sharpish chin and intelligent eyes with a propensity for disappointment. He was a man of high expectations—for himself, for his work, for the world at large, and it had resulted in considerable success for him. When he applied those high expectations to his eldest son, however, the results had to be far less satisfying.

Tobias took a seat, every fiber in his body strung tight as piano wire, and Papa sat across from him, crossing his legs and folding his hands in his lap.

"I brought you in here to discuss your internship." Papa's gaze raked over Tobias. "But I see now that's something for later. Are you all right?"

This again. And again and again, it seemed. "How do you mean?"

"You seem upset."

"Do I?" Tobias's throat might've been lined with razor blades, the words came out so sharp.

His father looked taken aback, but only briefly. "What's happened? Are you all right? Has someone done something to you?"

"Yes." Something barbed and choking and vicious was rising within him. "You did."

His father's gaze went flinty. His pupils expanded, and Tobias's brain filled in the explanation for that absently— *fight or flight response. Fear or anger triggers the release of adrenaline, and one of the side effects is greater pupil dilation to provide increased visual perception to aid in a dangerous situation.* Nice to know his classes were good for something.

"You'll explain yourself now, please," Papa said, voice as rocklike and heavy as his stare despite his calm intonation. That was the worst thing about his lectures, generally. He existed in a state of perpetual rationality, so that even a hint of anger or defiance seemed grossly out of place, and yet the whole time he gave off an air of dominance so strong that to do anything but obey seemed potentially catastrophic.

It was so strong, in fact, that Tobias had yet to come across a more intimidating consequence in life than the disapproval of the man sitting across him. It seemed nonsensical, perhaps, that Tobias could love his papa, and know that he was loved in turn, and yet still dread being in Papa's presence when he had to admit to some failing—when he'd gotten lost on a shopping trip as a small child; when he'd broken his arm falling from a tree when he was eight; when he'd come out to his parents at eighteen, so tempted to apologize that he'd had to press his palm against his lips to hold it at bay. And while his parents had accepted his homosexuality with gradually increasing pragmatism over the years, he'd never quite forgotten the potency of his fear when he'd first begun explaining. His hands had trembled so much that he'd been forced to sit on them.

Now he waited for that familiar dread to overwhelm him, but instead he laughed. It filled the air, cutting as the crack of a whip and just as brief. He stood up and pulled the letter out of his back pocket. He dropped the stained, ragged thing on the desk between them so the address faced upward.

"How long has she been trying to contact me?" he asked.

Papa stared at the letter like it was an insect crawling toward him. "You don't have all the facts."

"That's an unfortunate side effect of being lied to."

"We had good reasons to keep her from you."

"Until I was eighteen, maybe." Tobias spun the letter with one finger. "It's a federal crime in this country to keep mail from someone, did you know that?"

His papa finally looked up, aiming the full weight of his disapproval at him. It rolled off like soap bubbles, gone in a flash. "Don't be ridiculous. We're not criminals. We're your parents. We do what's best for you."

"That's not for you to decide anymore!" Not once had Tobias raised his voice at his papa, and certainly not like this, with every muscle in his body coiled, with such volume that he heard Manman exclaim down the hall.

Papa had gone still, his eyes two burning holes in his

face. "You were fragile back then, Tobias. And there are things about your adoption that you don't know—"

"You mean the part where she threw me in a Dumpster, right?" Tobias asked, and Papa's mouth dropped open, his eyes widening, and it felt so good to finally get a reaction. "Yeah, I know about that. I've known since I was ten, when Tante Esther let it slip."

Tante Esther was much younger than Manman, hip and bold and adored by his siblings, but Tobias's relationship with her had always been rocky. Even now, almost fifteen years later, he wasn't sure if she'd told him the truth about his adoption because she felt he deserved to know or if she'd simply been carelessly cruel. Not that it mattered at this point.

"Esther," Papa muttered. "Of course."

"I looked it up on the microfiche at the library afterward and read all about the case. And I—the thing is, I understand that. You didn't want a kid to know that he'd been treated like garbage, and yes, I was angry at the time, but I understand it. This—these lies, for years, even once I was old enough...this I don't understand."

"Tobias," Manman said from behind him. He turned, and the letter must've become visible, because her confused gaze dropped to the envelope and went hollow with clarity. "Oh, Toby."

"Don't call me that," he said quietly, and her expression twisted. He refused to feel guilty.

"You protect family," Papa said stiffly, and Tobias turned back to him, surprised at the response. It was so obvious, wasn't it, that they'd done wrong? But perhaps not, and Tobias considered for the first time that the reasonable expression in the older man's eyes wasn't reason at all, but rigidity.

"You're not sorry." Tobias couldn't believe it. "You lied, and you're not even sorry."

"You don't understand—" Manman began.

"No, *you* don't understand. There is no explanation that makes this okay." Now Tobias had yelled again, leaving them both staring at him, and he didn't care. He didn't want to try to calm down. He never would've managed it, and besides, this anger was both pleasurable and warming—he wanted to keep it. "You're liars. This isn't protection. This is control."

In the ensuing silence Tobias could hear Ruby crying in the living room.

"You can't behave like this around your siblings." Papa climbed to his feet, and it should've been a sign of his impatience, a minor aggression even, but it wasn't. Andre Alcide, for the first time in Tobias's life, appeared small. "You absolutely cannot speak to me this way."

"No?" Tobias reached down and picked up his letter. "You keep forgetting that I'm old enough to do what I want."

Papa's spine straightened, his gaze hardening. "While you're here, as a member of this household, there is a standard of behavior, young man. I understand that you're upset, but there's a right way and a wrong way to handle it. You owe your best to the people who love you, to your dignity, and to your responsibilities."

And like that, Tobias was done. He was just...done. He tuned his father out and headed for the hall, gently edging his mother out of the way. In his room, he grabbed his backpack, dumping it upside down over his mattress so that everything spilled out. He shoved his laptop, his allergy pills, and a couple T-shirts and changes of underwear inside, not bothering to close the drawer again. He grabbed his wallet and his toothbrush and everything else that his shaking hands could grasp. After a brief hesitation, he picked up his textbooks as well.

When Tobias shut his door behind him, his parents were in the hall, Manman begging with her eyes, Papa watching with his mouth flat and stunned.

"I'll come back for the rest of my things." Tobias pushed past them, still gentle, because he couldn't hurt them, not like that.

Ruby was downstairs on the couch, her face screwed up tight as she sobbed, her cheeks wet. Mirlande was beside her, rubbing her back, watching Tobias somberly. He sank onto the cushion beside Ruby, tugging her into his arms. She clung to him.

"I love you," he said. "So much. I'll call you. Tell the others I'll call them too, okay?"

"Toby," she gasped, shoulders heaving, and he kissed her forehead and peeled her hands from his waist.

"I love you," he said again. To Mirlande, he murmured, "Call from your cell if you need me."

She nodded, her hand landing warm on his forearm to squeeze once.

"Tobias," Manman choked out. "Wait, please."

He could sense Papa on the stairs watching, but Tobias didn't look at him or say anything to either of them.

He left.

The motel room smelled like cigarettes and wet dog.

Tobias sat on the orange and blue duvet, his backpack beside him because he didn't dare risk bedbugs by setting it on the floor, and stared at the blank screen of the television. The crickets were calling on the other side of the window. It was too warm; he should get up and turn the air-conditioning unit on, assuming it worked. But in a minute. He needed a minute. Right now he needed to sit on his hands until the urge to break something passed.

He expected to feel guilty, but he didn't. He felt wired. Like he was on one of those amusement park rides that spun and spun until the centrifugal force seemed on the verge of flinging you in to the air. Terrifying and thrilling at once.

He needed something to do. Needed...something. Weirdly, what came to mind then was that strange moment on the sidewalk when Sullivan Tate had praised him. The feeling that rose in him at the memory was unfamiliar. He worried at the sensation, picking it apart, trying to understand, but he couldn't make sense of it. He thought he liked it, though. It was warm and electrifying.

He *did* know the name for what he'd felt when Sullivan stood next to him in the cramped dark, his warm breath puffing against Tobias's ear and jaw, his mouth almost close enough to brush Tobias's skin. He hadn't been able to concentrate on that shivery feeling at the time, what with the bad guys who might be the same Krayevs from eight months ago in the other room.

But yes, that one he knew.

He thought about Sullivan's competency, the way he'd acted in the condo, swiftly and without doubt. The way he'd laughed at the idea of stalking potentially dangerous people, like there was nothing frightening about it. Maybe there *was* nothing frightening about it, not for someone like Sullivan, who wore his hair as if professionalism had never entered his mind, whose black tattoos ran the lengths of both arms and marked him as rebellious at the very least. Maybe even dangerous. Someone who didn't care what anyone thought of him, someone wild, who took chances, acted recklessly. Someone who took what they wanted and never minded the consequences.

Tobias didn't know how to be any of those things. He wasn't sure he wanted to be any of them. What he did want wasn't nearly so exciting; he wanted to stop doing things that made him feel bad—which was most things, in retrospect—and do things that made him feel good—which was a much shorter list. He wanted to say yes where he normally said no. And he wanted that to be okay. He didn't want to be afraid that the people he loved would lie or leave simply because he wasn't easy anymore.

With the wild, spinning itch of anger under his skin, it seemed reasonable. Possible.

A new Tobias. One who got what he wanted, did what he wanted. Damn the people who wouldn't stand by him in his happiness. If Church or his parents or his college advisor or his…his birth mother couldn't respect that and wanted to leave, let them. He didn't need any of them.

But Ghost.

Unlike everyone else, Ghost wouldn't blink twice at Tobias's rebellion. He wouldn't sneer at this crappy economy motel that was all Tobias could afford, considering that it might take weeks for him to find a new place and a job that could pay the rent better than his lowly work-study at the writing lab. Ghost wouldn't see the water-stained carpet as a sign that Tobias should put up and shut up. There was no consequence severe enough to make Ghost cave when he didn't want to do something; a motel or a few arguments wouldn't even ping on his radar.

No, Ghost was a different sort of problem. More than anyone else in Tobias's life, Ghost *left*.

Frequently, and without concern for how others might feel in the process.

The new Tobias couldn't—*wouldn't*—stomach it.

Ghost's leaving might not be leaving, though. It might be kidnapping or running or… Tobias ran out of guesses. But the point was that getting hurt or being frightened was something Tobias—new or old—could forgive. Abandonment was not. And before he could decide if the new Tobias could allow Ghost to remain in his life, he needed to know which one it was—desertion or evasion.

To find out, he would need help. He could hire Sullivan, maybe, though he had an instinctive dislike for the idea because it meant sitting here while Sullivan went out and did whatever it was he did. It meant waiting for the phone to ring, waiting for someone else to deign to pay attention to him.

Everything in him thundered with a resounding *no* at the very idea.

And he was going to listen to that *no* this time.

He was done reacting and waiting. This time, he was going to be the one calling the shots. Starting with finding Ghost. Starting with Sullivan. He got out the business card Sullivan had given him and went to his laptop.

# Chapter Six

Sullivan woke up fidgety on Thursday with thoughts of Nathalie whirling in his mind: whether he was being foolish to hope she might truly be alive, wondering where she'd been for the past two and a half decades if she was, if she needed help, if there was anything he could do to give her back her life once he did find her. And on a more pragmatic, self-interested level, he couldn't stop thinking about the other perks of finding her—impressing the hell out of Raina and starting the reputation of his future detective agency on the right foot by breaking a case like this.

He was jittery through coffee and cereal, and he knew, after long years of experience, that if he wanted to get anything done today, he'd have to burn the extra energy out of his system with a run first. The miles blew by in a haze of distraction and *more, more, faster.*

He'd been the definition of hyperactive as a child. He'd even been tested for ADHD, but ADHD tended to have a negative impact on people, and other than having exasperated his parents and a few learning professionals, Sullivan had always functioned fine. He was simply curious, easily bored, and generally obnoxious in the way that overly energetic people could be.

It was just that the world was so interesting, and it was unfair that at any given moment he only had access to a very small part of it. He didn't understand how anyone could take a look around and not be fascinated by the things and people in front of them. Puzzles abounded, questions were posed, and there was so much out there that sometimes he could barely contain his need to do all of it.

He had sharp memories of that—sitting in the buggy at the grocery store reading about how the archaeologists had unlocked the mysteries of ancient hieroglyphics, fiddling with a Rubik's Cube while his mother chatted with her friends over coffee, sitting on the grimy floor at the dry cleaner's with the excavation kit he'd gotten at the museum, and in each instance losing interest as soon as the concept had clicked. It had to have driven his mother crazy, especially when he threw a fit at being told to play with whatever he'd brought, because she didn't understand that he'd gotten everything he could from it and needed something new.

He was the youngest of five and the only boy; they hadn't had much money or many toys, so he'd spent a great deal of his childhood playing imaginative games like racehorses and tea party. And while he made an excellent cup of imaginary Darjeeling, if he said so himself, there were only so many times you could appease your sisters by jumping over lawn furniture while neighing before you started to worry that your formative years were being spent on unproductive activities. That was how he'd found the library and Arthur Conan Doyle and, eventually, his life's work.

When he'd run himself into the ground—took about seven miles, not his best day, but not his worst—he got cleaned up and made his way into the office around nine, where he sat at the table in the kitchen at ASI, listening to the janky fridge complain while he thought about how to work around some dead ends.

He'd gotten pictures of both of the Russians, at least, but he'd had little luck trying to match the faces to any names. He'd spent yesterday doing research into Riviera Condominiums—the complex where Ghost, real name unknown, currently lived in the late Margaret Trudeau's condo—a process that had been time consuming and ultimately useless.

As far as he could tell, Riviera hadn't knowingly sold the property to a dead person as part of a scheme or anything. The firm that owned Riviera owned another complex, but after spending twelve exhausting hours looking at the property records for every single condo at both properties, Sullivan had confirmed that they were all owned by living folks. Riviera didn't have any red flags in other arenas either, not financial or human resources.

The research into the Realtor who'd brokered the sale didn't give him any red flags either, and the guy, a septuagenarian whose partner had had cancer at the time, unfortunately had no memory of the person who'd fraudulently bought the condo under the name of a dead woman.

The lies were all grouped solely on the side of the condo's buyer.

Two days down, and zip to show for it.

Which made Tobias Benton, currently in possession of Ghost's phone, his next best lead.

He was in the middle of wondering how best to go about getting the guy to answer some more questions, when Raina yelled down the hallway to pick up the extension because the guy who'd tried to rat him out for snooping was calling.

Speak of the devil. Sullivan snatched up the receiver. "Hello?"

"Sullivan? This is Tobias Benton. From the condo the other day?"

Sullivan was busy thinking that he needed to avoid sounding like the kind of shady PI who wanted to steal Tobias's buddy's phone for nefarious purposes, all while scrambling for scratch paper to take notes on, so it took him a second to phrase an answer. Tobias apparently thought that pause meant Sullivan didn't remember him, because he heaved a small sigh and added, "The concerned citizen?"

Sullivan laughed before he could help it. "No, I know who you are. I didn't run into that many law abiders this week. So what can I do you for?"

"Do you have time to meet up? I have some things to talk about."

"Okay." Sullivan forced himself to count to three so he wouldn't sound like a teenage boy getting asked out by his crush. "Here? Where you are?"

"Wherever."

Sullivan hesitated because Raina had appeared in the doorway, looming like a disapproving parent, and he resented the implication. "Yours, then."

Tobias rattled off the address of a local motel. "Can you—now? Are you free?"

"I'm on my way."

"Thank you."

After he'd hung up, Sullivan got his things together, all under Raina's watchful eye. "Concerned citizen wants to meet up. Might have some info."

"So I gathered."

He told her the name of the motel, and when she merely raised an expectant eyebrow for more info, he said, "I've got this. If I need help, I'll ask. I'll protect our firm's reputation and I won't get thrown in jail, I promise. Just…a little leeway, okay? To do this myself? Tiny bit? Five inches' worth. You trust me five inches, right?"

She pointed at him with a threatening crimson fingernail. "You better have a comprehensive summary for me in twenty-four hours."

"So comprehensive you'll die of old age before I shut up."

The address Tobias had given him was an unimpressive brown and yellow structure that looked more like a parking garage than a motel, with rooms that opened onto the lot. Bushes gone brown from the heat wilted in cracked cement planters, and the pool had been drained despite the warm weather. A more politic person might call it affordable. Sullivan would call it a dump.

Sullivan rapped on the door.

When he answered, Tobias looked ten years older than he had the last time Sullivan saw him—his curls were uncombed, his eyes red rimmed, and his body language managed to be lethargic and agitated at once. He still resembled a Renaissance angel in a holy war painting, but it was a war he was definitely losing.

"Wow," Sullivan said, following him inside. "This is a relaxing getaway. Getting some good rest here?"

"I'm fine. But thank you for asking." Tobias smiled politely, an expression which did nothing to conceal the fact that he thought Sullivan was being a dick. So much for setting up a friendly rapport.

The room had a king-size bed with the covers tugged up in a halfhearted nod to neatness, a TV, a desk, and a small closet. There was an unzipped backpack with clothes spilling out on the mattress, and the air smelled of bacon and eggs—from the takeout containers in the trash—damp canine, and bitter smoke. On the nightstand were a book, an iPod, a wallet, and a ring of keys. A plastic bag from a local corner mart sagged on the desk, revealing snacks and bottles of juice and tea.

"Are you on the run or something?" Sullivan asked.

"No." Tobias sank onto the bed and gestured to the desk chair across from him. "It's unrelated to the case."

"Right." Sullivan took the chair. "What's up?"

Tobias pursed his lips. "You said you were at Ghost's because you were tracking down a missing person."

"Yeah."

"But it's not Ghost, is it? The person you were hired to find, I mean."

"No. I'd love to talk to him, though, if you've heard from him yet."

Tobias shook his head. "No, I—no."

"Mind if I take a look at his phone? Maybe I can get something that'll help both of us. Direct me to my missing person, help you find your buddy?"

Tobias ignored his question. "I want to hire you to find Ghost. And I'll answer your questions and let you look at his phone, but only if we work together."

"Work together."

"Yes."

"Like, you want to tag along? To…watch?"

"No. I want to help. I'm going to help."

Sullivan sat back in his chair and studied him. Tobias stared back, his brow heavy and determined, his gaze almost combative. He appeared to be expecting a no, which was a good call, but Sullivan suspected he was going to have a fight on his hands, and that wouldn't make it easy to get the answers he needed.

"I'm not going to be able to go that route." Sullivan tried to sound apologetic instead of irritated.

"This is nonnegotiable."

"Oh, is it?"

"It is."

Sullivan lifted an eyebrow. "Sorry, Tobias, but I'm calling your bluff. You want your buddy safe more than you want to play detective. I'll find Ghost for you, but I'm the professional here, and I'll do it alone."

Once again, Tobias ignored him. "Here's what's going to happen. I'm going to pay you and we'll work *together* to find both of our missing people. You'll be getting paid twice for the same work, and it'll be easier having me on the case, because my information will save you an enormous amount of trouble. This is a good deal for you."

On the surface maybe. Until Tobias got hurt or screwed something up, or Raina caught wind of their new teammate. The Raina part he would especially like to avoid—she'd kill him, maybe fire him, and he'd end up starting over from scratch someplace new, losing a couple of years in the process.

Just the idea of putting all of that at risk had his pulse speeding. While Sullivan considered himself a pretty easygoing guy for the most part, feeling cornered was a guaranteed way to get him to push back. Hard. "No. Answer my questions, give me the phone, and I'll let you know if I find your buddy over the course of my investigation. Keep arguing with me, and I won't even do that much."

"No. I'll pay you, I'll give you what you need to get the job done, and you'll let me help. That's the deal."

"I don't need your help to do my job," Sullivan said flatly. "I'll get the answers I need without you."

"Trust me, knowing what I know, that's not remotely true."

A dark thought occurred to him, and Sullivan tilted his head to one side. "Were you and Ghost in a relationship?"

It seemed to take Tobias a second to see where Sullivan was going with that, and then his jaw tightened. "I'm not a stalker. I would never hurt him."

"But you'll slow down my investigation so you can play junior detective?"

Tobias's mouth went taut. "Are you agreeing or not?"

"I ought to haul your ass into the precinct. If you know something that can help resolve an open case, that's obstruction of justice." Sullivan was lying. Tobias wasn't under any legal responsibility to report illegal activity, and he could lie to a PI all he wanted. The cops would laugh in their faces, but Sullivan was betting Tobias didn't know that. "So we can have a chat here, or we can bring the cops in. What's it going to be?"

Tobias stood, blowing out a breath like he was resigned to a fight. Sullivan rose too, not liking the way Tobias loomed over him, already considering how he'd respond if Tobias did take a swing and for a second, as Tobias shifted his body sideways to go around Sullivan, they were standing too close to each other. He could smell the cheap motel soap on Tobias's skin, feel the warmth radiating from his body. It was claustrophobic, too much of an invasion of space for how angry Sullivan was, and he wanted to shove Tobias back, anything to get some breathing room. Or, he thought, as an old, familiar impulse rose within him, maybe he wanted to shove Tobias to his knees right at Sullivan's feet.

Instead, he watched as Tobias walked toward the nightstand, where Tobias paused and said, "All right. We can go to the cops if you want, but it's going to be harder to solve this case when you're in a jail cell. Which is where you'll be, for breaking and entering."

Sullivan felt a slow, creeping dread inside him. "What did you do?"

"Nothing yet." He picked up his wallet and slid it into his back pocket. "I just think the police would be interested in knowing that a local private detective is committing crimes while conducting investigations."

Sullivan hesitated. "You won't tell anyone about us being in Ghost's condo. You'd be in more trouble than I would. You were the one with the rock."

Tobias stared back at him evenly. "Why would I need a rock when I have a key?"

Sullivan's gaze flew to the ring in Tobias's hand. It was bullshit, wasn't it? He cast his mind back. Had Tobias pocketed the key Ghost had left on the counter? Sullivan had seen Tobias pick up the phone, but the key... he couldn't remember.

"You probably won't get in any real trouble," Tobias continued, sliding the keys into his jeans pocket. "I mean, the complex might not press charges, since it'll be a lot of money and time to do so on behalf of a resident they can't find. Still, imagine what your boss would say when you get arrested for breaking and entering. They'll have a witness, after all." He waved a couple fingers to indicate himself, then picked up his room keycard, sliding it into the opposite back pocket. "But I'm ready to go if that's what you want to do."

Sullivan looked Tobias over again, top to bottom, from his tousled curls to his forthright blue eyes, to the hard line of his jaw, to the strong shoulders and flawless posture. "Quite the transformation. From the concerned citizen afraid to break a pane of glass to cold-blooded blackmailer. I misread you. You're a completely different person than I thought you were."

For some reason, that made Tobias's lips curl into a tiny smile. "Maybe I am."

Sullivan tried to work through the angles, wondering how best to handle things so that Raina didn't get wind of any of it, because she would break their deal in a finger snap. That urge to push Tobias back on the defensive, to push him until he broke or knelt, grew stronger.

"Well?" Tobias asked, watching him carefully.

Sullivan had no idea what was on his face, but whatever it was had Tobias circling back around the foot of the bed toward his original seat. "Good. Let's move on to the part where we get some work done."

It was Tobias's bad luck that he was right next to Sullivan when that last little bit of bravado sank in, because Sullivan moved without thinking, his hands finding Tobias's upper arms, his body turning until Tobias was stumbling over his feet, back fetching up against the wall with enough force to knock the wind from his lungs.

"You picked the wrong guy to fuck with," Sullivan said quietly, leaning in until they were pressed close together, using his weight to help keep Tobias contained. Not that Tobias was fighting. He was slumped against the wall, his gaze startled and wide. Sullivan could feel Tobias's heart knocking hard, and the speed of it pleased him.

"I'm not doing this to screw you over." Tobias's voice

wavered. "I just need to find him. And I need to be the one to do it."

"Stop trying to make it sound reasonable. If you're going to pull shit like this, be man enough to admit what you're fucking doing."

Tobias's expression hardened. "Fine. I'm screwing you over. Happy now?"

Sullivan leaned in closer still, letting his fingers dig into Tobias's biceps. "Not even close."

Tobias's breath stuttered warm across Sullivan's skin, eyebrows folding in confusion even as his gaze dropped to Sullivan's mouth. His biceps flexed under Sullivan's hands, but he didn't try to free himself, apparently content with Sullivan trapping him against the wall, controlling him, probably hurting him.

Tobias's next breath was more of a sigh, which was… not a normal reaction to this sort of thing, and for a second, Sullivan was tempted. To push. To see. To know what Tobias would do if Sullivan cupped the back of his neck and shoved him toward the floor. Would Tobias go down smooth or fight? Back when he'd thought Tobias was a demure college student, he'd have assumed the former, but now Sullivan wasn't sure. He also wasn't sure which he would prefer. He liked the idea of Tobias thrown open, all resistance gone, utterly submissive. He also liked the idea of breaking him open as he struggled to hold the shattered pieces of himself together.

Sullivan was half-hard in his jeans and getting harder fast. He tightened his grip for the span of two seconds, three, watching the way Tobias's lips parted, the way he swallowed, and then Sullivan pulled back. Lowered his hands. Tobias's skin had turned red with the pressure of his fingers, and that…fuck, that hit him good.

He sounded hoarse when he said, "I won't forget this."

Tobias didn't sound much better when he replied, "I wouldn't expect you to. And for what it's worth, I know this is unfair. You might not believe me, but I am sorry."

"Not sorry enough to take it back, I bet."

"No."

Sullivan stared at him for another second, taking in the flush on Tobias's cheeks, the way his eyes clung to Sullivan, and Sullivan forced himself to step away. If he didn't get some space to think, he would do something incredibly stupid. "I'm going for a walk. Twenty minutes. Be here when I get back."

Tobias's expression creased—disappointment first, relief following. Then that dissipated too, and he mostly looked exhausted again. "I will."

## Chapter Seven

When the door slammed behind Sullivan, Tobias fell into the nearest chair with rubbery legs. His heart thundered. He'd won, and the triumph at the knowledge wasn't small. But what stole his knees from him was the way Sullivan had shoved him against the wall, his grip painful and mean. Tobias had silently debated the merits of struggling, but under his worry that he wouldn't be able to get free had been the terrifying realization that he…didn't actually *want* to.

Sullivan had known, somehow, what was going through Tobias's head. That narrow, bony face had shifted from fury to surprise to awareness with electrifying speed. Tobias had felt exposed and uncertain and quivering, like a bit of kindling might feel seeing the match approach, and Sullivan had been inches away from doing…something, God, Tobias wasn't sure what, but he wanted to know. He wanted to push, wanted Sullivan to push back, wanted it to burn.

Tobias had liked it.

He was hard.

"Jesus," he whispered, wondering what the hell was wrong with him. He should be focused on finding Ghost, on making sure he gave Sullivan enough information to get the job done, but not so much that he didn't need Tobias's help anymore. He needed to be on his toes, not distracted by whatever twisted sexual tension had managed to spring up between them.

His phone buzzed, and he sighed, the irritation bubbling up even before he looked at the screen. Manman again. He'd been avoiding her calls, and it was probably unfair, but he wasn't sure he had it in him to talk about anything without yelling yet. He let it go to voicemail, deleted it without listening to it, and sent a text: I'm safe, but I don't want to talk. Unless it's an emergency, I'd appreciate some space.

After a couple of minutes, she replied: All right. We love you. Let us know if you need anything, and be safe.

He stared at the words for a second before putting his phone away.

Sullivan came back when he said he would, his knock crisp and loud. Tobias let him in and returned to the bed. The brown hair at Sullivan's temples had darkened with sweat and he had a laptop bag slung over one shoulder. Some of the wild energy he'd been trying to curtail earlier had faded, although his tone remained hard when he said, "There are rules to this."

"If I agree, perhaps."

"No. If you don't agree to these, you could get someone hurt—maybe yourself, maybe me—and I'd rather take my chances getting fired or going to the cops. These are my nonnegotiables. If you don't like them, you can fuck off."

The inflexibility in his voice tipped into aggression by that last bit, but when Tobias lifted an eyebrow, Sullivan took a deep breath and reined it back in. "All right?"

"No promises," Tobias said slowly. "But let's hear them."

Sullivan dumped the laptop bag on the desk, then turned to lean against it, folding his arms. "Rule number one. If you lie to me, even once, we're done. I don't care if we're talking about whether you like pickles on your hamburgers."

That made sense enough, so Tobias nodded. "No problem."

"Rule number two. You will not display initiative of any kind. Sometimes things like this end up going to court, and that means everything has to be done a certain way. Having a random citizen sticking his fingers into the case would make my testimony questionable. I'm not having someone get away with a crime on my watch because you decided to take a peek at something that wasn't your business."

"And if I have a good idea?"

"Tell me. You can help plan strategy and you can be present for some things if we agree upon it in advance, but you're not going to be interviewing witnesses or sneaking into people's offices to find murder weapons, so get that sort of thing out of your head now. Don't take it upon yourself to investigate something if I haven't given you permission because you might end up shooting me in the foot without meaning to."

"Okay."

"Rule number three," Sullivan said. "You do what I say when I say it."

"But—"

"No buts. My word is law when we're in the thick of things. I'm not always going to have the time or the inclination to explain why something should be done to my specifications, but between the law and standard practices and safety, sometimes things simply have to be done inefficiently. We can argue until the cows come home when we're talking like we are now, but I have the final say. Even if you don't like it, you need to obey."

Tobias's jaw tightened even as his belly went unnervingly warm and liquid at that word: *obey.* What on earth was wrong with him? "Fine."

"Fine." Sullivan pulled a laptop out of the bag and booted it. Once he'd found what he wanted, he spun the laptop around so Tobias could see the screen. "Read this. Type your initials below the fee chart. Note that while I won't unnecessarily reveal information about you, my client, I make no such promises about the facts of the case, particularly if addressed by law enforcement officers. I reserve the right to use my own discretion in these instances. Type your name at the bottom—it'll count as an electronic signature."

Tobias read through the metric ton of legalese, signed, and wrote out a retainer check.

Sullivan put it in his pocket. "Now tell me who's in the pictures I took at Ghost's place yesterday."

"Not yet."

Sullivan rounded on him with such visible antagonism that a thread of unease crept up Tobias's spine, and it took considerable effort to hide it. "I want to know about your missing person first. I don't know what information to give you until I know how it might go together."

Very quietly, Sullivan said, "If you're fucking with me, you're not going to like what happens."

Tobias's unease grew stronger. "I'm not. I'm just covering my bases."

There was a beat of silence before some of the hostility began to fade from Sullivan's expression. "Okay. Bare bones…back in 1992, an idiot who wanted to be a crime lord got himself and some of his thugs killed in a turf-war thing. He also managed to get his hapless housekeeper killed at the same time. The housekeeper's ten-year-old daughter, Nathalie, went missing. My client is a family member and he's been looking for her ever since. I followed a stupid hunch, and got a hit—the dead housekeeper somehow bought property about six years ago. Can you guess which property that was?"

Tobias's forehead creased. "Ghost's condo."

"You can see why I'm interested in talking to him. And the people who had keys to his front door."

"Yeah."

"Do you know who they were? The Russians?"

Tobias hesitated. From what Sullivan had said, there was a very good chance that the Krayevs were the owners of the condo where Ghost had been living—or someone in their organization was. He'd suspected as much, but he wasn't sure how they could move forward without confirming the connection first. "I have a good guess."

"A guess?"

"I know someone who can confirm it. I need your pictures, though."

Sullivan's jaw worked as he went back to his computer. He sent the pictures to Tobias's email, then waited impatiently while Tobias forwarded them to Church, along with the message: Are these two of the Krayev brothers?

A minute later, Tobias's phone rang. He glanced at Sullivan and gestured to the door. "I need some privacy for a few minutes, please."

After a long, baleful moment of *are you kidding me?* Sullivan shoved his laptop in the bag and took it with him on his way out, slamming the door behind him for the second time in half an hour.

"Sorry about that," Tobias said into the phone.

"What the fuck, dude?" Church sounded halfway to panic. "What—where—what are you doing? How did you get these pictures?"

"Is it them? The Krayevs?"

"Where did you get the pictures?"

"Church."

"Yes, it's them, all right? Seryozha's the handsome one and Yasha's the stupid-looking one. Now how did you get these pictures?"

"From my private investigator."

"You hired someone to find Ghost?"

"Yes."

"Is he any good?"

"His firm has a good reputation. I checked."

"This is a horrible idea," Church said. "You're going to get yourself hurt."

"Your lack of faith in me is duly fucking noted." Tobias clamped his mouth shut, shocked at himself. He didn't talk to Church like that. He didn't talk to anyone like that. He heard Church's indrawn breath, felt the pause between them as tangible as a wall, and...and he couldn't make himself apologize. "It's not like I'm going to wander up to them and ask if they've hurt my friend. I'm not stupid."

"They almost killed me." Church's voice was low, almost tentative. He didn't sound like himself at all. "They almost killed Miller. You've seen what they did to his hand, Tobias. I didn't mean you can't do shit, I meant... the Krayevs don't fuck around. If they think you're asking questions because of what happened eight months ago, they'll put a bullet in your brain."

"You're the one they'll expect trouble from. They're not going to care about me. As far as they know, I'm a college kid who hired someone to find his buddy. Okay? Let me handle this."

Church's unhappiness radiated through the phone. "This feels wrong."

"It doesn't make you a bad friend to keep Miller safe," Tobias pointed out. "I've got this. I'm only going to see if I can find out where Ghost took off to. I'm not going to start a war with the Russian mafia. You're doing the right thing by staying out of it. You know I'm right."

"The hell I do. I know Ghost and I know this sort of situation, and I know… I know I can't let you get hurt."

"I'm not asking for permission." That snap had come back to his voice, and again Church's side of the conversation went tentative.

"Let me come to your place, yeah? We can talk this out, I'll eat some of that beef stuff that your mom makes and we'll figure—"

"I'm not living there anymore."

"You're—you moved? Why does everyone keep moving without telling me?"

*Sucks getting left out, doesn't it*, Tobias thought, but only said evenly, "You're not my babysitter."

"I know, but—"

"I moved because I don't want to live at home anymore. I'm tired of the bullshit."

"What's going on with you, man?" With uncharacteristic, awkward gentleness, Church asked, "Is it like what happened before, the shit that landed you in Woodbury?"

"So if I'm angry, it's because I have a mental health issue?"

"That's not what I meant—"

"I'm not talking about it right now." Even this had been enough to get that red, raw anger broiling inside him again.

For a long minute they breathed silently into the phone.

"You better not disappear on me the way Ghost has," Church snapped finally. "Dude, I fucking mean it."

"I won't," Tobias promised, affection rising within him as it always did in the rare moments when Church's sharp edges thinned enough to reveal the good heart he tried so hard to hide.

"Send me updates."

"I will."

"Damn it," Church muttered, and hung up.

Tobias collected himself and tugged the door open. "I'm done."

"Swell." Sullivan came back inside, his movements jerky. He threw himself into the chair at the desk and raised his eyebrows. "So? Ready to talk?"

"Within limits."

Visibly exasperated, Sullivan pulled a small digital recorder out of the laptop bag, setting it between them. He pressed the record button. "This is Sullivan Tate, private investigator, beginning interview one with Tobias Benton on the matter of Nathalie Trudeau's disappearance. Interview is taking place on August 3rd, 2017, at 10:28 a.m. Mr. Benton, you're aware that I'm recording this and you give permission, right?"

"Yes."

He turned his laptop to face them, tipping the screen so they could both look at the photograph of the Russian men from the day before. They were both dark-haired and somewhere in their late twenties or early thirties. The hulkish big guy had a vapid expression on his face, while the other, movie-star handsome, looked far cagier.

Sullivan said, "This is a photograph that I took outside of 2435 Ann Arbor Drive at the Riviera Condominium Complex on August 1st at roughly 4:00 p.m. Do you know who the men in the picture are?"

Tobias nodded. "They're Seryozha and Yasha Krayev."

"Jesus fucking Christ."

"You've heard of them, I guess."

"The Krayev name pops up from time to time when you're looking for scumbags, but…" As he spoke, Sullivan opened his browser and ran a quick search for a name. A second later, he spun the laptop one more time in Tobias's direction. "But in this case, it's because Vasily Krayev's body was found in a shallow grave on Lookout Mountain about a month ago. He'd been there for quite a while apparently."

"Oh." Tobias's eyes flew over the first few lines of the search results, all article names like *Suspected Meth Dealer Murdered*, *Man Guilty of Assaulting Cop Found Dead*, and *Shooting Victim Found on Lookout Mtn. Has Mob Ties*. He and Church had kept an eye on the news for weeks after everything had gone down eight months ago in case something that could bite them in the ass ended up in the hands of the press or the cops, but as time had gone by without reports of meth, dealers or related violence, they'd eventually quit monitoring. "Oh, that's bad."

"No shit, Sherlock." Sullivan pushed the laptop back. "Don't suppose you have any thoughts about this dead meth dealer?"

Tobias paused. "I never met him, but I know who he is."

"Do you know his relationship to the guys in the picture? Seryozha, you said? And Yasha? Vasily's brothers? Cousins?"

"Brothers. They're nicknames, though. I don't know what they're short for, but my friend said that Seryozha's the smaller guy, and that he's really smart. He said not to underestimate him."

"And your friend knows this how?"

Tobias reached over and turned off the recorder. "If I tell you about crimes, will you go to the cops?"

Sullivan dragged a hand through his hair, the strands tangling around his fingers. "To be clear, I have zero legal obligation to report criminal activity I stumble across during a case. I'm not law enforcement. That being said, if keeping my mouth shut will get someone hurt, I'll sing like the proverbial canary. I have ethics."

"You care more about people getting hurt than seeing bad guys go to jail," Tobias clarified.

Sullivan frowned. "In the general sense, yes. In the specific sense, it depends on the situation."

Tobias huffed a breath. "Are you going to turn my friend in or not?"

"Did he kill someone?"

"No."

"You sound sure."

"I am sure. He wouldn't do that."

"Sexual assault? Torture? Kidnapping?"

"*Torture?* Are you kidding? No."

"Not even a meth dealer? No one likes meth dealers."

"Not even Vasily Krayev." Tobias's chin lifted. "Not anybody. But I'm not sure about everything that he had to do to stay safe, so… I mean, there might be smaller stuff. I don't know."

"I'm not worried about smaller stuff. We're good." Sullivan restarted the recorder and picked up a pen. "Start at the beginning."

It took about an hour from start to finish. Without using Church's name, Tobias explained his hiring at the bakery owned by the youngest Krayev brother, Matvey, a good man who wanted to live outside of his family's criminal activities. He talked about how the older Krayevs had brought their clumsy, burgeoning meth business into Matvey's bakery without his consent, resulting in Church's subsequent, accidental witnessing of some very illegal drug-related behavior. Cue a landslide of harassment from the oldest Krayev son, the now-deceased Vasily, who'd had a temper problem the size of a moon crater, and the eventual involvement of the Krayev matriarch, who had agreed to let the situation resolve without murder in exchange for Church's silence about the meth and a favor from Ghost.

"There're five Krayev brothers?" Sullivan asked, making notes. "Well, four, now that Vasily's dead?"

"Yes. But Matvey's not going to be a problem. He's a good guy."

"And this matriarch—"

"They called her Mama."

"Right, she's in charge, huh? Do you know her real name?"

"Give me a second." Tobias texted Church: What was Mama's first name?

The response came gratifyingly fast: Yalena? Yellena? Something like that everyone called her mama tho and fuck, you better be careful.

Tobias sighed and passed the message on.

Sullivan kept writing. "But you don't know the specifics of what happened between Mama and Vasily and your buddy?"

Tobias jerked a shoulder. "I just know that on that last day when everything happened, Vasily went after my friend. Mama stepped in, Ghost agreed to do a favor for her, and neither me nor my friend have seen Vasily or any of the other Krayevs since."

"Hmm." Sullivan stared at his notes. "This was eight months ago?"

"Yes."

"And it was around this time that Ghost moved into the new condo?"

"Not long after."

"Think *K* in his phone stands for Krayev?"

"I don't know. I think so, but..."

"But not sure. Fine. And you have no idea what the favor was?"

"No." Tobias licked his lips. "What do you think?"

"I think we're going to need to be careful."

"I mean about Ghost. All of this is definitely connected to him being gone, right?"

"Well, I don't buy that he suddenly fucked off to San Diego to visit Sea World." As he spoke, Sullivan tugged one of Tobias's bags of chips out of the grocery sack and opened it, popping a couple in his mouth, chewing thoughtfully.

"Help yourself," Tobias said dryly.

Sullivan blinked down at the bag in his hand as if he wasn't sure how it'd gotten there. "Oh. Yeah. Well, maybe people who live in glass houses full of blackmail shouldn't throw stones at a little casual potato chip theft."

"It's fine. Just go on."

"So Ghost is either on the run or he got grabbed." Sullivan spoke with his mouth full. "But if he was grabbed, I don't think the Krayevs took him."

"You don't?"

"The Krayevs came to Ghost's place for a reason. One of them stuck his head into the room while we were in the closet, right? Not long enough to find something, but long enough to see that someone wasn't there."

"They were looking for him, too," Tobias said slowly. "Maybe that's why one of them hung around for a while. Waiting to see if Ghost would show."

"Maybe."

"What's next?"

"Next I want to know how Ghost and the Krayevs are related to a dead housekeeper and a missing girl from 1992. Any thoughts on that?"

Tobias shook his head. "I have no idea. There was never any mention of any of that."

"I'd like to talk to this buddy of yours anyway," Sullivan said. "Can you arrange for him to meet me?"

"Not going to happen. I'll ask him whatever you want, but I'm not telling you his name or how to reach him. Consider me your contact."

Sullivan's jaw muscle worked, but all he said was, "Fine."

"Fine."

Sullivan reached into the grocery sack again, helping himself to a bottle of iced tea. "In the meantime, let's talk about Ghost. What's his legal name?"

Tobias's brain shorted out for a good five seconds. Finally, when Sullivan's eyebrows were halfway up his forehead, Tobias admitted, "I don't know."

"You don't know your best friend's name?" Sullivan's tone was flat.

"His name is Ghost. That's the name he likes. It's the one that matters."

"Not when it comes to finding him," Sullivan said. "But let's move on. Don't suppose you know his social?"

"No. Sorry."

"Date of birth?"

"January 30th." This, at least, Tobias was certain about. When they were in Woodbury, there'd been a cottage party for Ghost on that date.

"Year?"

Tobias shook his head. "I'm not sure. He claimed he was fifteen when we first became roommates but his age tended to change based on what he wanted at any given moment. It's either '96 or '97, though. I'm pretty sure."

"Why were you roommates?"

"It doesn't matter."

"Why don't you let me make that call?"

Reluctantly, and with the same hot flush of embarrassment he always felt speaking about it, Tobias admitted, "We were in a residential treatment program together. I was eighteen, he was a few years younger." He could feel Sullivan's attention like a physical hand on his skin, picking at him, searching for weaknesses.

But all Sullivan said was, "So he'd be twenty now, assuming he told the truth about his age."

"Yes."

"Has he lied about that sort of thing in the past?"

*He lies about everything*, Tobias thought bitterly. "I'm not sure."

"Any other addresses he's lived at?"

Tobias rattled off the one for the gray dump Ghost had stayed at before he moved into the Riviera condo, but he didn't know any others. "Will that help?"

"Probably not. Leases aren't like mortgages; it's a lot harder to find out who's paying the bills when names aren't part of the public record. But neighbors might—"

Tobias shook his head. "He's not very sociable. They won't know anything about him that I don't."

Sullivan nodded. "Have any pictures of him?"

"No. He doesn't like having his picture taken."

"Parents' first names?"

"I don't know."

"Where's he from?"

"I don't know."

"Where's his family from?"

Tobias's face burned. It was humiliating, knowing how much of his life he'd given to Ghost and how little Ghost had given him in return. Tobias knew it was wrong to think that way, that secrets and intimacies couldn't be bartered, couldn't be demanded in equal amounts, not when different people had different needs and different abilities to trust, but it had never been so baldly shoved in his face before.

"Don't know that either, huh?" Sullivan asked.

"No." Tobias hated how hoarse he sounded.

"What about that shoebox back at his place? Would we find anything helpful in there?"

Tobias shook his head. He'd seen inside the box only once, when by chance he'd been standing close by enough to see a staff member search through Ghost's things when Ghost had been brought in for his third or fourth visit to Woodbury. The box was filled with assorted odds and ends—pictures cut from magazines, a broken piece of pottery, an old necklace with a broken clasp, a worn rubber stamp, amongst other things—but only Ghost knew their meanings.

"Let's go back to this treatment place. What were you two there for?"

"It's not related," Tobias gritted out.

"We don't know that. You might have details about Ghost's life that you don't realize are—"

"It's…it was a long time ago."

"That doesn't matter—"

"He was a kid. *I* was practically a kid, and he's three years younger."

Sullivan chucked his pen on the table with enough force that it bounced to the floor. "Why the fuck does Mama need a favor from a twenty-year-old street kid? You really think it's unrelated to the sort of shit that gets a guy in trouble with the system? Use your head."

Stung, Tobias jerked back. It wasn't the way Sullivan had spoken to him—which seemed reasonable, considering how they'd gotten to this point—so much as that Sullivan was right. Tobias hadn't thought it through. Finally he said, "He was there for prostitution. But I don't know the specifics. I don't know why that would matter to Mama."

"You said you're his best friend."

That one cut deep, and Tobias spoke more sharply. "I am."

"But you don't know anything about him."

"I—I know other things. Things that won't help us here, that's true, but that doesn't mean I don't know him."

"You promised you wouldn't lie."

"I'm not lying!"

Sullivan opened his mouth, paused, and then closed it again. He studied Tobias for what felt like a long time before he finally—and very gently—asked, "What *can* you tell me about him, Tobias?"

*He's beautiful,* Tobias wanted to say. *He's smart and sarcastic and surprising. He saved me once, back before we were friends, simply because he could and I needed it. Where other people are soft, he's hard. Where other people are dull, he's sharp. He's like the knives he uses, and he always wins. I know he doesn't care that much about me, but it's still more than anyone else gets from him, and that has to mean something, doesn't it?*

But in the end, all he could manage was a soft, "He doesn't need me, not the way I need him. He doesn't need anybody, but he lets me stay."

Something in Sullivan's expression shifted, a minute twist that meant *oh, I get it.*

"It's not like that," Tobias said, weary at the very idea. "I told you, we weren't in a relationship, and I'm not in love with him."

Church had once accused him of being in love with Ghost, and Tobias supposed from the outside that it probably looked that way. Heck, there had been moments when Tobias had wondered it himself, but after weeks of examining the feeling, he'd come to the conclusion that the phrase *in love* was fundamentally untrue. The better word would be *crush*, and even that was misleading. It was the sort of crush teenagers got on their teachers, the sort of crush that you looked back on later with a cringe, painfully aware of all the reasons why you should've known better, thankful that you'd dodged a bullet.

Yes, he found Ghost fun and intriguing. Yes, he laughed more around Ghost, who was canny and witty. And he'd be lying if he said he didn't think Ghost was attractive.

But in all honesty, what he most frequently felt around Ghost was the anxiety of knowing he had to make Ghost

happy so Ghost would want to stay. When he was successful, Tobias felt a profound satisfaction at being worthy. But in a dark, secret part of his heart, he resented
having to earn Ghost's presence over and over. In that
part of his heart, he harbored a sharp, potent anger that
he could never just be enough.

No, it wasn't love. It was addiction, and it wasn't even
Ghost he was addicted to. Tobias was addicted to being
chosen, and being chosen by someone like Ghost, who
found so few people worth his time, was the best high
of all.

## Chapter Eight

"That's enough to find him, isn't it?" Tobias asked, as if he thought Sullivan could just enter a street name and a last known address into a national database for missing hookers and get what they wanted.

"Not remotely." Sullivan turned the recorder off and put it away. "We've got a couple of options. I'd like to go through Ghost's phone to see if we can't find out who some of these numbers belong to."

Tobias pulled a face but took Ghost's phone out of the duffel. His fingers clenched around the casing for a moment before he finally held it out. "You can track them down with just the numbers?"

Sullivan took it. "Can usually get at least a billing address or a name. The real question is what to do once we know. We could start calling people to ask them about when they last saw him, but the ones most likely to know something useful are people we're probably better off avoiding at this point. Like K, for example. I'm assuming that's a Krayev, and that means balancing the gain against the potential bad of letting them know someone's peeking into their business. Plus, anyone we talk to might contact Ghost. Could be good if he needs help, but…"

"But if he's running, he'll go deeper into hiding," Tobias said.

"That'd be my guess. If there's nothing else, that's what we'll do. But for now, you go do whatever you do, and I go to my computer and run a bunch of searches."

Tobias frowned. "I'm going to help."

"This kind of research is a one-person job with a million little details to keep track of, and explaining everything will just slow me down. It's a bunch of database reading. And I have other cases to work on. You have homework anyway, don't you? Don't you have classes today?"

Tobias took a second to respond. "But Ghost could be hurt or…there's got to be something I can do. Isn't there a place I could… I don't know, go look around? Like in the Russian district or something." He paused. "Does Denver have a Russian district?"

Sullivan didn't miss Tobias's lack of answer about school, but he was too busy trying not to tear at his hair like a deranged person to deal with that at the moment. "Hit the brakes, Kamikaze."

"But—"

"Hey, shut it for a second, huh? Listen to me. I'm invoking rule number…" Sullivan tried to remember the order, then shrugged. "I forget which one was which. But the one about you having initiative. That's the one I'm invoking."

Mulishly, Tobias's jaw set. "I don't think—"

"You're gonna go insane if you keep this up. I understand you're worried, and I know it's hard not to think about all the horrible things that could be happening to your friend, but you've got to be patient. Rushing will lead to mistakes and missed threads and possibly getting us or Ghost hurt."

Which was possibly a bit manipulative, but if it got the guy to chill, he'd use it.

The skin around Tobias's eyes tightened. "Sullivan…"

"No. There's only so much that can get done in a day. We need realistic expectations for what we can accomplish at any given moment."

Tobias sat there vibrating for a good ten seconds, before all of the energy abruptly rushed out of him. "I feel so helpless," he whispered, staring at the floor, and against his best efforts, some of Sullivan's anger wavered.

"You'll get your chance," Sullivan said grudgingly. "And we'll meet up again tomorrow."

"Right." Tobias nodded. "Tomorrow."

When he got back to ASI, Sullivan began researching Tobias Benton.

He was twenty-four, had been born in the States, and had been adopted by Haitian immigrant physicians— Mom worked in a clinic that catered to impoverished families and Dad was a famed oncologist. They were both active with several charities, as were their children, and there were multiple photographs of ribbon cuttings and benefit dinners with the family. Tobias stood out as the sole white member; fewer publications and articles made note of the fact than Sullivan's cynical side would've expected, focusing instead on the impoverished backgrounds of Tobias's siblings. Typical media narratives.

Sullivan rocked in his chair and gnawed on the end of his pen, Sleater-Kinney's "Modern Girl" blaring through his earbuds. Why would a Haitian couple who later adopted five children of Caribbean descent start by adopting a white baby boy from the States? Unlike their other children, Tobias would've almost certainly been adopted and given a good start in life—racism and American homogeneity being what it was, a healthy white baby boy simply wasn't going to languish in the system the way that traumatized black children from an impoverished nation would. So why would doctors who clearly valued helping the people who slipped through the cracks start with Tobias?

More to that point, why was Tobias the only one of the kids who still had his original last name?

It was an anomaly.

Sullivan dug deeper.

Tobias had graduated from a Catholic high school in a district equitable with two doctors' salaries, albeit a year and a half later than normal students would've. That time in the residential treatment facility, Sullivan supposed. Tobias didn't have a criminal record, and for the past four and a half years he'd been a student at Metro State University of Denver, studying Cell & Molecular Biology. He was likely to graduate this upcoming winter.

There was nothing concrete about Tobias's adoption. He found a few mentions in local papers of a teenage girl with the same last name abandoning a baby back in the day, but he couldn't tell for sure that she was the birth mother in question. If she was Tobias's mother, though, it was pretty fucked up.

After staring at the results for a long while, Sullivan decided he wasn't going to be sympathetic. Tobias's adoptive parents might be decent human beings who liked to help others, but whether or not they'd gotten around to giving their kids the whole don't-blackmail-people lecture didn't matter. This rested on Tobias's shoulders and didn't buy him any slack.

He got out the Nathalie Trudeau case file and tapped a finger against the photograph of the girl. She couldn't have been a more storybook representation of innocence, with her slightly bucktoothed grin where her adult teeth had come in too big for her face.

"What happened to you?" he muttered.

When he was tired of feeling maudlin, he put the photo aside and got to work.

He ran searches for every variation of Yalena/Yellena, Seryozha, and Yasha Krayev that he could think of, then realized he'd skipped ahead and did some research into Russian names. When he went back to Google, he changed Krayev to Krayeva for Mama's searches because Russians used gendered last names. He wished he had their patronymics—Russian children had a middle name denoting their father's family—because that would really help narrow things down, but he couldn't find anything.

He *was* able to nail down a mug shot photo that made it clear that Yasha's real name was Yakov, and there was a woman named Yelena Krayeva who'd done a charity thing for abused women at a local restaurant a few years back, but there was nothing conclusive, and there were no pictures attached. He couldn't be sure that Yelena was the same person as Mama.

Unfortunately, whoever Mama was, she'd covered her tracks well.

Next, he went through the list of Ghost's contacts. The text messages and code names marked almost all of them as clients, but Sullivan checked them anyway. He used online reverse directories mostly, and ran the unpublished numbers through a PI database that private citizens couldn't access, and probably wouldn't want to, since they charged about fifty bucks a number. For now, the only nonpublished number that he was willing to pay for was the cell phone of the mysterious *K*.

But he got nothing. The number was unassigned, belonging to a burner phone. A dead end.

After he'd gotten everything he could from Ghost's phone, he started some searches for his actual job, quickly getting what he needed to serve one of his dirtbags with a bright, shiny subpoena.

The answer was just *sitting* there. Waiting. Like the universe had cleared every potential obstacle out of his way.

It kind of pissed him off.

"How'd it go?"

Sullivan jerked his head up, finding Raina in the doorway. He blinked at her, wondering where the hell she'd come from—she was damn sneaky for someone who wore heels all the time—and she clarified, "With the concerned citizen?"

Right. Sullivan shrugged and let some of his annoyance show. A half-lie was always more believable than one made up wholesale. "He's kind of an asshole."

She pulled a yogurt out of the fridge. "A useful one?"

"Maybe."

"I hope this isn't the report so comprehensive I'll die that you mentioned earlier, because it leaves something to be desired."

He explained everything up to the point where Tobias had requested to play assistant, instead saying that he was sure that Tobias knew more, and that with some finessing, Sullivan might be able to get the break he needed. He also pointed out that he wasn't behind on his regular work.

Raina made doubtful, noncommittal noises, but she did that a lot when Sullivan said things, so he didn't read too much into it.

Not long after, he was following Jasper Giff, a disability-hosing loser in his forties, into a grocery store. Sullivan made his move in the freezer aisle, and barely had time to say, "Jasper Giff?" before the guy dropped his toilet paper and margarita mix and ran for it. Giff managed to make it through the parking lot and behind the wheel of his car before Sullivan caught up, and proceeded to laugh at him through the windshield as he fumbled to start the engine. "Too late!" he called.

Sullivan slapped the packet of paper down on the hood and called back, "This counts as being served, and it'll hold up in court. Have a nice day, dickhead." He left the packet on the hood and, with Giff's furious curses ringing in his ears, crossed the lot to where he'd left the Buick.

His irritation didn't fade with the success of the chase. As he filled out the form he would send to the district attorney's office to show that he'd delivered the papers, he was tempted to do something juvenile, like punch the dash.

All too easy. The usual channels, the usual answers, the usual outcome. Giff had been right where any other disability-hosing jerkwad would be hiding—at his girlfriend's house. All it had taken was waiting for the idiot to come out where Sullivan could get to him, and bingo. Four hours from start to finish, and not an original thought required or a single challenge found at any point in the process. Even the stupid chase had been predictable—guys like Giff always ran.

ASI and other investigatory agencies like them only got the tricky subpoena cases; the district attorney's office and the bigger law firms had their own people to serve papers to those witnesses and defendants who weren't trying to hide. Sullivan was only sent after the dumb asses who couldn't be quickly located by an intern.

Giff and the other guys like him were supposed to be the hard cases, and it had still been by the numbers. Textbook. Easy cash.

Unsatisfying.

That familiar discontent settled over him like a blanket, and he could feel himself getting moody. As angry as he was about Tobias's manipulative blackmail attempt, at least that was interesting. The contrast between the work he'd done just now and the work he'd been doing on Nathalie's case had never been so clear, and for a second he couldn't help acknowledging that he was worried that he wouldn't be able to solve it. He'd go crazy doing nothing but serving subpoenas for the next year.

After dinner, as he was nodding off on the couch to a nature documentary about wasps, his cell rang. He checked the screen, saw Caty's name, and set it aside. The ringing continued until voicemail kicked in, then stopped. For a moment, anyway, before resuming. Went to voicemail. Ringing resumed again. Over and over.

There was a long pause. Nearly three minutes passed.

He was beginning to think he'd weathered the storm when his cell rang again. Lisbeth's number this time, and he sighed.

He answered with, "I'm not talking about it. I'm not. I'll hang up first."

Even before she said a word, Lisbeth's habitual calm wafted across the line like a subtle perfume. Pleasant. Soothing. Sweet. Especially compared to Caty's yelling in the background. He only caught about every third word or so, but he got the gist from *coward*, and *delusional* and *bastard*.

Lisbeth said, "I don't want you to talk about your feelings, Sullivan."

"Good. How's work? Write any confusing contract lingo today?"

"Nope, we're not doing that, either. You're going to listen while I explain something, and then, once you've thought about what I've said, you're going to call Caty and deal with this like an adult."

"No promises."

She waited silently.

Eventually, when it became too awkward to stand, he said, "All right. Fine. God."

"Thank you." She was serene in her victory. "Please hear me out before you respond. I won't take long."

He turned off the television and resigned himself to misery.

"We're not friends because we like each other, I think you'll agree. We're friends because you love Caty and she loves you and she belongs to me, which means, by extension, you do as well. And since I have no motivation to sugarcoat uncomfortable truths to protect your feelings, I think you might find my read on things more objective than hers. So here it is: you've been unkind."

Sullivan sucked in a breath. In the background he could hear Caty's yelling elevate to a more fevered pitch.

"One moment, please, Sullivan." There was a rustle on the other end of the phone, then a *thud* that might've been a door closing. Caty's shouts became distant.

"Sorry about that," Lisbeth said, placid as ever. "Now, I think you'll agree with me that the situation with Nick was badly handled on your part, although I suspect we would give different reasons for why we think so. That you've reacted by adopting celibacy leads me to believe that you're suffering a persistent insecurity."

"Jesus," he muttered. "Is there anything Caty doesn't tell you?"

"There are no secrets in a healthy Dom/sub relationship," she replied, only a little smugly. "Where was I? Yes, I think you've been unkind—to *yourself*. You've allowed him to warp your opinion of yourself, and since his opinion is very limited in experience and open-mindedness, you're judging yourself by an inferior standard."

"Lisbeth—"

"There's nothing wrong with you," she explained, so brutally plain about it that it made an actual lump rise in his throat. "I know it's difficult not to internalize the judgments of people we care about, but it's something we all have to learn not to do, because the alternative is to be miserable and subject to other people's whims. You gave yourself impossible expectations to live up to, and you've been cruel to yourself ever since you decided—erroneously, I might add—that you failed."

"Lisbeth—"

"Be quiet, please."

He closed his eyes.

"The relationship failed because you attempted to change yourself to make him happy, not because you're monstrous. You're not an animal; you're a dominant. That he couldn't see the difference is a flaw in his thinking, not yours. Punishing yourself like this is both wasteful and blind to the reality of the situation."

"You can't know that." He sounded like he was choking.

"Have I ever lied to you?"

"No."

"Have you ever thought me kind?"

"No," he murmured. "No, you're not kind."

"Then hear me, Sullivan. What Nick said was untrue, ignorant and cruel. And, to my way of thinking, unforgivable when said by a lover or a friend."

His chest hurt. Fuck, it hurt like a boulder lay on it.

"Do you understand?" she asked.

"Yes."

"Call Caty when you're ready." Lisbeth hung up on him.

Sullivan rolled over on his couch and pressed his face into the cushion. His skin felt hot and too tight, his stomach sick, and that damn boulder was still there, crushing his chest into fragments. He smothered his wet, ragged breaths into the couch cushions and pretended that he couldn't still hear Nick's words in his head.

*This is disgusting. You're like an animal. These things you want...they're monstrous.*

*Why can't you just be normal?*

He had to force himself to tune those out, to hear Lisbeth's words instead: *there is nothing wrong with you.*

Eventually he slept.

He woke up to an eleven-mile dawn.

The morning was full grown and his legs were jelly by the time he was done. In the shower, he sat on the floor of the tub and let cold water beat down on him. He toweled off and drank half a Gatorade. He managed to get dressed before the last of his energy became apathy and he stretched out on the couch again. He needed to close his eyes for a minute. Just to catch his breath and regain his equilibrium. Just for a minute.

* * *

"This is pathetic."

Sullivan cracked open an eye and saw a tall brunette with fawn-colored skin wearing a red pantsuit staring down at him in disdain. She was perched on the battered steamer trunk that he used as a makeshift coffee table as if she were afraid she might catch anthrax from the surface. She was peering around at the streaks of paint on the ancient hardwood floor and the grimy windows with the expression of someone witnessing an autopsy. He blinked, the blankness in his brain slowly taking shape.

Raina.

"You live in a crack den," she informed him.

"Why are you here?" Since he was almost flat on his face, the couch ate most of his words. Perplexed, he began to lift his head, and then froze. "What time is it?"

"Nearly noon."

"Shit. I overslept."

"Apparently." She flicked him on the nose hard enough that tears sprang to his eyes, then sniffed him while he lay there wincing. "You don't smell hungover."

"I'm not." He sat up, patting his aching nose gingerly.

"I thought perhaps you'd stumbled onto your concerned citizen's dirty laundry and been murdered."

"Your luck's not that good. Bad night, that's all. I'm sorry I didn't call. Won't happen again."

Those sharp brown eyes picked at him like he was a tangled knot of string that she was determined to unravel. It was disconcerting and familiar at the same time. He'd gotten that look a lot last year. He hadn't told Raina much about the Nick situation—he and Raina were a strange mixture of friendship and professionalism and cutthroat competition that didn't exactly invite confidences—but

she was a keen observer and it wasn't like the signs of
a bad breakup were hard to read. Getting dumped happened to everyone; the symptoms were universal.

Well, except to Raina. If the man who would dump
Raina existed, he probably wouldn't be alive for long
after it happened. Sullivan certainly wouldn't dare, not
that he would make a move in the first place. No matter
how much he appreciated her legs when she wasn't looking, they worked together, and besides, Sullivan's sexual
tastes ran in a direction he was pretty sure would result
in Raina extracting his intestines.

"I'm fine," Sullivan insisted, and grabbed a packet
of nicotine gum from the floor where he'd dropped it
last night. "See? Not smoking. Awake. I'm good to go."

She continued to stare at him. "If the case is too much
for you..."

"It's not. I'm fine. I just overslept." He frowned at her.
"Wait. How did you get in here?"

She stood, the ring of keys in her hand—which apparently held a copy of his house key that he definitely
had not given her—jingling, and gave him a cold smirk.
"The front door was unlocked." She walked out of the
living room, stepping carefully over the rotting boards
piled in the entryway.

"It fucking was not," he yelled after her. Her only response was to laugh as she left.

He supposed he shouldn't be shocked that a professional snoop had broken in with an illegally obtained key.

He raked a hand over his face. He felt marginally better than he had earlier. More capable of handling the activities of the day, which meant finding his blackmailer,
doing some investigating, and snitching his house key
off of Raina's key ring.

He needed to call Caty, too. Not today. Soon, though. She would probably yell. She liked to yell, and she was good at it.

He took a second to feel very put-upon by the demands of the women in his life. It occurred to him—not for the first time—that he needed to keep Caty and Lisbeth and Raina from meeting at all costs, because if they did, they would take over the world, creating some kind of amazon utopia, which wouldn't bother him if not for the part where he—as a male—would be too dead to enjoy it.

He stopped for breakfast on the way to Tobias's motel, getting a cup of coffee large enough to decimate his stomach lining by the end of the day, and pounded on the door with the flat side of his fist. It opened so swiftly that he felt a rush of air against his face.

"Where have you been?" Tobias asked, the words stiff and bitten-off.

"Hello, Tobias. I'm fine, thank you for asking. Yes, it is a lovely day, isn't it?"

Tobias's eyebrows crushed together, and Sullivan watched with growing, vindictive amusement as Tobias fought the urge to be polite. Finally, resignedly, he said, "Sorry. Hello, Sullivan. How are you?"

"Fine."

"Great. Where have you been?"

Sullivan rolled his eyes and went inside. "Chill. I overslept."

Tobias closed the door behind him with an air of such perfect control that Sullivan knew that he'd been tempted to slam it. "Half the day is gone."

Sullivan put his bag of food on the table. "I have a life outside of following your every impulse, you know."

Tobias's shoulders tensed. "What are the plans for today?"

"Today we're going to commit a crime."

That crease between Tobias's eyebrows deepened. "I—I don't—"

"Don't try to pretend that's crossing some sort of line for you." Sullivan eyed him darkly and crammed half of a greasy hash brown patty into his mouth.

Tobias's next breath was pointed and slow, the breath of a parent trying not to lose his temper with an unruly child. "What kind of crime?"

"How much cash do you have on you?"

When they'd marked out the plan—such as it was, seeing as bribery wasn't that complicated—they left the motel and headed for Sullivan's car. Tobias paused beside the passenger door of the Buick. "This is your car?"

"Yeah." Sullivan glanced at it, trying to see it the way Tobias would. It was dented and primer was showing in a couple places and the seats were kind of janky, which were all proof of how damn cool his car was. "What of it?"

"It's not bad or anything," Tobias said. "I only thought, you know, that it looks like a gangster from the seventies should drive it."

Sullivan frowned. "Stop trying to butter me up and get in, will you?"

Tobias studied him across the roof. "You're very odd, you know that?"

"You're very judgy, you know that?"

Tobias clamped his mouth shut and got in.

The security guard on shift at Riviera Condominiums was a big white guy with beady eyes who wore a short-sleeved yellow button-down, sweat stains discoloring the fabric at his armpits and the small of his back. He eyed Sullivan's hair with disdain and fiddled with the offered business card while Sullivan explained the situation. "And you think maybe someone took the guy in 121 against his will?"

"Maybe." Sullivan nodded to the bank of monitors against one wall, trying to look unimpressed. He could only hope that Tobias, who was standing by the door behind him, was managing to do the same. "Do you have any security footage of that parking lot?"

"Maybe," the guy parroted. His smile turned sly. "But I'm pretty sure you're supposed to have a warrant or something."

"Not a cop. Also, not if you let us." Sullivan no longer had to pretend to be unimpressed. People were so predictable, honestly.

"Oh, I don't know if I could do that. Sounds like an invasion of privacy to me. There are rules, you know."

"You don't say."

"I'd hate to get in trouble."

"Let me guess. You've got hungry mouths to feed."

"I do."

Sullivan gave a mental sigh. "How's fifty sound?"

"I was thinking more like two hundred."

"Seventy-five."

"Two hundred."

Tobias interrupted with, "I only have a hundred on me, sir." Both Sullivan and the guard glanced at him and he offered an apologetic smile.

The guard frowned.

"That's better than nothing," Sullivan added.

The guard shrugged. "That'll do, I guess. But you've got to look at it here."

"We don't know when he went missing," Sullivan protested. "It could take ages to find the—"

"Not my problem. When a copy gets made, the security system automatically notifies the corporate contact, and that's my boss. You've got to do it here. Now gimme my money."

Tobias paid up and the guard set a stack of CDs in front of them. "That's the lot outside of 121. They're organized backward from today, two twenty-four-hour periods per disk. Load 'em there, scroll forward and back with this button thingie here, print stills here, and don't touch anything else."

"Best behavior," Sullivan promised, and the guard gave him a suspicious look.

"You better do this fast. If I see my boss coming, I'm kicking you out whether you've gotten what you want or not."

The guard headed for the front door down the hall to keep watch, and Sullivan sat down at the terminal and kicked the other chair back for Tobias, pulling Ghost's phone out at the same time and passing it over. "Look up the date of the last text message he sent."

Tobias thumbed through the list. "Last outgoing text is on the 21st of July."

"Let's start there." Sullivan grabbed the stack of discs.

The camera's angle didn't show Ghost's condo, but it caught the parking lot and most of the sidewalk out front. That was lucky, as it meant that his and Tobias's breaking and entering earlier that week hadn't been recorded. Over the next forty fruitless minutes, they worked their way through the disc, fast forwarding when they could, slowing down during peak times, and eventually moving on to the 22nd of July. The guard stuck his head in five times to glare and complain that they were taking forever, and it sure as hell felt that way to Sullivan, but on minute forty-one, Tobias sucked in a breath and jabbed his finger at the screen.

"There! There, that's him."

"You sure?" The picture quality wasn't great—Sullivan mostly got blond and slim—but Tobias nodded.

"Yes!"

Ghost was carrying a big duffel bag over one shoulder and was followed by a balding man in slacks and a polo shirt.

"Who's that?" Sullivan asked.

Tobias squinted at the screen. "No idea."

They were definitely together, though. Ghost paused at a sedan near the sidewalk, waiting while the balding man unlocked the door and popped the trunk. Ghost put the bag inside before he circled the vehicle to get in the passenger seat. The car drove away, and that was that.

"No sign of distress." Sullivan backed the disc up so they could watch it again. "His body language is calm. Don't you think?"

Tobias nodded. "He looks all right. He might be all right. Ghost could've run and he didn't."

"There are other kinds of coercion besides force, as you well know," Sullivan said, not a little bitterly.

Tobias nodded again, not looking at him.

Sullivan grabbed a nearby pen and a scrap of paper and scrawled out the date—July 22nd, thirteen days ago—and started making notes about the car, only to decide that was dumb. Instead, he took a quick screen capture, both printing it and emailing it to himself, remembering to log out of his account because he was basically a professional badass. "Light-colored sedan. Maybe a Nissan? Can you see that?"

"Here, wait until he pulls out." Tobias reached over to the desk and turned off the light so only the overhead was on, killing the glare.

Sullivan leaned closer. "Regular Colorado plates. That's a Q, isn't it?"

"Yeah? I think? Then an F?"

"E."

"F." Tobias hummed thoughtfully. "That's definitely an F."

"That's definitely a line at the bottom."

"That's definitely mud."

By now they were both so close to the screen that their noses were practically touching. Sullivan muttered, "Mud my ass. That's an E."

Tobias made a dissatisfied sound. "Then a L. Then an 8."

"3."

"8."

"You know, I'm the private detective here." Sullivan turned his head, ready to give Tobias a pointed look, only to realize how closely they were sitting.

"Doesn't mean your vision's better." Tobias's raised eyebrow was somehow dour and civil at once, at least until he realized what Sullivan already had—too much proximity.

Sullivan's heart jumpstarted in his chest. Up close like this, it was hard not to notice the strong planes of Tobias's bone structure and the clear, pure blue of his thickly lashed eyes. He didn't move, testing the tension in the air, and Tobias didn't either, except to let his lips part on an indrawn breath. Which he then held.

Tobias felt it too.

The knowledge only pissed Sullivan off further. And got him hard. He thought of his hands digging into Tobias's arms the day before, thought of the red marks he'd left behind when he released him. Thought of Tobias letting him, not saying no or stop or don't.

Thought of Nick saying *monstrous*.

He sat back abruptly and opened his mouth—not that he had anything of value to say, because his brain was completely blank—and sent a silent thank-you to the patron saint of stupid people when he was interrupted by the guard hurrying in, shooing them to their feet. "Go, go, she's back, go, get out."

Sullivan managed to snatch the notes and his printout of the security camera pic before he and Tobias were hustled down a long hallway and unceremoniously shoved out a rear door that locked behind them, the sudden heat like a slap in the face.

Sullivan led the way back to the car, ignoring the way Tobias had gone quiet and watchful, as if considering what he should say. Sullivan sure as shit wasn't going to discuss this thickness in the air between them, and rather than give Tobias the chance to do so himself, he said, "I'll put in the request to run the plates tonight, but we won't see anything until Monday, so we should meet up again then."

Instantly distracted, Tobias said, "That's *two days* from now."

"Good job. We'll work on counting to three next. Watch out for four, though. That's where it starts getting difficult."

Tobias's jaw set hard, the muscle going rigid, and Sullivan smiled a mean little smile of vindication.

Maybe it was immature, but being a dick to Tobias under these circumstances was kind of fun.

## Chapter Nine

His stomach was acidic from too much coffee, his eyes felt dry with weariness from yet another bad night of sleep, and if Sullivan kept saying things like, "So I'll come by the motel when I've got the results from the DMV. I'd wish you a happy weekend, but I think we both know I wouldn't mean it," Tobias was going to be committing assault in addition to bribery today.

They'd barely gotten anything done yet.

Tobias reminded himself to remain calm. Losing his temper wouldn't help; it might even push Sullivan's frustration into something else, something closer to that raw darkness that he'd seen yesterday in the motel when Tobias hadn't backed down. The rawness that made Tobias's stomach hot and fluttery, his skin tingly. Part of him wanted to know what it would be like if he pushed a hair's breadth further, what Sullivan would do with it.

The rest of him knew that it might be more than he could handle, and he couldn't afford to lose control of this. "That's not all you're going to be doing between now and then, right?"

"No, but it's all background stuff. More research. Nothing for you to do."

Tobias wondered if he was lying. "There has to be something."

"Nope. Sitting at the computer. Boring. One-man job. Go away."

As Sullivan went to unlock the door to the car, Tobias considered the likelihood of Sullivan leaving him here in the parking lot, and decided it was all too believable. He darted a hand in and snatched the keys from Sullivan's fingers.

"Hey! Give me those."

"If it's just sitting at a computer, you can do it at the motel." When Sullivan made a lunging grab for the keys, Tobias put a hand up between them and held the ring up in the air behind him with the other. "I'll buy us food later. You can work and I'll watch."

Sullivan gave Tobias a small, frustrated shove so that he bounced back against the side of the Buick, the hot metal burning him through his T-shirt. It wasn't violent enough to hurt, but adrenaline spiked through his blood anyway. Tobias pushed against Sullivan's chest to keep him back, the sensation of that lean muscle against his palm making every nerve in his body light up.

Sullivan ground his teeth together. "You're seriously going to watch me do research?"

*The job,* Tobias told himself. *Concentrate on the job at hand.* "Yes."

Sullivan reached for the keys again, forcing Tobias harder against the car. Tobias held them farther out of reach, and Sullivan finally snapped, "Fine. Whatever. Give me the keys and we'll go."

Instead of obeying, Tobias pushed gently against Sullivan's belly. "Step out of the way."

For a long few seconds, Sullivan didn't move. He

simply stared at Tobias from inches away, his whole body tense, and it... God, it was intense being pressed up against him like this, Tobias's bracing hand the only thing keeping them apart, Sullivan's expression bordering on vicious, and Tobias wasn't sure he was breathing by the time Sullivan took a small, deliberate step back.

The message was clear—Sullivan hadn't moved because Tobias had told him to, but because he'd chosen to.

Tobias shivered despite the million-degree sun reflecting up off the asphalt, suddenly aware of nothing more than how much he wanted to lean forward and catch that annoyed mouth with his own.

"What is this?" Tobias asked, unthinkingly. His experience of romance until now had been simple, almost careless in comparison to the way this thing with Sullivan was building with countless small collisions and subtexts that Tobias couldn't keep up with. He didn't understand how Sullivan worked, how he kept making the ground beneath Tobias's feet seem like thin ice, how Tobias could hold all the cards and yet still feel like Sullivan was the one winning the game.

He ran his gaze over Sullivan, looking for some clue to this strange hum between them. Sullivan wore jeans, big black boots, and a snug, plain gray T-shirt that showed off the stark black tattoos that covered both arms all the way up to disappear under the fabric. If he'd put gel in his hair that morning, it'd already given up, because the brown strands were loose and soft and barely out of his eyes where they'd fallen to one side. He looked good. Really good. But there were other attractive people in the world, and Tobias had never felt desire like this— razor-tipped and biting and all too capable of dragging his attention away from the important things. There was nothing romantic about it.

Sullivan's face went blank. "This is business."

Tobias swallowed back the sharp tang of disappointment, reminding himself that Sullivan was right; this was business. It *should* be business. Anything else was a distraction from what Tobias really wanted—to find Ghost on his own terms. He eased out from between Sullivan and the car, went around to the passenger side, and got in, unlocking the driver's-side door from inside. When Sullivan was behind the wheel, Tobias wordlessly held out the keys.

The drive back to the motel was silent.

"What are you going to be looking up?" Tobias asked, pulling his textbooks out of his bag. They seemed heavier than usual, like they'd transformed into lead weights while he was out doing other things.

"I'm going to send requests to the DMV for all the possible plate combinations on the bald guy's car, try to track down Nathalie's father, and look at the property records for the houses surrounding the Howard residence where Margaret Trudeau was killed. If the Krayevs are the ones who bought Ghost's condo under Margaret's name, someone in the family must've known her, maybe been a neighbor or a friend. I'm wondering if someone associated with the Krayevs—Yelena or whatever her name is—might've been a neighbor or a friend back then. If nothing else, I might be able to scrounge up someone to talk to who lived in the area during that time. I mean, if that's okay with you, boss?"

Without waiting for an answer, Sullivan sketched a sarcastic salute, put his earbuds on, and started typing away. Tobias shot him a disapproving glare, pulled his biochemistry book onto his lap, and began to read.

After about an hour, Sullivan snapped, "For God's sake, why are you reading that if you hate it so much?"

Tobias jolted and lifted his head to find Sullivan watching him. "I don't hate it." His back hurt after so long bent over the book, and he arched, popping his spine in several places. Instant relief.

"You said you wouldn't lie," Sullivan reminded him.

"I'm not lying."

"You always make that pained, miserable face when you're reading?"

"This is just how my face looks."

Sullivan laughed, low and dirty and a little mean, and Tobias refused to find it sexy, ignored it entirely, in fact, refocusing on the page. *Transplantation of the mes/met junction results...* No, that wasn't where he'd been. He skimmed through several paragraphs and realized he'd already read them several times and still wasn't sure what they'd said. He'd have to start over.

He was on the verge of getting absorbed in the material again when Sullivan said, "Could you shut up?"

"I'm not saying anything."

"You keep sighing. Loudly. I can hear you over my music, that's how bad it is."

"I'm not sighing."

"You sound like a dog whose owner left for vacation without it."

Tobias closed his book with far less force than he would've preferred. "Is there something I can do that would help you concentrate?"

"Yes, you could stay here like a normal client while I go back to my office and do my damn job."

Well, he'd walked into that one. "You know that's not going to happen."

Sullivan stood up and cracked his neck. "Fuck it. I'm going for a walk. I'm crawling out of my damn skin here."

Tobias began to set his books aside, beyond grateful for the excuse, when Sullivan added, "Alone."

Tobias went still, considering him.

Sullivan said pointedly, "The sort of alone where I'm by myself, in case that wasn't clear."

"Don't make me have to come find you."

"Quick question. The next time I go to the bathroom, are you planning to tag along and shake it for me?"

Tobias returned that hostile gaze evenly. "If that's what it takes."

Sullivan's lips pressed tight. He turned and left, and Tobias sagged back onto the bed.

He felt like a jerk.

Which was reasonable, since he was being a jerk. And selfish. He had no illusions about what he was doing or how unfair it was. He just…he needed to be part of this. Sullivan wasn't the only one crawling out of his skin for lack of something to do, but for Tobias the sense of stagnation and claustrophobia existed on a nearly catastrophic level. And being near Sullivan while he worked was the closest thing to relief he could find.

Maybe after they found Ghost, he could do something nice for Sullivan. Something to make up for what he'd done.

To assuage his conscience.

It wasn't like he was killing anyone. Or robbing anyone. He was simply *helping*. He didn't expect Sullivan to like it or to forgive him, but to Sullivan it was an inconvenience at most. To Tobias, it was crucial.

When Sullivan returned, he got back to work without a word, and Tobias did the same even though the idea of more reading was about as attractive as getting dental work.

He didn't sigh.

Later, as he shut the door on a pizza delivery boy while juggling a 2-liter of soda, Tobias said, "Take a break."

Sullivan looked up from his laptop with the confused air of a man who'd lost all sense of time and place. After he blinked a couple times, he tugged his earbuds loose and tucked them inside the collar of his T-shirt once more. He closed his laptop and accepted a handful of napkins before tearing into his first slice, and for a few minutes, they ate silently.

When they'd put a sizable dent in the pizza, Tobias asked, "What have you found so far?"

"Nathalie's father is Brock Trudeau, and he lives in California. He's married to a teacher and they have three kids."

Tobias took a small sip of soda, savoring it. His parents hadn't let him and his siblings have much processed food growing up, so he had a secret love of most things sugary. Soda was toward the top of the list. "It's good he managed to recover from his wife's death."

"Not sure how much recovery he needed. They weren't married at the time she died—there'd been a divorce a few years before, fairly rancorous, I'm assuming, seeing as he remarried about five minutes after it was finalized. He did file for custody of Nathalie in the divorce, but according to the police report, Nathalie chose to stay here with her mom and Dad accepted it. And from what

I can tell, Mom never accepted a penny of alimony or child support."

Tobias glanced at the papers strewn around Sullivan's laptop, finding a picture of a young blonde girl.

"Is this her?"

"Yeah."

"She's pretty."

Sullivan threw a balled-up napkin into the trash with a little too much force. "I guess."

"Can this whole divorce/custody thing actually be related to the murders? I mean, it really comes down to who killed Margaret, right? You said the homeowner, Lawrence or whoever—"

"Lawrence Howard."

"Yeah, him. You said he was a crime lord. So that makes it sound like another gang would've had reason to want him dead, which sort of implicates the Krayevs, but if the Krayevs did it, why would they kill someone they cared enough about to memorialize with a condo? But if Nathalie's dad was the one pulling the trigger, it seems like a risky way to go about it—going up against a guy like that and some bodyguards."

At the very least, if Margaret had been the target, it made sense to wait until the guy and his bodyguards weren't at home.

Sullivan was watching him with a considering eyebrow lifted. "Not bad."

"Oh." Tobias cleared his throat. "Thanks."

"Calling Lawrence Howard a crime lord's being a bit generous, though," Sullivan said, his mouth twisting wryly. "Small-time criminal overreaching his capabilities is more accurate, but either way, I doubt there's a connection. Nathalie's father was a person of interest at the time, and the cops looked pretty hard at him, but he seems to have had a pretty airtight alibi back in California."

"Dead end."

"Most likely."

"Find anything else?"

"No one with the name Krayev, Yellena, Yalena, or any of the brothers' names has ever lived in that neighborhood that I can find." Sullivan stared up at the ceiling. "But one of the neighbors has lived down the block since the mid-eighties, so tomorrow I'm gonna go talk to him. See if he remembers anything."

"We," Tobias reminded him, and Sullivan exhaled hard. For a second he looked like he might finally lose his temper and yell, and Tobias braced himself, but Sullivan's shoulders slumped.

"We," Sullivan repeated, sounding weary. "Can I go home now?"

"Yeah." Tobias got up and stacked his school things on the table, clearing off the bed so he could get some sleep. The guilt in his gut seemed to grow with every passing hour, but he refused to let it sway his path. "I'd do this differently if I had a choice, you know."

Sullivan paused in the act of shoving his feet back into his boots. "You do have a choice. You just made the one that screws me over. That's fine, whatever, be a dick if you want to. But don't lie about what your options are. I can see the bullshit from a mile away."

With that hanging in the air, Sullivan finished tying his laces and grabbed his laptop.

Tobias was still standing there, hands aching from holding his textbook too tightly, long after Sullivan was gone.

Saturday dawned bright and already warm, and Tobias was awake to see it, eyes gritty as sandpaper, his thoughts sluggish. He'd been snatching hours of sleep here and there, uncomfortable on the unfamiliar mattress, his thoughts too loud to muffle, his stomach in knots.

When he'd showered and eaten, he halfheartedly tried to study some more, but he mostly spent the time with his thoughts in a whirlpool made up of the phone call and letter from Ashley Benton, his parents' lies, the likelihood of Ghost being hurt, and this whole mess with Sullivan.

He'd made little progress with his books by the time Sullivan knocked on the door.

He was wearing jeans and another Henley, and looked nearly as tired as Tobias felt. "Ready to go talk to the neighbors?" he asked, voice blank.

"Good morning to you too," Tobias said under his breath, and followed him to the car.

They parked across the street from the Howard house, and Tobias got his first look at the sprawling ranch with the stone wall and gated drive where Margaret Trudeau, Lawrence Howard, and a handful of bodyguards had died.

"A ten-year-old could get over that wall easy," Tobias said, noting the uneven gray blocks that jutted out along the entire surface. "If she needed to."

Sullivan nodded, squinting in the morning sunshine. "That's what I was thinking. Kinda defeats the purpose of a security wall."

Beyond the gates, Tobias could see a two-car garage and several old elm trees. "Nice place."

"Yep." Sullivan glanced at the plated numerals on the gate and jerked his head down the street. "This way."

Three doors down was a smaller bungalow. Lots of windows, but no gate so they walked up the drive to where a portly man in his mid-sixties was giving a beige

Lincoln a wash. He wore a polo shirt, khakis, and loafers wet with soap suds.

"Hi," Sullivan said. "Are you Ray?"

"Yeah." Ray tipped his chin up in greeting. "You'd be the private detective I talked to this morning?"

"That's me." Sullivan gestured to Tobias and introduced him.

"Hello." Tobias gave a little wave that instantly made him feel juvenile. He was definitely not cool enough to work in this business. "Thanks for letting us stop by."

If Ray thought Tobias was an idiot, he hid it well. "Not sure what all I can tell you, but I figure there's no harm in asking a few questions."

Sullivan grinned. "A man after my own heart. You mind if we record this?"

Ray glanced at the recorder with a gleam in his eye. "No problem. Let's go up to the porch, though, and get out of this sun."

The porch had a complete set of wicker furniture that managed to appear weathered and expensive at the same time. Tobias sank into an armchair with a plush cushion as Ray went to the door and warbled, "Barbara, they're here. Bring out the lemon water, sweetheart."

He glanced back at Tobias and Sullivan. "My wife. She's home all day, so she keeps an eye on things around the neighborhood."

"Hello!" A woman shouldered the door open while holding a tray with tall glasses full of ice and a big pitcher of water. She was short and plump with curly graying hair and a wide smile. "I hope you're thirsty! I've brought enough for everyone. My, it's already hot out. This weather, I tell you." She smiled at them all, her cheeks pink and round.

She was basically Mrs. Claus, Tobias realized, thanking her for the glass of water she passed to him. All she needed was a red velvet dress with white fur hems.

"No trouble at all," she said, patting him on the knee. She handed a glass to Sullivan as well. "I like your hair, Mr. Detective. It's downright adventurous."

Sullivan was startled into a laugh by that, and Tobias did his level best to pretend that it wasn't an attractive laugh at all, no matter how soft and warm it was. "Thank you. It pays to be adventurous in my line of work."

"Oh, I imagine it does."

"Now, Barbara, leave the young men alone." Ray shook his head and tugged his wife onto the loveseat beside him. It creaked under their combined weight. "They're here to talk about murder. It's not a cheerful subject."

Tobias noted dryly that Ray looked every bit as enthusiastic as Barbara did. Sullivan must've had the same thought, because he sounded amused as he ran through his spiel for the recorder. When that was done, he said, "Well, before we get to the murders, do you think you could tell me a little about the people who lived there?"

"We didn't know them that well, I'm afraid," Barbara said. "Larry—that was his name—was…how to put it?"

"He was an ass," Ray said bluntly.

"Ray! Goodness," Barbara admonished. She looked at Sullivan and Tobias apologetically. "He was though, a bit."

"How so?" Sullivan asked.

"Full of himself," Ray explained. "Pompous. You know the type. Puffed up a lot. Needlessly so, in my opinion."

"He wore a sport jacket to an evening wedding," Barbara whispered to Tobias, still loud enough that everyone heard her anyway.

"I see," Tobias said.

"Next day, he bragged about having been invited," Barbara continued. "Held Ray up at the mailbox for ages talking about it."

"Like it's any great compliment to be invited to one of Carole-Anne's weddings," Ray said. "Anyway, Larry seemed to have forgotten that we've been to three of them now, including the one he'd been at, a point he did not appreciate me making."

"She's on husband number five," Barbara murmured to Tobias. "Such a shame."

"That's too bad," Tobias managed.

"Was there anything in particular that Larry was pompous about?" Sullivan asked. "Did he ever mention work?"

"We didn't really speak to him much," Barbara said. "Neighborhood events only. I seem to recall there was an incident at a barbecue. He got into a tiff with someone over parking, I believe?"

"It was Wayne," Ray said. "They got into it over all those cars that were always parked in front of Wayne's house."

"The cars?" Sullivan asked.

Barbara nodded. "Lots of them. Parked up and down the street at all hours—"

"Black sedans," Ray interjected.

"—and always these big men coming in and out of the place—"

"Wore sunglasses," Ray interrupted. "Sometimes at night, even. Ridiculous. Although I suppose it makes more sense now, why he thought he needed a bunch of bodyguard-types."

"—and Wayne and Larry got downright loud about it." She leaned toward Tobias and spoke with that same stage-whispered confidentiality as before. "It was very dramatic."

"That was the last time Larry came to a neighborhood function, I think," Ray said, squinting like he was trying to remember.

"He went to a lot of them before that, though?" It struck Tobias as odd that a guy involved in small-time crime would be interested in neighborhood functions in the first place. "Was he interested in meeting women at the barbecues?"

"Lord, no," Barbara said.

"He had a girl." Ray took a sip of his water. "I did not approve of the way he spoke of her, did not approve at all."

"Can you be more specific?" Sullivan asked.

"He kept talking about her…ah, *attributes*."

"Attributes," Sullivan repeated.

Ray huffed. "I asked what she was like and he told me her cup size."

"Ray, please," Barbara said in a low voice.

"Sorry, sweetheart." Ray gave Sullivan and Tobias knowing looks.

"I thought he had a daughter too," Barbara said quickly, shifting the conversation back. "But she turned out to be the maid's girl. All that horrible news about the search when she went missing."

"Was this her?" Sullivan asked, holding out the school picture of Nathalie.

Barbara and Ray both slipped reading glasses on

and took turns holding the picture out at arm's length to squint at it. They both nodded.

"She would sit and read on the porch," Barbara said. "Saw her from time to time on one of my walks." She gave Tobias a sweet smile. "I take walks around the neighborhood. For my blood pressure, you know. Sometimes I'd wander that direction."

She would've had to wander pretty close to the gate to notice someone on the porch. Tobias suspected that Barbara was bored out of her mind.

"Did you ever meet Larry's girl?" Sullivan asked. "The one with the, uh, attributes?"

Ray shook his head, but Barbara said, "I did, once, about five or six years before the murders, back when she first arrived. To welcome her to the neighborhood, I took over a coconut cake of Hanna's—Hanna's our cook, she's glorious—and the maid answered the door. Nice woman, very pleasant, and then Larry's girl came up." Barbara's gaze went distant, as if she saw not her own crisp, elegant yard and rosebushes, but a front entryway from thirty years before. Her words slowed to a thoughtful crawl. "She didn't fit Larry's description a whit. I was expecting someone voluptuous and obvious, but she was so young, barely more than a child really, a slip of a thing but for this enormous pregnant belly. She was far too pregnant for how long she'd been in the country, so Larry couldn't have been the father. I always wondered if that was part of his distaste; he could be such a low man. Her dress was far too large for her—I remember that so clearly. It was this cheap, spaghetti-strap sundress, and it kept slipping off one shoulder. She was standing in the shadows, looking at me with these enormous eyes, spooked, like a startled colt. She made me…mmm, I don't know. Sad, I suppose. Uneasy. As if…"

"Never came to the neighborhood functions," Ray said, disapproving, and Barbara startled, blinking twice at her husband.

"Never came out of the house," Barbara corrected, her manner brisker now. "Not once that I recall. Maybe she had trouble adjusting to the States."

"Adjusting," Sullivan repeated, glancing over at Tobias with a warning gleam in his eye, somehow guessing that Tobias was about to squirm out of his chair with excitement. "She wasn't American?"

"Larry called her his 'foreign beauty,'" Ray said, and if a tone of voice could roll its eyes, his would've.

"She asked the maid something while I was there. Had an accent. Russian, maybe." Barbara pursed her lips, thinking about it. "Or it could've been Ukrainian."

Sullivan leaned forward. "Did Larry ever mention her name?"

Barbara and Ray looked at each other, brows pinched in identical frowns, and as one said, doubtfully, "Lena, wasn't it?"

There it was. Tobias stared at Sullivan, fighting the urge to reach over and shake him, to say *that's her, Yelena Krayeva—Mama!—was Larry's girl way back then, she was living there*, but Sullivan looked every inch the chill detective.

"What about around the time of the murders? Did you hear anything about her then?"

Barbara shook her head. "I remember being surprised that Lena never showed up in the news. She wasn't listed as one of the victims, and the police never asked about her. I mentioned her to the nice police officer who talked to us right after everything happened, but he didn't seem to know who I was talking about."

"You think something happened to her?" Sullivan asked.

"No." Barbara considered. "Larry had stopped talking about her altogether well before the murders, now that I think about it. It's entirely possible that they broke up and she moved out, perhaps years before everything happened. I suppose we'll never know now."

"It's her, isn't it?" Tobias asked when they were back in the car. "Larry's girl? Lena? That's Mama, isn't it? And Margaret Trudeau must've been the maid Barbara mentioned. Lena and Margaret were probably friends."

"It's likely." Sullivan didn't start the engine, instead staring into space. "Interestingly, I don't remember reading about Lena in the police reports I've got. My client passed on what he had access to, and I've read it pretty thoroughly. There's no girlfriend mentioned, Russian or otherwise, throughout the investigation."

"Sloppy? Or did she leave so long before the murders that she wasn't relevant?"

"Good question. Probably impossible to answer, but good. What was the thing with the sports jacket?"

"She was saying he was new money."

Sullivan frowned. "How's that?"

"Evening weddings are usually formal. Sports jackets are more informal, and they're made for, like, afternoon events. It's the kind of stupid social expectation that some rich people tend to think denotes someone's value."

"Huh." Sullivan was giving him a mildly unfriendly look now.

Tobias pinched the bridge of his nose with two fingers.

He wasn't sure why Sullivan's opinion should burn, not when Sullivan didn't know him and couldn't understand, but it did. "I know what you're thinking."

"Oh?"

"Poor little rich boy whining about how hard his life is. But I'm not."

"Says the man who can afford to live in a hotel."

"It's not exactly the Bel-Air," Tobias said, trying not to sound snide or juvenile, "and I meant that I'm not whining. Besides, I'm paying for the motel out of my savings."

"Not the money you use to go to 'functions,' I'm guessing."

Tobias gritted his teeth. "I've been working since I was fifteen, and I've been living at home to save for school, so no, it's not 'function' money. It wasn't handed to me."

"Okay."

"My parents put themselves through undergrad and medical school while working full-time. They're not spending weekends at someone's hunting estate, for crying out loud."

"Okay."

"Don't talk about my family."

"Okay," Sullivan said, and this time, instead of doubting and bland, it sounded gentle. Not apologetic exactly, but calming. "Okay."

"Fine." Tobias heaved a breath. "What's next?"

"That's a very good question." Sullivan started the car. "Let's get sandwiches and brainstorm. You're paying."

## Chapter Ten

The house Sullivan drove them to after picking up food was located a few blocks from the cutoff between nice Denver and crappy Denver, although if he'd been pressed, Tobias wasn't sure which side he'd say it was on, because the place was a nightmare. For a good ten seconds, all he could do was sit in the car and marvel. The clapboard had been painted a sickly pastel orange and the little bit of trim that hadn't rotted away was a dingy, faded purple. The portico was half collapsed over the front door, several of the big windows were cracked or boarded up and the rest were filthy. The yard was bare dirt, the privacy fence sun-bleached almost white and sagging so low as to be useless, and the driveway was so pitted as to be a long stretch of rubble.

"Why?" Tobias wondered out loud before deciding that he sounded kind of snobby and should probably shut his mouth. If someone wanted to live in that…thing… they should be able to. But God, it was awful, especially compared to the neat, pretty houses with blossoming rose bushes and white porch swings that lined the rest of the street.

"You mean why are we here?" Sullivan asked. "Because that motel is claustrophobic and depressing and it's killing my soul to work there. Plus I want to save my updated notes on my external drive while I'm thinking about it or I'll forget."

"I mean why is it like this?"

Sullivan glanced at the house as if trying to figure out what the problem was. "You don't like it?"

"You're joking, right? I can't tell. Please be joking. I can't believe you live here."

Sullivan sighed. "You rich boys and your unreasonable standards."

"Knock it off with the rich boy thing. Not wanting to get rabies is not unreasonable." Tobias followed Sullivan across the street reluctantly.

"You're far more likely to get tetanus than rabies. Let's not be silly."

Tobias was taken aback by the urge to smile.

Instead of leading him up the sidewalk, Sullivan headed for the edge of the property and the open gate to the backyard. They waded through a mass of weeds on the other side. "Why are we going this way?"

"Front door deadbolt died this morning, so I've got a cement block keeping it closed from inside," Sullivan said over his shoulder.

"Doesn't that violate the fire code?" Tobias asked, and Sullivan laughed, which was not at all reassuring.

There were white-painted cement stairs to the left leading up to a sun porch with a screen door clinging halfheartedly to its hinges, and a bright red sign—the only intact thing on the whole property so far—taped to it. Danger, Fumigation Chemicals Present. Do Not Enter. May Cause Death.

Tobias stopped short. "Did you bring me here to kill me?"

Sullivan laughed again as he tugged on the doorknob, and the door swung open easily because there was no spring to resist. "That's meant to scare off invaders until I get a new door installed."

The inside of the sun porch had been stripped clean so that the stanchions stood exposed, as if someone had been putting work into the structure of the thing. Sullivan led him through a pair of tidy French doors.

With the weak sunshine that leaked through the filthy screens, Tobias could see that the family room, at least, was in pretty good shape. The hardwood floors shone and the crown molding over the doorways was lovely, and the mismatched but lived-in decor gave the space a cozy sort of atmosphere. The sofa and armchair were the overstuffed, comfy kind that begged to be napped on, an old, beat-up trunk served as a coffee table, the surface watermarked and scarred, and a painting hung on one wall.

It was a painting of a seagull wearing yellow rubber rain boots, but still. It was art.

And there were books everywhere.

Two wide bookshelves were stuffed to overflowing, paperbacks jammed horizontally above double-stacked rows, and leaning towers of hardcovers rose to knee height everywhere except where a narrow bare path wound through the room and led deeper into the house.

Standing in front of the nearest shelf, Tobias turned his head sideways to read the titles. *The Logic of Alice* by Bernard M. Patten, *The Book of Divination* by Ann Fiery, *Cookie Dough Delights* by Camilla V. Saulsbury, *How to Build and Modify GM LS-Series Engines* by Joseph Potak and *Twilight* by Stephenie Meyer.

Sullivan owned *Twilight*. This time the threatening smile made it to Tobias's face. "You have eclectic taste."

"Yeah, a bit." Sullivan had gone through the alcove into the dining room, which was still mid-renovation; a card table and two folding chairs took up most the space, a hole gaped in the ceiling where a chandelier was probably meant to go, and the baseboards had been ripped up.

Tobias wandered over to the painting, charmed by the whimsy of the seagull. All told, it was not the kind of place he'd have expected a guy with a mohawk and tattoos to live.

"Do you feel bad about judging me now?" Sullivan asked, although his tone didn't reflect insult at all. He sounded almost amused. When Tobias winced, he added, "You can say it. You thought I lived in a crack den."

"Yeah. Sorry," Tobias admitted grudgingly.

"Nah, I'm not offended. One of my sisters and her husband flip houses for a living. I like moving around, so every few months when they get a new place, they cut me a serious break on rent in exchange for some manual labor and running off the occasional would-be squatter." He patted the table and Tobias realized he was standing there staring around like a yokel, with his arms full of food.

"Lot of books to move every few months." Tobias dumped everything on the table.

"I don't take most of them. Most of my favorites are on my Kindle, and anything else goes to libraries or used bookstores on moving day. When I'm settled in a new place, the whole accrual cycle starts again."

While they ate, they talked—Sullivan with his mouth full occasionally, Tobias with far more civility because he had manners.

"Okay, so let's lay out what we know," Sullivan said, one foot bouncing under the table. "Back in, what, '87, '88? We've got Larry the crime lord wannabe with his young Russian pregnant girlfriend who eventually turned into Mama, the legit crime lord."

"Lady," Tobias interjected.

Sullivan rolled his eyes. "Whatever. Roughly five years later, in February of '92, he's dead, along with a bunch of his bodyguards and his housekeeper, while the girlfriend-slash-crime lady and the ten-year-old girl are nowhere to be seen. Six years ago, someone bought a condo in that dead housekeeper's name. And that same someone has been, of late, housing a prostitute in that condo in partial payment for a 'favor.' That prostitute accepted a ride thirteen days ago from a stranger in a vehicle that we have not yet identified." Sullivan dipped a chip in ketchup and jabbed it in the air toward Tobias. "Stop making that face."

"Come on. You're thinking it too. Nathalie's with Mama."

"We don't know that. Mama-the-girlfriend could've left years before the murders."

"But it makes sense."

"No, it makes coincidence. We need to find out when the girlfriend left before we start jumping to conclusions."

"You're excited about it." Tobias glanced pointedly at Sullivan's bouncing foot.

"I always fidget," Sullivan said defensively, going still. "My mother called me the patron saint of perpetual motion. And if I am excited—which I'm not—it's only because I like outlandish theories. But since I have more than five brain cells, I'm aware that the outlandish theories often turn out to be bull. It's Occam's razor. 'When you have two competing theories that make exactly the same predictions—'"

Tobias finished with him, '"—the simpler one is the better.'"

Sullivan stared at him.

"You're not the only person on the planet who reads, you know."

"Sometimes I wonder. But okay. Good. It's good. That you read, I mean."

Tobias shrugged that off. If Sullivan wanted to be weird, let him. "But you know what's really strange? That the wannabe crime lord's description of Lena didn't match what she really looked like."

"It's hard to mix up voluptuous sexpot and skinny waif," Sullivan agreed.

"It's almost like he didn't get what he was expecting." Tobias nodded when Sullivan gestured to the remains of his sandwich, sliding his plate over so Sullivan could finish it. "You know what that sounds like, right?"

"That's gotta be a movie cliché or something, though." Sullivan opened his laptop and entered the password, then paused, looking back and forth between Tobias's leftover sandwich and his laptop before pushing the computer toward Tobias. "No one really gets a Russian mail-order bride."

"Of course not." Tobias handed Sullivan a napkin, then opened a browser window for a new search. "That's not a thing people do."

After half an hour of badly translated sleazy websites advertising hot foreign brides and another half hour on sites working to end human trafficking, it was clear that yes, mail-order brides were very much something that people did, and in far more messed-up ways than Tobias had expected.

"Some of these scenarios are basically sex slavery. This girl was rescued from a basement where she was kept chained up for months." Tobias's sandwich sat heavy as stone in his stomach. Some of these girls were younger than Mirlande. His fingers jerked toward his phone instinctively before he reminded himself not to be ridiculous—his sisters, at least, were safe.

"Ugh, don't read that next case study." Sullivan closed his eyes and put his head down on the table so that his words were muffled partly by the wood. "I'm going to take a moment to be disgusted by both my gender and my species."

Tobias couldn't look at the pictures anymore. He got up, swallowing hard against the urge to be sick and collecting their lunch trash. "I'll take care of this," he muttered, and headed in the likely direction of the kitchen.

He had to pick his way through a hallway filled with debris and paint cans and a haphazard stack of half-rotted boards, but Sullivan's kitchen, like the family room, was farther along. He was greeted by bright yellow and white tile, a wall of gutted cabinetry, expensive stainless-steel appliances, and a big six-burner stove that his mother would kill for, but no visible trash can. As he searched in all the reasonable places, he tried to focus on the case. He called, "You think that's how Lena came to this country? Made a deal for a husband and a fresh start and ended up a prisoner in some monster's house?"

"Seems like a pretty common situation." Sullivan appeared in the doorway, his gaze thoughtful on Tobias, his soda cup dangling from one hand. "No wonder becoming a crime lady looked like a viable option. Most of these women aren't here legally, and even if they are, they're told horrible things about the police to keep them from trying to get help—and coming from a place like Russia, you're probably inclined to believe the stories. Most of the men they're given to never marry them or arrange for green cards like they claim they will, so deportation is another threat that can be used. It's not like you can learn the language or get job skills if you're tied up in a bedroom for months. You know, I read this thing a while back about how education in foreign countries doesn't always transfer to the States because we have this attitude here that our learning institutions are better than the ones in other countries even though it's frequently the other way around, especially in K-12—"

Tobias had run out of cabinets to search now, and he kicked the one under the sink closed. "Where on earth is your trash can?"

"—so that immigrants have to… Hmm?" Sullivan blinked. "Oh, it's in the bathroom."

Tobias aimed an exasperated look at him but didn't say anything, only picking his way back through boards and debris to find the bathroom. Sullivan pointed him toward a secluded hallway, at the end of which was a closed door which, when Tobias pushed it open, fell off its hinges and crashed into him, knocking him to the floor and startling the hell out of him in the process.

"What the—" Tobias cried, shoving the door away as Sullivan burst into laughter at the mouth of the corridor. "Why did you let me do that?"

Sullivan only laughed harder.

Tobias climbed to his feet, telling himself to calm down. He wasn't hurt, and it wasn't rational to expect Sullivan to be nice. Tobias was blackmailing him—Sullivan's little rebellions were almost predictable, given the context, and as far as pranks went, this was downright harmless. But his breath was strangling in his throat, much as it had the other day back at home. He was so tired and his eyes had been scraped with sandpaper and he was surrounded by a chaotic mess and the reins holding his temper in check were slipping through his fingers. "I suppose I shouldn't be surprised, but do you seriously not have a kitchen trash can?"

Sullivan's laughter trailed off and he hitched a hip against the table, so that he leaned inelegantly like some insolent hick, only lacking a stalk of wheat to chew on. "Well, now, I don't know how y'all do things up in that fancy neighborhood you live in, but down here in our neck of the woods, we just throw that shit right on the floor."

Tobias flushed. He'd meant that because of the state of the house, it was understandable if the garbage can hung out in whichever room Sullivan or his sister had been working in last. "That's not what I meant," he said stiffly. "I meant I can see that you wouldn't always have the inclination to drag it from room to room—"

"That's very kind of you," Sullivan continued, a saccharine simper on his lips. "We don't all have maids to serve our entitled asses with whatever our hearts could want in any given moment, regardless of how it might affect the little people—"

"Buy another trash can!" Tobias yelled, and threw the bag of crumpled sandwich wrappers at him.

Sullivan batted it out of the air easily, his dark eyes flashing with equal parts anger and *that's the best you can do?* and that was it. Tobias wanted out of this damned house and away from this ass, who was determined to interpret every word out of his mouth in the worst possible way. He headed back toward the family room and freedom, picking up steam as he went, but Sullivan didn't move. He braced his feet like a colonist protecting his square of uncharted land—*I claim this disgusting hall-way in the name of juvenile hair and too many tattoos.* He clearly meant to force Tobias to squeeze around him, and probably break an ankle on the pile of wood, at which point he would *smirk*—

"Move," Tobias gritted out, stopping directly in front of him.

"Giving me orders in my own home, now?" Sullivan snorted. "It suits your social class, I suppose."

"I swear to God—"

"Have we gotten to the threats already? Please do tell me what you intend to do to me for standing in my own fucking hallway."

Tobias was moving before the idea registered in his thoughts. He had Sullivan by the upper arms and was shoving him aside, and Sullivan stumbled over the loose boards. Tobias had caught him so much by surprise that he'd have fallen if Tobias hadn't used the wall and his own body to keep him on his feet, Sullivan's breath exploding from him in a huffed *uh*, and Tobias felt a thrill of victory that had his heart thumping wildly in his chest.

*You didn't think I had it in me,* he wanted to shout. He hadn't thought he had it in him, either, actually, because Tobias didn't fight. He'd never put his hands on someone in anger before in his life, and—God, what had he done?

Tobias lost the wild spree of fury that'd left him reacting so blindly. His fingers loosened, his mind spitting out *oh, God, did I hurt him, he's going to be livid, I just wanted to leave, wanted him to get out of my way, how did this go so wrong*—

Sullivan's eyes—wide and startled—narrowed and

hardened, and he shoved back, harder and with far more determination, his body twisting in a way that took Tobias not only into the other wall, but with enough force that it hurt. Tobias struggled, shoving back, trying to get free rather than cause pain, rapidly becoming aware that while he might outweigh Sullivan slightly, he was slow and clumsy in comparison, so he finally went still. He wasn't—he wasn't sure what to do, how to get out of this, but he knew he didn't want to fight, not like this, and he was angry but not angry enough to hurt someone, so he prepared himself to lose his first fistfight, and then abruptly he realized that they weren't fighting at all.

Sullivan was restraining him but not hurting him, and as Tobias simply stood there, Sullivan's grip loosened further until his hands were only resting on Tobias's arms.

Sullivan's gaze was uncompromising, but pleased, too, the tilt of his head somehow… Tobias didn't have the word for it, but it sent fear and craving tumbling madcap together through every nerve in his body.

It was the same thing he'd seen in Sullivan's eyes the other day in the motel, when he'd pushed Tobias against the wall, when the air between them had shifted and gone loaded and raw in a way that had made Tobias's blood go heavy and slow and bewildered. Something seemed to click inside him now, some switch that flipped so that his brain stuttered to a halt, and he just, he just…

There weren't words for what he was feeling, but his body knew what he meant, what he wanted.

He went to his knees.

Well, this was interesting.

Tobias couldn't fight for shit—if Sullivan had been

interested in doing more than containing him for a minute while they got their tempers in order, there'd have
been no contest—so Sullivan wasn't surprised to feel
him give up and sag against the wall. Sullivan wasn't
surprised that his dick was hardening, either, because
Tobias was attractive in addition to being an asshole, and
it was deeply satisfying to finally feel like he had one up
on that superiority complex.

He was more surprised about the whole Tobias-going-
limp thing.

Or not limp. He was going down, down on his knees,
and that took a second of adjustment, because he hadn't
expected Tobias to reach for Sullivan's fly, to tentatively
rest his hands there for a moment in a silent question before opening his jeans, especially not in this dingy, clut-
tered hallway, with their tension and anger still emanating
from the walls around them.

He hadn't put any real thought into Tobias's style of
getting down, but if he'd been forced to guess, he'd have
imagined some mildly snotty Harvard girl who went to
college as much to find a husband as to study, a girl who
started a fashion line but crapped out on it a few years in
when she married her med-school boyfriend, who seemed
like a nice guy on the surface but took advantage of people without blinking. Sullivan would have guessed at a lot
of missionary, except on the rare Saturday nights when
Tobias and his fictional fiancée had a couple too many
and busted out a little doggy-style. Maybe, if the vibes
he'd been picking up were accurate, the Harvard girl
might be a Harvard boy, but the tone wouldn't change.
It'd be bland and manipulative and occasionally sweet in
a superficial sort of way.

Wow, had he been off.

"Will you let me? Can I?" Tobias's words were slow and heavy, almost like he was drugged. Tobias's hands were slow and heavy too, as they worked his zipper down, hesitating again to give Sullivan a chance to protest, and then, when Sullivan didn't, they tugged his dick out through the opening in his boxers, and God, that felt good. It'd been more than a year since he'd known a hand other than his own, and it was such a simple touch, an easy, too-dry brush of skin on skin, but Sullivan's spine went liquid all the same.

"Let me?" Tobias whispered. "I want to. I...want to give you something, I need—" He stopped, looking confused and frustrated and searching.

Letting himself be guided by an instinct that had gotten him in trouble more than a few times, Sullivan reached down and tunneled one hand into those romantic curls, taking hold and tugging, hard enough that it would hurt.

Tobias's eyes slipped half-closed and his breath shuddered out. "Yeah, that's... I need... I don't..."

Holy shit.

Tobias might not know the word for what he needed but Sullivan did. He'd heard subs talk about the ravenous emptiness that echoed inside them sometimes, the desperate need to give, to *serve*, and the way it became vital to everything they were in that moment.

If there was a Dom alive who could resist a sub in that headspace, he'd never met them.

"Fuck," he said, and eased Tobias forward. Tobias showed no sign of disliking Sullivan's regulation, instead pressing his face against Sullivan's hip, breathing in, mouthing at the skin, nuzzling the crease of his thigh.

His fingers tightened around Sullivan's dick, giving it a couple of idle pulls, and then Tobias was taking him deep.

Too deep, actually, because he jerked back and coughed. "Easy," Sullivan bit out, and Tobias leaned in again, his tongue working eagerly, his mouth wet and hot, and sucked hard, and oh, this wasn't going to take long at all.

They hadn't talked about limits or preferences or even a safe word, and Sullivan was probably the shittiest Dom in the world for going ahead with this anyway, but in his defense, it hadn't been clear they'd need them until his dick was already out of his pants. He shook his head once, trying to clear it, and guided them into a shallow, slow rhythm despite the impulse to use Tobias's mouth like it was his, to push and shove until he was practically in Tobias's damn lungs, to watch Tobias's eyes tear.

Sullivan had to keep it together, because it was one thing to suck off a guy you barely knew in his firetrap of a house, it was another thing to let that guy fuck your mouth like he'd paid for it. There were degrees to how shitty Tobias might feel about this later, and Sullivan didn't mind pissing off someone screwing him over, but there was a damn ravine's worth of distance between that and fucking someone up sexually.

Tobias apparently disagreed. His hands went up to close on Sullivan's where they were in his hair, gripping hard, the question in his blue eyes sharpening into a demand as they stared up at him, and Sullivan thought *yep, okay, he wants this, this is actually happening.*

Sullivan tightened his fingers and pushed forward into that impatient mouth once, a test of sorts. Tobias closed his eyes, let his hands fall to rest on his own thighs, and made a sound of such wrenched, hungry gratitude that

Sullivan stopped worrying about how his interpretive
skills were functioning.

It didn't take long at all after that. He didn't go as deep
or hard as he would've liked, but no one could say he was
holding back either, and Tobias knelt there and took it,
expression going somnolent, his whole body receptive
and willing. Thank God for it, too, because Sullivan was
sweating and grunting and completely losing his shit.

He came with a last series of hard thrusts, deeper than
any so far, the sensation of Tobias choking around him
less arousing than the fact that Tobias's hands remained
docile in his lap the whole time.

He opened his eyes to find that he was slumped forward over Tobias, one forearm propping him up against
the wall, and Tobias was pushing against him, wrench-
ing against him, and fuck—he'd, had he taken it too far?
But no, Tobias was trying to get his jeans open while
he was kneeling like this so he could jerk off, and his
mouth was still working, gentle and sweet around Sullivan's cock, so gentle, in fact, that post-orgasm sensitiv-
ity wasn't a factor.

Sullivan pulled back anyway, ignoring Tobias's moan
of protest, and dropped to his knees as well. He pushed
a few boards aside and guided Tobias flat on his back,
yanking at his jeans until he could pull out Tobias's
dick—thick and pretty and hard, dripping at the tip. He
stretched out beside Tobias and took him in hand, jerking slowly to start. Tobias made a soft, high sound, practically writhing, his kicking heels making drumming
sounds on the boards at their feet, turning his face into
Sullivan's shoulder shyly, and that was so surprisingly
charming that Sullivan had to lean down and put his
mouth on Tobias's throat, had to jerk harder and faster,

had to lick against his skin and taste the salt there. He got lost in the wild moans Tobias gave up, in the way his hips moved, in the way he whispered *please, please* and Sullivan, helpless, said, "Take what you need, sweetheart," and Tobias groaned and his dick jerked as he came all over his belly and Sullivan's hand.

## Chapter Eleven

Blissful silence.

Blissful stillness.

He was boneless and lying in a bag of cotton balls. It was so soft here. It was so *nice*.

He was dimly aware of Sullivan moving against him, and he thought maybe he should make something of that, but Sullivan whispered something soothing, and Tobias settled back down into the sleepy, perfect haze of quiet.

Warm wetness settled against his belly and he blinked his heavy eyes open, caught sight of Sullivan cleaning him up with a washcloth, his touch considerate, and it was impossible not to smile. Then he was murmuring that Tobias should get up, and he really, really didn't want to, but Sullivan was asking, and he probably had a good reason for it. He struggled upward, unworried when the boards shifted beneath him because Sullivan was ready, already holding him tight and close against his body. He was ushered into another room and eased onto a couch, and that was nice too, it was so plush and soft, and he sat there for a second breathing and staring at nothing, and it was all so very, perfectly quiet.

He had a glass of water now, and he was drinking it, and then Sullivan was guiding him to lie down, and Tobias put his head on Sullivan's firm thigh, and there was a blanket and there were fingers in his hair, stroking, and he was safe and insulated and warm, and it was so wonderfully, exactly what he needed.

All he had to do was follow Sullivan's directions. Sullivan would take care of everything. He'd made sure that Tobias came apart in a way that felt good, and he'd wanted Tobias and taken everything Tobias offered and he'd been grateful, Tobias had seen it in his face how much Sullivan had needed it too, and it'd felt so right to give Sullivan what he needed, and it was so soft and safe and quiet here that he just…floated.

He hadn't been sleeping, so he didn't really wake up per se, but there was definitely a span of time during which he had been distant from reality and a moment when he became aware of it again.

Sullivan was still stroking his head, and the TV was on, the volume low on some construction show and Tobias came back in bits and pieces until he realized he was concerned for the nice people whose bathroom had been wrecked by a shady contractor. He still wasn't quite all there when the episode ended, so he missed some of the summation.

"Did they find him?" he asked, referring to the contractor who should be in jail. Wow, his voice sounded thick as syrup.

"I don't think so," Sullivan said quietly. "But the host guy fixed it for them. They're all right."

"That's good."

"Back with me?"

"I think so?" Tobias thought about it for a minute. "Yeah, I think so."

"Want to sit up?"

That was the last thing he wanted, but he was starting to need the bathroom, so he supposed he didn't have
much choice. His head swam when he was upright, but
Sullivan steadied him.

He should explain. He'd sort of gone to pieces, but he
wasn't sure he could explain why, and besides, Sullivan
didn't look mad or like he expected an explanation. He
seemed thoughtful more than anything else. Tobias asked,
"The good bathroom's upstairs?"

"Through my bedroom, last on the right."

Tobias went up the creaking stairs at a quicker pace
than his legs were interested in, but the need was becoming downright urgent, so he didn't take the time to notice
much about his surroundings until after he'd peed and
washed his hands. His belly was dry and clean, and he
distantly remembered Sullivan cleaning him up.

He stared at himself in the mirror and wondered why
he wasn't upset about what'd happened.

He'd have thought it would be inevitable. He wasn't
good with change, especially abrupt change, and this
qualified, didn't it? This—this angry sex that'd given
way to a feeling entirely new and possibly dangerous, it
was a big thing, wasn't it? He should be obsessing, but
instead he felt calm and centered.

The more he thought about it, the more certain he became, too. He didn't know how to describe the experience, but it hadn't been alien. Somehow he'd known this
existed, even before he had the words to describe it or
the knowledge to look for it. He must've known, because
when Sullivan had taken him by the hair, he'd thought
*yes, right, this.*

In relationships in the past, sex had given him a frustrated, empty feeling. He'd be overcome by the sense that he was too mobile, too jagged, a puzzle piece jammed into a bad-fitting space. Like he was waiting for something he desperately needed but couldn't define. And without that definition, he couldn't know.

He knew now.

He knew how it felt to slip into a place like he belonged there. Knew how much peace there could be in the little pocket of time when he'd been tethered to the earth, seemingly, by Sullivan's will alone. A strange, edged quiet had taken up within him, a quiet that still hadn't fully dissipated, and it was sublime. This wasn't a change at all—it was an unlocking.

It wasn't only the peace he wanted, though. He swallowed hard and it hurt, the ache in his throat enough to make him feel hazy again. He wanted everything that came before the peace too: Sullivan sliding hot and large and demanding into his mouth, pulling his hair, forcing his way deeper near the end. It'd hurt and frightened him and made him choke even as he'd closed his eyes and thought *more*. He flushed red at the memory, getting a delicious thrill from the shamelessness of it, and his dick twitched in his jeans though he should've been satisfied by this point.

It was like meth. Tobias had read up on it after the whole thing with Church and the Krayevs eight months ago, and he knew that for some people trying meth just once fundamentally changed their brain chemistry, creating profound addiction that would rock the rest of their lives. He thought that might be what he'd experienced. He already craved more.

Tobias supposed they'd had casual sex.

He wasn't innocent, but he'd always preferred to know

a partner well before embarking on something physical, both because he liked the intimacy of it and because it helped him feel less anxious about pleasing his partners. He'd never slept with someone outside of a relationship; he was admittedly out of his depth.

Still, he'd expected casual sex to feel sort of…casual, and this had been anything but.

To him, anyway.

At that thought, his stomach rolled over, and the last of his lovely buzz vanished.

Who knew what Sullivan was thinking? Tobias hadn't asked for what'd happened, not with words anyway, but neither had Sullivan, now that he thought about it. Neither of them had said yes or no or if or how. They'd followed some unspoken form of communication and it'd been perfect—on his side, at least. He hoped it was true for Sullivan as well.

He'd had sex with a man he'd known for all of five days, a man who should hate him. A man who had tattoos and a mohawk and worked as a private detective and was impossibly cool, not to mention decent enough to take care of Tobias when he'd been vulnerable despite all the reasons he had to be a jerk. Sullivan was a good man, a slightly weird, moderately hyper, hot-as-sin, occasionally annoying good man.

A man who liked to live by the seat of his pants, no doubt. He probably didn't do relationships. He'd probably be uncomfortable if Tobias suggested otherwise. In fact, this would probably last only until the case was over.

Fine. That was fine, actually. Tobias could be casual. He was doing all sorts of things lately that he'd never thought to do. And people had casual sex all the time. Why shouldn't he be one of them? The more he thought about it, the more he liked the idea. Tobias Benton could be the kind of person who followed his urges and didn't think about the consequences and had casual sex with tattooed private detectives. In fact, that sounded downright *excellent*. He'd milk this dark, strange power between them until he'd gotten what he wanted, and once he'd found Ghost, he'd say good-bye to Sullivan with a little wave and a thank you kindly and move on.

Before going downstairs, he paused to take a slow look at Sullivan's room. There wasn't much here: a box spring and a mattress without a bedframe, the sheets and pillowcases mismatched, one of those Rubbermaid four-drawer storage containers full of clothes, an old milk crate of odds and ends, including a bottle of vitamins, a Kindle, some wires and cords.

Everything Sullivan owned was designed to be transitory. He'd said it himself earlier—he didn't like to stay in one place. Sullivan was a guy with wanderlust. It wouldn't be long before he wandered away from Tobias, too.

His phone buzzed in his pocket, making him jump. He found a text from Mirlande: where are you? Ruby's performance starts in forty-five minutes. Are you riding with me and Guy? If you are, you better be on your way.

"Oh, shit." Tobias hurried downstairs, typing out a reply that he would meet everyone at Boettcher, freaking out about how he was going to manage to get back to the motel, shower, and still make it on time—he was *not* going to his little sister's concert reeking of sex—and... he didn't have his car. It was at the motel. Sullivan had been driving all day.

He blundered into the living room at full speed. "Can you take me to the motel?"

"What?"

"I have to go. I'm sorry. I'm—my sister, she's—I have to go."

Sullivan climbed to his feet. "Is she all right?"

Tobias had no idea where his car keys were. Where the hell had he put his keys? "Yeah, no, it's nothing like that, it's... I promised I would be there for her performance— she's a violinist—and I forgot. I'm so late, and I can't beg off; she's got abandonment issues. Well, we all have abandonment issues, I suppose. Adopted kids. It's pretty standard. And I'm her favorite, though God knows why, since I can't seem to—"

"Here." Sullivan held out Tobias's keys. "They fell out of your pocket while you were lying on the couch."

"Oh, thank you, you're..." Tobias stuttered to a halt, struck by the tension in Sullivan's mouth, in the way his brow pinched. He realized suddenly how this looked. "Hey, so about, uh, the sex."

As he spoke, he lifted a hand to try to straighten his hair, because he no doubt had sex hair, and Sullivan... Sullivan *flinched*.

Tobias dropped his hand. It took a full five seconds for his brain to come up with "It was really good," but he said it with far too much vehemence, because he was suddenly furious at that stupid flinch. He tried to soften it by adding, "I'm good if you are." He cleared his throat. "I didn't realize I needed that."

Perhaps not the most graceful postcoital compliments possible, but at least Sullivan didn't look like he was anticipating a punch anymore. He mostly looked sort of startled, and Tobias's mouth was still running on without his permission. "Thanks for being decent. I mean, you don't have any reason to like me, and I know casual things don't come with a lot of expectations, so it could've been…but you were good to me, and thanks."

Something flickered in Sullivan's expression, something that Tobias began to interpret as annoyance, but then it shifted, lightning-quick and impossible to parse, and finally Sullivan's features settled into a mask of distance. Tobias wasn't sure why at first, but then realized that he'd basically implied that he would've expected Sullivan to be a crappy human being rather than a decent one, and he belatedly added, "Sorry."

"For?" Sullivan asked, still distant, and this had gotten awful and awkward, and Tobias would've pushed, maybe, if he had time for it, and maybe if Sullivan didn't look quite so much like Tobias was a complete stranger he'd bumped into on the street instead of someone he'd had sex with half an hour ago. But he didn't have time, and Sullivan didn't seem to want to hear it anyway, so he didn't push.

He muttered, "Never mind. Look, uh, I know it's inconvenient, but I'd really appreciate a ride to the motel so I can get my car."

Nothing on Sullivan's face changed, but he grabbed his own keys and his wallet and headed for the door, and Tobias thought *forget it then*.

Tobias arrived at Boettcher Concert Hall with dripping wet hair, a damp collar, a small bouquet of roses, and a healthy amount of dread brewing in his belly, but showing up at the last second had one perk—there was no opportunity for small talk with his family. He snuck into the auditorium out of breath, just before the doors closed, and barely had time to exchange some nods of hello. After a brief intro from the conductor and the obligatory tuning of instruments by the orchestra, the first guest soloist began.

Unfortunately, he couldn't avoid intermission the same way. The concert was a showcase of young talent, and since Ruby hadn't played yet, they didn't even have the topic of her performance to discuss.

In a lobby humming with the polite conversation of well-dressed patrons in line for wine at the bar, Tobias shook his papa's hand, kissed Mirlande and his manman on the cheek and gave Guy a not-too-hard shoulder bump. "Where are Marie and Darlin?"

"Darlin's got one of his migraines, so Marie stayed home with him." Manman was wearing the emerald green dress she'd worn to Tobias's high school graduation. She joked sometimes that it was her proud parent dress, because she'd noticed one day that by sheer coincidence she'd worn it in four photographs of various school events. "They'll be sorry they missed seeing you."

"Yeah, me too." Tobias shifted his weight as he considered what other safe subjects he could bring up.

"When are you coming home?" Guy asked, and when Mirlande kicked him—not subtly—in the shin, he said, "What? I didn't promise I wouldn't ask. I said I'd *think* about it."

"Nice," Mirlande hissed under her breath.

"Please," Manman said, in the voice she used when she was not to be disobeyed. "Not here and not now."

"Sorry," Mirlande and Guy said immediately.

"How are your classes proceeding, Tobias?" Papa asked, mercifully before Tobias could be expected to answer Guy's question, not that Papa's was easier.

He couldn't say that it'd been days since he'd gotten through more than a paragraph in his textbooks without wanting to tear his face off, could he? "They're fine, thank you."

After a minute of incredibly uncomfortable silence, Tobias asked, "Did anyone else recognize the girl who went first? We've heard her before, haven't we?"

"She was good," Mirlande said, and heroically carried the conversation for several minutes. He squeezed her forearm in gratitude.

Eventually the chime rang to let people know that intermission was over, and they trooped back to their seats to watch another boy perform with his cello before finally it was Ruby's turn.

Tobias would never be half as good at anything as his sister was at the violin, and as proud of her as he was, Tobias worried too. Ruby had an entire global music community breathing down her neck. Conductors and music directors and recording companies from around the world called after hearing her play. Her teachers talked about her career in terms of decades, about her responsibilities to her gift like she'd been touched by the finger of God.

The very idea made Tobias's throat want to close up.

She started with one of Paganini's Caprices, an excruciatingly difficult piece that would satisfy even the most discerning doubter of her talent and a piece which had driven the entire family mad over the months it'd taken her to master it. Her second choice was Sarasate's majestic and unnerving Zigeunerweisen, one of Tobias's favorite pieces of music.

He closed his eyes and let the notes take him away.

After flowers and congratulations and autograph signings, Ruby was finally free to leave, and the family made a plan to get ice cream to celebrate. Night had fallen, warm and blue and breezy, and Tobias drove with Ruby in the back seat watching him in the rearview mirror and Guy in the front, fiddling with the radio on low volume.

"So?" Guy asked. "When are you coming home?"

"I'm not," Tobias said.

"I knew it," Ruby muttered.

"I'm twenty-four. I can't live at home forever."

"It saves school money," she argued.

"I have enough saved up," Tobias lied, because living in a motel was the worst way possible to maintain a savings account. "It's time for me to be more independent."

"It's because you had a fight with Manman and Papa." She gave him an *I see through your bullshit* look in the mirror.

"The fight doesn't matter. As an adult, sometimes you need more breathing space, that's all."

"He means he doesn't want to be single anymore." Guy's gaze tracked the scenery as his thumb flicked through channels. "Men have needs."

"Oh, who cares?" Ruby rolled her eyes so hard they nearly popped out of her skull. "Women do too and you don't hear us whining about it all the time."

Guy twisted around in his seat to snap at her, and Tobias said quickly, "Everybody has needs and everybody whines, except when they don't. Okay? You're both right."

They gave him matching dubious looks but settled down.

After a minute, Ruby said, "Are you lonely? Is that why you want a boyfriend?"

He was absolutely not going to think about Sullivan or kinky sex while in a car with his little brother and sister. "I don't want a boyfriend. I want—" Hell, he wasn't sure what he wanted. He just didn't want what he'd had. "That's not the point. This doesn't mean I'm not going to see you guys. When I get a place and I'm all set up, you can come hang out any time you want. And we can still talk on the phone or text."

Guy asked, "Did they do something wrong? Or was it you?"

Tobias wasn't touching that with a ten-foot pole. "It's complicated."

"That's what adults say when they think you're too stupid to understand," Guy intoned, and Ruby snorted.

Tobias sighed. "That's what adults say when they don't want you to be depressed about how hard life can be sometimes. Or when we don't want to give you ideas that might get you screwing up your own lives. Or when we're being stupid jerks and we don't want to admit it to kids because it's embarrassing and you'll bring it up later as evidence for why you shouldn't have to listen to us."

They were both looking at him again, this time with matching, satisfying expressions of *whoa*. He found himself curiously unmotivated to take any of it back, either.

At the ice cream shop, when everyone had gotten their cones, they filed over to the small picnic tables, where their parents and Guy sat separately because Ruby claimed "star's rights" and commandeered Mirlande and Tobias at another.

"You were amazing," Mirlande told Ruby. "The caprice sounded perfect."

She ducked her head, her smile pleased and shy. "It was okay."

"After the number of hours you put into it, I think you can admit it was better than okay," Mirlande said.

"It was really hard," Ruby admitted. She lowered her

voice. "I threw my bow once when I was practicing. Don't tell."

"Manman would've killed you if you needed a new one." Mirlande gave Ruby an appraising, impressed look. "You would be dead right now. In the earth, child."

Ruby giggled. "I know. I almost peed my pants when I thought it might be broken. It was fine, though."

Tobias cleared his throat. "Is it worth it? This part, when everyone's proud and we're celebrating? Is it worth wanting to throw your bow?"

"No." She took a big lick of her ice cream. "Being on stage is, though."

"Oh. You—you still like performing?"

She nodded.

"It's not frightening up there in front of all those people?" He could feel Mirlande watching him and tried to keep his face neutral, as if he were asking about the weather or something equally insignificant.

"It's…" Ruby stared off into the distance. "It's like being on fire. In a good way."

"And that's what makes all the awful parts okay?"

She frowned. "It's not awful."

"No, I mean…what do you do when you hate it?"

"What are you talking about? I don't hate it."

"I mean when you don't want to play. I mean the moments when it's hard and you're frustrated and you kind of hate it."

"I never hate it. Even when I'm frustrated, I don't hate it. I still love it. The hard parts I almost love more, because they're like a buildup. They make it so that when I do get it right, it feels bigger."

"But you almost snapped your bow," Tobias reminded

her, a bit embarrassed by how hard it was to keep his voice down. "That's—I can imagine what that feels like."

"But I love the hard parts too," she repeated, her nose wrinkling as if she thought he was being stupid on purpose.

"Because everyone's proud when you work hard," he told her. "That's why."

"No, because they're good."

"Tobias," Mirlande started, but he shook his head and spoke over her.

"But what makes them good? Like, what do you do to make them feel that way?"

"I don't know, they just *are*." Ruby sighed hugely. "It's like, why is ice cream good and spinach is nasty? They just are, Tobias." She licked her ice cream, one eyebrow lifting in a look that reeked of Mirlande, judgmental and worried and about to be way too pushy on his behalf, and it didn't help that Mirlande was right beside her with the exact same look on her face.

"I'm fine," he told them, trying to nip it in the bud.

Ruby talked with her mouth full. "Guy says that when people try to tell you that your feelings are wrong it's because they're describing how their feelings are. He says he knows it because he's deep."

"Well, there's a reliable source." Mirlande held out napkins. "Finish your bite before you speak."

For a split second, Tobias thought he'd gotten away clean, but Mirlande turned to him. "Are you doubting your career path?"

"Guy is fourteen and not remotely deep," he said. "He is the opposite of deep. He thinks nursery rhymes count as poetry."

Ruby asked, "What parts don't you like?"

*All of them*, he almost said, and nearly bit his tongue off trying to keep the sentence contained. "It's fine. It's hard right now, that's all, but it'll be fine."

"Because you'll get back to the easy parts soon and then you'll love it again," she said uncertainly.

*I never loved it.* "Right."

Mirlande was eyeing him with insulting sympathy.

"I'm fine," he insisted.

"Oh, Tobias. You're such a mess." Mirlande shook her head and went back to eating her cone, and he tried not to look across the lot at his parents, both successful doctors who'd spent years in a high-pressure field taking care of the sick and the poor, flawless examples of everything he was supposed to be but wasn't.

## Chapter Twelve

Roughly four hours after Tobias ran out on him, Sullivan turned off the documentary about serial killers that he hadn't been paying attention to anyway, and bit the bullet.

She answered the phone by saying, "Caty's House of Pain."

"I fucked up."

She hesitated. "Is there a body?"

"What? No."

"Oh. Okay. What'd you do?"

"Do you seriously think I would kill someone?"

There was a pause. "No."

"Jesus."

She laughed. "C'mon, I'm joking. When you avoid someone for weeks because you're a big, ugly coward, you should expect some shit."

"Fair enough. I'm sorry about that, by the way."

"No, you're not."

"No, I'm not," he agreed. "But I want to be sorry."

"No, you don't." She sounded downright amused by it.

He grinned. This. This was why he adored her. "No, I don't."

"So what'd you do?"

"I fucked someone I shouldn't have fucked."

There was a tiny pause. "If you're not here for dinner in twenty minutes, I will come over there and pull you out of that shit hole you live in by your hair."

Then she hung up on him.

This was *not* why he adored her.


Caty and Lisbeth lived in a bungalow not far from his place, a charming slate-blue one-story with a yellow door, which opened before Sullivan had a chance to knock. Caty stood there in all her big-haired blonde beauty, her low-cut purple top revealing the upper swells of her large breasts, her black leather collar latched around her throat as usual. Her skirt was pink tweed and short enough to reveal the knee-high lace-up boots she was wearing.

"Nice." He nodded appreciatively, because good boys might be his kryptonite, but bad girls definitely had their charms too, and he knew Caty would take it as the compliment he meant it as. "It's very Barbie Does Dallas."

"Get in here," Caty snarled, yanking him inside by the wrist.

"I missed you, too," he said, unable to curb his smile.

"You've been an uptight little non-boner for over a year—a year!—and you've been avoiding me for weeks—weeks!—just because I tried to get you to give someone new a chance post-fuckface, and out of the blue you're all 'oh, I fucked someone, oh, it's so dramatic' and now you're trying to be chill about it? Fucker!"

Lisbeth appeared at the far end of the hallway, small and brunette and slender in her quiet blouse and trousers, lovely in a sedate way. "Hello, Sullivan. How are you? Was it a pleasant drive?"

"It's hot as balls out here."

"Classy," Caty sneered, and smacked him on the back of his head.

"I'm wearing a button-down." He'd even taken a shower so he wouldn't be all sweaty. "Ungrateful wench."

"We're having rigatoni with a white wine sauce," Lisbeth said serenely. "Does that suit you?"

"Sounds delicious." He followed the women into the kitchen, a bright, airy room thick with the scent of butter and herbs at the moment. "Smells delicious too."

"Thank you." She stirred something in a pot and gave him a soft smile. "Caty mentioned you've been busy at work. Trouble with a case?"

"I did not say he's been busy at work," Caty said hotly. "I said he was pretending to be busy at work to *avoid* me so he wouldn't have to crawl out of that dank hole in the ground he's squatting in."

Lisbeth nodded. "Oh, that's right." She added salt to the sauce. "What's the pretend trouble at work?"

"Oh, my *God*," Caty groaned.

"It's actual trouble these days. Boss Lady finally gave me a case of my own."

Lisbeth smiled. "Congratulations."

"Thank you."

"How'd you con Raina into that one?" Caty asked.

Sullivan nobly ignored that in favor of going to the fridge and peering inside. "I'm looking for a missing girl, and one of the leads I stumbled onto is a college guy who…" He stopped with his hand midair, reaching for string cheese. He wasn't sure how to finish that sentence.

"Context," Caty demanded. "Now."

So he explained the whole mess, starting with the ineffectual blackmail and stumbling to a halt before he got any more specific about the sex than he already had.

This wasn't the kind of thing he would normally bite his tongue on—people in the kink community generally had very few boundaries when it came to discussing this sort of thing in a group—but something told him Tobias wouldn't like it, so he kept his mouth shut.

When he'd finished, Lisbeth made a humming sound. "You're right. He's an inappropriate person to sleep with."

"You're telling me." Sullivan licked a drop of wine from the lip of his glass.

"You don't sound mad that he's blackmailing you," Caty said slowly.

"Oh, I'm mad." He paused. "I *was* mad." He peeled off another string of cheese and considered it thoughtfully. "I'm still mad if I think about it for too long, but it's hard to be mad about it all the time because it's sort of stupid. I mean, they might arrest me, but even if the apartment complex pressed charges for breaking and entering, what am I really going to get?"

"I'm not even sure they can file charges on behalf of a resident, especially if he hasn't been determined to be missing yet. Hmm. I'd have to check. Either way, if you didn't steal or vandalize anything, I'd say you're fine," Lisbeth said. "Slap on the wrist at most."

"Exactly. And it might be neat to get arrested once. To see what it's like, you know?"

"You're so weird," Caty said.

"Honestly, if it weren't for how Raina would react, I'd say fuck it and see what he does."

"Raina would shit a brick, wouldn't she?" Caty asked.

"Yeah." Sullivan slumped in his chair. "There's the rub, as they say. It wouldn't be the end of the world if I had to continue my training at another firm, but it'd eat up a lot of time, and I'm not ready to be on my own yet.

Getting arrested would be more of a pain in the ass than anything else, but getting fired would cut."

"So you're letting him help," Caty prompted, eyeballing him over her glass.

"Yeah, I'm letting him help. He's not entirely useless, at least."

"Uh-huh."

Propping one hip against the counter and taking a sip of her wine, Lisbeth said, "Considering what the case means to you, sleeping with him does seem self-destructive."

"That's lawyer speak for stupid," Caty said helpfully. "And it figures that after a year of non-boners, you're getting actual boners for people you shouldn't be getting boners for."

"Boner? Really? What are you, fourteen?" Sullivan said.

"Boner, boner, boner."

He swallowed the last bite of string cheese and threw the wrapper away. "How big a deal would you say unnegotiated kink with a newbie is, ethics-wise?"

Caty lifted a slow eyebrow. "My, my, my. I'd say it depends. Is he psychologically vulnerable in a way that'll make it hard for him to interrupt play? Was he upset afterward? Was the consent explicit even if the kink was sort of wandery and play-it-by-ear?"

Sullivan blinked. "No? Yes? I'm not—that was a lot of questions. Wandery?"

"Wandering. Wanders. To wander." Caty stared at him balefully. "Prick."

"How did his cues read?" Lisbeth asked.

"Green. And afterward he said it was good."

Both women studied him for a minute. Lisbeth finally said, "Why are you asking? You know as well as either of us that play should be safe, sane, and consensual, and that's what it sounds like you orchestrated. Where's the problem?"

Sullivan didn't know how to describe the flinching sensation in his gut. It'd started once Tobias got up to go to the bathroom, and it had grown fast, tempered by Tobias's reassurances that the sex had been good, but the flinch was still there, squatting inside him, waiting for the blow.

"Nick really fucked you up," Caty said, more gently than she'd ever said anything to him in the years he'd known her, and it was *awful*. "He's got you questioning everything, and maybe some of that is okay because that's how you stay a good person, but there's nothing wrong with the way you like to fuck. I wish you'd stop acting like you're trying to cage a beast or something. It was cruel of him to imply that."

"He wasn't being cruel," Sullivan replied wearily, though he wasn't sure why. He wasn't going to change her mind at this point. "I scared him. He couldn't give me what I wanted. There's no fault in that."

To Nick, Sullivan's desires were a corruption, a betrayal of years of friendship filled with bicycles and baseball and private detective movies and grape popsicles and homework sessions and bad prom photos with girls whose names they could barely remember. By the time they'd been old enough and brave enough to exchange confessions about their adult sexualities—Sullivan bisexual, Nick gay—the nature of their bond had been well defined. Sullivan had violated their unspoken contract. He'd changed the rules. He'd stumbled through an excruciating confession that'd felt so much like the others they'd made, up until the moment Nick had yanked his hand out of Sullivan's and stared at him like he was a predator.

*Have you always been like this? Have you been wanting to hurt me all these years? What kind of monster gets off on hurting the people he claims he loves?*

Losing his boyfriend of several months over a fundamental difference in sexual interests hadn't been pleasant, but losing his best friend had been another kind of pain altogether.

Lisbeth pulled a colander from a cabinet. "Are you going to see the college boy again?"

"It's a complicated situation."

"No, it is not." Caty kicked him in the ankle hard, laughing when he yelped.

"I do what I want," Sullivan snapped, rubbing his ankle.

"Read my lips, loser. He. Is. Blackmailing. You."

"Ineffectually." He swallowed hard. "I *know*. But…"

"But?"

Sullivan remembered the small jerks of Tobias's body, the eager way he'd sucked Sullivan deep, the way his eyes had gone dark and desperate. The way he'd laid his head on Sullivan's lap after, letting Sullivan play with his hair as he swam up from that altered headspace, vulnerable and trusting and sweet. The way he'd taken it so in stride, as if the part of Sullivan that Nick had been so disgusted by were something to be craved. It was like the universe had conspired to give him one perfect moment. For the first time since Nick left, all his pieces had been in harmony, all the planets aligned.

Sullivan pretended his voice wasn't hoarse when he said, "It was really good."

"Of course it was really good, but it's not because of

*him*. His dick isn't magic." Caty shook her head so hard her hair bounced all over. "It's because you haven't boned anyone in over a year! Plus, he's blackmailing you, which is exactly the sort of weird, interesting shit that you're attracted to in a person. Of course it was good!"

"I don't like being blackmailed," Sullivan corrected. "It pisses me off. There are better ways to not be bored. I'm just still all postcoital, so it's hard to keep my energy up for bitching about it. There's this bonding hormone called oxytocin. It floods your system after orgasm, and it's been shown in studies to facilitate monogamy in men. Well, straight men. Don't think any bi or gay men were in the study. I should look that up. It's also been found in women as they breastfeed their children, which is less applicable here, but—"

"Sullivan," Lisbeth said.

"—it's— What?"

"You're monologuing."

"Oh." He blinked. "Sorry. But you get my point."

"Oxytocin makes you forget you're being blackmailed," Caty said, flatly doubtful.

"It doesn't make me forget anything. I just like the people I'm sleeping with more than I did before I slept with them. That's a perfectly normal thing. I like them a normal amount. And it's not like he'll let me get all twisted up over him. He wants something casual. So no big."

"Silverware, Caty, please." Lisbeth pulled a block of parmesan out of the fridge.

"You can't keep boning the college guy." Caty rose and opened the silverware drawer. "You're in a vulnerable place right now. You're back on the market for the first time post-fuckface, and you're so hard up that the boning will be amazing and then he'll leave because he doesn't want something serious and you'll be left lying around in a pool of oxytocin hormones."

"I'm aware of that," he snapped. "And stop saying *bone*. It doesn't even sound like a word anymore."

"God, you're going to keep boning him and you'll fall in love and he'll trash you," Caty moaned.

"Plates, Caty, please," Lisbeth said, in a tone that meant she was exhausted with their drama.

Caty dragged herself to the cabinet with the petulance of a teenager, calling back over her shoulder, "There are other attractive, kink-minded people in the world, Sullivan. You can always role-play blackmail scenes."

Sullivan groaned.

Sullivan woke up the next morning to his phone buzzing with a text message. Tobias.

Are you alive?

Sullivan sent back: no leave me alone.

The reply was prompt: Are you home?

Sullivan ran the heel of one hand over his eyes and tried to clear the fog from his brain. He sent back: no.

A split second later, he got: Your car is here. I'm going into your backyard. Please come and let me in.

"I'm not boning you," Sullivan muttered, and started the long, unpleasant process of dragging himself out of bed. Only once he'd staggered downstairs did he think to check the time, and then he let out a groan of disbelief.

Tobias knocked on the back door and Sullivan yelled, "It's *9:45*, you ass! On a Sunday!"

There was a long silence. Then a more respectful knock.

Sullivan decided to ignore him.

He made coffee and a bowl of cereal, chewing while standing over the sink, ignoring the knocks that came with increasing frequency and volume as the minutes passed. His phone buzzed several more times, but he ignored that, too. It wasn't until he saw Tobias's irritated face appear in one of the windows at the side of the house that he realized he was going to end up with a broken pane of glass if he didn't let the guy in. He went outside and stuck his head around the corner of the house.

"I thought you had manners," he said, watching Tobias struggle back out of the bushes.

"I do," Tobias replied, sounding offended.

"You're a peeping Tom who doesn't respect the sanctity of sleeping in on Sundays." Sullivan went back inside, leaving the door open behind him.

"I wasn't peeping." Tobias brushed dirt off his well-fitting khakis—which Sullivan was pointedly not noticing—before following. "I was making sure you hadn't gone back to sleep."

"You weren't trying to catch me in my frilly nightie?"

Tobias's eyes narrowed. "No."

Despite himself, Sullivan laughed. "You sure? I think I look pretty good in it." Which was sort of flirtatious, and probably not helpful to the whole not-boning plan, but it was worth it for the way Tobias's cheeks went deeply red.

With stiff dignity, Tobias said, "What's the plan for today?"

Sullivan shrugged. "I haven't gotten that far yet."

"Well, get started." Tobias gave him an admonishing frown. "Every minute that we hesitate is a minute of progress we lose."

"This isn't charming," Sullivan pointed out. "This bossy micromanaging thing? It's not cute at all. Also, it's ten a.m. on a Sunday. You're lucky I'm forming complete sentences and not killing you. Why are you dressed up?"

"I was at Mass."

"Oh." Sullivan looked at him askance, then decided he didn't care. "Better you than me."

"Fine." Tobias sat at the table and folded his hands together like a well-behaved fourth grader. "I can wait, but out of curiosity, do you think you'll be much longer with whatever it is you're doing?"

Sullivan rolled his eyes and opened his laptop. "Christ. All right. You want to help? Let's see if you can track down a possible source at one of those trafficking sites. Someone based here in Denver who could talk to us about what the girls usually do after they get away."

"You want to know where Mama would've gone after she left."

"Yeah, I do."

"Because she has Nathalie with her."

Sullivan gave him a dirty look. "I'm going to take a shower. Don't peep."

Tobias's blush went all the way to his ears this time.

## Chapter Thirteen

Over the next eight hours, they migrated from the hard-backed dining room chairs to the living room. Sullivan sprawled on the sofa, his long arms and legs akimbo, laptop balanced on his thighs, and Tobias sat in the over-stuffed chair and tried not to watch him.

It took more effort than he liked.

He kept thinking of the day before. Sullivan looming over him, eyes blown dark, his mouth half-open, his grip verging on painful as he guided Tobias's mouth over his cock. He thought about them lying on the floor together, Tobias long past self-consciousness, his heart pounding like it could burst out of his chest, his face buried in Sullivan's throat, the taste of salt on his lips where he couldn't help nuzzling as Sullivan's hand took him apart. And he thought of Sullivan's voice somehow soft and firm at the same time as he said *take what you need, sweetheart.*

If Tobias had the nerve, he'd ask how Sullivan could act so normally after everything that'd happened yesterday. He seemed resigned to Tobias's presence finally—or at least there hadn't been a return to the obvious anger of the days before—but it'd been replaced by a conversational tone. Like he'd missed the way the whole world had turned on its side yesterday.

But then, for Sullivan it hadn't been a big deal. Sullivan hadn't needed to be held for half an hour on the couch afterward. He probably did this all the time. It was only Tobias who was affected, clearly.

"I've reached the limit of my skills on this." Sullivan dumped his laptop on the steamer trunk coffee table with a *thunk* and stretched his arms over his head, revealing a strip of firm belly where his T-shirt rode up.

Tobias quickly looked at his own notes. The search for a contact had not gone well. Part of it was that it was Sunday and people weren't at work, but part of it was that the folks most likely to have the kind of inside information they needed weren't going to be promoting themselves on a website. He'd sent some emails, but he wasn't holding his breath. The first task that Sullivan had given him, and he'd made zero progress.

"Okay." Tobias pushed his notebook away with nervous fingers. "And, um. What do we do until then?"

He glanced up and found Sullivan watching him, his eyes shadowed in the late-afternoon light creeping through the dirty windows. "That depends," Sullivan said slowly.

"On?" Tobias's stomach filled with butterflies.

The air seemed to thicken during the long pause that followed. Tobias's skin felt oversensitive and he knew exactly what he wanted to happen, but he wasn't sure how to ask for it. He thought of Sullivan's hand in his hair the day before, thought of Sullivan's cock in his mouth, and started to get hard. He was—

"Why are you looking for Ghost?"

Tobias jolted. "What? I mean, he's my friend, and he's in trouble, so…"

"I mean why are *you* looking for Ghost." Sullivan

didn't sound angry so much as curious, but his eyes were eagle-sharp on Tobias's face. "Why couldn't you pay me like everyone else does and go home and do your home-work like a normal college student whose best friend is a missing prostitute?"

"Ha-ha." Tobias chewed on his lip. "You'll think it's stupid."

"Maybe. But right now I'm thinking that you have something underhanded going on, so stupid is probably an improvement."

His stomach was tight now for a whole other reason. "I told you, I'm not in love with him, and I'm not some jeal-ous boyfriend. He doesn't owe me money or anything."

"Then what is it?"

God, this was hard to say. "You know how I said yes-terday that I have some abandonment issues? Ghost aban-dons people." Instantly he shook his head and clarified, "That's unfair. I mean that he takes off. It's not aban-donment. Still, there's only so much of it I can take." Hushed, like a confession, he added, "I don't think I can take much more. It's one thing if he ran because he's in trouble, but…"

"But it's something else if he took off because he doesn't give a shit."

Tobias dragged a hand over his mouth, suddenly tired. "Yeah. And this search…it's so many things at once. If he did drop me, I don't want to be someone who stays put where I get left, if that makes sense. I need to see for my-self. So I'll know if I should—should get over it or not."

"Why haven't you kicked him loose already? This is all…" Sullivan pursed his lips, searching for words, maybe. "It seems very effortful."

Tobias hesitated. "You remember I said I'd been in a residential treatment facility?"

"Yeah."

"I was… Everything in my life was sort of crushing me. Up until then, I'd had this idea that if I could just make it through high school, things would be different. *I'd* be different. And then one day my guidance counselor made me fill out this little card about what my eventual career field was going to be and I realized I was going to have to write medicine, and I couldn't. It was too much. It was the whole rest of my life smothering me and I didn't see a way out and I—I wasn't trying to kill myself."

Quietly, Sullivan asked, "But you hurt yourself?"

"Yeah." He paused, wondering why it was so easy to tell Sullivan what was so difficult to tell anyone else, and decided it had something to do with the nature of casual. He didn't need to impress Sullivan, didn't need to wonder about how it would affect things. He could say whatever he wanted. There was power in that. "The next day I was in Woodbury."

"Where Ghost comes in."

"Yeah." Tobias tilted his head back against the seat. "My parents picked it because it was classified as a behavioral treatment place as much as a mental health one. I guess they figured it would look better if we could say that I'd just gone to too many parties as a teenager instead of that I'd had a nervous breakdown and spent some time on depression meds. I knew within hours that I'd been stupid to let them put me in there. I don't know what I'd pictured, but the guys there were… I was in way over my head. I was…"

Not to put too fine a point on it, he'd been terrified.

"Out of your depth?" Sullivan asked.

"Completely. I didn't know how to talk to anyone, and most of them hated me before I ever opened my mouth. You can probably guess why."

"My youngest sister was fourteen before she got nice jeans that weren't hand-me-downs five years out of style. I remember her crying about it she was so happy. Yeah, I can guess why."

"I didn't look down on them, truly," Tobias said softly. "We weren't spoiled, growing up, or at least I didn't think so then. My parents are really careful about that. They don't want entitled kids. But there are degrees to having and not having, and spoiled or not, I still had more. Within a week of my first letter home, Mirlande had brought me a bunch of clothes she'd gotten from Goodwill, and I gave her my watch to take with her, but it was too late. You can change your clothes, but it's a lot harder to talk in a way that doesn't show how much private school you've had. They knew I had things they didn't, and it's hard not to hate someone who rubs it in your face, even if he doesn't mean to."

"They kicked the shit out of you, huh?" Sullivan asked.

"A few times. Gibson—this big, skinhead guy—he was the worst. A constant onslaught. If it wasn't punches, it was words, and looks, and threats, and I'm—" He gave Sullivan a small smile. "You might've noticed I'm not very good at fighting. I don't like hurting people."

"And Ghost? He felt sorry for you?"

"Ghost doesn't feel sorry for people. He's not built that way." Back then Ghost had been skinny and pale and delicate with a loveliness that hinted at innocence. Tobias might've believed that lie himself if his first glimpse of Ghost hadn't been one of the younger boy grinning, his gaze empty and feral, the blade in his hand sparking the reflected light from the caged fluorescents overhead. Ghost hadn't done much, just hovered in the doorway and told some rambling story about a kid who'd died in a car wreck—nonsense completely unrelated to the spectacle of Tobias lying on his belly in the center of the now-still ring of boys. The long string of words barely made sense, but they didn't need to, not when they were delivered while that blade played with the light and his voice got lower and throatier and more eager, his body coiling like he might spring at any moment. At some point Gibson had lifted his hands in a calming gesture and said soothingly, "Ghost, hey, hey, we wouldn't have if you'd just said, man. All you had to do. He's yours, fuck, have at him. Keep him off my dick, though, yeah?"

Ghost had fallen silent like a carnival automaton that'd run out of quarters, and the boys had filed uncertainly past him while he stood there staring. By the time Tobias had hauled himself up and cleaned the blood from his teeth and nose, Ghost had been sweet and smiling. He'd started talking about this dog he'd seen get trampled by a police horse, a story that sounded every bit as bogus as the earlier story about the car wreck, and Tobias had followed him around mutely for days listening to the patter, never really taking a deep breath, scared to leave Ghost's side, but also scared to stay.

Once you'd seen the facade break down, it was hard to forget what Ghost really was.

But Ghost hadn't hurt him. Had, in fact, been surprisingly gentle with him, always receptive to Tobias's words and thoughts when he finally began offering them, and one day Tobias had realized that instead of being a half-wild prostitute and the guy he'd saved, they might actually be friends.

The only reference Ghost ever made to that day in the bathroom had been when he got out of Woodbury months later. On his way out of the cottage, knapsack over one shoulder, he'd called back to Tobias, "Stay off Gibson's dick, won't you?"

"I'm honestly not sure why he helped me," Tobias said now. "Maybe he was curious. Or bored. Or setting up some elaborate plan that I played a role in but which he later abandoned. Who knows? I just…he stopped them and let me stay by him and then I loved him."

He almost choked on his tongue trying to backpedal on that one, because he meant it, but he didn't mean it like *that*. "As friends, I swear. And that makes it sound like it was less of a bond, but it wasn't. It was huge to me anyway. Maybe he's walked out on me, maybe not. But I have to know, and it's… I can't wait around and hope he'll notice I need him anymore. Does that make sense?"

"He's your best friend," Sullivan said, a weary sort of acceptance in his voice.

"Yeah." It was the only term for Ghost that Tobias could apply, even if it was too small and too large at the same time. "Did you really think I was a stalker ex-boyfriend?"

"Not sure. I trust my instincts, and they're all telling me you're a pretty run-of-the-mill college kid."

"Thanks," Tobias said, unsure if that was a compliment or not.

"I'm in a weird spot, though, since my instincts are telling me one thing, and the fact that you're blackmailing me to play junior private detective tells me something else."

"I'm sorry about that. I didn't know what else to do. I

needed... I *need* this. It's wrong of me, and selfish, and I know it doesn't change anything, but I am sorry."

Sullivan's gaze was heavy on his face, almost intimidating, but Tobias sort of liked it. He felt centered. The minute stretched, endless and dense, and then Sullivan was rising, perching on the arm of the overstuffed chair and burying a hand in Tobias's hair, just as he'd done yesterday, if not as tightly. That hand was directing Tobias closer, tugging him in so that he could bury his face against Sullivan's side. He smelled like laundry detergent and warm skin, and Tobias wanted to stay there forever.

"I'm sorry," Tobias said again.

"Okay."

They sat like that for a considerably long time, until Sullivan's hand paused in Tobias's hair and began to pull away. Tobias pressed closer and muttered, "I want you to."

"Want me to what?"

His face flamed hot. "To...whatever you want."

After a moment that lasted an eternity—during which Tobias died waiting—Sullivan asked, "You want more of what we did yesterday?"

"Yeah."

"I'm not sure—"

Remembering how Sullivan had been forced to take care of him on the couch afterward, Tobias hurriedly added, "You don't have to put a lot of effort in. We can keep it easy." He swallowed. "You can do whatever you want."

Again, Sullivan's hand went still. Another interminable hesitation. "All right. There are some things we need to talk about first, though. Do you like the idea of telling me to stop and having me keep going?"

Tobias blinked, taken aback. "Um, no? I mean, if I say no, I'm probably going to mean it?"

"Probably?"

"I've never needed to before, so I don't know."

"Let's have you pick a safe word then, hmm? Just in case."

"What kind of word?"

"Anything you want. We could go with green, yellow, and red. Like stoplights. That's pretty common. You say yellow and I know to slow down; you say red and everything stops. Or we can pick something else."

"No, that sounds good." If nothing else, he'd remember that in the heat of the moment.

"What kinds of play do you think you'd be interested in?"

Tobias pressed his face harder against Sullivan's side, wishing his cheeks would cool off. "I don't know."

Sullivan's hand worked gently through his hair. "Did you like being on your knees?"

Tobias nodded.

"What did you like about it?"

"I don't know. I felt—like I was doing something you'd like. That made it good."

"Okay. Did you like it when I fucked your face?"

Tobias swallowed as a wave of heat went through him, and nodded again.

"Like the idea of servicing me? Being used by me?"

He breathed, "Yes."

"What about when I called you sweetheart?"

Tobias shivered, and Sullivan laughed, low and pleased. "We'll consider that a keeper, then." He toyed with Tobias's shirt collar. "You're doing well. Beginners sometimes have trouble talking about what they like."

*Beginners.* Tobias wondered what that made Sullivan. "You've done this sort of thing before, haven't you?"

Sullivan's hand paused. "Yes."

"A lot?"

"Yes." There was a tiny hesitation. "Is that a problem?"

"No," Tobias replied honestly. "If anything, it's a relief, I guess. That you know what you're doing. It's... everything sounds okay so far."

"Okay." Sullivan's fingers started tracing through Tobias's hair again. "You're all right with ass play? Do you bottom?"

"Yeah." That came out breathier than Tobias had meant for it to, but at this point, he wasn't sure he cared.

"Mind some teasing?"

"No, that's actually—no."

"All right. Any questions before we start?"

"Um, no."

Sullivan stood up, tugging on Tobias's shirt to get him to rise too. "Take your clothes off for me, then."

Tobias's fingers shook as he pulled his shirt off, and it only got worse. He faltered when he got to his boxers, but Sullivan waited expectantly, so he pushed them down and stepped out.

Sullivan trailed a hand over Tobias's chest, lingering on the sensitive skin below his belly button. "Nice," he murmured. "Very nice."

"Oh. Um, thanks."

Sullivan smiled. "You sound nervous."

Tobias blew out a breath. "Yeah, I am."

"Good. Stay here."

Then Sullivan was gone. Tobias shifted his weight and a terrible sensation of discomfort welled up in him. He felt alone, which—of course he did, he *was* alone,

and that was a silly thing to be made uncomfortable by,
even as exposed as he was. Silly or not, though, it was
real, and getting stronger by the moment. Seconds went
by and turned into a full minute, and by the time Sullivan walked back into the room with a tube of lube and
a towel, Tobias was verging on jumping out of his skin.

"That wasn't good, huh?" Sullivan studied him. "Don't
like waiting?"

"It's the…" He gestured at his whole body, miserable that he'd somehow managed to mess this up already.

"Hey, no. That's good. I'm glad we figured it out. It's
a small thing, and now we know that you don't like being
left alone when you're feeling vulnerable. Won't happen
again." Sullivan pulled him in so that Tobias's face ended
up buried in his throat, and the feeling began to subside,
replaced by warmth and surprise that the mess had been
so easily cleaned up.

"Sometimes things hit us wrong or weird; it doesn't
have to make sense. That's okay." Sullivan's hand rubbed
firm and soothing along Tobias's spine. "For this to work,
we have to be able to share this stuff. It's good. You did
good."

Tobias nodded. Sullivan didn't seem to think anything
of it, so Tobias decided he wouldn't either.

"How are we doing now?" Sullivan asked. "Green?
Yellow? Want to put your clothes on and watch TV?"

Tobias laughed, and something about it made Sullivan's eyes crinkle like he was happy, which was nice.
He liked the idea of making Sullivan happy. "Green."

"Cool. Come on over here." Sullivan threw the towel
over one arm of the big, overstuffed chair. "Lie across
this on your belly. Feet on the floor, face on the cushion."

Tobias hesitated, a million thoughts rioting through

his brain. This felt different from yesterday, when he'd been caught up in the current. This was a choice.

He glanced at Sullivan, taking in anew the narrow, handsome face, the calm, dark eyes, the tattoo sleeves that disappeared under his T-shirt. He waited patiently, like he had countless hours to fill and this was one of a million unimportant ways to fill them. It might feel like a dive into deep water for Tobias, but Sullivan's body language said this was nothing special. Even if he agreed to do as he was told right now, there was no commitment to it. He could say *red* at any time, and Sullivan would back off.

He was pretty sure he believed that.

With his pulse thundering, he leaned forward over the arm of the chair until his face pressed against the seat. He didn't quite have to rise onto his toes, but his ass was up in the air, his most private parts on display. He was shaking; he was hard enough that the pressure of his dick against the wide, soft armrest felt amazing. He was tempted to rock against it for friction, but some instinct told him not to, and he was rewarded with an appreciative murmur from Sullivan, his hand sliding along Tobias's back and sides like he'd never touched anyone worthier.

"This okay?" Sullivan asked.

"Yeah."

"Good. Spread your legs for me."

"Jesus." Tobias whispered, and with heat curling in his stomach at the command—delivered so casually, as if it never occurred to Sullivan that he might be disobeyed—he did as he'd been told.

"Here's the deal." Sullivan sounded easy, like they might be talking about football or fishing. That was equal parts disorienting and reassuring. "You don't come until

I give you permission. It's okay to say that you need time to calm down, or if you need to say yellow or red—all fine. I'll never be unhappy with you for any of that. But don't come. Green?"

Tobias nodded, his cheek brushing the soft fuzz of the cushion.

"I want you to respond verbally when I ask for a color."

"Green," Tobias managed.

There was the sound of a lid opening and closing, and then Sullivan was sliding lube-wet fingers between Tobias's cheeks. The cold damp made him jump.

"You've done this before, yeah?" Sullivan explored that crease gently, taking his time. His hand left, then returned, wetter than before. "Anal, I mean?"

"Yes."

"Just been fucked? Or toys, too?"

"Just—just sex."

"Did you like it?"

Tobias was paying more attention to Sullivan's hand than his words; it wasn't until Sullivan dug his thumbnail into the sensitive skin of one cheek that he realized he'd let the conversation falter. He gasped, "Sorry, what?"

"Did you like it? Getting fucked?"

"Yes. No. I don't know."

Those fingers were clever and quick; one was inside him and gone again almost before he'd felt its presence.

"You don't know if you liked it?"

"I was—um..." Tobias bit his lip on a moan as Sullivan pushed inside him with two fingers this time, the lube plentiful, the sensation of intrusion more powerful than the friction.

"Try to relax. You were what?"

"I was always all locked up. In my head." Tobias

would've made a gesture toward his temple, but he was a bit occupied holding on to the cushion for dear life. "Thinking too much."

"Hmm." Sullivan prodded deeper with two fingers, thick and implacable, his thumb massaging the rim of Tobias's asshole, and Tobias made a harsh, embarrassing sound of greed. The nerves in his belly sparked something fierce. "Needed it slower?"

"No. No, I… I kept thinking there was something I should be doing, but I was never sure what."

"Maybe I can help you out with that." Sullivan's fingers searched inside him, as careful and delicate as an artist's or a pianist's, and a heartbeat later pleasure lit up in a golden, warm throb inside him. It traveled up his spine and through his limbs, leaving him shaking. "What are you supposed to be doing right now, Tobias?"

"Don't—not coming." Tobias swallowed hard, pressing his face into the cushion, and as Sullivan's fingers worked inside him again and again, the pleasure stabbing through him over and over, following that order seemed like a far harder task than it had a minute ago.

"That's right. Might be easier said than done, hmm? Look at you move. God, you're a needy little thing, aren't you?"

Tobias choked on air, flushed and too hot and humiliated in a way that felt so incredibly good. He wasn't sure if he was supposed to answer. Now that Sullivan had mentioned it, he was aware of the way his hips were rocking, of the way his whole body had gone taut, pressing back into Sullivan's touch. He tried to hold still, thinking perhaps Sullivan didn't like that he was…*needy*, but he couldn't seem to control it. And besides, Sullivan's voice was unsteady behind him as he added, "It's pretty. You look so sweet like this, Tobias. Eager for me. Aching for me. You'd like more, wouldn't you?"

"Yes," Tobias gritted out.

"Want my cock?"

Tobias couldn't even find words for that—he could only groan, his eyes squeezing tight, because he was close, he was so damn close, and he…he couldn't.

"Stop," he cried. "I—I'm gonna, I'm sorry, but—"

The fingers inside him went still instantly and the pleasure subsided in a slow, painful undertow.

"I'm sorry," Tobias muttered.

"Shh. No, Tobias, you were so good. You did exactly what I told you to do."

"I can do better." He was sure he could. The orgasm had retreated all the way. He could hold on for much longer now.

"This is exactly what I want. Take some breaths." Sullivan's left hand stroked up and down Tobias's spine, soothing as Tobias obeyed. "Ready?"

"Yes, I can do it."

"All right." Sullivan's fingers began to move inside him once more, and the pleasure grew in degrees, through small, almost indifferent brushes of fingertips at first, and then through more pointed, determined pressure, until Tobias was fighting not to grind his dick against the towel Sullivan had thrown across the arm of the chair.

The effects weren't only physical; deep inside, in a part of his mind he hadn't been actively aware of before, he could feel a sliding sensation. Like he was shifting or opening. Submerging—that was it. Like he was sinking into himself, into a new place in his own mind. It wasn't alien—he'd experienced it yesterday, when he'd been on his knees, far past thinking, little more than a creature of need and desperation. But that dip into thoughtlessness had been almost instantaneous, like Sullivan had shoved him into a pool and Tobias had gone over without so much as a caught breath. This was a slow immersion, Sullivan drawing him in slowly, temptingly. This was something he might be able to stop, if he wanted to.

He didn't want to.

The sensation built, Sullivan's hand sure and steady, demanding that Tobias's body give up its secrets, that Tobias give him everything. And the command in it, the surety, was impossible to resist. Tobias spread his legs and pushed back into it and gave.

"You're lovely like this," Sullivan murmured sometime later, when the last of the sunlight had vanished from the windows. "So desperate. So hungry."

Tobias didn't feel lovely. He felt wrecked—covered in sweat and lube, his whole body trembling, his mouth parched. He couldn't speak anymore, was long past thinking. All he knew was the impossible pleasure that ripped through his body until it almost reached a peak, and his own wild cries of "stop, don't, wait."

Sullivan had three fingers wedged into Tobias now, giving his prostate a brief break while he tormented his rim, the burn painful in a way that only got Tobias closer, in a way that made him yearn for something larger to fill him up. Sullivan added more lube regularly, never letting him get dry enough to tear, always careful.

Always maddening.

Again, Tobias cried out, and this time Sullivan pulled away completely. Tobias remained still, vibrating in place, the silence in his head huge and dark until Sullivan's voice came back: "I'm still here. I haven't left you. I'm just getting something. Be patient."

Dimly Tobias knew that Sullivan was being kind, but he was long past knowing why he thought so. He only knew that the words made him feel safe, and he didn't have to question the feeling.

A minute later Sullivan used one hand to guide Tobias into a standing position. He held a bottle of water up to Tobias's lips. "Drink," he said quietly. "Not too much at once."

Tobias sipped until Sullivan was satisfied. "How are we doing?" Sullivan asked. "How are your back and legs holding up?"

His mind was so starkly blank and open that it took a second for Tobias to *find* his legs and back, and several more seconds to assess their state of being. "Okay. Muscles are tight."

"No pain, though?"

Tobias shook his head.

"What about here?" Sullivan's hand dropped, his fingers prodding between Tobias's cheeks, sliding inside him without difficulty. "You seem all right. Wide open, actually. Soft and wet."

Tobias sucked in a breath. "I'm okay."

Sullivan kissed him once, small and tender, beneath the ear. Then with his other hand he pushed, slowly but irrevocably, until Tobias was once more bent over the arm of the chair. That hand stayed between his shoulder blades, just enough to let him know the weight, to let him know he couldn't move. Enough to center him and trap him and it was exactly what'd been missing. He sighed in gratitude.

"Good," Sullivan breathed, dark and pleased and strained, and shoved his fingers deep, hard enough that pleasure and pain swirled within Tobias and he lost track of the world all over again.

At some point, he became aware of more water, of Sullivan repeating his earlier questions. Tobias was sore and even copious amounts of lube couldn't kill the near-constant burn now, and his dick had leaked so much that the towel was dark and damp beneath him, and he could barely breathe for the pleasure that racked his body, and he jerked at the rough, impossible mixture of cruelty and appreciation in Sullivan's voice when he said, "You're trying so hard, aren't you, sweetheart?"

Tobias whispered, "Will you hold me down harder?"

Sullivan went still. "If you'll tell me why."

He didn't know how to say that he was on the verge of disobeying—all he could think about was coming. He knew he'd said he wouldn't come without permission, but he also knew he couldn't hold off anymore. His brain was too much of a mess to manage those words in the right order. So he went with, "Need to be good."

Sullivan made a small, punched-out noise, and his fingers inside Tobias were suddenly twisting in a determined, straightforward way that killed any chance of resistance.

"No, that's not—" Tobias started to lurch upward, half-panicked, because it was way too fast, he'd never hold out, not like this, and Sullivan forced him back down, both of them letting out harsh sounds in the process, and none of that was helpful in the not-coming thing, and Tobias cried out as Sullivan drove him straight to the cliff—

"Come, Tobias. Come *now*."

—and over, directly over the edge.

The orgasm bowed his back, flowing through him like jolts of electricity, and it fucking hurt, it hurt so good, and it went on for *ages*, for whole centuries, horrible and impossible and so overwhelming that when it was over Tobias's legs were useless. He lay slumped over the arm of the chair, shuddering, only faintly aware of Sullivan shoving his jeans down and sliding his dick through the mess of lube between his cheeks. His cock caught on Tobias's oversensitive rim several times, and it was downright painful, and each time Tobias jerked and each time it made Sullivan's breathing grow faster, and it wasn't long at all before Sullivan was coming across the small of Tobias's back and shuddering against him.

Sullivan had expected it to be a fluke.

He'd gotten caught up in the moment yesterday, that was all. Speed and impulse and high emotion—it would be hard for anyone to resist desire when it sprang at you from out of nowhere like that.

A staged scene would be different, he'd told himself. There was always an element of performance to it, and sometimes it was hard to get past the awkwardness of that. More than that, now Tobias had an idea of what was happening; self-awareness could impact a sub's ability to get lost in play.

After the conversation he'd had with Lisbeth and Caty, Sullivan had planned to let this thing between him and Tobias die a quiet death. Too much potential risk, too much drama, he had too much pride to sleep with someone who was manipulating him, blah, blah, blah.

One quiet confession of vulnerability and a heartfelt apology later, Sullivan's pride and maturity had taken a hard-left turn. When Tobias had haltingly said that Sullivan could do whatever he wanted with him—and don't think that hadn't gotten him hard, fuck—Sullivan had gone along with it like a teacher who gave a pop quiz on the last day of school before summer vacation—partially because he got off on being a bastard, partially because he had to fill time somehow. He'd told himself that if it worked out, they'd both get off; if it was shit, well, once the case was over, they'd never see each other again.

Oh, how the arrogant fell. *If it worked out, they'd both get off*—what the fuck kind of dumbassery was that? He'd thumbed his nose at the gods of kink, and now in punishment, he had a sub—a true, natural sub, not a partner doing him a favor or a date trying it out for fun, but someone who'd likely be unable to live without kink now that he knew what he'd been missing—sprawled helplessly in front of him, and this wholehearted abandon in the face of Sullivan's perversion was no fluke. This, *this* was magic.

It had only been a week. As of tomorrow, they'd have known each other for exactly seven days.

It felt like Tobias had left a deeper mark than that amount of time should allow.

When Sullivan had caught his breath, he pushed himself upright and tried to get his head in gear. Tobias was limp beneath him, covered in come and lube and sweat, and by all rights he should be about as unattractive as it was possible for a man to be, but he was so *gone* on the experience that he could only be described as beautiful.

Jesus, Tobias was beautiful.

And he'd taken it so well. There'd been nothing but obedience, nothing but the struggle to serve. Sullivan had pushed him hard, especially for someone so inexperienced, and Tobias had never quailed. He'd asked Sullivan to hold him down because he was that determined to be good.

Sullivan would be lying if he said that wasn't one of the hottest things he'd ever experienced.

"You did so well," Sullivan said, making Tobias's lips curve upward at the corners. "You were so good for me."

It took some elbow grease, but eventually he got Tobias up on his feet, where he wobbled, dazed and big-eyed. He followed Sullivan upstairs and into the shower, where Sullivan shampooed his hair and scrubbed his skin clean. He shuddered when Sullivan washed between his legs, front and back, his cheeks going pink, but he made no move to do it himself or complain. When Sullivan pulled him close and whispered, "That's right, sweetheart, let me take care of you," Tobias tipped his head down against Sullivan's throat and clung with both hands and sighed.

It was late. The bedside clock said after eleven. Sullivan hadn't expected Tobias to last as long as he had; a handful of rounds of edging, he'd thought, but because he didn't know Tobias's limits well, he'd intended to take it easy. He'd meant to leave plenty of time for aftercare before he dropped Tobias off at the motel.

Instead, he'd wandered off the map and was stuck with a sub who was still altered. Tobias was fucking adorable in this headspace, following him around like a baby duck, head tipping to rest against Sullivan's arm as Sullivan stood there thinking, and Sullivan might be a bit of a bastard when it came to tormenting his subs with pleasure, but he sure as fuck wasn't going to leave an altered sub alone in some dingy motel to deal with the likely endorphin drop on his own. And considering how hard they'd gone and how new to this Tobias was, drop was pretty fucking likely.

Sullivan sighed and got them tucked up together under

the covers, naked and sleepy, Tobias's face hot against his arm, before looking over the nearest stack of books by the bed. "All right, what've we got? *The Things They Carried*? Hard no on that, I think. Want to learn how to build industrial fans?"

Tobias didn't say anything, but a slight wrinkle of his nose told the tale there.

"Yeah, me neither. How about *The Lion, The Witch, and The Wardrobe*? Yeah?"

Tobias nodded and for the next hour, Sullivan read aloud about fauns and Turkish Delight, and rubbed his palm against the nape of Tobias's neck until he drifted off.

Sullivan looked up at his ceiling, and if there'd ever been a white flat surface capable of judging a human being, he'd found it.

"I think I might be fucked," he told it, and turned out the light. He fell asleep with Tobias's soft breaths in his ear and the reliable thud of his heartbeat under his palm.

## Chapter Fourteen

Tobias woke up with that itch beneath his skin again.

It wasn't that he didn't feel good. He felt great, actually. His body was loose and warm and he'd gotten his first deep, complete sleep in what might have been months. Since before the letter came, certainly. The room was downright cold while he was cozy under the covers with—with someone else's arm wrapped around his belly.

The night before came back to him. He'd slept with Sullivan again. Jesus, he'd done more than that. He'd let Sullivan turn him into a wordless animal. Sullivan had torn him into little pieces, wrung him out, and then put him back together so completely that the only thing Tobias could say about the whole experience was *thank you* and *again*.

That was the problem, actually. That little *again*. That itch beneath his skin was all about the *again*.

His ass was sort of sore, though. He shifted gingerly and, yeah, that was going to be distracting.

Sullivan hummed sleepily behind him, a long line of bone and muscle against his back, and Tobias went still. He was wonderfully comfortable and he didn't want to face the morning-after yet. He'd never before woken up with someone he wasn't in a relationship with, and he'd assumed that casual meant there wouldn't be any sleeping over. He had no idea about the protocol for this sort of thing.

Sullivan hummed again and shifted closer, his arm curving up so that his hand rubbed against the light chest hair over Tobias's sternum. His lips came to rest against the nape of Tobias's neck, and this was—this was definitely not casual, because this was cuddling.

He really liked it. He liked Sullivan against him, the lazy, happy sound Sullivan made as he nosed at Tobias's neck, and the—oh.

Sullivan's morning wood was pressing against Tobias's backside.

Not cuddling. Sex.

Which—okay. It was fine. And as Sullivan's hand trailed lower on his torso to play with the hair right above Tobias's dick, he could acknowledge that his own morning wood wasn't opposed to the idea. He certainly wasn't going to complain.

He pressed backward and had the pleasure of hearing Sullivan's breath catch.

"Hey. You good?" Sullivan murmured, the rumble of his voice broken with sleep, and Tobias melted at the sound of it, so intimate and rough.

"Hi. I mean, yeah." Tobias took a deep breath and started to turn over, but Sullivan's hand closed on his hip.

"Stay like that." As soon as Tobias complied, Sullivan's touch gentled. He stroked Tobias's side and belly for a while. "How's your puzzler?"

"My what?"

"Your head. Freaking out? Anxiety? Pleased as punch?"

"Green," Tobias whispered.

"Anything you'd take back if you could? Anything that didn't work for you?"

Tobias shook his head, perhaps with too much emphasis, because Sullivan laughed. "All right. Up for another round?"

Tobias hesitated. On the one hand, yes, he was up for anything and everything, and the more Sullivan touched him, the more his libido was waking up and insisting that going along with any of Sullivan's ideas was an excellent plan for the day. On the other hand, the more he shifted around, the clearer his soreness became, and the idea of something going inside him right now was intimidating.

"Say it." Sullivan didn't sound mad, only curious. "I always want you to tell me things like this."

"I want to do it again, but I'm kind of sore."

"Your ass? Or other places too?"

His back ached a tiny bit from holding that position over the chair arm for so long, but that was more the kind of ache that would go away with activity. "Just there."

"That's workable." Sullivan's lips landed on his nape again, kissing hot and damp across the skin, and Tobias shivered. This went on for long, lovely seconds while Tobias's bones turned into molten lava and his spine bowed, helplessly begging for more.

"God, you're sweet. Don't move." Sullivan shifted away, throwing the covers down around their lower legs and letting cool air into the bed between them, but he was back a second later, the sound of the lube cap snapping open and then closed, and Tobias was about to protest, to say *but I said I was sore*, when he thought *Sullivan knows*.

And maybe it was backward, but that thought hit him in the belly like a Molotov cocktail. If Sullivan knew Tobias was sore, that meant Sullivan didn't care. Or, more

likely he cared, but he'd decided that the pain was imma-
terial. That Tobias was here to serve him and this minor
soreness wouldn't be allowed to get in the way of that.
And Tobias shuddered at the idea of his body being so
intensely meant for Sullivan's pleasure that even being
sore wouldn't stop them. He abruptly wished he was in
more pain, because then it would take more out of him,
it would cost more, and he would feel every agonizing
movement, and each second could be a gift that he would
give to his—

He didn't have a word for the end of that sentence.

He didn't have time to consider how he felt about that
glaring absence, either, because he was jumping, startled.
Sullivan was smearing wet lube not between his cheeks,
like Tobias had expected, but lower, between his thighs.

Tobias tried to muffle his disappointment, but it came
out anyway, in the shape of a small unhappy noise.

"Uh-oh," Sullivan said, still working his fingers there
slickly. "What's up? Talk to me."

"I—it's nothing."

Sullivan's hand stopped. "Tobias, the way this works
is that you do as you're told. Which means that I get an
answer when I ask a question. You have a bit of a history of not saying things because you don't want to upset
people, yeah?"

Tobias had to admit that Sullivan had made the correct
inference, embarrassing as it was. "Yes, I do."

"Not with me, okay? I try to pick up on cues, but I'm
not a mind reader. I have to be able to trust what you tell
me. That's—that's *sacred* to this game we're playing,
okay? I might not always give you what you're asking
for, depending on what it is, but I have to know. You can
tell me what you feel."

Suddenly Tobias was stupidly, humiliatingly on the verge of tears.

"I want that," Sullivan continued, twisting the knife, opening Tobias up in a place that had nothing to do with sex. "Really. Tell me stuff. I'll never punish you for being honest with me. Okay?"

Tobias stared straight ahead at the wall, afraid of what his voice might do if he opened his mouth.

"Hey." Sullivan propped himself up on one elbow and nudged Tobias to lie a bit more on his back so they could see each other's faces. He lifted his hand, then scowled at it for being wet with lube, before making a noise of mild frustration and pressing his lips to Tobias's cheek. That was how Tobias realized a few tears had slipped loose after all. Sullivan couldn't brush them away, so he was kissing them away, and Tobias snuggled backward, closer. Sullivan wrapped his arm around him again, careful to keep his lubed fingers off the sheets, and it was awkward and a little funny and Tobias liked all of it so very much.

"I want you inside me," he confessed. It was still hard to say, but oh, it was so lovely to have Sullivan nodding like it made perfect sense. "While I—while I hurt, I want to, um, give that, I think."

Sullivan was quiet for a long moment. "That's...if you just want to give, we can do it without pain. Or is the pain part of it?"

The pain made it more, Tobias thought, but he wasn't entirely sure that made sense, so he said, "It's part of it."

"Gotcha." Sullivan sounded fine, but something in his expression went slightly rigid. "I can work with that. No problem."

"Are you—" Tobias started, uneasy, but Sullivan

pressed another small kiss to his throat, making a soothing humming noise, and the moment when Tobias might've pushed it slipped away.

Sullivan eased Tobias back onto his side, and his hand slid between his cheeks so that his wet fingers brushed against the raw skin there. Tobias arched, pain and pleasure rocketing up his spine, and the combination of the two meant he was very tight when Sullivan's fingers pressed inside, two at once.

"Oh," Tobias whispered. Those fingers worked inside him, too much, and he couldn't breathe. He was so hard. His dick jerked with every thrust of Sullivan's fingers and that was without any contact against his prostate.

"Stay still," Sullivan murmured. "Give me this, Tobias. I want you to feel this for me. Can you do that?"

Tobias nodded frantically.

"That's it. Give it up for me." Those fingers were moving faster now, demanding and gentle and rough all at once. Tobias squeezed his eyes closed tight and listened to Sullivan's morning-hoarse words as they crawled inside him. "There you go. I want more, Tobias. Can you give me more?"

Tobias's back arched without his permission, his ass shoving back, desperate for it. He was already close, already so close, and he wasn't sure if he was allowed to come, if that rule had just been a rule for last night or if it was an all-the-time thing, but it never occurred to him to come now and apologize later. He'd hold on. If there was a chance that this was what Sullivan wanted, he would hold on. He would've asked, but his jaw was locked tight against coming, especially now that Sullivan had apparently decided that it was time to get Tobias's prostate in on the act and was jabbing at him there, quick, hard little pulses that hurt so good.

He could hear himself distantly, making soft, keening noises interspersed with harsh grunts when Sullivan laid into him particularly hard, and he was on fire, everything hurt, and it was so… God, he couldn't hold on. He had to, he wanted to, but he couldn't, but he *had* to.

He wanted Sullivan inside him so badly. More than fingers. He shifted his leg up, begging with everything he had in him, and behind him Sullivan sucked in a breath.

"Fuck," Sullivan muttered, and he bent down, his mouth finding Tobias's shoulder, his teeth sinking in, the pain almost blinding, Sullivan's breath fast and hard against the damp, sensitive skin.

Tobias's hips couldn't hold still—he was pulling away from the force of those thrusting fingers, and pushing back into it, and wanting more, always more, he wanted Sullivan's cock deep inside him, stretching him wider, making the burn brighter. He wanted Sullivan to feel just as good, wanted Sullivan to have everything Tobias was, everything he could give, and if his body could deliver on any part of that, he wanted it.

Sullivan's fingers pulled out, and for a heartbeat, a lovely, perfect heartbeat, the head of his cock was there, pressing against Tobias's rim, far larger and hotter, and even that small contact was far too much, but he pushed back anyway. He made a sound that could only be termed a whine, and maybe he'd be embarrassed about that later, but for right now, he just fucking *wanted*.

Then Sullivan was growling, "Goddamn it," and pulling away. There was a flurry of movement behind him, the shocking, cold sensation of more lube, the tearing sound of a condom wrapper being opened.

"I want to fuck you," Sullivan bit out. "It's going to hurt. Color."

"Green," Tobias moaned, "God, please, do it."

And then Sullivan was finally, *finally* sliding his cock inside him. He sank in completely with that one thrust, an unspoken demand that Tobias's body yield everything. Even loose and relaxed, Tobias still found it too much, and he cried out in wordless protest instinctively, scrambling away from the intensity of the sensations.

He was hugely, deeply satisfied when Sullivan didn't hesitate for a second, using leverage and his weight to keep Tobias where he wanted him, already withdrawing and shoving back in, angling for Tobias's prostate, and Tobias cried out again. It did hurt, badly enough that he couldn't lie still, couldn't stay quiet, but it was also immensely good, contributing to the pleasure, the fullness and weight of Sullivan inside him far more important than the burn. He was on fire, the pain sharp and acute and raw, the pleasure dagger-edged and welling up, impossible to resist, and he couldn't come, he couldn't, not until he knew—

His jaw unlocked. "Please, Sullivan, can I? Please. God, I have—"

"You—Jesus." Sullivan sounded startled, and vaguely unhappy for a split second. But the unhappiness was gone when he continued with, "Yes, sweetheart. Go ahead."

With a low, throaty cry, Tobias did, only dimly aware of Sullivan making a deep, punched-out noise and following. He slumped on top of Tobias like a lead weight.

"Jesus," Sullivan whispered. "Jesus. You're—*Jesus*."

"No, I'm Tobias," he said into the pillow. His voice was lazy and thick like he'd been drugged or something, and it was a horrible joke, but Sullivan laughed anyway, because Sullivan was nice. He was soooo nice. He had nice hair and nice arms and Tobias liked the stark black tattoos and the muscles there, and he liked the way Sullivan's body smelled, especially now, first thing in the morning when he was warm and a little sweaty and recently asleep. Tobias had made a stupid joke and Sullivan had laughed, and this was all so nice that he giggled.

"You're nice," he said.

"You're completely high on endorphins, aren't you?" Sullivan asked.

"I don't know," Tobias said, still giggling. Sullivan pulled out of him and slumped to one side, smiling dozily, all those long muscles lean and graceful. God, he was hot.

"Yeah, hold on to that as long as you can."

"I'm gonna be so sore." Somehow that was really funny, and Tobias started laughing in earnest. Sullivan was laughing too, like he thought Tobias was being silly, and maybe he was, but he felt so good that laughter was the only thing possible.

Sullivan was fucked. He was so fucked.

Because Tobias was sweet and eager and he'd instinctively wanted permission to come even though Sullivan hadn't asked—it hadn't occurred to him that Tobias might think Sullivan expected it this morning, which was pretty shitty Dom behavior—and there'd been zero self-consciousness in the asking. It was outrageously hot.

And worst of all, Tobias had laughed afterward.

He hadn't shown any sign of feeling tormented or scared or guilty. He wasn't second-guessing the kind of sex they'd shared. In fact, as Sullivan cleaned Tobias up and smoothed a cooling gel gently over the raw skin between his cheeks, Tobias was nuzzling into the sheets like a damn puppy, warm and happy and spent, halfway back to sleep, and Sullivan wanted to slide down beside him and settle in for a nap.

Instead, he tucked Tobias in, rubbed his head until he was asleep—which took thirty seconds tops—and went into the bathroom for a shower.

He had to get a grip. This was a mess, and he had to figure out what the hell was going on so he could institute some kind of control over the situation. Logic. That was what he needed.

Okay, so he was clearly ready for sex with other adult humans at this point. Fine. Sex was good and healthy. He should have more of it. No reason it had to be Tobias, right?

But as he forced himself to consider finding another sub, his stomach flipped over in distaste. The idea of getting formally back into the scene didn't appeal at all. Some people in kink got off on the feeling of the dark and taboo; Sullivan wasn't one of them. No, what Sullivan wanted was sex and kink with someone that felt *good*. Nothing dark or twisted, no leather or emo music or filthy porn or leather clubs or munches run like city hall meetings. No choosing a partner based on how many similar boxes they'd ticked on a kink checklist. Just this—a playful, naturally occurring connection to another person that made Sullivan feel like a decent, normal human being who could be wanted and trusted.

Maybe it made him stupid that he was having fun with a guy who'd threatened his job and his future, but he was. It reminded him of what he'd had with Nick before the whole thing fell apart. Friendship. As important, if not more important, than the infatuated rush of love and passion that'd eventually overtaken it. Their friendship hadn't survived Sullivan's sexual preferences, but with Tobias, the two elements seemed almost to amplify each other. Maybe they weren't exactly friends, but it was in there. It wasn't casual and it wasn't just sex, because if it was either of those things, picking someone else wouldn't be such a problem.

Shit. He liked Tobias. He *really* liked Tobias.

*Don't think like that*, he told himself as he dried off with sharp, punishing flicks of his towel. He had to remember that Tobias was experimenting and he wanted casual sex and his life was in a period of upheaval and this case was *temporary* and Sullivan needed a goddamn hormone condom.

By the time Tobias came downstairs into the kitchen, his brown curls still damp against his temples from his shower, Sullivan had managed some semblance of emotional maturity.

"Hey," Tobias said. His shoulders were tense, his hands in the pockets of his jeans. "Um. Sorry."

Sullivan looked at him blankly. "For what?"

"I fell back asleep?"

"Oh. Nah, forget it." Sullivan finished stirring the bowl of pancake batter he was working on. "Was gonna wake you up in a minute anyway to eat. Sit down."

Tobias's body jerked in the direction of the table before he hesitated, and Sullivan realized they hadn't had that particular talk yet.

"You're not my slave." Sullivan wiped up a spill with a paper towel. "When we're fucking, that's one thing, but what we do in the bedroom doesn't have to match what we do outside of it. The rest of the time, I'd really prefer that you tell me to fuck off if you don't want to do what I say. Does that work for you?"

Tobias nodded, and went to the table. "How do you navigate all this? It seems so much more complicated than other sorts of relationships. Even casual ones."

"We're navigating it right now." Sullivan poured batter onto the griddle and forced himself to hear *casual* with more emphasis than any of the other words. "Just like anything else that people do, it's a series of small decisions, you know? People in the kink community learn to be more explicit about it, that's all. We talk shit to death. It's exhausting sometimes, but it's nice to know where you stand and get what you need."

As they ate, Sullivan checked his email, where he found a reply from his contact at the DMV. He'd submitted all three plate numbers—anticipating that two of them would be wrong because of the mud that'd partially obstructed their view—and the results were gratifyingly helpful. One was unassigned, one belonged to a hearse in Pueblo, and the other belonged to a beige sedan registered to Cindy Jackman, the owner of a home on Josephine Street in Denver.

Sullivan passed the news along to Tobias.

"The guy picked up Ghost in his wife's car?" Tobias asked, nose wrinkling in a way that Sullivan firmly told himself was not adorable.

"Could be a sister or a friend." Sullivan jerked a shoulder. "I'll check her out, see if I can learn anything about the balding guy, and then I'll track him down. I'll give you a progress report—"

Tobias sighed, long-suffering, and Sullivan almost smiled before reminding himself that he needed a *hormone condom*.

"Let me guess." Sullivan raised an eyebrow. "You're coming with me."

"Yes."

"And school?"

Tobias blinked, once, twice, three times.

"Forgot about that little detail, huh?" Sullivan finished his pancakes while Tobias stared at his plate, apparently doing some sort of mental gymnastics, judging from the way his mouth had pursed and his brow had furrowed. Finally, Sullivan prompted, "Well? What's the verdict?"

"I'm not going to class."

"Okay. We'll get through this stuff today, and you'll have plenty of time for homework later. I don't know, maybe they'll give you a makeup or something—"

"No, I mean I'm not going back. Ever."

Sullivan took another bite of pancake. "Cool."

Tobias slowly lifted his gaze, and his eyes were wide, almost stunned, and his cheeks were flushed. His fingers clamped around his fork. "I'm never going back."

Sullivan chewed, watching him, and Tobias's chin lifted mutinously, as if he thought Sullivan might try to make him go, which was stupid, because Sullivan generally thought that doing things you hated was a bad idea in principle, let alone in practice. When it became clear that Tobias was waiting for an answer, Sullivan swallowed and said, "Congratulations. You're a wild man."

"I'm not, really," Tobias said, more to himself than Sullivan, perhaps. "I don't do impractical things."

"Sure," Sullivan said, although he thought that was mostly bullshit, considering the things Tobias had been doing the past few days, and that was only the things Sullivan knew about.

"I think I could, though," Tobias continued, still probably to himself.

"Cool. Can I have your textbooks?"

Tobias glanced at him. "You're not going to argue with me?"

"I'm not your mom. Do whatever the fuck you want."

"You're bossy enough," Tobias muttered and Sullivan grinned. "But you don't think it's bad? Dropping out?"

"I'd be an asshole if I did. You're looking at one and a half semesters of college right here, baby."

"Oh." Tobias's face made a cramped, half-smothered expression, and Sullivan's grin widened.

"You're judging me, aren't you?"

"No," Tobias said quickly.

"Yes, you are. You think I'm one of those guys who partied my way out of school."

"No, I don't," Tobias said, earnest enough that Sullivan believed him. "I just think it's odd because you're clearly well-read and interested in learning. College seems like a natural choice for you."

"I thought so too, which is why I tried it. But college wanted me to pick one thing to learn about and then take a bunch of tests, and I'm more of an eclectic, non-test-taking sort. So. We broke up. And if you consider the hell I put my professors through with all my off-topic questions, it was probably mutual."

"Oh. I thought maybe it was a money thing."

"Well, my parents weren't going to manage six college funds on their salaries, so it didn't help. I don't know. Might've given it a better try if I hadn't been fighting so hard to pay for things, but it seemed stupid to put that much cash and effort into getting something I wasn't sure I wanted."

Tobias chewed on his lip, a slight pinch to his features. Sullivan said, "Not much point in you feeling guilty for having access to an education I turned down, you know."

"I'm paying for most of it on my own," Tobias said. "My parents matched me my first couple of years so I wouldn't drain my savings, but yeah, I know how expensive it is. Everyone should have access to education. Everyone."

"Says the newly dropped out."

Tobias's lips quirked into a small, dawning smile. "It's a sign of how out of my head I am that I like the sound of that. I think education's important, but…"

Sullivan studied him thoughtfully as Tobias considered his words. He wasn't sure how he felt about Tobias's description of himself: *out of my head.* Tobias could be in sub-drop. Endorphins and adrenaline were magical things—they got people through marathons and rescuing babies from tigers and…well, nothing else was springing to mind, but the point was that sex in the scene could produce a lot of the same chemical changes in the blood and brain that dangerous or physically taxing activities could, and eventually, when those chemicals were filtered out, a person's emotional state could drop into the toilet until things settled. Aftercare was crucial post-scene to help with that, because in addition to feeling shitty, occasionally drop ended with people doing wacky things.

Sullivan could've kicked himself. He should've stayed in bed and cuddled, been there to reassure Tobias that everything was fine. Or maybe not, since cuddling wasn't casual and he needed a hormone condom, but at the very least he could've gotten the guy a glass of water and told him that he'd done everything right.

Maybe this wasn't about school at all. Maybe this was a sign of bad treatment from—

"I hate medicine," Tobias blurted, jolting Sullivan out of his thoughts. "I've hated it for years."

"Sounds like you're making a good choice, then." Sullivan let out a slow breath. Not chemical.

"I've never admitted it. It's been getting worse. It's worse than it was in high school, and I thought that was the low point, and I never said anything."

Sullivan tilted his head, considering the speech Tobias had given him yesterday about how much he hated being left behind while other people made the decisions. "You're naturally sort of repressed, huh?"

Tobias's brows settled low over his eyes. Sullivan was on the verge of apologizing—it *had* been rude—when Tobias said, with fresh, untried iron in his voice, "Not anymore."

Sullivan was starting to realize that Tobias was a far more complicated guy than he appeared to be. The blackmail and breaking and entering said *asshole*, but none of it—including the running away from home and the kinky sex—fit the image that Tobias painted of himself in the moments when he talked about his past. In those moments he was a guy who had to work up the nerve to express anger at his parents and spent most of his time swallowing his feelings and followed an academic path he hated for…for some reason that wasn't clear. But the point was that instead of the asshole Sullivan had thought he was dealing with, Tobias was looking more and more like a decent guy in the middle of some crisis of character. In fact, Sullivan was starting to suspect that he was part of some elemental rebellion that existed outside the bounds of Tobias's natural personality.

Further proof that this whole thing between them was temporary.

Tobias would revert. People always did.

## Chapter Fifteen

Tobias's pancakes were cold, but he didn't care. He could've been eating paper and he wouldn't have minded.

He wasn't going back.

Sullivan kept staring at him with mild interest, like he was expecting fireworks to explode out of Tobias's head or something. It wasn't a bad read of Tobias's emotional state; a kernel of revolt burned red-hot in his chest. He wanted a ridiculous number of ridiculous things suddenly—to go on a bender at a grimy bar; to pick a fight in a parking lot against a trucker twice his size; to drive in a random direction for hours with the radio as loud as it could get, not stopping until he hit something golden and strange. He could do any of those things or none of them; the only restraint, he realized, was *him*. His own limits of *have to* and *don't be selfish*.

It was a small change, objectively. Lots of people dropped out of school. But when Sullivan had mentioned class and that old sense of dread had risen again, it had occurred to him that he could just…not…go. He was twenty-four, not twelve. He wasn't going to get in trouble. He didn't have to go, he didn't want to go, and so he wouldn't. And with that choice, he'd forged some new, blazing ground inside himself. Maybe he *was* exploding. It certainly felt like the old Tobias had been permanently destroyed.

He had to clench his fingers around his silverware again to avoid chucking them gleefully through the air. He could only imagine how Sullivan might look at him then, but that wasn't why he held himself in check. The truth was, if he let any of this feeling out into the world, he wasn't sure he'd be able to regain control, and thrilling as it might be, the size of it frightened him too.

Who knew what he might destroy before that wildness was sated?

An hour with the laptop proved that Cindy Jackman had never been married and had no siblings, so the guy who'd used her car to pick up Ghost must've been either a friend, a boyfriend, or a car thief who'd politely returned the vehicle when he was done with it. Which apparently meant a stakeout.

They found her exactly where her social media page had suggested she would be—at her job as a receptionist at a small nonprofit serving veterans with PTSD. They pulled into a parking lot that served several businesses in the strip mall and parked far enough away that they wouldn't attract attention, but close enough that they could see both the beige sedan and the door to the nonprofit.

"It's nice out," Tobias said from the passenger seat of the Buick, grateful he'd taken Sullivan's advice and stopped off at the motel for shorts and a white T-shirt. Jeans would mean heat stroke by this afternoon. "For the moment, anyway. You won't be alone and bored with me here. I don't know why you're so down on this."

"You are painfully young and innocent," Sullivan retorted.

"You're what, three years older than me? Four?"

Sullivan shook his head grimly, still staring out the window, and Tobias ignored it. He wasn't going to let Sullivan's pessimism ruin this—instead of being in his biochemistry class, he was on a stakeout. An actual, real-life stakeout with an actual, real-life private detective. Sullivan had said that stakeouts were miserable, horrible, awful, terrible, no-good things, but so far Tobias was having a lot of fun. And if he wasn't so damn sore that he kept needing to shift his weight from one butt cheek to the other, it would be perfect.

Actually, it was kind of perfect anyway.

Sullivan eyed him sideways for a few seconds, his lips turning up at the sight of Tobias fidgeting. "You know, I almost put a butt plug in you before we left," he said conversationally, like that was a thing people said all the time.

"What?" Tobias managed, his heart thumping double time.

"I like the idea of you sitting there with a plug stretching you open, right where you're most sore. Making it worse. Every time you shifted or moved, you'd get a little burst of pleasure and a little bit of pain. You'd be fidgeting even more than you are now. You'd be miserable."

Sullivan sounded almost dreamy at the prospect, and Tobias shifted again, his cheeks going bright red. He could imagine it all too easily, and he was already getting hard in his shorts.

"Why didn't you?"

Sullivan's small smile grew. "God forbid we have to run anywhere."

Tobias laughed. "This isn't what I would've expected. From kinky sex, I mean. It's more fun than I would've thought. Or maybe it's only that you're good at it."

Sullivan didn't say anything for a long minute. Then, "Thanks, but that's kind of a rookie analysis. I've made a few mistakes that a more experienced sub would probably call me out on. Or should call me out on, anyway."

"Like what? It all seemed good to me."

Sullivan shrugged. "Little things. Should've stayed in bed with you this morning. I've been too light on the aftercare, I think. Want to ramp that up next time. It's tricky, because it's sort of a balance between what's good for you and what's too...well, that's neither here nor there. But I've been moving too fast, now that I think about it. You're still new at this, and I've already asked a lot from you."

"I'm fine." Tobias cleared his throat, wondering what, exactly, was neither here nor there. "I've enjoyed it."

"I know. But that's sort of in spite of things, not a sign that I did everything right. I'm out of practice." He glanced at Tobias. "I'll be more careful with you. I promise."

Tobias's heart thumped hard. Sullivan's gaze was direct and warm and honest, and Tobias could only fumble out a nod. "Thanks."

Sullivan went back to staring out the window at the nonprofit's front door. "Shit, I'm thirsty. Bust open that cooler, yeah?"

Firmly warning his pulse to slow down, Tobias reached into the back seat and grabbed the cooler Sullivan had packed that morning. "Why are you out of practice?"

Sullivan selected a cold bottle of water. He took a

drink and fiddled with the cap, his expression going tense. "You know, can we not?"

"Oh. Sorry. That's none of my—"

"No, it's fine that you asked. Really. I'd just— It's sort of heavy, and I don't want to deal with it right now. Maybe some other time."

"Sure. You don't have to tell me, if you don't want to."

"I know. We'll see."

Tobias nodded and took a sandwich from the cooler, disappointed but unwilling to push. He wasn't sure what to say next, though. Any number of other topics might also be too private for this casual thing they were doing. None of Sullivan's history was his business.

Finally he said, "It's crazy hot."

Sullivan tipped his head back against the rest. He looked vaguely displeased, but only said, "Yeah."

At five-thirty, Cindy Jackman finished her shift, calling good-bye to coworkers. She was a solidly built brunette with cat's-eye sunglasses, dark slacks, and a bright pink polo shirt, and as she crossed the lot to her beige sedan, she was talking on her phone a mile a minute.

"That's her, right?" Tobias asked.

"According to the pic on her Facebook page, yeah." Sullivan started the car.

As Cindy ran errands at the grocery store and the bank before heading home to a little green house with a thirsty brown yard, Sullivan maintained a careful tail, finally parking slightly down the block and across the street from where she lived.

Bored, they got to talking about television—Sullivan liked the hard-edged stuff on HBO, Tobias preferred sit-coms. They'd both watched the entirety of *Gilmore Girls* though, roped in by sisters initially and staying of their own volition, and they argued for far longer than the topic deserved about the love triangle involving Jess (Sullivan) versus Dean (Tobias) before admitting that neither of the guys were perfect for Rory—Dean was intellectually lazy and Jess could be mean.

There was no sign of the balding man from the video at any point.

By midnight, they were both exhausted and starving and stiff, and Sullivan said, "I'm calling it."

"What does that mean?" Tobias had entered a sort of meditative state by this point, and would've been half-asleep if he weren't so physically uncomfortable.

"It means human bodies need a rest and we've reached the point where it's unlikely anything's going to happen. Give me five minutes. Stay here."

Sullivan got out of the car and popped the trunk. He fiddled with something Tobias couldn't see through the rear window, then walked down the street until he was behind the beige sedan. He bent down by the right rear tire for roughly three seconds, and then kept walking. A few minutes later he circled around to the Buick and climbed back behind the wheel.

"What did you put behind her tire?" Tobias asked.

"A cheap wristwatch. If she leaves, the tire will crunch the watch, and we'll have an idea of what time she took off. That way when we come back tomorrow—"

"We'll know to be here around that time in case she does it again."

"Yup." Sullivan started the car and pulled out onto the street. The cool night air rushed through the windows.

"Smart," Tobias said.

"Can't take credit. It's a tool of the trade. Everybody does it."

"Oh. Well, in that case. Loser."

Sullivan gave him a wry smile. "Are you hungry?"

After they left Cindy Jackman's, they stopped for burgers, and at the exit of the drive-thru line, Sullivan let the car idle. Tobias realized that a left turn would take them back to the motel, and a right would take them to Sullivan's place. In the dim red light of the restaurant's sign, Sullivan looked uncharacteristically uncertain.

Tobias said, "We're both tired. It's been a long day. I understand if you don't want to. I'd like to, but I understand."

"It's not that." Sullivan licked his lips. "I'm—my friend Caty says—" He paused. "Oh, fuck it."

He turned right. Tobias let out a breath.

The place looked subtly different than it had when they left. Tools had been moved and a pile of debris had gone missing.

"No burglars," Sullivan said. "My sister Therese must've been here, working on the place while we were out."

"Oh."

After they ate, they showered off the sweat of the day, and Sullivan cornered Tobias against the cold tile and jerked him off, his other hand resting against his throat. Sullivan didn't press at all—in fact, his thumb stroked gently along his pulse the whole time—but the symbolism was clear, along with the threat: for now, at least, even the breath in Tobias's body was Sullivan's to control.

Sullivan whispered filthily in his ear the whole time: "I can do whatever I want and you'll let me, won't you? I'm tempted to bend you over right here and make you come on my cock. Do you think you could? Come without a hand on you? Ever managed it before?" His rhythm paused, his fingers teasing until Tobias shook his head. Sullivan made a considering noise and went back to jerking him, pulling rough cries out of him with a tight fist. "I bet if I drew it out long enough you could. Maybe that's what I'll do, make a rule that you don't come unless you come on my cock. How long do you think it would take? How many times would I have to fuck you before you gave it up? I like the idea of that, of you walking around on edge for days, desperate for my cock, begging for it, ready to cry because it's been so long and it's so hard to get there without my hand, but you don't have to be scared, sweetheart, I won't give in before your body does."

Tobias came the second permission was granted, half-startled Sullivan had allowed it at all, given the way he'd been talking. Tobias stood dozily under the hot water while Sullivan jerked himself off too, his gaze hot as it lingered on Tobias's throat, where his palm still gently cupped the vulnerable flesh.

Sullivan nudged Tobias out of the bathroom so he could clean up, and by the time he wandered back into the bedroom, Tobias was out cold on top of the duvet. Sullivan sat on the edge of the mattress and watched him sleep, telling himself he should wake the guy up and kick him back to the motel where his ass belonged.

The idea of it made him feel like an asshole.

*He wants casual. Casual doesn't sleep over. At least, casual doesn't sleep over when one of the people involved gets hormones from cuddling and shit.*

He should kick Tobias out. He really should.

But Tobias had faint purple smudges under his eyes, and he looked so boneless and relaxed that Sullivan tugged the sheets out from under him, climbed in beside him, and turned off the light.

Sullivan got up at six, his internal clock overridden by the hum beneath his skin. It was going to be one of those mornings, and with a long day of sitting in a car ahead of him, he didn't dare try to go back to sleep. He laced up his sneakers, got a podcast going, and wrote a quick note in case Tobias woke up. After his run—six miles, hopefully enough to forestall his jitteriness later—he took a quick shower, refilled the cooler, and prodded Tobias awake so they could eat cereal at the sink before taking off.

On the way to Cindy Jackman's, Sullivan stopped at the motel so Tobias could change. When Tobias came out with his backpack in hand and a rebellious look on his face—*what are you going to do about it?*—Sullivan said nothing, just popped the trunk so he could sling his things inside.

The guy deserved access to his toothbrush at night, that's all.

Sullivan circled the block once, darting out to grab the watch from behind the beige sedan's rear tire, before parking on the other end of the street this time, four houses down from Cindy Jackman's address, and seven houses down from where they'd parked the day before. Tobias yawned into the thermos of coffee Sullivan had poured him.

"Did she leave?" Tobias asked.

Sullivan looked down at the unbroken face of the watch. "No."

They waited.

While Cindy went to work and then hit a local book-
store and café with friends, Sullivan and Tobias followed,
talking movies for hours before shifting to books. It
wasn't long before Sullivan had contributed a dozen novels to Tobias's new to-read list, which Sullivan scrawled
on the back of an old receipt. This was the result of a conversation that included Sullivan yelling, "You've never
seen *Blade Runner*? How are you a living, breathing person who exists?" and a long spiel that worked its way
through the classics of both sci-fi and hard-boiled detective noir from there. Tobias promised to try *Do Androids
Dream of Electric Sheep*, the book *Blade Runner* was
based on, although Sullivan suspected it was primarily
to shut him up.

They left when the last light in Cindy's house went
dark, and got dinner before driving back to Sullivan's.
After they ate, Sullivan lounged on the sofa, his fly open,
watching as Tobias sucked and licked and moaned around
his dick, petting his soft curls. By the time Sullivan came,
he was so deep in Tobias's throat that he was practically
in his chest, and he couldn't remember an afterglow as
satisfying as the one that followed, during which Tobias
begged to come in a voice that was completely trashed,
his words hoarse and running together into a long string
of *pleaseletmepleasepleaseletme*.

Sullivan jerked Tobias off hard and fast so that he
came in hot, damp pulses in his hand.

"Good boy," Sullivan whispered, and Tobias shivered.
He didn't look as exhausted that night as he had the night
before, but Sullivan still didn't mention the motel. He
simply guided Tobias upstairs and into the shower.

"Something's going to happen sooner or later, right?"
Tobias asked later, brushing his teeth and bemoaning the

ineffectual nature of stakeouts at the same time. "I mean, we've been following her around for ages."

"Two days isn't ages." Sullivan stretched out on the mattress, tired and curiously content despite finding several smug texts from Caty about her certainty that Sullivan had already caved to the lures of the college boy. He put his phone aside without replying; he sure as hell wasn't going to confirm it for her.

On Wednesday, they followed Cindy to work, the gym, and then out to a movie and dinner with a handful of her friends. For most of that time, Tobias read aloud, pausing only to drink from the bottles of water Sullivan kept pushing on him. At Sullivan's behest, they wandered through five different books, starting and ending at seemingly arbitrary points in *Lady Chatterley's Lover*, the *Bhagavad Gita*, *The Gospel According to Judy Blume*, *Slaughterhouse Five*, and *The Portable Dorothy Parker*. Tobias was a good out-loud reader—careful, not too slow. When they got bored with that, Sullivan went on a long, enjoyable spiel—monologuing, Caty would say, but she wasn't here, so whatever—about the strengths and drawbacks of the wah-wah pedal.

"Do you even play guitar?" Tobias asked him during a lull.

"No. Why?"

"No reason." Tobias smiled and Sullivan shook his head. Tobias asked the weirdest questions sometimes. But he also gestured for Sullivan to tell him more, so Sullivan figured he could put up with it.

Later, while Cindy and her friends dined on the restaurant patio, they somehow got onto the subject of guilty pleasure tasks.

"You stress bake," Sullivan repeated. "For fun, you stress bake."

"Yes."

"What does stress baking mean?"

Tobias pulled out another bottle of water and shoved it at Sullivan. "It means I bake when I'm stressed, what do you think it means?"

"I don't know." Sullivan wasn't thirsty, but he felt somehow unhappy at the idea of rejecting the offering. He decided not to think about why that could be and immediately began pulling the label off with his thumbnail. "I thought maybe it was like you have to produce a certain number of cupcakes in an hour or they blow up your pans or something."

Tobias laughed. "No. It takes a lot of concentration, so I can't worry about other things, but it's not high pressure in and of itself. It says a lot about you that you thought there might be something dangerous in it, you know."

"Hey, cherry pie done right is very dangerous."

"For the waistline, maybe."

"In *every* way. Come on, that's a sexy pie. If apple pie's the good girl, cherry pie's the filthy minx."

Tobias laughed again, and when they left Cindy tucked in for the night, they ended up at a twenty-four-hour grocery store shopping for baking ingredients.

Which was how they ended up covered in flour at three in the morning, eating steaming cherry pie out of the tin. Sullivan had enjoyed helping—if you could call snitching cherries and flicking sugar at Tobias's face helping—almost as much as he enjoyed the pie itself. The pastry was golden and flaky and buttery, the filling the perfect mixture of sweet and tart. Sullivan ate three pieces before he collapsed onto the counter, too full to move.

Tobias smirked, drawing a film of plastic wrap over the pie to keep it fresh. "You could've stopped at one piece."

"She seduced me," Sullivan moaned. God, he was going to explode, and he wasn't sure it wouldn't be worth it.

"Come on, get up." Tobias tugged on his arm. "Let's clean up. I'm so tired."

"You made a mess of my kitchen." Sullivan turned his wrist over so he could trail a thumb over a smear of flour on Tobias's hand. "And you're not in much better shape."

"That's what happens when someone bakes something for someone."

Sullivan stood up straight, struck dumb by the flutter of warmth in his chest at Tobias's words. "Did you bake it for me? Or did you just bake it?"

Tobias's cheeks flared crimson. "I prefer *konparèt*."

"I have no idea what that is," Sullivan murmured.

"It's Haitian," Tobias said, staring at his mouth. It was the middle of the night and they were both riding a mixture of exhaustion and sugar high, and Sullivan maybe wasn't thinking straight. He could decide if those were good excuses or not tomorrow. Now, he simply gave in to the urge to press a ripe-cherry-red kiss to Tobias's mouth, tentative and slow, little more than a brushing of lips. Tobias kissed him back instantly, angling his body so that their chests brushed and that was good. Sullivan leaned back against the counter, his hands finding Tobias's hips, tugging him closer, and that was even better. They kissed for what seemed like hours, slow, thorough, drugging kisses, the need less like a fury and more like an inevitability.

Sullivan didn't think of himself as the kind of man who was kissed; he did the kissing. He liked the action of it, the dominance of it, and he'd been told by a high school girlfriend that he was a bullying sort of kisser to boot, a complaint he'd taken as a compliment, but he felt help-less here, overwhelmed and stupid and shocked, and all he could do was keep kissing Tobias, keep kissing him as if they would never stop, not until the sun expanded and the world went up in flames. It still might not be enough.

They didn't fuck that night. They were too tired, too locked into this one simple act. They stumbled upstairs only when they were too weary to stand anymore, and then they lay in the dark in the cool sheets, legs entwined, fingers linked, mouths still brushing lightly, lips sore, until they slept.

After that, it was like a dam had broken. If Tobias stood still for more than five seconds and they weren't actively working, Sullivan's mouth was on his. Tobias would com-plain if Sullivan weren't so damn good at it. Sullivan kissed him like Tobias was *his*, his to use and enjoy and take care of, and Tobias—Tobias couldn't remember ever feeling this full, this safe.

All day Thursday, as they once more followed Cindy Jackman through her day-to-day life, Tobias thought about those kisses. In fact, the only thing that seemed to wipe the idea of kissing from his mind entirely was when Sullivan passed his laptop over to where Tobias was slumped in the passenger seat of the Buick reading aloud from *Android*.

The class catalog for Metro State University of Denver had been downloaded.

"Here." Sullivan tapped the casing until Tobias reluctantly set the book aside.

"What is this?"

"It's a computer," Sullivan said helpfully.

"No duh."

"Okay, leaving aside the fact that you're an eighth-grader, it's a random thought activity."

"Random thought activity," Tobias repeated, pretending he hadn't been busted for saying something lame enough to pass for a middle schooler.

"Indulging a random thought for the sake of it. Pick one class that you could bear taking. You won't actually take it. You don't even have to tell me what it is. There are only two rules. The class can't be in the hard sciences, and it has to be something you don't already know a lot about."

"Subtle," Tobias said wryly.

"You're the one who keeps saying you're not a spoiled rich boy. At some point you're gonna need a job, yeah?" Sullivan smirked. "I've heard great things about Underwater Basket Weaving 101."

Tobias didn't know what to think of the activity, to be honest. He'd been locked into medicine for so long that he'd never considered what other options were out there, so it might be interesting. He couldn't be Sullivan's lackey forever, after all. If he felt a small twinge of unhappiness at the idea, he brushed it off. He was here for Ghost. This was temporary.

"Thanks," he said, and Sullivan nodded, already watching out the window again, as if he really thought either Cindy Jackman or the balding man who'd used her car to pick up Ghost might show up any second, something Tobias was less certain about every day.

He worked his way through the class catalog, losing track of time so thoroughly that he didn't look up again until Sullivan ordered him to go get them some sandwiches from the shop at the other end of the strip mall.

"Did you find anything you liked in the catalog?" Sullivan asked, once they were eating.

"Not yet, but I'm only through F. It's kind of fun."

"Yeah?"

"Yeah. Thinking about what I might do with the rest of my life. There are possibilities there that weren't there before, and it's… I'm excited about it. For the first time that I can remember, the idea of moving forward feels good instead of terrifying."

Sullivan was licking mustard off his fingers, eyeing Tobias like he'd done something perplexing, like taken his clothes off to dance a jig. "I don't understand why you didn't do this a long time ago."

Tobias fiddled with one corner of his sandwich bread, tearing it and rolling it into a ball. "When I was four or five, one day someone asked me what I wanted to be when I grew up, and I said I wanted to be a doctor so I could spend all day with my papa."

Sullivan grinned. "That's adorable. You're an adorable boy, Tobias."

"You're not the only one who thought so." Tobias tore another piece loose, then a third. "My papa was so proud. He told the rest of the family and all his colleagues and friends and it turned into a whole thing. At one point, back in high school, he was talking about the two of us practicing together."

"Snowballed on you, huh?"

"Yeah. It was cast in stone from so early on that for years I didn't stop to think about whether it was a good thing or not. That was the way it was, you know? Tante Esther was mean, you saved mangoes for Saturday pajama mornings, and I was going to be a doctor. For a long time it wasn't any big thing, you know? What does a ten-year-old care about a career path? It wasn't until high school that it started to feel real."

"That was part of the breakdown, huh?"

"I tried rebelling like a normal teenager for a while. Parties. Staying out past curfew. Little rebellions like that." He gave Sullivan a sheepish look. "It didn't last long. I wasn't very good at it, and it only made me feel worse. My parents didn't understand. Of all my siblings, I was adopted the youngest, and I haven't had a lot of the same problems, so I could tell they didn't know where it was coming from. I didn't know how to say that the idea of graduating from high school was making me wish I could hibernate until it was all over."

"You thought hurting yourself was preferable to telling them the truth about how you felt?" Sullivan was mostly watching the nonprofit building, but he was glancing over frequently, his brow furrowed. The fact that he cared helped counter the anxiety of the subject matter.

"I didn't want them to hate me."

As soon as he said it, he felt stupid. Of course they wouldn't hate him; they loved him. Even as angry as he was with them now, he knew that. But feelings didn't always reflect reality, and they didn't have to make sense. He had to train himself out of that kind of thinking. Train himself *into* thinking of his needs and opinions as equally valid, as well as being the ones that he weighted the most when it came to decisions like this.

"That wouldn't happen," Tobias said, when it looked like Sullivan was about to ask how likely it was. "But he'll be hurt when I tell him I'm not going to be a doctor anymore."

Later, while Tobias read in the living room, Sullivan got caught up on his subpoenas, cursing under his breath the whole time. He also called his sisters—all five of them in a row, and spent nearly three hours altogether in his bedroom in conversation with them about various jobs, men, children, sports, and parents-in-law. Tobias and Sullivan made dinner together afterward, talking about a million small things, none of which were related to the case.

It was oddly, satisfyingly domestic.

That night, tired and pressed for time, Sullivan slid on top of Tobias and pushed his thighs apart with his knees. Sullivan kissed him deeply, rocking their dicks together in a slow-building, shuddering rhythm until Tobias couldn't breathe through the heat. "You love that I make you feel like this, don't you?" Sullivan asked, his voice low and smug.

Tobias nodded helplessly.

"Yeah, I thought so. For a good boy, you're awfully needy. I'm going to have to give you a lot of cock to keep you satisfied, won't I, Tobias?" Sullivan was looking at him with dark, expectant eyes, and he knew exactly what Sullivan wanted to hear.

"Yes," Tobias whispered. His face couldn't be more painfully red. Perhaps tomorrow he would be horrified by the things they were saying, but right now it was a fire in his blood.

"Do you know why?"

An answer crept to the tip of his tongue, but Tobias

couldn't say it. Could he? Sullivan was still watching him, probably expecting something along the lines of *because I'm a bad boy*, but somehow the real words came out, tiny but daring, "Because I'm a slut."

Sullivan's breath caught and his eyes widened. "Oh, that's good, sweetheart." Sullivan leaned down, nosed at Tobias's jaw, pressing a kiss there in reward. "God, you're so good for me."

The praise sank into Tobias deeply, made him shudder with warm, sweet pleasure. It was almost enough to override the heat that came from Sullivan's continued words. Almost.

"Maybe I'll make you beg for it," Sullivan murmured thoughtfully. "Make you beg to get fucked. Make you beg suck me. I can do anything I want and you'll like it. Because you're a slut, aren't you?"

"Please." Tobias had felt filthy and overwhelmed when he said that forbidden little word—*slut*—but it was so much hotter when Sullivan said it. He was so close. He lifted his hips, trying to get more friction. "Please let me come."

"Not yet. Not until you admit you want it."

He couldn't think, his mind hazy and blank, but he obeyed instinctively. He gasped, "I want it."

"That's my good boy. Go ahead and come, sweetheart."

"I want it," Tobias repeated, just for himself, and came in a long rush against Sullivan's belly.

"I know," Sullivan replied, and he came too, his mouth hot and demanding against Tobias's the whole time.

Are you allowed to kiss people like you might be dying during casual sex? Tobias typed out in a message to Church while Sullivan was in the bathroom getting a washcloth for cleanup.

He didn't send it.

On Friday, after they followed Cindy home from early dinner with her girlfriends, they parked down the street and waited. Eight-thirty was too early to assume she was in for the night.

"It's been a week." Tobias rolled his window up, grimacing and slapping at the gnats and no-see-ums. Sullivan didn't blame him; the tiny annoyances were legion after dark. "At what point do we go ask Cindy about the guy who took her car?"

"At the point when otherwise we have to abandon the case."

"And we're not there yet?"

"You said it yourself—it's been a week. Do you see everyone in your whole life every week? Patience is a virtue."

"I'm patient." He fidgeted in his seat for a second. "Okay, but what about K in Ghost's phone? We have to call at some point, right?"

"Nope. The logic there hasn't changed. We don't want anyone to know we're looking." Sullivan flicked him on the leg. "Chill. It'll happen sooner or later."

When a trace of mulish rebellion crossed Tobias's face, Sullivan smiled. The guy might pretend to be mild-mannered, but still waters ran deep.

Almost challengingly, like he could sense that Sullivan was amused by him and he wanted to undermine it, Tobias asked, "Why haven't you spanked me?"

Sullivan's smile slipped off his face. He considered

and discarded a half-dozen responses before finally saying, "Why would I?"

Tobias shrugged. "It all goes together, doesn't it? Whips and chains and BDSM…spanking's part of it."

"You know that how?"

"CSI."

"Jesus." Sullivan might've laughed if he wasn't feeling like he might suffocate any minute. "Kink doesn't have to include pain. Not everyone likes it. So I didn't bring it up."

"Kink doesn't have to include edging or anal, either, and you brought those up without knowing if I'd like them." Tobias darted a glance at him. Whatever Sullivan's expression was doing—he honestly wasn't sure—made Tobias add, "It's okay if you don't want to, but… do you want to hurt me?"

Sullivan considered lying. It was the sort of question with a clear right answer; social expectation demanded a *no*. It would be easier to lie, too, because then they could be done with it. He wasn't sure what could be gained from this conversation in the first place. Tobias might seem all right talking about the subject theoretically, but pain wasn't like other elements of kink. Wanting to tease someone wasn't the same as wanting to hurt them. Sooner or later Tobias would see that, and it would get ugly between them, and however the blackmail thing had twisted them up to start, they'd somehow settled into something far less angry. He liked Tobias, far more than he'd expected to. He liked how light it was between them, both in bed and out, liked how they fit, and taking this into that area of kink would only screw everything up.

At the same time, it had been so long, and now that Tobias had brought it up, he couldn't stop picturing it:

Tobias lying naked across Sullivan's thighs, his breathing fast, his cheeks firm and ready for Sullivan's hand, all that perfect skin, warm and unblemished and...that was where Sullivan's brain started to short circuit. He should say no, because anything else would ruin everything. But he really wanted to say yes.

In the end he didn't say anything at all.

The silence stretched and stretched.

He realized he'd been clenching his hands around the steering wheel when Tobias started trying to peel his fingers off.

"Easy," Tobias said quietly. "I'm not going to judge you. You're not in trouble, and I'm not going to be mad. It's not like I can't guess just from your reaction."

Of course he had. Tobias was a lot of things, but stupid wasn't one of them. Sullivan pulled his hands free and shook out the aching joints. "You sound like a mom."

Tobias sat back, startled. He glanced out the window at the little green house, mouth turning somber at the corners. "That's the sort of thing Manman says when me or one of my siblings is upset. I guess the shoe fits."

"You miss her."

"Yes. And don't change the subject."

"I'm not changing the subject. Why don't you call her?"

"Because I'm still angry. And that's the definition of changing the subject. We were talking about your desire to hurt me and segueing into a talk about how to make that happen, and then you were all about—"

"The fuck we were segueing into making that happen." Sullivan took a breath, forced himself to talk more slowly. "I can change the subject if I want to. It's my con-

versation too. Also, no one's saying you can't be angry.
You can call someone while you're angry."

Tobias sounded insultingly calm when he said, "Okay.
We don't have to do anything. And it's better if I calm
down first. Or I might end up saying something I regret."

"If you aren't chilled out by now, you're never going
to be. Plus, not to be a dick, but your problem doesn't
seem to be about saying things you regret so much as
not saying anything at all and pretending everything
is fine. You can't get mad at people for believing your
bullshit when you're selling it to them this hard. Maybe
you should try telling the truth for once; you wouldn't
have this problem."

Tobias's expression went slack with shock. "Wow.
That's…that's quite the read on something you know
nothing about."

"Am I wrong?"

Tobias set his jaw. "Are you going to admit you want
to hurt me?"

They stared at each other.

Neither of them answered.

Four silent hours later, when all the lights in the green-
house had been off for a while, they left for the night. Sullivan drove Tobias to the motel without a word.

A week shouldn't be long enough to get addicted to the
feel of someone else in bed breathing softly in the dark
with you, Tobias decided around four in the morning.

Sullivan woke up to a ten-mile dawn.

*Two weeks*, he bitched to himself as he ran, earbuds
in, the Single Mothers' "Negative Qualities" blaring because it matched his mood. *Two fucking weeks you've*

*known the guy, and you're all out of joint. Two fucking weeks and you're acting like a sulking teenager. Get your shit together.*

Even after he'd run himself into exhaustion and taken a hot shower, he still felt unsettled. His skin had somehow shrunk overnight, and he didn't fit right in his own body. Nothing fit right.

## Chapter Sixteen

Because he was determined to act like an adult, Sullivan made a thermos of coffee for Tobias as well as himself before he went to the motel. They hadn't explicitly said they'd meet up today, but Sullivan had enough experience with Tobias's determination by this point to know he wasn't going to get away with avoiding him just because they'd argued. He was unsurprised to find him waiting outside, hair still damp from a shower, eyes bloodshot and heavy.

Sullivan drove them out to Cindy Jackman's house and collected the cheap watch from behind her tire. Once again, she hadn't driven anywhere after they left. Then they sat in silence for several long, strained minutes until, almost in unison, Sullivan said, "We should talk," and Tobias asked, "Can we talk?"

After a jumble of "Yeah," and "go ahead," and "no, you first," Sullivan threw himself on his sword.

"I'm sorry. You threw me with the spanking thing, and I might have some issues with that, and I took it out on you, and I'm sorry."

"No, you didn't. It's fine. It's none of my business, and I shouldn't have—"

"You didn't do anything wrong."

"I was the one who started the whole conversation. It was my fault. I'm sorry."

"I was the one who acted like a dick."

"If I hadn't brought up the spanking thing, none of this would've happened."

Jesus, Tobias was uptight. No wonder his damn head was a mess. "You think you shouldn't have brought it up?"

"I upset you."

"Oh, my God." Sullivan dropped his head back against the rest. Where was the guy who'd stood up to him so well a week ago, who'd argued and squared his shoulders and spoke his piece? That guy had been an asshole, but at least he'd been *real*. He wanted to get back to that.

In fact…he was going to get back to that. Tobias had to be able to say what he honestly felt, and yeah, he'd gotten pretty good at that when it was easy shit, but it wasn't always going to be easy shit.

Sullivan took a deep breath. Being analytical about it hadn't gotten them anywhere. Best to hit it head-on. "I'm mad at you."

"That's why I'm apologizing."

"No, I mean I'm mad at you for apologizing."

"That's— How are you mad at me for apologizing?"

"You didn't do anything wrong."

"It takes two to argue."

"Exactly. And you're not arguing, you're rolling over, and it's not—it's so damn polite I can't see straight. I don't like it."

Tobias frowned at him. "You don't like politeness? But it's good to be kind."

"Polite and kind are two different things. Kind is crucial. Polite is superficial. I mean, it's great to say thank you and all, I'm not arguing that, but you not saying shit isn't polite. It's manipulative."

Tobias sucked in a breath. "I am *not* manipulative."

"No? So you're not changing your behavior to get a particular response from the people around you, without ever once explaining what you're doing or why?"

"You're twisting it around."

"You make it impossible for people to legitimately like you."

"Because I'm a manipulative liar who—"

"No," Sullivan interrupted, "because you don't show them *you*. Of course people like this fake, polite, nice bullshit you dish out, because it's easy, and it gives them what they want, but they're not getting *you*. You do it on purpose so they'll like you, but it's disingenuous and manipulative and I don't fucking like being lied to."

Tobias jerked back as if he'd been struck, his cheeks flooding with color. He opened his mouth, froze, and finally said, "You're right, I should've—"

"Oh, for fuck's sake, would you *say what you're fucking thinking*?"

"I think you're being an *asshole*!" Tobias shouted.

"Well, so do I!" Sullivan shouted back, and then laughed out loud at the shock on Tobias's face. "Jesus, you make it hard to get an honest answer out of you. You're not my slave, remember? I don't want polite, doormat Tobias. I want the guy who blackmailed me and stood up to me and shoved me in my own hallway and, like, went after my dick with zero advance notice. That version of you isn't very polite, but at least it's honest. You can yell and call me out and say what you want, even if you think I'm not going to like it. That's not going to drive me away. The only thing that's guaranteed to drive me away is that manipulative, bland politeness you pull with everyone else."

Tobias's fingers plucked at the hem of his shorts, his face tipped away. "I appreciate what you're trying to do, this whole save-Tobias-from-himself plan you've got going, but it's not that simple."

"It was easier when I was just some guy you were screwing over, huh? Let's practice. Tell me how it made you feel that I was a dick to you yesterday." Sullivan reached out and took Tobias's hand, and Tobias's head snapped around so he could stare at their intertwined fingers. Sullivan could see the indecision on his face, the warring impulses to follow the same script he'd followed his whole life or to do as Sullivan was suggesting. It wasn't unlike a scene, now that he thought about it. Setting up conditions that made it safe for a sub to come apart, and then helping them pick up the pieces afterward.

Still staring at their hands, Tobias muttered, "You really hurt my feelings."

Sullivan's heart turned over in his chest with something close to pride. It was both alarming and embarrassing, actually. "Good," he murmured. "You're doing good. Keep going."

"It felt like you went right for one of my most vulnerable spots."

"Yeah, that's because that's what I did. Keep going."

"I wasn't trying to make you mad yesterday. I was trying to ask for—ask for what I wanted."

"I know. It's all right that you did that. I should've listened. Explained."

"It's not easy to have someone spring something like that on you, though. I get why you were upset."

"Whose side are you on?" Sullivan asked. "Stop helping me. And if I'm not okay, I should say that I need time to think, not say a bunch of dickish things."

"Well, that's true." Tobias glanced up, his gaze searching Sullivan's face, and whatever he saw there seemed to reassure him. "And I know you were frustrated and maybe you're okay fighting the way we just did, but I don't like it."

"Sometimes yelling clears the air."

Tobias visibly bolstered himself. "I—I—*no*. I really don't like yelling. If one of us isn't listening, we can try different things, but not yelling."

Sullivan squeezed Tobias's hand. "Fair enough. I promise. No yelling."

"And I'm sorry about yesterday."

Sullivan grumbled in exasperation, and Tobias's jaw set. "I can be sorry if I want. If I should be able to say the bad things I feel, I should be able to say these too. I don't like that I made you feel threatened. I don't want to do that again, even accidentally. I want to approach things like this differently."

"I don't know if *threatened* is the right word," Sullivan started, but Tobias just looked at him, clear and sweet and vaguely admonishing. "Yeah, all right, good word."

"Maybe I didn't do anything wrong, but I can still be sorry that you felt that way."

Sullivan supposed that made sense. And if it was what Tobias felt, well...wasn't that the whole point of this? "Okay. Thanks."

"Okay." Tobias's shoulders straightened. "I feel better."

"Yeah? Me too."

"Although I'd like to ask some questions, if I can. Figure out where we stand. We haven't talked much. About the sex stuff, yeah, but not about where we're coming from and what we want, so—"

"You mentioned casual, that first day," Sullivan said slowly. "I don't know how much casual sex you've had, but this—what we've been doing—doesn't fit my definition of it."

"It doesn't feel casual," Tobias admitted. "Maybe that first day, a little, but it shifted. I'm not sure how to get back to that first day. Probably less kissing? Sleepovers are…maybe not…" He sounded unexcited at the prospect at another night at the motel, which was a small comfort.

"I don't think I want to. Go back, I mean." Sullivan's stomach tightened at the surprised pleasure on Tobias's face.

"You don't? You like where we are?"

"I like kissing you. I don't want to stop kissing you."

Tobias's cheeks flushed again, and his lips curved in a small, shy smile. "I don't want to stop either." He squeezed Sullivan's fingers and opened his mouth to add something else, and then stalled out.

"Say it." Sullivan nudged his knee.

"No, I will. I'm just not sure *what* to say. I don't trust myself."

"What do you mean?"

"My life is a mess right now. I don't know what I'm doing, I don't know where I'm going or how, and I've been making a bunch of huge decisions in a short span of time and it's all sort of awful."

"Oh."

"Except for you," Tobias added hurriedly. "You're the only part of my life right now that I'm not half-tempted to drop in a lake, but I've been feeling very impulsive lately. I like it, but it's probably not a great time for me to make any promises." He paused, his thumb tracing over Sullivan's hand like he was relishing the texture of Sullivan's skin. "You're amazing and I like you a lot, but I don't want to give you false expectations. I want this, but I don't trust my mental state enough to know that I'll keep wanting it. That sounds really mean, I know, but you wanted me to be honest, and that's where I am. Is that okay? I understand if you want to go back to being professional."

"If it's what you feel comfortable with, it's okay." Sullivan didn't have to like it to respect it. He also didn't think he was required to lay on the line how much the idea of Tobias deciding that all he'd wanted was a fling bothered him. That was his problem, and saying so might make Tobias feel guilty. He was giving Sullivan the honesty he'd asked for, daring to trust Sullivan to handle it the way he'd claimed he would. Sullivan wasn't going to screw it up now just because it wasn't the answer he'd wanted.

And as much as Tobias might think otherwise, this *was* an answer. If Tobias thought he should keep one foot out the door, there was a reason for it. Maybe it was because he was making a bunch of changes. Maybe it was because he already knew that this new, better person he wanted to be wouldn't have the same inclination for dirty sex with some guy he'd known for two weeks.

Either way, Sullivan wasn't going to hold his breath.

He said, "I'm cool with playing things by ear. We'll stick with maybe, and when things get a bit more settled for you, we'll talk about it again. Yeah?"

"Yeah." Tobias smiled, the tension in his shoulders dissipating.

Sullivan heaved a deep breath. He would just have to keep his head together.

Tobias asked, "Does that mean I get to ask you nosy questions about the spanking thing or not?"

Sullivan's throat went tight and he reminded himself to chill. "Yeah, ask what you want. I promise this time that if I don't want to talk about something, I won't be a dick about it."

"Okay. But first…" Tobias leaned in, gaze searching, and kissed Sullivan's mouth. Sullivan kissed him back for as long as he dared, and it wasn't enough by far, but eventually he pulled back.

"On a stakeout," he reminded them both, licking his lips, and Tobias nodded.

"I know. I just needed to do that."

Sullivan's heart did a stupid tumbling thing in his chest, and he directed his attention to Cindy Jackman's front door. "No problem."

"So…" Tobias was still holding his hand and playing with his fingers. It was soothing, and even though Sullivan should probably take his hand back, he didn't. It might make the rest of this conversation easier. "Before we get back to the question of whether or not you want to hurt me, I thought maybe I should ask why you seem so unhappy about answering me. Is it related to the reason why you're out of practice with, um, the kind of sex we're having?"

Sullivan gave him a wry glance. "Do you make a habit out of being insightful? It's annoying."

"Sorry." Tobias didn't sound sorry so much as amused.

"Yeah, I guess it is."

"You don't have to tell me. I'll understand. But if you

want to, whatever it is, I'm not going to laugh or be mean. I'm a good listener. Or so I've been told."

Sullivan studied Tobias's smile, the kind curve of it. It was a lovely smile, one that both reassured and warmed. "My last relationship ended badly. We were buddies since we were kids, and we tried to make the leap into something else, but he wasn't into kink. Which he explained, in great detail, when I told him what I wanted."

Tobias winced. "In a nonjudgmental, whatever-makes-you-happy sort of way?"

Sullivan laughed without humor. "Not hardly."

"I'm sorry."

It wasn't the token apology that most people offered in this sort of situation, fulfilling the day's allotment of social expectation. He sounded like he was truly touched by Sullivan's pain. It was earnest and endearing and hard to take. Sullivan looked down. "Thanks."

After a brief hesitation, Tobias asked, "Did you love him?"

"Yes." Sullivan thought he sounded embarrassingly hoarse, but it wasn't because of Nick, exactly. Or at least, it wasn't because he was pining for their romantic relationship. His love for Nick had been platonic for a long time, partially because they'd been young when they met and partially because Sullivan had never dared to let himself hope for more, and he'd have been able to make the switch back to friendship if given the chance. It would've hurt, but he could've done it. Instead, within two days of Sullivan's confession about what he needed in bed, both Nick and all evidence of his presence in Sullivan's life had been gone. He hadn't gotten the brushoff. He'd gotten a swift and brutal ejection.

Nick had left the gifts Sullivan had given him over the years in a pile on his front stoop, for fuck's sake.

No, he might be upset, but he definitely wasn't pining.

"I don't think some handcuffs and a little wax play would've been enough to make him hate me, but the rest of it..." Sullivan tipped his head back against the rest, concentrating on where Tobias's fingers had tightened around his. "I said I wanted to hurt him. He said I was a monster. It wasn't like he didn't have a point, you know, but—"

"Whoa, that's—" Tobias's eyes had gone wide. "He did not have a point. What he said is not okay, Sullivan. You're not a monster. He doesn't have to like what you like, but it's not okay to vilify people for wanting or liking different things. He could've said no, he could've walked away, but trying to shame you and humiliate you because he didn't have the same views on the subject— *that's* what's monstrous."

"Hey, hey, easy." Sullivan tugged his hand loose, but only so he could wrap his fingers in the curl by Tobias's temple, tugging gently, stroking the skin there with his thumb. "I'm okay. Take a breath."

Tobias did, but the tension in his lips didn't fade. "I *hate* that. When people assume that different is bad. Someone doesn't have to understand your choices or agree with them to accept that you still have the right to make them. We don't all have to be the same. We can be different without letting it make us afraid or mean or careless. It's so stupid."

"It is," Sullivan agreed, and his voice sort of broke because he hadn't expected this. Caty had been fired up, no doubt, but she was always fired up, and her anger had been of the protective, *don't hurt what's mine* sort, not this, this acceptance from someone who knew what Sullivan wanted to do to him and was still all right with it.

Tobias kept going, "And if I want you to beat me from here to Port-au-Prince, that's my prerogative. Someone doesn't have to want that too in order to back the fuck up and let me have it."

"Wow, that's—Port-au-Prince?"

"The capital of Haiti. Learn some geography." Tobias scowled fiercely at nothing in particular.

"I know where it is, you just don't get a lot of references to it in kinky conversation. At least, not in my experience. You know, I don't think I've ever heard you say *fuck* before." Sullivan's lips twitched. Tobias cursing was cute. Sort of like a fluffy animal from a kid's movie busting out gang signs. "Do it again."

"Oh, shut up." Tobias knocked Sullivan's hand away from his face, but gently, so he couldn't be too angry. "I sound like my Tante Esther. Every other word out of her mouth is an F-bomb."

Sullivan laughed. "You disapprove?"

"She's kind of mean sometimes." He stopped short, then said slowly, "Actually…she's not."

Sullivan raised an eyebrow.

"She's honest," Tobias said. "She's the one who told me that I'd been found in a Dumpster as a baby."

Sullivan had to swallow hard. During his research on Tobias, he'd seen mention of a teen girl abandoning her newborn, but he hadn't known for sure that Tobias was the infant in question. And what had been a random fact about a stranger before felt like a bruise in a very tender place now. "I'm sorry."

"It's all right. My birth mother was very young when she had me." Tobias glanced out the window, away from

Sullivan. "I think she panicked. Didn't know what to do. My parents never told me about it. I'd resigned myself to the idea that they'd kept it from me, but then I found a letter from her in the trash. And then she called me. She... it was sort of horrible. I think she wants to meet me, and I get why my parents would be afraid of that, but I don't want to meet her, and if they'd asked, I'd have told them that, but they never asked. Even though I'm an adult, they just made the choice for me, and that's why I left."

"Shit. I should think so."

"We'll be okay," Tobias said, but quietly, like the reassurance was meant for himself more than Sullivan. More briskly, he continued, "Tante Esther told me when I was ten. I thought she was being mean at the time— she often said things that hurt people's feelings, or so it seemed to me when I was a kid. But honesty does hurt, doesn't it? Sometimes at least. Doesn't mean it's not worthwhile. Maybe she thought I deserved to know the truth. Or maybe she refused to lie. Who knows? Anyway. Where were we? Oh, right. Your ex is a d-bag who needs to learn that just because something doesn't fit his experience of the world, that doesn't make it invalid."

Sullivan studied the solemn, determined expression on Tobias's face. "I would very much like to hurt you, if you think you'd enjoy it."

Tobias's solemnity shattered into a large, sunny grin. "Oh, sure! Let's try it tonight."

Waiting was *torture*.

After a year of hating this small, central part of himself, and after almost eighteen months of going without satisfying it in any shape or form, Sullivan felt like a smoker still an hour out from his next cigarette. Time slowed down. A glacier could've melted in the time it took for Cindy Jackman to go to work, have dinner with friends, and return home for the night.

By the time they got back to his place, Sullivan's hands were shaking.

Tobias dumped their stuff on the counter, his gaze running over Sullivan. He asked kindly, "Can you wait a bit longer so I can shower?"

"Sure."

Tobias smiled like he knew what that cost him. "I'll be quick."

Sullivan spent the ten minutes pacing in the kitchen, thinking about what was coming. He had to make it good, and not only so Tobias wouldn't regret it and say they could never do it again. He thought Tobias might find spanking to be a blessing in disguise. Lots of high-strung subs preferred a dirty, playful punishment to spending weeks beating themselves up over a mistake. And it would be sweet to soothe him afterward, to touch him until he lost track of everything else, to let him know that he was still wanted and valued, to bring him pleasure in exchange for his trust.

When the shower cut off, Sullivan went upstairs and found Tobias standing in a towel in the center of his bedroom. Water drops beaded along his shoulders and belly, and his hair lay dark and curled at his forehead and nape. His gaze was bright and interested; Sullivan saw no sign of fear.

"How do you want me?" Tobias asked.

"I don't…" Yeah, Sullivan's words were actually wavering. "I don't know. It depends on what you want."

"What do you mean?"

Sullivan hesitated. "Are you under the impression I'm

going to thrash you or something? It's a spanking, not a beating. You get a say in this."

Tobias laughed. "No, I know. But it's been a while for you and I thought you might want to…sort of…well, bang it out. I don't need anything fancy. At least I don't think I do."

Sullivan almost choked. "Bang it out? What the hell?"

Tobias shrugged. "I don't mind."

"Well, I do. I want it to be good for you."

Tobias's gaze softened. "It already is. I can tell how bad you want this. I can see it. It's—God, Sullivan, I love that you want this so much." He licked his lips, then pulled the towel from his hips and tossed it in the direction of the bathroom. He was half-hard and filling fast. "I like the idea of it. I want… I don't know what I want, but I know it'll be good. You'll make it good."

"You trust me?"

"I do."

Sullivan's knees were fucking weak. He sat on the bed, surveying Tobias from his broad shoulders to his lean arms and legs. "Turn around."

Tobias did, and Sullivan stared at his ass. He'd looked plenty of times before, but now he let himself see what he'd refused to consider all those times before: that ass was *made* for play, round and pert enough to bounce under a hard blow, the perfect tapestry for bruises and welts. His thighs were strong and lightly hairy. He didn't have much fat on his build at all, and Sullivan would have to be careful not to cause damage along with the pain.

"Come here," he said, and he heard the catch of Tobias's breath.

Tobias was fully hard now, and when Sullivan took hold of his wrist and tugged, he went easily, folding across Sullivan's lap like a dancer, his erection coming to rest in the space between Sullivan's legs. If it hadn't been for the wild beat of his pulse, Sullivan might've thought him calm. Not that he was calm, himself. He couldn't seem to tear his eyes away from Tobias's ass, and he definitely didn't have control of his hand, which stroked that fine, lightly downy skin as if it were sacred.

"Color?" he asked.

"Green."

There was nothing left but to do it, then. Sullivan lifted his hand, ignored the trembling in his fingers, and brought it down. The sound rang through the room, louder than he remembered it being, and at the same time an electric shock of pleasure burned through his belly. He watched Tobias's flesh move, distantly aware of Tobias's breath catching again, and lost a few seconds staring at the reddening skin where his palm had made contact.

"Color?" he asked.

"Green."

He brought his hand down again. Harder this time, to hear the way Tobias inhaled sharply, jolting against the pain. "Yeah?"

"Yeah."

And again. A fourth time. His fingers lingered this time, squeezing. "How's…is that all right?"

"I'm good."

"But do you like it, I mean?"

"I don't know yet," Tobias replied, sounding mildly exasperated. "You keep stopping."

Right. Sullivan was killing the mood with all the check-ins. Obvious mistake. He should shut up and do it. Instead, he said, "I want you to know you can trust me."

Tobias sat up, going to his knees on the mattress beside him. He surveyed Sullivan's face closely enough that Sullivan wanted to fidget. "What?"

"I think the question is whether or not you trust me."

Sullivan frowned. "What's that got to do with anything? I'm the one with all the power here—"

"I wouldn't go that far. I'm the one with the power at the moment, and I'd really like to switch that back around, so tell me what you need." Tobias's tone was relaxed, like this was the kind of conversation that took place every day.

Sullivan only stared at him.

Tobias sighed. "If I safe word, you'll move heaven and earth to fix whatever's broken, won't you?"

"Of course," Sullivan said, a little offended.

"So if I know it, why don't you?"

"I—"

"I will tell you if I need out. Or if it's not doing anything for me. You're not going to hurt me." He paused. "I mean, you will, but you *won't*. Because I won't let you. Trust me to tell you. And until I do, assume we're green, okay? That's how I want it. That's how I want *you*. Fully loaded, okay?"

"Swear it. That you'll stop me if you need me to."

"You know I will," Tobias replied steadily. "And until I do, I'm yours, all right?"

Sullivan kissed him. He had to; he was half-convinced he'd suffocate if he didn't. The kiss was brutal from the outset, little more than teeth and naked demand, and Tobias submitted instantly, following where Sullivan led, his mouth soft and hot and open. Sullivan felt a wild stab of triumph in his gut—*mine*—and guided Tobias down across his thighs once more, his left hand tunneling into those pretty curls, his right stroking along the bottom curve of one cheek. "If you do like this, we're going to

end up doing it a lot," he said, his voice far calmer than
he felt. "I think you've got a secret bratty side to you."

"I do not," Tobias protested indignantly.

"Quiet," Sullivan snapped, and spanked him. And this
time, he *really* spanked him.

Tobias's whole body seized, his hands tightening into
fists. The skin of his ass flooded cherry red under the
blow. That one would leave a mark, and that was... Fuck,
that felt good.

"God," Tobias whispered.

Sullivan hit him again, hard enough that his palm
stung riotously. "I said *quiet*."

Tobias's body abruptly went liquid. He turned his face
on the duvet, his features somnolent, his eyes half-closed.
His lips were pink and parted, his breath quick. He liked
it. He *liked* it.

Sullivan let go.


"Will you do it again? You said you would. Please?"
Tobias asked later in the dark, his words still soft and
slurred around the edges from coming.

"As much as you want, sweetheart." Sullivan tugged
him closer, pulled the covers up higher. There was a cool
breeze coming in through the open window, and he didn't
want Tobias to catch a chill. "As far as I'm concerned, if
you like the idea of never being able to sit down again,
we can make that happen."

"Good. You hurt me so good." Tobias laughed softly, a
thick, heavy, happy sound, and Sullivan had to swallow,
had to press kisses against his forehead and cheeks, had
to blink hard. Tobias was the one with tiny pink welts
decorating his ass and thighs, but Sullivan, somehow,
was the one who felt deeply, dangerously defenseless.

## Chapter Seventeen

It didn't hurt.

Tobias peered over his shoulder at his own ass in the small pocket of fogless mirror he'd wiped the condensation from. There were no bruises. His butt bore two barely raised welts, but they didn't hurt. Not unless he pressed hard. As much as it had hurt at the time—and it had, gloriously—the spanking hadn't left any serious marks.

For a second he wondered at the faint sliver of disappointment that the thought raised. He thought maybe he wanted the marks, perhaps more than Sullivan did—Sullivan, who had looked at those small welts in the shower a little bit ago as if he didn't quite know what to make of them. Sullivan, who'd had this dopey happiness radiating from him ever since he'd woken up.

He'd touched the welts with fingers light as feathers, and Tobias had shivered, thinking of how much his cheeks had been burning the night before as Sullivan rubbed off on him, his cock hard against Tobias's sore cheeks, the movement of his hips lighting up those sensitive nerves with every thrust.

But it didn't hurt now. And the marks would fade soon, maybe by nightfall.

Tobias wanted to find Ghost, he did. Maybe he was

using Sullivan, using this ridiculously good sex to distract himself from all the questions about his friend—where he was, what he was doing. Once he let the topic of Ghost's circumstances take priority in his mind, it became difficult to think about anything else.

But a small, ashamed part of him was grateful that it was taking so long. That part of him wanted to spend the day teasing Sullivan, stealing ground an inch at a time with the sort of comments that Sullivan would term bratty, until Sullivan got that look on his face, that hard, uncompromising look that he'd had last night once they'd finally gotten him past his nerves. When Sullivan looked at him like that, Tobias knew that nothing less than total submission would save him. He knew he could push as much as he wanted, and Sullivan would only push back harder, forcing Tobias down, forcing him still, forcing him into that blissful quiet where all the noise in his head vanished.

When Sullivan had finally shifted Tobias off his lap to lie on his belly on the bed, even with his ass on fire, Tobias had thought *don't stop yet*.

He'd wanted more. The sex had been brilliant, as always, but he'd known, at that moment, that nothing Sullivan could want from him was going to make him say no, not on this front, anyway. He couldn't imagine a scenario where he would want to. The thing was, he was starting to think he was addicted to that little itch under his skin that told him to say yes where he would've said no only a few months ago. He wanted more things to say yes to, wanted to test those boundaries further, whether that meant choosing a new career or letting Sullivan turn his ass red. He got to decide. It was his choice, and he wasn't going to apologize for any of it.

\* \* \*

That morning a balding man pulled up to Cindy Jackman's house in a battered truck and trundled out of the cab wearing faded jeans, a plaid shirt with the sleeves rolled up, and a sweat-stained John Deere cap.

"That's him." Tobias grabbed Sullivan's arm, comparing the pic from the security camera video to the man across the street, wishing the quality was better. It was happening. After what felt like countless hours, here was the break. "Isn't it?"

"Just like that, buddy," Sullivan muttered, his fancy camera already clicking. "Look right over here."

The man knocked on the front door. Cindy Jackman answered, throwing her arms around him in welcome. He hugged her back, patting her on the bottom.

"An ex, you think?" Sullivan said. "I'd bet a million dollars it was 'mutual' but it was actually her decision. She's out of his league."

"He's built the same as the guy in the video."

Sullivan made a thoughtful humming sound.

Tempted to poke him in order to prod a more excited reaction, Tobias added, "Same height."

Sullivan lifted an eyebrow. "Let's see the picture." They stared together, darting glances back and forth between the grainy page and the man on the porch now brushing a dark lock of Cindy's hair behind her ear.

"It's him," Tobias said. "That's the guy who took Ghost."

"If it isn't, it's a hell of a coincidence."

The balding man went inside, but was back outside in fifteen minutes, getting not into his truck this time, but into Cindy Jackman's beige sedan. Sullivan started the Buick.

Tobias didn't know much about how to follow some-one, but after the long week of stakeouts, he figured Sullivan was more than competent. He always kept two cars between them when he could, and seemed to have a sort of sixth sense for when to hang back before yellow lights and when to assume the balding man would demonstrate a lead foot. All the same, Tobias wanted to tell Sullivan to go faster, to make something happen. He knew it was counter-productive, but he couldn't help it.

The balding man stopped in front of a brick-red ranch house, and was knee deep in four shouting kids by the time Sullivan had found a place to park. A woman stood on the stoop, a backpack dangling from one hand; she held it out for the man to take, then produced a car seat from behind her, which she shoved into his arms as well before disappearing back inside, shutting the door firmly enough behind her that the kids fell silent for a beat. Then they went back to swarming the man—their father, Tobias figured, and a fairly absent one at that, judging from their near-panicked devotion. All of the children were talking at once and the balding man nodded and listened as he carried the backpack and car seat to the sedan, where he spent several long minutes getting everyone situated.

"That explains why he switched vehicles," Tobias said. "Can't take four kids in a truck. He must've picked Ghost up either right before or right after he hung out with his kids."

"So Cindy got in the middle of the marriage but didn't stick around to be the new mommy," Sullivan mused. He'd already started taking more pictures. "Write down that address, will you?"

"Yeah." Tobias grabbed the notepad, thinking about what Sullivan had said. "That's very cynical. She could

be a friend who doesn't mind lending him her car so he
can have his kids for the day."

"Could be. Isn't, though."

"You don't know that. You don't know he cheated on
his wife."

"Yeah, I do. See how mad she was? Even now, after
it's final? World's full of deadbeats."

Tobias eyed him. Sullivan didn't look upset or angry;
if anything, he was far too calm, sitting there cracking
his knuckles with his hair hanging in his eyes, espousing
a bitter belief system that Tobias rejected on principle.
Before he got a chance to argue, the balding man got behind the wheel of the beige sedan.

"He's leaving," Tobias said. There was a low pulse of
excitement in his stomach. He doubted the balding man
would be taking his kids to wherever he'd taken Ghost,
but later, eventually, it was going to happen. They were
getting closer. "Come on, let's go. Hurry."

"Don't get ahead of yourself," Sullivan said, and put
the car in gear.

"No, I can feel it." Tobias leaned forward, wishing he
could will the clunky Buick to move faster. "We're finally moving."

"Not gonna lie, this is not what I expected," Sullivan said.

Tobias had to agree.

They were standing on the cement path between the
two main lakes in City Park, watching the nearby hub-
bub of picnickers on the grass. Wooden tables with paper
tablecloths littered the area in front of a low stage with a
podium, and there were people clustered in small groups
eating and drinking, the men in T-shirts and jeans, the
women in shorts, the kids shrieking and running around.

The faint odor of animals drifted on the inconstant warm breeze from the zoo, which lay at the northeast boundary of the park; stronger was the damp duck smell from the green water nearby. Geese were honking in the distance. Strung above the small stage was a big banner which read, in black letters, *Congrats to Chief Spratt!* Below that, in smaller, red type, was the slogan *And Justice for All!* At the end of the banner was the logo of the Denver Police Department.

Which made sense, because for every person in street clothes, there were two in uniform.

"Wow, that is a lot of cops," Sullivan murmured.

"Are we crashing a government picnic?" Tobias asked, his heart pounding enjoyably. "I've never crashed anything before. We should definitely go in." He started forward and Sullivan caught his arm.

"Hold on, Kamikaze, let's think about this for a minute."

"What's to think about?" He tugged his arm free. "There's like, two hundred people here. No one's going to know we shouldn't be here. Assuming it isn't come one come all."

"I'm not worried about getting caught crashing. I'm worried about who we might run into."

"You mean a Krayev?" Tobias asked doubtfully. "Considering how many cops are here, I find that unlikely."

"No, I—"

"Even if we get busted, what are they going to do? Shoot us? They're *cops*. We're not going to get hurt." He started walking again.

And again, Sullivan caught him. "Tobias, so help me, if you don't slow down and—"

He jerked away hard enough this time to make his shoulder twinge. "God, Sullivan, we've been sitting still for so long and we finally have something and you want to stand here some more?"

"That's not what I'm trying to—" He broke off, the muscle in his jaw working. "You know what? Go sit in the car."

Tobias could only sputter for a second as betrayal, hot and choking, rose inside him. "Excuse me? Are you joking? No. *No.* I'm not—I am not getting sent to the car like a damn—"

"Yes, you are. I don't have the time or inclination to argue with you about this. Just do as you're told and wait—"

"The hell I am." Tobias didn't sound like himself. He sounded angry, maybe mean, and he liked it. He liked it a lot, and Sullivan was out of luck if he thought he could muzzle Tobias now. Sure, they played at the submission game when it was convenient, but this wasn't sex, and Tobias wasn't waiting anymore. Sullivan had said he wanted Tobias to be honest. Now he could reap what he'd sown.

Tobias said it again. "No."

He took off across the path, ignoring the way Sullivan cursed and said his name, walking quickly enough to shake off the hand that Sullivan almost managed to catch him with, and then he was on the grass, losing himself in the group of attendees. He didn't slow down, wedging his way through the crowd well enough that when he glanced back, he didn't see Sullivan anywhere.

Good. He'd catch up eventually, of course, because he wasn't incompetent, but Tobias was deep in the thick of the picnic now, and Sullivan wouldn't make a scene, wouldn't want to risk attracting attention.

The speakers gave a cry of feedback, and a woman at the podium began talking about the state of justice in Denver. Tobias tuned her out for the most part, concentrating on winding his way through the attentive crowd and looking for the balding man.

As he got closer to the stage, he saw more people in suits and dresses, their jewelry and watches more expensive, the average age increasing sharply. There were more cops, many in patrol uniforms, a bunch in business casual with badges pinned to their waistbands. There weren't as many kids, either, which was part of the reason that the four children making a minor ruckus and drawing annoyed glances from the adults nearby stuck out. Tobias surveyed the nearest faces, and found the balding man talking with a strikingly red-haired man in his fifties, sour-faced with small brown eyes and ruddy cheeks.

Neither of them spared the children or the annoyed attendees a second's attention.

The woman wrapped up her speech with a loud and enthusiastic, "So let's give a warm welcome to the man who will be taking over the job, Benjamin Spratt!"

There was loud applause, and she stood back, clapping as the man who must be Spratt walked on stage. He was tall and slim, elegant in his charcoal-gray suit, his salt-and-pepper hair handsomely styled, his thin face a pleasant mixture of noble decency and stern, hard-eyed strength. He looked like a cop should look, Tobias decided.

He listened to enough of Spratt's speech to catch on that he was talking about updating the police department and helping the community. Tobias went back to watching the balding man hiss something into the ear of the redheaded man.

When the speech ended, Tobias circled around, trying to edge closer to the foot of the stage, where the balding man and redheaded man were still talking in low voices. By the time he got within hearing range, they'd been joined by Spratt himself, smiling and nodding as people passed. He'd been given a flute of champagne at some point, and one long finger tapped at the glass as the balding man muttered at him.

Tobias eased around a clutch of attendees, coming at Spratt and the two unnamed men from behind. There were fewer people standing on this side, fewer voices to try to hear past.

"—the bitch knew we were coming...had the middle one there already...and the big fucker...by surprise..."

Tobias grimaced. He wasn't close enough to get all of it. He took a couple of steps closer. He was exposed now; if one of them turned, they'd see him head-on, but it was easier to hear from this spot, at least.

Spratt said, "Was the mysterious Kellen there?"

Tobias frowned. Kellen. He knew that name. From... he couldn't remember, but he *knew* it.

The balding man replied, "No, we only saw the others."

"Pity." Spratt shifted, nodding to one attendee, then extending a hand to another for a brief shake.

The balding man said something else, more softly now that others were closer, and Tobias eased another step closer. He wanted to hear more about Kellen, wanted something to jog his memory of how he'd heard—

"And the boy? Any progress there?" the balding man asked.

"It's a matter of time," Spratt said.

"Assuming he doesn't act up anymore." The balding man squinted at the sun as if its glare was purposely designed to afflict him. "Assuming he can trust a guy doing what you're doing."

"A caged animal is a safe animal," Spratt said, and Tobias thought *Ghost*.

A hand clenched on Tobias's elbow all of a sudden, and then Sullivan was edging in front of him, planting himself between Tobias and Spratt's circle, his back to them.

Tobias tried to shrug him off. He needed to *hear*.

Sullivan leaned in and hissed, "If you don't come with me right now and without a fuss, we are fucking done. Deal off, case over."

Tobias jolted, stung. Sullivan's expression matched his words, and Tobias swallowed his own anger, allowing himself to be prodded back toward the car after one last, lingering glance at Spratt.

"Not a word," Sullivan said when they were in. "Not one damn word until we get back to my place."

Tobias complied, but only because he had some things of his own to say, and he didn't want to get noticed yelling at Sullivan any more than Sullivan wanted to be noticed yelling at him. Tobias didn't like yelling as a rule, but the itch under his skin was becoming downright painful, and he thought he could manage a yell very nicely at the moment, thank you very much.

For the next hour, Sullivan took photos and wrote down tag numbers for the cars in the lot. Tobias took out his phone and texted Church: who is Kellen? Why do I know that name?

A minute later, he received a handful of texts in rapid succession: fuck that dude works for mama when vasily and his brothers beat me up i guess kellen was the one who stepped in to stop it for mama.

And: even vasily jumped when keelen said to.

And: *Kellen* fuck i never saw him but he must be a scary bastard to make vasily nervous.

And: are you being careful fuck man you better be careful.

Wrapping up with: should i come over where are you.

Tobias sent back: I'll fill you in soon. And don't worry. I've got it all under control.

They didn't make it into the house before Tobias's temper broke.

"Wait in the car." Tobias slammed the car door behind him. "That's what you said to me. Wait in the car. Like I'm a child or your...your *slave* or something. But getting on my knees for you in the bedroom doesn't mean I owe you obedience at any other time."

"The fuck you don't. Three rules, remember?" Sullivan countered, lifting the heavy, sagging gate so he could give them room to pass. Tobias refused to appreciate the way the muscles in his back worked under his T-shirt in the process. "Do as I say in the field. Obey when it matters because I might not have time to explain and you might fuck up my case out of sheer ignorance and stubbornness. It's not about slavery, you ass, it's about knowing what the hell you're doing and being able to follow when you don't. You promised, remember?"

"I thought you meant if we were getting shot at or something like that." Tobias followed him into the house, slamming that door too. "This wasn't like that. They were talking about Ghost, Sullivan. They called him a caged animal. That guy, Spratt, who gave the speech? He knows where Ghost is. It was important, and it wasn't even dangerous. We were *finally* getting somewhere and you wouldn't—"

"Not dangerous? You sure about that?" Sullivan stopped in the living room, yanked open the camera bag, and turned on the Mark III. With a sharp flick of his thumb, he flipped through the pictures he'd taken, then showed the screen to Tobias. There was a shot of the redheaded man who'd been speaking to the balding guy and Spratt. "Do you know who that is?"

"No," Tobias said stiffly, because he could sense where this was going.

"I do." Sullivan set the camera down with such careful restraint that Tobias got the distinct impression he'd been tempted to throw it. "That's my fucking client."

"What?"

"Yeah. My client, who has been searching for a missing girl since 1992, who claimed to be an insurance adjuster, who apparently hangs out with a bunch of cops. Why didn't he go to his cop friends for help, do you think? Guess he didn't need to, what with that badge there on his belt. But why does a cop go to a private detective? Why does he lie about his job? And his name?"

Tobias's throat had shrunk. It took more effort than it should've to swallow. "I—I didn't know."

"Of course you didn't know. You were too busy going off half-cocked. Look, I get that you're having a nice time with the rebellion and all, but my case is not the fucking place or time for you to indulge it by losing fifty damn IQ points. I couldn't give a rat's ass what you do when our safety's not on the line, but if we're in the field and I tell you to do something, you're gonna fucking do it. Clear?"

"Clear." Tobias couldn't think past the panic bubbling in his veins. What if the client—the redheaded man— had seen Sullivan? Why would a cop lie about who he was? Why would he go outside the department to track someone down? What if he knew the private detective he'd hired to find a missing girl had somehow traced it back to him?

There was only one answer to the first two questions

that he could think of—the cop was dirty. And that made the potential answers to the third question much more frightening.

Tobias had put everything at risk with his impulsive, reckless decision. He'd put Ghost at risk, because the balding man knew where Ghost was, Spratt knew where Ghost was, which meant the redheaded man probably did too.

God, he couldn't think. It was all too confusing. None of it made sense. All he knew was that Ghost was involved in something that included not just the Krayevs but dirty cops.

And he'd put Sullivan and Ghost in danger.

"H-he almost saw you," Tobias stammered. "God, I'm sorry."

"Yeah, I'd hope so," Sullivan said, but his anger seemed to have shrunk; he sounded mostly frustrated and tired. He reached out with one hand, but Tobias flinched back. He wasn't sure why, because he wanted Sullivan to touch him. He didn't want Sullivan to feel rejected, either—it had only been last night that he'd taken that step of trusting Tobias enough to try the spanking thing, and was probably still feeling insecure about it, and having your... your...whatever Tobias was, having that person flinch from your touch couldn't feel good, but Tobias couldn't help it. He was jerking back before he had time to realize it was happening, and then his phone rang.

He took his phone out with numb, automatic fingers and answered.

"Now? Really? Nah, that's great, answer your phone," Sullivan was muttering, but Tobias's attention—what he was capable of producing at the moment, anyway—shifted immediately to the voice on the other end of the line.

"I just finished speaking with Clint Hammel," his father said, skipping *hello* entirely.

"Papa," Tobias managed. He should say that it wasn't a good time, but Papa was iron in his ear with that one sentence. What could he do against iron? What should he do? Why couldn't he think?

"Do you know what he told me? He told me you'd missed the appointment I set up for you."

What appointment? Tobias couldn't—

"He'd moved his schedule around for you, Tobias. For me. As not only a courtesy, but as the act of a colleague and friend whose opinion of me matters a great deal."

*I didn't have an appointment. Did I?*

"You couldn't even call him? You didn't—" Papa broke off, exhaling as if he were trying to stay calm. "I understand that you're upset, son, but this is… I wouldn't have expected you to do something like this. To undermine my professional relationship with someone so thoughtlessly? I…what am I supposed to think of this? Are you striking out? Did you do it to hurt me?"

"I don't— What appointment?"

"You don't remember?" There was a small, sharp laugh. "This is extremely unproductive behavior. This is an attack, both on my relationship with a colleague and on yours and mine as well, but never mind that. You've torpedoed a sterling opportunity for yourself. Do you know what an internship with Clint Hammel could do for your application to medical school? I'm at a loss to understand how you could be so careless with your future."

"What internship?" Tobias managed.

"The one that Clint Hammel was going to offer you at the meeting I set up for you," Papa snapped, the words vibrating right on that fine line that demarcated speech from yelling.

The itch was there, under his skin, making him fit so badly into the space he occupied, and Tobias said, "I didn't ask you to do that."

"You didn't have to. This is what fathers do for their sons, and you've thrown it in my face. I don't know where this anger is coming from."

"Don't you?" Tobias bit his lip so hard it bled. He couldn't say—he shouldn't...that itch was dangerous, it made him reckless and stupid, like it had at the picnic. It made him hurt people, people he loved and needed—

Papa sighed. "We wanted only to protect you. That creature who gave birth to you did an abominable thing. Of course we couldn't allow her contact with a child."

"I don't have a problem with that. I have a problem with you not allowing her contact with an adult." He closed his eyes. *Stop it*, he told himself. *Stop talking.* The itch didn't listen. He'd let everything out, and now nothing would go back where it belonged. "And I didn't know about the appointment. I didn't ask for it. You can't be mad at me for not showing up when I didn't know."

"I sent you the email. As I have whenever I've set up meetings for you in the past. How am I to know that you've—"

"My student email." Of course. Tobias had been checking it only infrequently since the blowup with his parents and he'd begun skipping class. He hadn't checked it once in the last week. "I didn't know—I didn't look."

"You're—you're not checking your email now? I—I am *bewildered* by this behavior. You've completely... I think you should see Dr. Thornton."

Tobias laughed, but it was a shocked, choked laugh. "What? I'm not—I'm not depressed, Papa. I'm—"

The itch wanted him to say *I'm finally living*, but the part of him that'd screwed up this morning told him to keep his mouth shut.

"You're behaving erratically. You should come home. I'll set up an appointment with Dr. Thornton. We can get you a new prescription, and—"

"No!" Tobias shouted, making Sullivan jump where he stood halfway across the room, leaning against the table and shamelessly eavesdropping. "I'm not sick! The problem is not that I'm sick again. It's that you're not listening. You don't *listen*, and then you're shocked when I resent you for it. I don't—*Bondye*, it's—I don't know how to talk to you, because no matter what I say, you don't care. You just…you try to wrap me back up in this box that I don't want to live in."

"You will not speak to me like this—"

"I dropped out of school! I dropped out. I'm not going to medical school. I'm not coming home. I'm not sick. I'm just tired of putting everything I want last, and it's been fucking me up for years and I'm not doing it anymore, do you hear me? I'm not—"

There was no sound in his ear. No sound at all. Tobias pulled the phone away and the screen was flashing numbers—*7:04*, the duration of the call.

Because his father had hung up.

"God," Tobias whispered. "Oh, God, what did I do?"

"You stood up to him," Sullivan said, gently prying the phone out of his clenched hand. "In a fairly destructive manner, yeah, but I'll bet it got the job well and truly done. So good work there, I guess. Breathe."

"I can't. God, I can't breathe."

"Well, you are, since you're talking, but I meant something deeper and slower. You're going to hyperventilate if you don't get it together."

"I'm sorry. I'm so sorry. I could've gotten you killed today."

"Breathe, Tobias."

"I can't. I don't—I can't."

Sullivan clamped a hand over his mouth, forcing him to breathe through his nose, and that helped a little, since no one could hyperventilate through their nose as easily. When he'd gotten some breath back, Sullivan peeled his hand away and kissed his forehead, but Tobias had almost gotten Sullivan and Ghost hurt, and damaged the case, and he—that phone call—God, what had he done?

He jerked back.

Sullivan's brow was creased, his gaze concerned, and Tobias didn't deserve any of it. "Don't do that. Don't—you can't."

"It's going to be all right," Sullivan said. "Maybe it feels like the end of the world right now, but it isn't."

Sullivan's voice had lost that diamond edge. It was soft and easy as cotton balls now, and it was too late. It made Tobias sick, because he hadn't earned it. Sullivan had been mad, he'd had good reason to be mad, and Tobias hadn't paid for it yet. His heart rate kept climbing. His pulse had gone loose and thin in his chest. He became aware that Sullivan was prodding him gently to the sofa.

"I think I might be sick." Which wasn't exactly true—or at least not physically. But he felt that same terrible, shaky feeling that came with being sick, that sensation of being utterly out of control and unable to stop a process that was already well underway.

Sullivan crouched in front of him and stroked a thumb

along the side of his face. Tobias slapped his hand away without thinking.

Sullivan sat back, his face going blank. "Sorry."

"Don't apologize," Tobias snapped, because that careful expression made him want to kick something. Tobias was the one who was a mess, the one who couldn't decide if he was furious or a horrible person, the one who kept saying and doing things that were wrecking everything, and now Sullivan was just *taking* it, just letting Tobias be a *dick*.

That pissed him off maybe more than anything else. "Don't do that. Don't be soft like that."

Sullivan's eyes narrowed. "You want some time alone? Want me out of your hair?"

Tobias lunged forward, his hand flashing out to catch Sullivan's sleeve. "Don't, don't—I, no—that's not—"

"Okay, okay, easy, I'm not going anywhere if you don't tell me to."

Again with that soft voice. What was Tobias supposed to do with that? He still wasn't thinking, clearly, because now he was reaching out and shoving Sullivan.

Not hard, barely enough to rock him. He wasn't trying to hurt Sullivan. He wasn't trying to do anything except get Sullivan to stop taking it, to stop letting Tobias treat him like this, to stop Tobias cold.

Please, God, let Sullivan be able to stop this.

Yeah, Sullivan had seen this coming from a mile away.

Tobias was a hot mess right now, and everything in his life was falling apart, and he needed an outlet. Everyone did, from time to time. Some people worked out, some people drank, some people played golf. Tobias had ad-

mitted to stress baking, but Sullivan suspected that soft
little hobby wasn't going to cut it here.

No, what Tobias needed was a complete disengagement.
An escape into a calmer headspace. No decisions, no responsibilities, no ambiguities. Just an expectation of obedience and a clear system of punishment or reward depending
on whether that expectation was met. Sullivan would've expected Tobias to prefer a reward-based system until roughly
thirty seconds ago, because liking pain wasn't the same
thing as wanting to be taken down hard, but that shove,
combined with the *don't leave*, was a pretty blatant signal.

Sullivan had never met a sub who'd fought back like
this when they didn't want it. They safe-worded or they
left. The broken ones, the ones who'd been abused, they
just buckled. The only ones who fought, who said *don't
leave* but picked a fight, they wanted to be reassured
that the world had rules and that there was safety within
them. The only way to trust those rules was to be made
to conform to them. They wanted the punishment because it meant order existed.

In the past, a nasty takedown wouldn't have fazed Sullivan. He had to be in the mood, but he didn't mind a sub
who needed something a little more violent to go under.
He didn't have a weak stomach for that sort of thing generally, but he'd only ever gone there with subs he knew
well, subs who weren't in the middle of a major personal
crisis. And it'd been well before Nick.

He'd had a little more confidence about his ability to
handle the cruelty back then.

Every line of Tobias's body was confrontational. His
hands were in fists at his sides.

"Do you have the first clue what you're asking me
for?" Sullivan asked.

Tobias shoved him again, harder than before, but still nothing to write home about. He meant to provoke, not harm, and the urge to push back, to push harder, flooded through Sullivan's whole body. He exhaled slowly.

He was already getting hard.

"You don't know how ugly this sort of thing can get," Sullivan warned him. "If there's a kind of scene that's more prone to going wrong, it's one like this. The fun scenes where you push and we both think it's a little funny that you're being naughty, that's one thing. I don't know how I feel about this, to be honest—"

Tobias shoved him a third time, hard enough that he had to take a step to keep his balance, and Sullivan knocked his hands away, grabbing him by the jaw and shoving him back. Then he kept shoving, even as Tobias stumbled, all the way until Tobias hit the wall with enough force to lose his breath.

"You do that again, and you aren't going to like what happens next," Sullivan said, and had the pleasure of watching Tobias's eyes go hazy. "I'm not saying I won't fuck you up, because I will, if that's what you want, I'll tear you into tiny pieces, but not until we talk about this, so slow your roll and keep your hands at your sides until I tell you that you can move."

He could see it in Tobias's expression, that he was tempted to rebel further, so he tightened his grip on Tobias's jaw so hard that Tobias winced.

"We are talking about this," Sullivan said. "That is nonnegotiable. You will say either *don't you dare* or *you can try.*"

Tobias mouthed the words, learning them, brow furrowing.

"I'm going to restrain you however I want. You'll be

exposed and humiliated and available to be used however I want."

Understanding snapped into place in those big blue eyes, and challenge dripped from every word as he snapped, "You can try."

"I'm going to hurt you badly. I'm going to take a paddle to your ass until you beg me to stop, and I still won't. I'm going to make you cry."

Tobias's lips curved into a furious, almost wild smile. "You can try."

"I'm going to fuck you until you can't do anything but take it."

"You can try."

"I'm going to be so sweet to you—"

"Don't you dare patronize me, you fucking—"

Sullivan squeezed Tobias's jaw until he writhed, a low pain noise coming from his mouth. Sullivan spoke over that sound even as it made him harder. "Yeah, that's what I figured."

After, then. There'd be room for sweetness when Tobias had gotten this out of his system and he could let himself grieve and refortify for whatever consequences his choices had stuck him with. Then Tobias would be receptive, probably in need of comfort and support, and in all honesty, if this got as rough as he was expecting it to, Sullivan might be in need of some, too, so yeah, he could see a lot of cuddling in their future.

But first he needed to fuck Tobias up. And then just fuck him.

His jaw ached.

Long after Sullivan released his face in order to take his arm and drag him up the stairs, the bone throbbed, and Tobias focused on that as he struggled, as he made Sullivan work for it. He made Sullivan put his back into it all the way down the hall into the bedroom, where Sullivan threw him bodily onto the bed. By the time the world righted, Sullivan was pulling a trunk out of the closet and shoving the lid open. Tobias slid off the bed slowly, wondering what Sullivan would do if he ran for it. He thought Sullivan would come after him and haul him back, but he wasn't entirely sure, so he stayed put.

He didn't want to get away.

Sullivan pulled out a mess of black leather and silver chain, tossing it on the bed, then took off his T-shirt. His tattoos stood out stark against his skin in the afternoon sunlight coming through the window, and his face was rigid with aggression. He was visibly hard in his jeans, and Tobias wanted to touch him. He wanted to lick him and touch him and fight.

"List the colors," Sullivan ordered.

Tobias didn't—God, he didn't want all of this crap. These limits—they were the opposite of what he wanted. But he could see from Sullivan's expression that he wasn't getting around this one, so he said through his teeth, "Green means I want more, yellow means I'm close to my limit, and red means stop now."

"Good. You can throw as much of a temper tantrum as you like, but if you try to kick me, you won't like the consequences."

"I'm not throwing a tantrum." He watched as Sullivan turned the mass of leather into two wrist cuffs with silver buckles and a short chain.

"Turn around," Sullivan said.

"No."

"If I have to make you, you aren't coming tonight."

Tobias's breath caught. He—he was so angry already, and the idea of having to go along with it chafed, but his blood was on fire. He turned around.

Sullivan wrapped a cuff around each of Tobias's wrists, then used the chain to bind the cuffs together at the small of his back. He gave it a few seconds before touching Tobias's fingers. "How's that feel? No numbness or tingling or anything?"

"Are you going to pull this babysitting crap all night?"

"I'm going to do whatever the fuck I feel like." Sullivan went back to the trunk and this time came up with a piece of wood roughly the size and shape of a large, square hairbrush, albeit without the bristles. A dozen holes had been drilled into it except on the narrow strip that would function as a handle.

A paddle.

He tossed the paddle onto the mattress, and sat down on the bed, perched on the edge as he had the night before. Nothing else was the same though, not the hum in the air or the way Sullivan wrenched Tobias down and over his legs. It wasn't a comfortable position by any stretch—he felt a bit like he might fall, at least until Sullivan's left hand wrapped around his wrist, centering him.

"Spread your legs," Sullivan ordered, using one foot to nudge at his calves, leaving Tobias both more exposed and more stable with the wider stance.

Sullivan spanked him with his bare hand. Once, twice, three times. The blows kept coming, and Tobias's frustration grew. His chest tightened. His urge to sit up and quit the whole process became impossible to ignore. His head was heavy and he was just—he didn't like it. It didn't feel like last night, when it'd been fun and he hadn't been thinking, hadn't felt on the verge of shattering. He didn't like it at all and now he was mad at Sullivan for not making this work on top of everything else. He didn't want to do it like this—no, he didn't want to do any of this *at all*, didn't want to be on his belly like this, like some low, subservient thing, spanked like a child, like he couldn't manage his own adulthood, his own life or choices. His whole body vibrated with unspoken denial and the blows *kept coming*, stoking the fire and it hurt, it just hurt, there was nothing arousing or fun or dirty about it, he wanted to yell and fight and…and…

"For a sub on the verge of throwing a fit, you're pretty fucking hard," Sullivan said, sounding calm and amused and so smug, and Tobias had somehow, weirdly, sort of forgotten that Sullivan was there, that he was the one committing these spanks. This wasn't something that was happening to him, this was something that Sullivan was *doing* to him, that Tobias had asked for, if not in so many words. Tobias was suddenly aware of two competing realities, realities that somehow existed at the same time without contradicting each other. First, he was aware that Sullivan wasn't wrong—he *was* about to throw a fit, and he *was* very hard. Painfully hard, which struck him as odd because he didn't feel turned on in any other way. The second reality was that Sullivan was also fundamentally wrong, because in that moment Tobias didn't feel submissive at all; he was livid and edged and feeling every bit of his own power and he wanted to smash all of that anger and power directly into Sullivan's face.

*Make me*, he wanted to shout, not caring that it was a complete non-sequitur. *Just try and make me.*

"Oh, I will," Sullivan said, low and unafraid and firm, and Tobias realized he'd actually said the words, actually *yelled* them. He'd refused, he'd raised his voice, and

Sullivan… Sullivan wasn't backing down. He wasn't letting Tobias go.

He hit Tobias again, harder, and Tobias yelled again, louder. No words this time, just fury. He couldn't stay still, kept yanking at the cuffs, kept shouting, kept thinking that he wouldn't yield, he wouldn't submit, not this time, not ever, that he hated this, hated every moment of it, hated his whole life and everyone in it, and he'd never wanted to destroy anything so much as he wanted to destroy the world right then.

"Color," Sullivan said grimly, and Tobias wanted to laugh, wanted to say *fuck you*, and *you can't make me* and *stop it right now*—

And his mouth opened and said, "Green."

"I thought so," Sullivan muttered, and the spanks paused for a heartbeat, a stutter of a heartbeat, long enough for all of Tobias's loaded fury to pause, shocked at his answer, because he'd meant to say "red," and then another blow landed, different and louder and impossibly, brilliantly painful. The paddle. It lit up every nerve from head to toe, and he howled at the bright, crimson burn.

"Fuck you," he gasped, and Sullivan laughed. He *laughed*, the bastard, and the paddle fell again and again, moving to his thighs now, and the blows weren't as hard there, not nearly, but it didn't take as much to register the same level of pain in that place, and he coughed out a furious sob. It was electricity and fire and burning, and it didn't stop, wouldn't stop.

He was dimly aware of Sullivan saying, "Color," and of his own voice saying, "Green."

But seconds or ages later, he was pulled out of it by the sensation of fingers in his hair. "What…" he mumbled. "What…"

"Breathe, sweetheart." Sullivan didn't sound angry. "Come on. Take a breath for me."

Tobias did, and only then did the lightheadedness start to dissipate. He hadn't realized he'd been holding his breath, and Sullivan stayed beside him, rubbing his back and saying over and over, "Breathe. That's it. Keep going."

"I can't," Tobias whispered, and he didn't mean the paddle, although that wasn't inconsiderable. He meant that yawning, terrible feeling from downstairs that had backed off briefly with Sullivan here beside him, but which hovered in the distance. It wasn't gone. "I can't."

"You can."

"No more." He might've been crying. The part of him that had watched a lot of TV and movies told him that crying during sex was bad, but it didn't feel bad to him. And it was sex, somehow. He was still hard. Hard to the point of dripping. He was pretty sure he'd been rubbing against the bed.

"You can take a lot more than this," Sullivan said, not unkindly. "And you will."

"Sullivan, please."

"Color?"

Tobias sobbed once. "Green. God, green."

"Take a breath."

Tobias did.

"Another."

He did that too. Sullivan leveraged him to his feet, then pushed him down on the mattress on his belly, easing his feet wide so that he was exposed.

"Between every blow, take a breath. Think of each blow as the first. Don't tense up. Your mind will follow your body, so try to keep your body relaxed."

Tobias sucked in another breath and another, and when he'd met some unknown criteria, Sullivan nodded his satisfaction and stepped back. Tobias knew what was coming, knew that he had to brace for it, but Sullivan had said not to. Sullivan had said *breathe* and *don't tense up*.

He obeyed, and Sullivan hit him again.

It hurt. No amount of breathing could possibly take the pain away. But the brilliant agony stayed in his body, didn't touch his mind. It hurt good, in a way that went beyond words. He'd never be able to explain why. It simply was. Sullivan was hurting him and Tobias liked it. His legs were spread wide open and he was exposed and humiliated, and he liked it.

That nervy urge to comply that he'd known every other time they had sex was finally building. All he had to do was breathe and be here. Sullivan would handle the rest. Sullivan was strong, Sullivan was in charge. Tobias could go away for a while, and Sullivan would take care of him. Tobias put his head down, breathed, and submitted.

He had no idea how much time went by. He only knew that sweet, perfect quiet, that warm, bubbling happiness brewing behind it.

At some point the pain hit a sharper note and Tobias felt a tiny tendril of worry in the quiet. Without thinking, he mumbled, "Yellow."

Sullivan stopped. "Good," he murmured. "That's it. Good boy, Tobias. That's perfect. I'm so proud of you."

The praise slid into the quiet and he closed his eyes, shivering with the pleasure of it. He could sense Sullivan moving behind him, could feel hands on his body, on his ass, pulling his cheeks apart. The skin felt tight and swollen and sensitive to the gentlest touch.

"You like this?" Sullivan asked.

Tobias nodded. Wet fingers slid inside him, opening him up, and he was so relaxed that it seemed effortless for his body to obey.

"You're so good," Sullivan whispered. "Look at you, so soft for me, you're so good."

Tobias made a wordless noise of contentment, the feeling of being full starting to creep up on him. Sullivan's fingers rubbed that spot inside him that made him cry out into the duvet.

"That's it, sweetheart." Sullivan's other hand was stroking the tormented skin of his ass, the sensations immense and awful and wonderful all at once. "Give it up for me."

He was on the verge of coming, Tobias realized. He was rocking into the bed, dick dragging against the fabric, and he wanted nothing more than to have Sullivan closer for when he came, close enough to touch and hold on to.

"You!" he cried.

Sullivan's hands paused. "What about me?"

"Want you."

"You have me. I'm right here."

"No——" His mouth wouldn't work. Words seemed to take years to make it from his brain to his lips. "Want you. Here. Inside me."

"Tobias…"

"Fuck me," he managed, and that, *that* was what he wanted. "Please, please fuck me. Please?"

"All right," Sullivan soothed, pressing his forehead against Tobias's shoulder. "Shh, all right. Give me a moment. I'll be out of sight, but I'm not leaving you."

Tobias knew that on some level that he didn't question. Sullivan knew he didn't like being left, and Sullivan wouldn't leave. Tobias could be angry, he could shove and yell and curse at Sullivan, he could push back and be... be bad and mean and immature, and Sullivan wouldn't leave. Sullivan would listen and understand and when Tobias needed to push, Sullivan would push back and push harder, he'd double down and take Tobias in hand and break down any wall between them until Tobias was here and small and safe and quiet and—

And Sullivan *still* wouldn't leave.

Tobias buried his face in the bed, the fabric damp against his skin, and at the sound of Sullivan coming back, the crinkle of a condom wrapper being opened a second later, he said into the blankets, "Please, Sullivan," all over again.

"Shh, sweetheart. I'm here. I'll give you what you need." Sullivan's strong thighs pushed his own wider apart, and the head of his dick, hard and hot, pressed against his rim. "Anything you need."

Sullivan slid in on a single stroke, balls deep, coming to rest against Tobias's impossibly sore buttocks. He gave Tobias time to adjust to the thickness, and his eventual thrusts were slow, small rocking pulses of his hips. They drove his dick directly into Tobias's prostate, ground his pelvis against Tobias's burning skin, and it was excruciatingly good, the pleasure and pain mixing, warm and heady and filling him up. He couldn't move or think. He could only lie there, open and willing, and let Sullivan use him, trust Sullivan to take care of him in turn.

He felt Sullivan's fingers trembling against his skin, felt Sullivan's lips brush against his ear and shoulders and neck, heard Sullivan whisper his name in a shaking voice, and thought, *he feels it too.*

* * *

"You don't have to be what they want," Sullivan said, much, much later into the darkness. "You know that, don't you? You don't have to be what I want, either. There's nothing wrong with being what you want."

Tobias was cuddled up beside him, sleepy and spent and boneless. Even after the cooling gel applied to the welts on his ass and thighs and an hour of cuddling and *The Lion, The Witch, and The Wardrobe*, the world still felt muted and dull compared to where he'd been, in that silence where he didn't have to do anything or be anything. The whole world apart from Sullivan, that was, whose voice and hands and smell were the sun in the center of a cold universe.

"Isn't there?" Tobias asked, because he'd spent the past two weeks coming to that realization, but it'd gone so wrong today that he couldn't help doubting.

Sullivan's arm tightened around him. "No."

Tobias closed his eyes briefly at the certainty in that single word. "The last time I broke down like this was in high school. They sent me away. They sent me to Woodbury. I know why they're scared. This looks the same way to them."

"Maybe it does look the same," Sullivan said quietly. "But there's a difference between breaking down and breaking out. You can be happy without losing them. You just have to find the middle ground between getting your needs met and being a dick. You'll figure it out."

A car drove down the street, the headlamps casting orange boxes of light along the wall as it passed.

*I love you*, Tobias almost said, but he was so tired that he couldn't decide if he meant it for right now or for always. That itch was gone, and he was alone in his head for the first time in what seemed like months, and it'd been an emotional night. They'd known each other for two weeks. No one fell in love in only two weeks. Tomorrow the feeling might be gone, and then where would that leave Sullivan? So Tobias didn't say it.

But he wanted to.

*Part Two*

## Chapter Eighteen

If only the boy would fall into place, things would be
moving along nicely.

Benjamin Spratt drove past the gate and into the underground parking garage. He parked in one of his two
spots—the other he reserved for guests—and took the
stairs up to the street level. He exchanged pleasantries
when he caught his next-door neighbor leaving to walk
her prize show poodle. The animal didn't attempt to sniff
at his crotch or whine for treats as they spoke, which he
appreciated. He didn't mind pets when they were civi-
lized. A well-trained creature was a thing of beauty.

He let himself into his townhome and locked the door
behind him before resetting the alarm. He believed it was
important for the chief of the Denver Police—interim
now, but permanently in a matter of weeks—to live in
the heartbeat of the city. And you didn't get more Denver than Capitol Hill, which meant there was the occasional bout of crime as the rougher element mingled
with the wealthy.

Spratt didn't consider himself wealthy, despite the
gleaming hardwood floors, fireplace, high ceilings or
luxurious cream carpets. Those were perks, and unimportant ones at that. He enjoyed living well, both because

it suited his position in the community and because it was pleasant, but he didn't need any of these material possessions in order to feel powerful or accomplished.

Those feelings came from his work alone.

After setting his keys on the counter, he tilted his head to one side, listening.

The air was still. No hint of movement. No sound from the downstairs bedroom.

The boy would be hungry.

Spratt set about making dinner—a spinach and pear salad with a light vinaigrette, honey- and Dijon-seared salmon and roasted broccoli and turnips. He poured himself a glass of Riesling, and poured his guest some iced tea.

He would be thirsty, too. It'd been hours, unfortunately. Tidwell hadn't been able to stop by for his afternoon visit; some problem with his daughter at the dentist's.

Spratt hoped the boy hadn't pissed himself again. He grimaced at the idea and prepared the tray, using glass plate covers so the food wouldn't get cold. He carried the tray downstairs, where he set it on the small wooden armoire he'd moved to this spot for this very purpose. After unlocking the padlock, he pushed the door open carefully.

After the first altercation, he'd learned to be careful. The boy wasn't prone to fits of panic, but when he did lose emotional control, he was a formidable animal. That struggle had ended with both of them the worse for wear, and while there'd been no sign of hostility since, Spratt wasn't a stupid man.

But he needn't have bothered. The closet was closed and locked, the little silver key on its hook beside the jamb. He opened the door and immediately stepped back, prepared for violence, but the boy was as he'd been left—

sitting nude on the sheepskin pillow, hands cuffed above his head to the D ring set in the wall.

Ghost blinked in the sharp, sudden light pouring over Spratt's shoulder from the bedroom.

He was breathtaking. The boy brought to mind the 1665 painting *Girl with a Pearl Earring*, by the Dutch painter Vermeer. They didn't look much alike in shape or form, but it wasn't his youth or his looks, not the pale, perfect skin or the golden hair or the pale green eyes, like tender shoots of new grass, that sparked the comparison. No, what Ghost and the girl in the painting shared was a heartbreaking, wounded innocence, an awareness of their own vulnerability.

"I'm sorry for the delay," Spratt said. "Tidwell had a family issue arise and I couldn't get away. How are you?"

"I'm fine, thank you. Can I use the bathroom?"

"May I," Spratt corrected.

"May I?" There was no trace of sulking or sarcasm. Only a soft, perhaps sad, resignation. Spratt pursed his lips in defense of it.

"Of course. Wash up while you're in there."

"All right."

Spratt unlocked the cuffs around the boy's wrists, alert for any kicking, but Ghost waited until Spratt stepped back before climbing to his feet and vanishing into the bathroom. While the water ran and the toilet flushed, Spratt moved the dinner tray into the bedroom and set it on the floor.

Ghost emerged pink-cheeked and scrubbed, the ends of his shoulder-length hair dark with wetness from where it probably trailed into the sink while he'd washed his face. He wore his nudity with disinterest, a reminder of his oblique outlook on society and appropriate behavior,

and while Spratt thought they might be on the verge of
Ghost earning back some clothing, Spratt had already
decided the garments would be of his own choosing. He
didn't approve of Ghost's wardrobe, all too-tight shirts
and torn jeans, everything fitted in such a way as to ad-
vertise the boy's old profession.

"Come eat," Spratt said, and Ghost sat on the floor
before the tray.

After several bites, he said, "It's very good. Thank
you."

"You're welcome."

It'd been some time ago now that they'd first met.
Ghost had been fifteen, and it was pure happenchance
that Spratt had been in the passenger seat of a patrol unit
driving by as the drama unfolded. Spratt infrequently
picked up shifts with his patrolmen and patrolwomen,
less often with his detectives. He liked to keep his hand
in, and besides, a strong presence from command did
wonders for both morale and the precision of police work
in his stations.

Unfortunately, even in policing, you found those cal-
low individuals who were attracted to power and the
abuse of it. That sort tended to behave better when they
knew they were being watched. Spratt had keen eyes for
that sort of thing.

He'd been on an impromptu ride-along when he saw
the pale boy knocked clear off his feet by the attentions
of a rough, far larger man in a black leather jacket. Spratt
and his companion for the day had flashed their lights and
stopped, and one brief struggle later, the rough man was
in the back of the squad car, cursing in a mixture of Russian and English. The pale boy watched with a cautious,
uncanny gaze, his shoulders set, his chin lifting in small

degrees as Spratt approached. Spratt was windblown and out of breath, his lip bleeding from a lucky punch.

The boy trembled with fear.

"Are you all right?" Spratt asked, displeased by the bright red mark on the boy's cheekbone. "Shall I call an ambulance? Is there someone who can take care of you?"

For a heartbeat the boy's expression narrowed, as if he thought perhaps he was being made fun of, and then he dropped the act, his face tilting toward the ground. He meant to hide his expression, Spratt suspected, because it'd gone heavy and far too old for one so young.

The man was spitting foul language about the boy through the window, calling him words that should never be repeated in polite company, let alone directed at a child. The boy flinched from the vileness in that voice, and Spratt, without thinking, rested a light hand on his shoulder. He expected the boy's second flinch, but what surprised him was the way the boy took a shy, almost secretive step closer, like he craved the shelter of Spratt's company beyond the resisting of it.

"You're safe," Spratt murmured.

Later, at the station, wrapped in a blanket and drinking a cup of coffee—an inappropriate beverage for a child, but all the station had—Ghost explained the conflict. Krayev wanted to add him to his stable, Ghost had demurred, and the situation had escalated from there.

He'd arrested Vasily Krayev for assaulting not only Ghost—who'd refused to press charges—but Spratt as well, who had pressed charges. Thugs like Krayev didn't belong on the streets. Spratt had not been dismayed to find that the meth dealer and occasional pimp had been murdered eight months ago.

Spratt had made promises to Ghost that day, about

his safety and his future, promises that he'd since failed to keep, a situation that had, at times, haunted him. He didn't like failing his citizens, particularly those who were exposed to the vagaries of the world and their own flawed conditioning.

Getting the boy into residential treatment hadn't been difficult, as he'd apparently been there many times before, but keeping him on the straight and narrow when he wasn't in custody was trickier.

The streets had their hooks in his boy.

"How was it?" he asked now, as Ghost put down his fork.

"Delicious. Thank you."

Spratt nodded and began clearing the plates. He was on the verge of guiding the boy back into the closet when he said, "Please may I come upstairs?"

Spratt frowned. "Ghost…"

"I'll be good," the boy said hurriedly. "I'm so sorry I hurt you. I know I've damaged your trust in me, and it's—it's unforgivable, what with everything you've done for me, I wasn't trying to hurt you, I swear, but I forget, sometimes, that I can trust you, and I do stupid things and try to leave. Not because I want to…it's just…familiar."

"I will always come back for you," Spratt said.

"I know that now. I should've had faith."

Spratt considered him. "The closet is the safer place for you. You can't get into trouble there."

Ghost leaned away from the closet, a movement so slight that a less observant man would've missed it altogether. "Please. Let me stay with you. For a few minutes more at least. Please? I'll be good."

"You won't try to leave?"

"I don't want to leave you. Just the closet…it's claustrophobic in there."

"I imagine it is." Spratt pursed his lips. The boy was incredibly slippery. He'd run from foster homes countless times, and reverted to the bad habits he'd picked up on the streets when given the opportunity. He might try to flee if Spratt allowed him out of the room. At the same time, though, Spratt didn't care for leaving the boy in there indefinitely. It was far too much like captivity, and that wasn't what this was about.

"All right," Spratt agreed. "You've earned a bit of a break. You've been very well-behaved of late. Wait in your closet. I'll lock the door and get you some clothes, and then you can come upstairs with me for a bit."

"All right."

After Ghost was secured, he took the tray upstairs and obtained some clothes for the boy, as well as his spare set of handcuffs. It would be easier to restrain Ghost within the closet against his will later this way, if necessary.

When Ghost was dressed and cuffed with his hands in front of him, he had Ghost lead the way upstairs. He encouraged the boy to sit on a stool at the island, then turned his attention to the dishes in the sink. The salmon had left a tough film on the skillet.

"Will you tell me a story?" Ghost asked. "About your day? Please?"

He was lonely. Of course he was. So Spratt talked about work for nearly an hour, telling the few stories he had which were child-appropriate.

By the time the clock read eleven and he was thinking of bed, Ghost was asking many questions, drawing the minutes out, his words rushing together as the seconds ticked by.

"It's time," Spratt said apologetically.

"No, please. Five more minutes. You don't have to talk. We could just sit here."

"I'm afraid I'm rather tired."

"There's bound to be—"

"Ghost." The boy jerked, and Spratt softened his tone. "Don't. I need my rest in order to be satisfactory at my job."

"May I sleep with you?" Ghost asked. "I could. There are things I could do. For you." He tipped his head to one side coquettishly, biting his lip and glancing up at Spratt through his eyelashes. In the hands of a common whore it would've been obvious and tacky. Ghost was neither. He appeared nothing more than an innocent tempted by a force larger than himself. A stupider man—or one desperate to believe the lie—would've found it convincing.

Spratt sighed inwardly. Every time he thought they'd gotten past this behavior, it reared up once more. Would there ever come a time when Ghost would trust him? When Ghost's first response to fear wasn't to sacrifice his body to the lusts of other men? They'd been doing so well.

Spratt crossed to Ghost and cupped that sweet face in his palms. Ghost tensed, but reached his cuffed hands up to work at the top button of the too-large oxford Spratt had given him to wear. Spratt shook his head, brushing those questing fingers gently aside. "Haven't I told you that I will never touch you that way?"

Ghost's gaze darted away. "Yes."

"Even if I didn't prefer women, even if I were the sort of man who was attracted to the sorts of vile things you've experienced in the past, I could never harm you, Ghost. If you would only talk to me, I could help you in so many ways."

Ghost shifted his weight from foot to foot, still staring at the wall. "I can't," he muttered finally. "I would,
but I—I can't."

Spratt ignored the twinge of anger and disappointment
he felt whenever Ghost refused to discuss the Krayev
matriarch.

"Why do you hold to this fiction?" Spratt leaned down
and pressed a gentle kiss to Ghost's forehead. "We both
know she sent you here. We both know she's using you,
that you're expendable to her. I can protect you."

Ghost shuddered against him, and Spratt pulled him
close. "Dear boy. I wish you would allow me to help you."

Ghost merely allowed the embrace at first, his lean
body almost vibrating, but slowly, when Spratt only held
him and ran a tender hand along the curve of his upper
back, he relaxed. He leaned in closer, and his voice deepened, less of that sweet tenor and closer to a full-grown
man's voice when he said, "I don't know what to do."

"Shh. You'll figure it out." Spratt kissed him again,
the top of his head this time.

Ghost didn't say anything for a moment, only peered
at him with a curiosity that made him seem older than
twenty. He murmured, "I've almost told you. Several
times. I—" His eyes widened. His lips parted. "I—I—
shouldn't have said that." Almost inaudibly, he said, "I
didn't mean to say that."

"None of us can live without trusting someone," Spratt
said, even as his heart began to thunder. It was working, as he'd known it would. Ghost was becoming de-
pendent, coming to need him, coming to see how safe
he was, here in Spratt's home, away from the threats of
Yelena Krayeva and her murderous offspring. He would
talk soon enough. He'd explain where the woman was,

explain her business, explain how he'd been roped in,
too young and innocent to possess the tools necessary
to survive free of her influence.

Ghost would tell him everything. Soon.

He reached out and ran his fingers through that golden
hair, tugging on the strands. "You're mine," he said.
"Mine to protect. You know that, don't you? There's nowhere you could go where I wouldn't save you and bring
you back."

Ghost's lashes lowered, his expression hard to read.
A heartbeat later, he pressed his face into the palm of
Spratt's hand. Lovely. So sweet, so lovely.

"I know," he said quietly.

"Good." He dropped a last kiss on that button nose.
"Now it's time for you to return to the closet."

# Chapter Nineteen

While Tobias slept, Sullivan crept down into the living room, turned on a solitary lamp and his laptop, and tried not to panic.

It was only nine-thirty, but by rights he should be out cold, just as Tobias was; neither of them had gotten much sleep this week during the stakeout. But while they'd been cuddling in bed earlier, Tobias had recounted what he'd overheard from the cops by the stage. The mention of Yelena Krayeva, the mention of the mysterious Kellen that Tobias's friend Church had confirmed was Krayeva's lackey. Spratt's reference to a caged animal. Sullivan wasn't convinced that the deputy chief—soon to be actual chief—of police's caged animal talk referred to Ghost, but it was suspicious either way.

Hardly traditional pillow talk, and it was enough to ensure that his mind wasn't going to settle for a while yet. If he didn't loathe the idea of Tobias waking up alone to find him gone, he'd go for a run.

What the hell had they stumbled into here?

He would have to bring Raina in at some point. If Klein realized Sullivan had figured out he'd lied about his identity, Klein might involve her, and Sullivan didn't like the idea of her being blind to that risk. Not that he was looking forward to the reaming he was going to get over Tobias's involvement in this. It would take her five seconds to realize that he and Tobias were sleeping together, too, and that would be another tick against him.

He had a feeling he was going to get fired.

Fuck.

Fuck, fuck, *fuck*.

This was the part Raina had warned him about when he'd first taken the case. With subpoenas, he'd always had the law on his side, always had a pretty clear view of where to go next. Now every choice struck him as a potential landmine, and for the first time, he wasn't sure he could pull this off. Maybe he deserved to get fired.

But even if he did, he sure as hell wasn't going to quit. If Nathalie was alive, shitty detective or not, Sullivan was all she had, so after several minutes of feeling sorry for himself, he shook it off and tried to figure out where to go next.

He'd taken pictures of every car in the lot at the picnic, and he got those tag numbers started at the DMV. It took all of five minutes to look up the property records of the house where the woman and her children were living—it was still in the name of Matthew and Nicole Tidwell, so that the was the balding man sorted out. A brief search there only ratcheted his tension higher— Matthew Tidwell worked in Internal Affairs. The cop whose job it was to keep other cops clean apparently made a routine out of picking up prostitutes and consorting with guys who pretended to be other people.

In theory, Tidwell could've been picking up Ghost because he was a material witness who had valuable info about the Krayevs. He might've used Cindy Jackman's car to pick him up because his truck was in the shop or something, not because he wanted to hide his own involvement. The conversation at the picnic could've been about a legitimate police operation. All of it could be on the up-and-up. In theory.

Except, of course, for Sullivan's client's involvement, the redheaded cop who was searching for a missing ten-year-old from an unsolved murder in 1992 loosely involving Yelena Krayeva. If it was legitimate, why couldn't he do it at work? Why couldn't he use department resources? If he was following up a cold case on his own time, why lie about his name? He had more clout as a cop than he did as a family member, so it didn't make sense.

Also, how the hell had the redheaded man gotten away with pretending to be Nelson Klein for so long? Sullivan didn't have to look far for confirmation that his client was a damn liar—it only took twenty minutes to scare up a photo of Nathalie's actual uncle from an old magazine article about the case, and he didn't look anything like the sour, redheaded man who'd pretended to be him.

It was hardly unheard of for clients to be dirtbags. Raina and Sullivan had a process they followed to check out every new client—or lawyer, in Sullivan's case—for exactly this reason, but the Nathalie Trudeau case was a holdover from the previous owner of the firm. Raina had taken it over years ago when she'd been less experienced in the game, and she probably hadn't thought it necessary to double-check the grizzled vet's work.

A rare rookie mistake on her part, and a damn lazy bit of detective work on the old owner's part.

Sullivan went to the case file for Nathalie Trudeau. After more than two decades of work, it was thick and full of assorted odds and ends—things turned in by his fake client, and things accumulated from Raina and the original PI's research, including the police report from that long-ago night. Sullivan hadn't paid much attention to the minutiae before, but now he checked the bottom of each page generated by the Denver Police Department.

At the bottom of each page were spaces for the signatures of the investigating officers. On each page were two names: Matthew Tidwell and Yannick Holt. Beneath that, where there was a space for the signature for the supervising officer was the same name on each page: Benjamin Spratt.

"Holy fuck," Sullivan breathed.

He went to his laptop; it only took a minute to track down a picture of Yannick Holt, and there he was, Sullivan's redheaded fake client.

Sullivan got out a piece of paper and sketched a quick flow chart. At the bottom he put boxes containing the names Matthew Tidwell and Fake Nelson Klein/Yannick Holt. He drew a line from Tidwell to another box marked Ghost, and a line from Klein/Holt to a box he labeled Nathalie & Margaret. Then, from the two cops, he drew a third line upward, where he wrote Benjamin Spratt and a question mark. Finally he drew a circle around the whole thing and scrawled Yelena Krayeva/Mama on the outside.

He stared at it for a minute, then turned back to his laptop.

A handful of minutes later, he felt like he knew everything about Spratt anyone could need to know. The *Denver Post* had called him the "hammer of justice." The American Bar Association had interviewed him and called him the "last clean cop in America." The guy was married to the job, had been cited six times for bravery, had saved several cops' lives, had several publications to his name in academic journals on the topic of criminal justice, and there was shaky cell-phone footage of the man taking a bullet for a six-year-old black girl when gang violence had erupted on a street corner a couple years back.

The new Denver chief of police was a hero.

Again, in theory.

But if this was true, what did it all have to do with Nathalie Trudeau? He wondered which officers and detectives had worked the Larry Howard case back in 1992, and had a sneaking suspicion that his client had been one of them. Possibly Tidwell and Spratt, too.

What had Nathalie seen that would ensure a dirty cop would still be searching for her all these years later?

"Fuck," Sullivan whispered into his quiet, dark living room.

The next morning, Sullivan woke up to find Tobias wide awake beside him, lying on his back, staring at the ceiling.

Sullivan held him for a long time, running his fingers through those light brown curls, and Tobias nuzzled his face into Sullivan's shoulder. When the morning was threatening to turn into early afternoon, he finally got them both into the shower. He went down on his knees on the hard porcelain and took Tobias in his mouth, sucking and licking until Tobias was arching his back, until his hips jogged in tiny, helpless thrusts, until he came with a soft shout that echoed off the tile.

When Tobias had come, Sullivan turned him around and jerked off against his buttocks, catching his breath afterward while watching his come drip down the curve of muscle decorated with deep, rapidly purpling bruises.

He ran his palms over the marks, listening to the pleased, satisfied little sighs and moans Tobias made as the sensation grew with the pressure.

"Are you in much pain?" Sullivan asked.

"It's perfect, thank you."

"We're going to be in a car all day. Might feel different in a couple of hours. I've got some over-the-counter painkillers around somewhere."

"Okay. For later. But I like it right now."

"About yesterday…"

"I'll listen to you better about case stuff. I shouldn't have done what I did. I'm sorry."

"You're already forgiven. But I meant the stuff with your dad. Are you okay there?"

"I feel…" Tobias watched a drop of water wend its way down the tile as he considered. "Better, actually. Not good, but it feels like the other shoe has dropped and now there's nothing to do but ride the fallout. Yesterday helped a lot. I got most of it out of my system, I think."

"Good."

"Are you all right? We were sort of rough on each other. I'm okay, you know. I wanted all of it. I just couldn't say it. You know that, right?"

"I know. I liked it," Sullivan admitted. He also liked that Tobias was checking in, knowing he might feel guilty for what he'd done. It struck him as sweet. "I wouldn't be up to going that hard every day or anything, but it had its charms, I guess you'd say."

Sullivan was tempted to rub his fingers between Tobias's cheeks, to get them damp with his own come and slide them inside Tobias's body. But they hadn't discussed unprotected sex yet, and it wasn't really a good time to add yet another potentially stressful conversation to the mix. Later, he told himself. Later, maybe he'd be able to mark Tobias with more than bruises.

Assuming Tobias still wanted to be here, anyway,

and that this whole thing he had going with Sullivan wouldn't prove to be one more casualty of his attempts to find himself.

He rinsed his come from Tobias's skin, then turned the water off. "Come on. We've got a lot to do today."

"Do we start with Spratt? Or your client?"

"Not sure yet." Sullivan dried off with rough swipes of the towel, explaining what he'd put together the night before.

"So Tidwell and your redheaded client guy——"

"Yannick Holt."

"——Holt, maybe worked for Spratt back then on the murders of Larry Howard and his bodyguards and his housekeeper."

"Yep."

Tobias bit his lip. "Heck of a coincidence."

"Yup." He hung his towel up and cocked a hip against the counter, watching Tobias dry off as he considered the options.

"What did you find on Spratt?"

"His rep is solid. He seems to genuinely like helping the innocent and fighting bad guys."

"Bad guys like Mama."

"Like Mama," Sullivan agreed.

"But he was talking about Ghost——"

"He was *maybe* talking about Ghost."

"——so he at least knows where Ghost is."

*"Maybe."*

"You think there's any chance Tidwell picked up Ghost for legit purposes?" Tobias asked, sounding hopeful. "Ghost did go with him willingly. Maybe that's the favor. Mama told Ghost to act like he's going along with it, but he's actually feeding them bad info."

Sullivan cocked his head. "You know, that might not be far off the mark. If she's worried about Spratt's people closing in, an informant to lead the cops astray might seem like a good option to undermine the investigation." He lifted an eyebrow. "Any chance Ghost double-crosses her and helps the cops legitimately?"

Tobias snorted. "Ghost wouldn't ask a cop for help if he was bleeding to death, let alone trust one to watch his back."

"Yeah, I figured. I like the idea of Ghost being a false informer, but if that's the case, anybody could've done it. I mean, what's the point of tracking down a reluctant hustler outside of your organization when you've got any number of folks who could wander in and start lying. Why Ghost?"

Tobias shook his head slowly. "I don't know."

"Ghost's never mentioned Spratt? In any capacity? Did Spratt or one of his men ever arrest him? There has to be a reason Mama would think Ghost was the only guy who could get it done."

"He's never talked about specific cops or arrests or anything that I remember." Tobias gnawed on a thumbnail. "Although…"

"What?"

"It's sort of dumb."

"I'm not grading you."

Tobias took a deep breath. "You said Spratt likes helping the innocent. Ghost is really good at looking innocent. He's good at being whatever someone wants him to be."

"Yeah?"

"He's super manipulative, actually." Tobias winced. More of that patented Tobias Benton loyalty, Sullivan suspected. "He was in and out of Woodbury half a dozen times and he still had the staff convinced he was this abused, helpless sweet kid with tragically low self-esteem. If Spratt did pick him up for hustling at some point, he probably pulled the same act."

"Spratt doesn't strike me as a man stupid enough to fall for the hooker with a heart of gold shtick."

"Maybe not, but I guarantee you that Ghost wouldn't sign up for this favor if he didn't believe he'd be successful. He must've had a reason to think it would work. He doesn't put his head on the chopping block for anyone, not even Church."

"Or you?"

"Or me." Tobias looked away. "He told me once back in Woodbury that the key to winning was to let people underestimate you. It meant you always had the element of surprise. If you made the first strike a killing blow, you never lost."

Sullivan headed for the bedroom, shaking his head. "No offense, Tobias, but I really don't see the two of you as friends. What did you talk about back then?"

"Not much, at first. I mostly followed him around in the beginning. It got easier once Church showed up. He balances us out."

"Huh."

"The real question," Tobias mused, "is what would Mama want Ghost to do to or for Spratt and his team?"

"Probably nothing good."

Tobias hung his towel up, then froze, arms still extended. "Oh. Oh, jeez. That's gotta be it."

Sullivan lifted his eyebrows. "Well?"

Tobias spun around. "Blackmail."

"You have a predilection you should look into," Sullivan said, only half joking, but at the same time, Tobias's answer struck him as sound. "Makes sense, though. Why else does someone involved in organized crime send a prostitute to the top cop in your city? To get him under your thumb. Even if he's clean until that point, a few pictures of the guy with a hooker's not going to look good. Mama would know that her kind of business can be investigated on the federal level, too, so it wouldn't be enough that Spratt has guys in Internal Affairs. RICO statutes, you know? She'd be aware that Spratt would want to keep any connections to Ghost quiet, because the Feds wouldn't hesitate to take a hard look at him if there was even a whiff of questionable activity. And if Mama had reason to believe that Spratt would fall for the noble, suffering hustler routine as long as Ghost was the hustler in question, it makes sense that he alone could get the job done. Damn, that's playing the long game, though."

"Ghost wouldn't mind screwing over a cop that way." Tobias's mouth turned soft and worried. "But your fake client asked Spratt if they'd made progress with Ghost. If Ghost could trust someone who was doing whatever Spratt's been doing to him. What if they figured out why he's really there? God, what if they've hurt him?"

"Hey, now." Sullivan kissed his temple. "He's still alive, at least. They can't be treating him too badly or he'd never trust them. And you said Spratt talked about him needing to feel safe, right? We've got a little time, at least. Yeah?"

Tobias nodded. His lips landed, sweet and warm, against Sullivan's collarbone.

Sullivan rested his forehead against Tobias's for a second before forcing himself to pull away. "Spratt's the link to Mama, though. She's not going to be concerned with a couple of mid-rank cops when she can go after the big fish. Let's start with him. Let's figure out what he's up to."

After two hours with the county courthouse property records, Sullivan grabbed his keys.

Benjamin Spratt owned a townhouse roughly ten minutes away in Capitol Hill.

Sitting in the car was delicious torture.

Tobias's buttocks were sore. Like, absurdly sore. And if he rocked his weight without thinking, the sudden remembrance of why the pain was there sent heat flooding through his whole body. At this rate, he'd be hard half the day.

Or maybe not. As they drove downtown, his phone rang. His manman.

"You gonna get that?" Sullivan asked, turning the radio down. More of that gritty seventies stuff he liked.

Tobias stared at the screen. He was still enjoying the centered stillness he'd gotten from the scene last night, and he wasn't sure he was up for more argument. "No. I think—no. Should I?"

"That's up to you, sweetheart."

That—he glanced at Sullivan, startled. He'd called Tobias sweetheart before, of course. A bunch of times, by this point. But never outside of the bedroom. Never like this, casually, like the pet name was more than a tool in their BDSM toolbox.

Sullivan was startled, too, his brown eyes going wide where they were watching the road. The silence grew awkward until they hit a red light, when Sullivan looked over, his eyes tracing Tobias's expression. "I didn't—that just came out. Sorry."

"No," Tobias said quickly. "I don't mind."

"No?"

"I like it when you call me that." Tobias's heart was thundering, warmth crawling up into his face. He liked it a lot, and never more so than here, in completely ordinary circumstances, as far from the bedroom as they could be. "Don't be embarrassed, please."

Sullivan cleared his throat. "Cool."

Tobias grinned, then glanced at his phone. She'd left a voicemail, and maybe he couldn't handle arguing, but he could at least listen, couldn't he?

He put in his code and held his breath. Her voice was tinny over the line and she sounded tired. Resigned, maybe.

"Tobias, it's me. I wanted to speak with you about what happened on the phone with your papa yesterday. I—" She broke off and sighed. "We're at such cross-purposes these days. It seems like we can't stop hurting each other, doesn't it? But I want you to know that we aren't going to stop trying. We love you, and if you have things you want to tell us, we'll listen. We can't promise we'll understand or agree, but we'll listen. I hope... I hope you'll call, *cheri*."

She hung up, and Tobias lowered the phone to his lap.

If he looked back on the call with his papa logically, he could admit that a big part of the meltdown that followed had been about the fear of rejection. He'd learned about it in therapy, not that it took a genius to figure it out. Lots of adopted kids struggled with that, and he was no different. One of his earliest memories was— embarrassingly—of having a tantrum when he was four or five because his parents had closed their bedroom door in his face without realizing he'd been following them inside. It'd been such a tiny thing, entirely accidental, but he'd broken down completely, too young to know why he was so upset.

He also remembered Manman singing *"Dodo Titit"* to him, drying the tears from his cheeks with kisses and brushing his hair away from his hot face. He was loved, he knew it. His papa hanging up on him had hurt him in a place he was vulnerable, yes, but he'd never have done it if he'd realized how deep it would cut. Besides, Tobias couldn't expect the world to rotate around his issues; that was his responsibility and no one else's—his responsibility to make clear, and his responsibility to cope with.

For a moment he felt such a visceral longing for her and Papa and home that his chest tightened. He saved the message and thought, *later.* They might not be good at listening, but they would try, and that was all you could ask of someone, really.

And if worse came to worst and they pressured him to resume his studies for medical school, he'd say no. It wouldn't be easy, and it might change things irrevocably, but Sullivan had been right last night. Maintaining that boundary didn't make him wrong, and it didn't make him cruel. It made him himself, and if they truly loved him, they would love him even like this.

Sullivan was also right that it was unfair to expect them to change their behavior unthinkingly when he'd never set boundaries before. Unfair to get angry when they did as they had always done, what he had never protested.

Yes, they had made decisions for him as if he were still a child.

But he had let them. For far, far too long. He wished he knew why. Why had it been so impossible for him to stand up for his own hopes and interests? He'd known he was loved. When they'd realized they couldn't have the children they wanted, the children they could make together, his parents had done an amazingly decent thing to adopt him. They loved him. They wouldn't kick him out of the family for being too much trouble now that their legal responsibility to him was done.

He knew that.

He'd never trusted it though. Despite all the evidence, he'd never stepped out onto the uncertain ice and trusted them all to remain intact.

None of them were guiltless.

In fact, there wasn't a single relationship in his life where he'd done that, he thought now. No one in the whole world where he'd just been his entirely messy self and trusted that the other person wouldn't walk. Church probably came closest, but even with him, Tobias still watched that line. He wasn't himself with anyone except for...

Sullivan.

Tobias had done and said exactly what he wanted over the past two weeks with Sullivan, and Sullivan had never flinched. Despite Tobias's attempt to blackmail him, despite his massive amounts of drama, despite shoving him and arguing with him and impulsively breaking the rules they'd agreed on in the beginning of this thing, Sullivan was still here.

Sullivan liked him, mess and all.

Just like Tobias liked him.

Not that Sullivan had much mess to him. Except for his insecurities about what he liked in bed—which Tobias would punch his ex in the nose for if he ever saw the jerk—Sullivan pretty well had his shit together. He certainly wasn't making his decisions because of extenuating circumstances. This was who he was, and Tobias really, really liked him.

What came over him then wasn't the itch he'd been struggling with for weeks and weeks. It wasn't desperation. It wasn't some temporary, maddening thing. It was a quiet awareness of what could be.

After this case wrapped up, Tobias could rebuild his life into something closer to his own ideas of happiness. He could be the guy who studied…well, he wasn't sure yet, but something other than medicine. He could study whatever and get a job he liked and hang out with his friends. He could volunteer in the community, because he wanted to help people, but he could do it in a way that didn't make him anxious or resentful. He could keep dating Sullivan, too. He could listen to him talk about weird, rambling subjects and make sure the fridge was stocked with healthy snacks so Sullivan wasn't eating bare pieces of bread because he wasn't paying attention, and he could sass back enough to make Sullivan's face go dark and aggressive before he reached for the paddle.

Wow.

It stole his breath. The possibility of it all. The potential happiness waiting to be grabbed. And Sullivan could definitely be part of it.

He *should* be part of it.

He opened his mouth to tell him exactly that, only for Sullivan to say, "Few more blocks, I think."

"What?"

Sullivan jerked his chin toward the building beyond the windshield. "The place where Spratt lives. Next block. Keep your eyes open for places where we can sit and watch the street without getting busted."

Right. Work. Ghost. Tobias bit his tongue. It wasn't

really the time for that conversation, anyway. He'd need time to explain it right, especially if Sullivan had any doubts. And if everything did work out, Sullivan might want to have sex after.

He couldn't even imagine what Sullivan might choose to do, but it would be good. He shifted his weight, and pain sparked through his buttocks and up his spine and he shivered a little. It would be so good.

Fortunately, Sullivan was being professional and was therefore oblivious to the sheer number of small epiphanies Tobias was experiencing. On their second trip down the street past Spratt's townhouse, he pulled into a tiny alley that led to a small parking lot behind a diner bustling with early lunch-goers. The large front window would offer a good view of the red door across the street marked 2600 C, the address in Spratt's name in the courthouse property records.

They couldn't spend the whole day in the diner, of course. It was likely Spratt wouldn't be back for hours yet, and while it bugged Tobias to be reduced once again to sitting and waiting, he knew this would be far less effort than trying to track Spratt's or the balding man's locations down through the department. Even Tobias's limited experience was enough to be sure that poking around a police station and then surveilling it would be logistical nightmare, assuming they didn't get busted.

After eating, they left on foot, window shopping nearby, never out of sight of the townhouse, before going back to sit in the car for a few hours. The small parking lot was tucked away between two small stores and there wasn't much traffic. Sullivan took some pictures, then got out his binoculars to peer through the first-floor windows. "He's definitely not home. Nice place,

though," Sullivan said, handing the binoculars to Tobias so he could take peek. "Bet that television cost him
a few thousand."

"He's very neat," Tobias noted. "There's nothing left
out anywhere. He doesn't seem to own much, but what's
there looks like it costs a fortune."

"I read that minimalism as an aesthetic can be linked
to social class." Sullivan peered across the street at pe-
destrians. "It's easy to get rid of things you aren't using
if you have enough money to buy what you might need
at any given moment. Whereas if you've been poor, it
causes cognitive dissonance to get rid of things, because
you're afraid that if it turns out later that you need it after
all, you might not be able to afford to replace it. Weirdly,
having less stuff requires having more money. And in this
other thing, I read...hold up. Is that—shit, that's Tidwell."

He snatched the binoculars out of Tobias's hand, leaving Tobias to squint uselessly at a balding figure walking
down the sidewalk. "That looks like the back of somebody's head. I have no idea if that's Tidwell."

"It is. He was wearing the same coat at the picnic."

Tobias glanced at him and admitted—if only to himself—that he was a little turned on by Sullivan's obser-
vational skills. "Good catch."

"Uh-huh. Hey, look who has a key."

"I can't look. You took the binoculars."

"I bet you can make an educated guess. It rhymes
with *bidwell*."

Tobias gnawed on his lip. "Would you give an underling a key to your very expensive townhouse?"

"I tend to live in places that have holes in the walls
and I've never had an underling, so I'm not one to judge."

Once inside, Tidwell stood right by the front door for

a good ten seconds. "What the heck is he doing?" Tobias asked, unable to see. "Is he staring at the door? Fiddling with the wall?"

"Alarm system, I bet."

Made sense—only a few seconds later Tidwell turned away and went deeper into the living room. Tobias said, "That means he has the code. Spratt's got to know he's here."

They traced Tidwell's progress through the windows; he was in the kitchen for a while, putting a plate together with a sandwich on it, then disappeared downstairs. He came back up about fifteen minutes later, made a second sandwich that he ate at the counter before cleaning up, resetting the alarm, locking the door behind him and vanishing down the cement steps that led to the parking garage.

Tobias closed his eyes and tried to breathe. "He's in there. Ghost's in that townhouse somewhere."

"We don't know that."

"Come on. Give me one other guess who it could be, if not Ghost?"

"The whole point is that you're guessing. We need proof before we do anything."

"And in the meantime he's just stuck in there? Sullivan, if he had free rein of the place, he could make his own sandwich. He's…he's tied up or something. We have to help him."

Sullivan sank back into his seat. He watched Spratt's townhouse for a long, quiet minute. "You know this is shitty, right?"

"Of course it's bad. He's in trouble."

Sullivan still didn't look at him. "I didn't mean…

whatever. If. *If* he's in there. And even then, we don't know that we'd actually be helping him."

Tobias frowned, wondering what he did mean, but then the rest of the sentence caught up with him. "You think he wants to be there?"

"You think he'll thank you if he's been working the situation for a month to get to wherever he is and we blunder in and ruin it because we think we know best?"

"Sullivan—"

"And you're the one who keeps saying Nathalie's alive and with Mama—"

"She *is*, it's the only thing that makes sense—"

"So what happens if breaking in to Spratt's house falls back on her in some way. Ghost isn't my only responsibility here."

"Or helping Ghost could give us a lead to finding her."

"I'm not saying it won't. I'm saying not yet. We don't know enough to be sure that we won't make things worse. I don't think we'll do him or ourselves any favors if we yank him out of there and it screws something up for Mama."

"I don't understand why you're fighting this. It's like you don't want him to be in there."

"Of course I don't want him to be in there," Sullivan snapped. "Do you…haven't you put together what's going to happen if he *is* tied up in the basement? Don't you get what you're signing us up for? So don't blame me for wanting to double-check everything first. We don't know enough yet."

No, Tobias hadn't considered what would happen next, what it would mean if Ghost was being held there against his will. He'd only thought of finally finding him, and suddenly the size of the whole thing hit hard. Look at how much time and effort the redheaded cop had put into finding Nathalie; look at the lengths Spratt would go to in order to get what he wanted. They wouldn't give Ghost up easily. If they weren't careful, Tobias and Sullivan would have these two dodging their every step, and with every advantage of the system that a cop could finagle.

He tipped his head against the passenger window. The glass was hot against his face, and through it he focused on the red door of Spratt's townhouse. "We're so close," he murmured.

"So let's not fall on our faces at the finish line. We confirm he's there first."

They sat in the car for another hour, then parked someplace else and sat there for another hour. They didn't talk much; Tobias was vaguely annoyed—more with the reality of the situation than Sullivan specifically—and he suspected Sullivan was aware of it and was giving him the space to deal with it. It was thoughtful, and later, when he wasn't as frustrated, he would appreciate it.

Eventually, near dinner time, when the staff at the diner had changed shifts, they went back to eat again. They were wrapping up a late, interminable meal and guiltily ignoring their exasperated waitress when Spratt emerged from the stairwell leading to underground parking across the street.

It must've shocked their waitress to spend nearly two hours with a slow-moving pair only to have them suddenly throwing money on the table and rushing out.

When they'd made it back to the car, Sullivan immediately pulled the camera and binoculars out, handing the latter to Tobias. It wasn't quite dark out yet, so they could still see everything with relative clarity.

They watched Spratt move through his rooms with

the air of a man staying in for the night. He removed his suit jacket and hung it in the closet before heading into the kitchen to wash his hands and start preparing food.

He didn't get far before he abruptly lifted his head like he'd heard something, then turned and disappeared into the basement. Tobias scooted forward on his seat as if those extra three inches could help him see down the stairs. "What's he doing, do you think?"

"I don't have any more information than you do," Sullivan replied, though not unkindly. "But I don't think he'll hurt whoever is down there. It looks like he needs Ghost—if it's Ghost—to trust him, remember?"

Sullivan proved to be right; not five minutes later, Spratt returned to the main floor, this time with Ghost in tow. Hair tousled, feet bare, wearing a too-large button-up shirt that was on the verge of slipping off one shoulder, and a pair of black shorts. His hands were cuffed in front of him.

"Oh, God, that's him," Tobias whispered, too horrified to even say *I told you so.* Not that he would, but still.

He watched through the binoculars with his stomach roiling. "I figured it would be something like this, but I didn't want it to be true. But why else do you send a prostitute, right?"

"He doesn't look hurt, at least. He really is…" Sullivan trailed off.

Resigned, Tobias said, "You can say it. He's gorgeous."

Sullivan was quiet a second. Then he said, "I was going to say hard to read."

Tobias slid a glance at him, found Sullivan still staring at the camera screen. "You don't think he's attractive?"

"I think he's nice to look at, yeah," Sullivan replied, brow creasing. "But so are lots of people. It's not going to change my life. Are we really having this conversation right now?"

"No." He ignored the warmth in his chest currently competing with his disgust at what he was witnessing, instead refocusing on the kitchen, where Spratt was talking, gesturing with one hand, and Ghost was listening and watching, his expression attentive but somehow dull at the same time.

"Could be consensual," Sullivan said, though he didn't sound like he believed it. "The sex slave thing—it's not an uncommon fantasy for Doms, but there's usually more, well, sex, in the whole sex slave thing. Or at least lust."

"Handcuffs take it a little far, but I agree about that last part," Tobias said, because there was no discernible chemistry between the two men in the kitchen. Weirdly so, considering one of them was an attractive hustler who looked like he'd just crawled out of a client's bed.

For the next hour, as Spratt cooked and Ghost sat at the counter watching, their conversation ebbed and flowed like that of any other couple making dinner, but the body language continued to be off. Tobias couldn't put his finger on it, exactly, but something niggled.

"Something's wrong," he said.

"He doesn't look injured." Sullivan took a couple pictures. "Stop making that face. I thought they might be torturing him or something, and when Ghost came upstairs like that, I was worried we were in for some pretty fucked-up shit too, but they've been perfectly civil. The restraints seem to be preventative, not punitive. Doesn't look like Spratt's even touching him. I'm less worried than I was, honestly."

"No, something's wrong."

Sullivan sighed, but Tobias grabbed his arm. "I know him. Something is wrong."

Sullivan studied him in the yellow glare of the sodium lamp beside the car. "Can you explain it?"

Tobias avoided his gaze in favor of watching Ghost carefully. It took a while, but he finally realized what it was. Ghost wasn't *playing*.

Ghost was always playing. He was always aware of what the people around him expected, and he reinforced it with every breath. Even with Church and—he forced himself to be honest—Tobias, Ghost was pretending. He was playing the role of friend. Tobias was never certain how much of that role drew from real life, but he couldn't pretend anymore that it wasn't a performance.

Perhaps the better way to say it was that Ghost was always acting. He was constantly in flux. Ghost was a verb, always, and sitting like a dull lump in Spratt's house, he looked very much like an object.

Tobias didn't say that though. It might feel true, but it would only sound stupid. Instead, he said, "I know all the different people he can be, but he isn't being anybody he's ever been—he's...he's *blank*. Ghost is never blank. He's always got something working. I can't make it sound right."

"Maybe this is who he really is," Sullivan said, but more doubtfully. "Maybe this is what he's like when he drops all the bullshit."

Tobias tried to keep his tone even rather than frustrated when he said, "Sure, his friends for years get the act, but a cop he's known for ten minutes who tied him up in the basement gets the real thing?"

Sullivan's lips twisted wryly. "Fair enough."

"And he's not here willingly or there'd be no need for

handcuffs. No. Something is really wrong. This isn't him playing Spratt."

Sullivan's shoulders tightened. "Okay. I believe you."

Tobias squeezed back, the air in his throat catching. "Thank you."

Sullivan's fingers tapped on the steering wheel in an erratic pattern for the next twenty minutes as Tobias watched Spratt and Ghost through the binoculars.

"A cop is going to have motion lights in his backyard," Sullivan said finally.

"Probably."

"He definitely has an alarm system. Whatever we do, it'll have to be fast. And quiet. We don't want any well-meaning neighbors calling the cops either."

"What do we do?"

"We do what any good PI does." Sullivan gave him a thin smile that didn't reach his eyes. "We snoop."

Apparently snooping consisted of a much smaller camera in Sullivan's pocket taking the place of the Mark III, a couple of enormous bottles of cheap malt liquor that Sullivan called 40s ineffectually hidden in brown paper bags, and a long amble down the alley behind Spratt's townhouse.

Where Sullivan waved his arms in a parody of drunkenness and purposely set off the motion light before setting his bottle down.

"Here." Sullivan lounged against the nearest fence and pulled out a new pack of Marlboros. He tapped the box against the heel of his hand several times, then tore it open and took two out.

"You don't have to inhale, but at least pretend to," Sullivan said quietly, lighting one and passing it over. "And we're thinking deep, drunken, middle-of-the-night guy thoughts, so get expansive."

Tobias figured that meant it was his job to keep the motion light on. So he pretended to smoke, which was ugh, disgusting, why did anyone do this—

"Oh, God," Sullivan groaned, sounding downright pornographic, and Tobias's whole body tightened before he realized Sullivan was reacting to the cigarette.

"This is a side of you I haven't seen before," Tobias said, equal parts repulsed and amused. "Where's your nicotine gum? Did you leave it in the car?"

"That stuff is horrible. It tastes like an ashtray."

Tobias brandished his cigarette, which was on the verge of going out because he wasn't smoking it. "*This* tastes like an ashtray."

Sullivan was unbothered. He only tipped his head back, blowing several smoke rings that floated into the night, pale gray in the sharp light from the fixture above Spratt's back door.

Faintly, Tobias heard the *click* of the camera working.

"Take a drink," Sullivan offered.

"Isn't this illegal? An open container or something?"

"Yup. But if anyone asks, they're Slurpees."

Tobias made a face. No one in their right mind would believe they were drinking Slurpees, but Sullivan was too busy reuniting with his lost love to care.

"I really hope this isn't going to take you back to day one." Tobias made a show of stretching his arms over his head. The light stayed on. "I've heard it's almost as hard to quit smoking as it is to quit heroin. How long's it been?"

"Four years."

"And you're still using the gum?"

"Look, I've heard quitting smoking is almost as hard as quitting heroin, okay?"

Tobias grinned helplessly. He liked Sullivan *so* much. "So you didn't kick the habit so much as you just switched delivery systems."

"Four cold, lonely years."

"Oh, my God." Tobias rolled his eyes, still painfully amused. He took another slug of his drink and winced. He didn't understand rebelling via substances. Between the alcohol and the cigarette, his mouth tasted horrible.

Sullivan angled his body to the right and poked Tobias in the stomach, making him jump. Sullivan laughed, turning still farther, and the camera went *click* again.

"Fuck," he said loudly. "I knocked over my bev-er-age."

Tobias laughed too, playing along, and waited while Sullivan went down on one knee and took a couple more pictures from that angle before standing up and starting to mosey farther down the alley.

They made their way to the cross street, where they turned left and came to the mouth of the underground parking garage. Sullivan hesitated there for a long second.

"Think it's assigned parking?" Tobias asked.

"If it is, I can find out what he drives." He flicked the cherry off his cigarette, then put the filter in his pocket. "Head back to the car. Take this." He shoved the small camera into Tobias's fumbling hands but held on to his drink. "Still have that business card I gave you? If I'm not there in twenty minutes, it means I got busted. Call Raina and tell her everything. She'll know what to do."

"I'm not leaving you."

"You promised to obey in the field," Sullivan reminded him, his dark eyes hardening, and Tobias stared at him for a long second.

"You better be so careful," he said finally, and shifted his things into one hand so he had another free to yank Sullivan in for a kiss. It started out angry, almost biting, but softened as Sullivan refused to bite back, instead cupping Tobias's face in his hands and gentling the pressure of his lips.

"I'll be fine," Sullivan whispered, and then he smacked Tobias on the ass—which, bruises, *ow*—and jogged away.

And Tobias headed for the car, pausing only to drain his 40 into the gutter. He kept the bottle to recycle later, though.

If it hadn't been for his worry about Sullivan, it wouldn't have chafed at all.

*Middle ground.*

That didn't make the twenty minutes go by any more quickly, though. On the plus side, he did get a chance to check his voicemail, where he found a message from the woman he'd called at the human trafficking website looking for a contact in the interest of tracking down Mama and—by extension—Ghost. She apologized for the delay in her response and gave a spiel about interviews and donations. Tobias deleted it. Even if it'd been what he was looking for, it was a little late now.

When Sullivan got back, he held up a hand before Tobias could say a word, and scrawled out some notes about the vehicle that'd been in the 2600 C spot. "Spratt drives a dark green Range Rover. Camera? Let's take a look at our options."

Sullivan thought of that kiss later. Tobias's fingers locked in his shirt outside the parking garage, his lips demanding and worried in the dark. It was an outlier.

He was pretty sure Tobias still hadn't entirely put together what was coming up. He was vibrating in the passenger seat like a shaken-up bottle of soda, his eyes always on the windows of the townhouse, as if he'd forgotten Sullivan was there.

Sullivan couldn't reconcile the two. A kiss like he couldn't bear to let go. Complete obliviousness to what he was going to ask Sullivan to do. As soon as he realized what had to happen, he would ask, and damn the consequences to Sullivan. Tobias might be sorry about it. He'd probably get those big blue eyes working. Hell, it wouldn't even be an act, because inside, he was soft. He didn't want to hurt people, didn't want to anger people. He'd feel bad, but that wouldn't stop any of this from unfolding.

Sullivan understood. Ghost's safety was more important than Sullivan's job or feelings. He even understood why Tobias felt that way. Tobias had hired him, Tobias wanted it casual, Tobias had always made his priorities clear, and Sullivan had never been at the top of that list.

That kiss, though. It hadn't felt casual or unimportant. It sure as fuck wasn't professional. It was…if Sullivan had dared to trust it, he'd have thought that kiss was evidence of something real growing between them.

But he didn't dare, because he wasn't stupid. That wasn't how the world worked.

## Chapter Twenty

As they drove back to his house, Sullivan wrestled with where to go next.

The obvious answer, of course, was to tell a reliable cop.

Unfortunately, neither he nor Tobias were in the habit of hanging around with cops, and walking into a precinct would be incredibly dangerous; there was no way of knowing whether they were getting someone who would rescue Ghost and catch the bad guys or if the cop in question would hand them over to Spratt and/or blow their brains out. Raina had contacts in the police department but wasn't close enough to any of them to trust their ethics without doubt, not with the risk of bullets in the brain as an outcome.

The district attorney's office wasn't much of an improvement. Both he and Raina knew plenty of lawyers, several who seemed ethical, but he wasn't sure he'd trust his life to any of them. The other problem with going the lawyer route was that it would take time. The district attorney's investigators didn't work like cops—they were meant to scare up evidence about existing cases and subpoena witnesses through guys like Sullivan. Even if Sullivan could find someone who took him seriously with the evidence he had against Spratt and Tidwell and the bald-ing man, it would likely take forever to go through back channels like that. Ghost might not have that much time.

Which left Lisbeth.

She was a contracts lawyer, not a prosecutor or public defender, but he figured that was as close as they were likely to get.

So after they dumped their stuff in the living room, Sullivan sent her a text.

I think I ran into trouble in the police department. U know someone local with impeccable ethics and a good rep?

"My friend's an attorney," he explained to Tobias as he typed. "Not criminal, unfortunately, or she'd have a much better idea of who to contact, but maybe she'll have a name she can recommend."

The response only took a couple of minutes—Lisbeth was nothing if not prompt—and it sent his heart into his shoes.

I have a contact I would trust with my life, but he retired about three months ago. He's somewhere en route to Yellowstone in an RV. He refuses to use cell phones these days, but I'll call his daughter.

Five minutes later, another text came through.

Daughter expects to hear from him in about a week. She'll tell him to call me and that it's urgent. I can tell him to call or come home then. Will that do?

"Damn," Sullivan muttered, turning the phone over so Tobias could read it.

"We can't leave Ghost in there for another week." Tobias caught Sullivan's wrist.

"I know." Sullivan eased himself free so he could send a text to Lisbeth thanking her. And, if he was honest, also because he didn't want Tobias touching him right now.

"So what do we do? Can we break him out? Is that... can we do that?"

And there it was. He'd phrased it as a *we*, but Sullivan knew what he was really asking. *Save him for me. Put yourself and your career at risk for a guy you've never met and for me, a guy who screwed you over and apparently isn't averse to doing it again.*

It hurt. A guy who could barely stir a finger to be Tobias's friend was more important than the risk to Sullivan's life and career. And yeah, Sullivan would do it anyway because it was the right thing to do—and if he was honest, because he didn't doubt Tobias would go in alone if he refused—but it would've been really nice for Tobias to at least seem conflicted about risking him for Ghost.

He took a deep breath and told himself to get his shit together. It wasn't like he hadn't known where he stood. "The alarm is probably only off when either Tidwell or Spratt is in there. So we either have to deal with the alarm or a cop."

"Yeah."

"I'm not attacking a cop," Sullivan said flatly. "Dirty or not."

Tobias shook his head, a little taken aback. "No. I wouldn't ask you to. I don't want to either."

"Then we need to go in when they're gone during the day."

"I don't suppose you know how to disarm an alarm without anyone knowing?"

"Nope. We'll have to be quick enough that the security system doesn't bite us in the ass."

"How long would it take someone to respond?"

"No idea. Minutes, though. I'd be shocked if it took more than ten."

"How's that work? Security guards?" Tobias lifted his eyebrows. "Actually—maybe that would be good. We could throw a football through a window, and when they come we'll say we heard someone yelling for help. They could go in and get Ghost."

"Not all security companies use guards. Some of them try to contact you and then, if they can't, they call the cops."

Tobias deflated. "We can't count on the cops to be reliable."

"Probably not." Sullivan paused. "But on the other hand, neither can Spratt. They aren't all dirty, not even the majority of them. He wouldn't be able to control who got sent to the scene, cop or security guard, so I'm not sure Spratt would go either route—you wouldn't want anyone in your home if you can't ensure they won't talk about the guy you've got tied up in your basement."

"Then what's the point of an alarm?"

Sullivan did a quick search for *home security*, and only a couple minutes later, he had a consumer review article about the different types and benefits and drawbacks. "Some systems are set up so you can get alerts on your smart phone. If I were Spratt, that's what I'd do. I bet the alarm isn't meant to keep people out so much as to keep people *in*. When we breach the alarm, he might come right home expecting to find Ghost trying to run."

"If we're in his house, can he just shoot us?"

"If he thinks we're there to commit a crime by force, yeah."

"What's force? In these circumstances, I mean?"

"Pretty much whatever he wants it to be. It's called the 'Make My Day' law for a reason. If you give him a shove on the arm, that's force. You don't even have to be armed."

Tobias blinked. "That's terrifying. Are we going to take one with us in case—"

"No. I don't like guns."

"But you're a PI."

"So?"

"So you carry one, don't you?"

"Have you seen me carry a gun? Why would I carry a gun? Someone could get shot."

"I just thought—"

"No." Despite what movies and television claimed, Sullivan didn't know a single private detective who carried; if there was a job that proved that guns started more trouble than they ended, it was his. Guns made people feel invincible, which was another way of saying that they did stupid shit because they thought being armed would protect them from the consequences. They picked fights they wouldn't otherwise pick, they stuck around when they'd be safer running, they tried to teach assholes lessons when they would normally call the cops. And almost all of it was avoidable if you did your job without getting your dick in a bunch. He cleared his throat. "Look, the second a gun shows up, you eliminate all the nonviolent options for resolving a situation. They make any situation life or death simply by existing, and I don't like life or death. It's usually a sign that someone fucked up ten steps back."

"Okay."

"And I'm sure as shit not breaking in to a cop's house with a gun."

"Okay," Tobias repeated, more softly. He was watching Sullivan with kind eyes. "I'm not advocating that. I don't want to get you in trouble. I know how much this could cost you. Maybe you think I haven't thought of it, but I do know. Thank you."

Sullivan gazed back at him, all blue eyes and tousled curls and earnest, open gratitude. He wasn't sure he believed that Tobias fully grasped just how bad this could go, but he got a warm pang from the words anyway. Helpless, he leaned forward and kissed him, deep and slow, once. "Yeah," he said, pulling back. "You're welcome."

Tobias smiled sweetly and cleared his throat. "So where do we go in?"

Sullivan straightened and pulled out the smaller camera. The pictures he'd taken revealed that there were six windows facing the backyard; two set near the ground that led to basement rooms, two on the ground floor and two on the second. Spratt had installed bars on both basement windows, black cast iron, delicate enough to be almost decorative, but thick enough to ensure that no one was getting in or out that way. "I think one of the windows by the back door is our best choice. We don't need to get complicated. Break the glass, pull out the screen, we're in. Run downstairs, find him, untie him, and back out exactly the way we came. Shouldn't take more than a minute or two, depending on what we find inside."

"We don't know what we'll need," Tobias said. "We'll

have to bring an assortment of things. Your sister probably has a ton of tools, right?"

"Yeah, that's not happening."

"But—"

"The first rule of this is that we can't take anything
that could point to us, because we might end up being
forced to leave it behind. They can't find out who we are,
or we'll be fucked. A small break-in and setting Ghost
up with Lisbeth's retired cop friend is one thing, but if
they know who we are, there's a good chance we're not
living through that. We have to walk out of there without
leaving anything behind that could be traced back to us."

"So we'll buy anything we use brand-new outside of
town with cash."

"Now you're thinking."

"And we'll have to get rid of anything we do use so it
can't be found in our possession later."

Sullivan nodded. "It's not likely, but he might have
exterior cameras. We can't bring the car too close. If
they see the tags, we're screwed. And…shit, he'll have
access to traffic cameras. We'll have to find out where
the cameras are so we can avoid them. God, I hope we
don't miss anything."

"We should make a list." Tobias glanced at the clock.
"It's almost midnight. Can we get everything done before tomorrow? What is tomorrow, anyway?"

"The fifteenth."

"I meant what day—wait, the fifteenth?"

"Yeah. Tuesday. What's up?"

"Tomorrow's Assumption."

"Tomorrow's a fact, actually," Sullivan said, just to
be a jerk.

"Ha-ha," Tobias said. "The Assumption of Mary. It's

a day of obligation. I'm supposed to go to Mass tomorrow. Ugh, this is the worst timing."

"I don't know. We could probably use some divine intervention. You should go. We'll never be able make the breakout work for tomorrow anyway."

"Sullivan—"

"I know this is driving you crazy, but there's way too much to do before tomorrow afternoon." Sullivan caught the way Tobias's eyes went pinched, and added, "It doesn't do Ghost any good if we get him out only to get busted again three hours later because we fucked something up by rushing. He's been there for weeks. Another day won't kill him, and it might be the thing that makes him safe in the long run. Patience, Kamikaze. Spend tomorrow morning praying. We'll do everything else tomorrow afternoon, and then the day after, we'll go get your friend."

"Right." Tobias nodded and squared his shoulders, as determined as any general, as resigned as any foot soldier.

Sullivan turned away to search for paper and a pen, asking casually, "You don't expect me to come with you, do you? To Mass, I mean. The only thing my family is devout about is not giving a shit, so I wouldn't be more than a religious rubbernecker."

"No." Tobias smiled. "You can stay here."

Sullivan lifted his eyebrows. "No arguments that I should? For the good of my immortal something-or-other?"

"No. I'm not going to guilt-trip you or proselytize. I love God, but I don't need other people to confirm my faith for me. If you want my opinion on the subject, you'll have to ask me."

"Really?"

"Really. What you do with your immortal something-or-other is between you and Him."

"Huh." Sullivan tapped his pen against the table. "Let's make a list of stuff to get."

When the plans were made as best as they could be, they set everything aside and went to bed. Tomorrow would be filled with assorted tasks: shopping, timing how long it took to get from the nearest precinct to Spratt's house, that sort of thing.

But now it was late, deep in the night, and there was nothing else they could do.

When Tobias slid close to him, Sullivan didn't push him away. He probably should; he was too tired to have sex, so this was unabashed cuddling, but Tobias smelled like Sullivan's soap and he was warm and he made a soft humming sound as Sullivan's arms came around him, settling in like he never planned to move.

It both soothed Sullivan and pissed him off. On the one hand, having Tobias close like this was probably the world's best high-blood-pressure medication; he could feel his heartbeat slowing. On the other hand, how had Tobias phrased it? *I want this for now, but I don't know that it'll stick.*

There was a good chance Tobias wouldn't be here in his bed in two days' time. Sullivan was part of Tobias's little rebellion, and maybe it felt real, but he'd have to be stupid to forget that Tobias had made no promises. He'd been honest, at least, but that honesty meant there was zero reason to hope Tobias would stick around once Sullivan had delivered.

It was a lie. Tobias here, in his arms, snuggled up like a damn kitten, sleepy and warm and heavy against

Sullivan's chest, was a lie. Maybe Tobias wasn't like his other dirtbags, pretending to be one thing while actually being another, but even if Tobias had the best of intentions, it was still a lie because nothing about what they were doing was his to keep.

Tobias was gone when Sullivan woke up, but was back, as promised, by eleven. He was wearing a blue suit and tie, his hair neatly combed, his shoulders straight, like something about the whole process had bolstered him, and Sullivan had to admit it: devout was a good look on him. And true to his word, there was no implication— spoken or otherwise—that Sullivan had failed him by staying behind.

Okay, then.

They spent the rest of the morning shopping in Aurora, buying clothes and gear before heading over to Spratt's place to watch out for Tidwell's afternoon visit. Tidwell rolled up exactly six minutes after he'd arrived the day before.

Once again, he made sandwiches. Once again, he was gone in roughly twenty minutes. Once again, no one came in or out of the townhouse until Spratt returned, this time at almost nine p.m. Ghost came upstairs with his wrists handcuffed again, apparently free to wander the place for an hour, but he instead haunted Spratt's footsteps like, well, a ghost, trailing him from room to room, quiet and attentive. At one point, while Spratt's back was turned, Ghost reached out as if to touch him, his expression was hard and soft at once, one hand knotted into a fist, the other outreached, tentative and slow-moving. But by the time Spratt faced him once more, Ghost had jerked away, his face tipping down and out of sight.

"We've got to get him out of there," Tobias said from the passenger seat, his face shadowed in the dark. "That's—none of that is *him*."

"We will," Sullivan said.

That night they got Chinese takeout and sat at the table to research which streets in Capitol Hill had traffic cameras so they could avoid them. In that way, they had some luck—as long as they avoided Speer Boulevard, West 6th Avenue and the highways, Spratt wouldn't be able to track where they went. It meant they could park closer, too.

They also figured out timelines. Cops usually didn't live in the jurisdictions they policed, but administration staff had more leeway. The Denver Police Administration building, where Spratt's office was located, was roughly a mile from Spratt's place—a six-minute drive in normal traffic. However, since Spratt frequently traveled to different stations in the city, they couldn't assume he would be in his office. The chance was small but real that he would be at the Division 6 station, which was even closer and would have a more straightforward route on the one-way streets. They decided to give themselves the smallest possible window to ensure the lowest likelihood of taking longer than they should. For that reason, they would need to be in and out of Spratt's place in fewer than four minutes.

It was after midnight by the time they finished, but Sullivan felt like sleep would be impossible. The hours until tomorrow pressed down with a near-palpable weight.

While they were cleaning up, Tobias said, "I can see why you'd be mad at me for all of this."

"I'm not."

"I know. That's what I don't understand." Tobias fiddled with a napkin, tearing it into shreds. "I know it's my

fault you have to break the law for someone you've never
met. If I hadn't blackmailed you, none of this would be
on your plate. There's a lot at risk for you. That would
make anyone mad. But you're not. You're…something,
I can't tell what, but you're not mad."

"No, I'm not mad."

"So what are you?"

Sullivan scrubbed at a bit of spilled soy sauce while he
tested possible answers. He couldn't come up with anything, though, because he was too wrapped up in questions of his own: *What would you do if I said no? Would
you blackmail me again? Would you still stay afterward
if I refused to help?*

He wasn't sure he wanted the answers. He wasn't sure
he could trust the answers. In the end, he didn't say anything.

"You're a good man," Tobias said, and Sullivan jerked
his head up. "To do all of this, risk so much, for a guy
you don't know? Yes, you're a good man."

*I'm not doing it for him,* Sullivan thought, but that
would be admitting too much. "You think so?"

"Yes." Tobias shrugged one shoulder, a self-conscious,
perhaps even embarrassed move. "You push me to say
what I think and feel and once you know those things,
you respect them, and that makes it so much easier to
share them. But you also don't let me hide, and that's—
you've helped me be better and happier. You wouldn't
believe me if I said how good I think you are."

Sullivan couldn't hold the eye contact, couldn't keep
everything he felt off his face.

"I care about you a lot," Tobias said, more quietly.
He put the napkin down and came to stand in front of
Sullivan, reaching up to cup Sullivan's jaw, directing

his gaze back up. He smelled faintly of soy sauce and spray cleanser, and Sullivan let himself be kissed, but he couldn't help feeling like he was standing on a slippery slope. Tobias might think he was a good man, might care about him a lot, but it didn't do him any good if Tobias didn't stay.

# Chapter Twenty-One

They dressed in the morning in the clothes they'd bought the day before—popular, cheap brands of tennis shoes in case they accidentally left footprints somewhere, light windbreakers that would be easy to ditch so as to be harder to track. They both wore thin polyester balaclavas, the fabric folded up at the crown so they looked like ugly spandex hats instead of masks. In case he had to ditch his jacket, Sullivan was also wearing a long-sleeved T-shirt underneath to hide his tattoos. The new backpack was already stocked with everything else they might need.

When dressed, they looked like poor, fashion-challenged college students.

They parked in the lot of the diner across the street from Spratt's while they watched for Tidwell. The smell of burgers and fries made Tobias nauseated; he was too nervous to even think of lunch. Fortunately, Tidwell arrived and left right on schedule, sandwiches delivered, alarm reset, and Sullivan and Tobias were free to get started.

The most difficult part of the plan was ensuring the Buick stayed concealed; if any of the cops involved got a glimpse of the tag numbers, they were screwed. The day before they'd scouted out the best area to park in; Denver was lousy with one-way streets, and they ended up parking upriver, so to speak, within two blocks south of Spratt's townhouse, and past an intersection with another one-way street. According to Sullivan, they couldn't have gotten much luckier; if Spratt wanted to follow them by car from his property, he'd have to go around the block first, while Sullivan and Tobias could run up the sidewalk against traffic, climb into the car, and immediately hang a left and be out of view. It had the added benefit of being far enough out of sight of Spratt's place that no matter what security system he had, there was no way he'd be able to identify the Buick.

Sullivan turned off the car. "Got the bag?"

Tobias not only had the bag, his fingers were locked around the strap so tightly they might never come loose. "Yeah."

Sullivan was watching him, his brown eyes narrowed and thoughtful. "We don't have to do this today."

"Can you promise he'll be safe until tomorrow?"

"You know I can't."

"Then give me a minute. I'll be fine. Just…one minute."

Sullivan nodded and Tobias concentrated on breathing. In and out, in and out, slow and steady.

He wished he was in Sullivan's kitchen baking *konparèt*. Or cherry pie. He wouldn't say no to making Baked Alaska at this point, and that was a nightmare waiting to happen. He didn't know anyone who'd made Baked Alaska. He wasn't sure it would be safe in Sullivan's firetrap of a house. All it would take was tripping over a hammer while the kirsch was on fire and they'd both die.

Which was an idea ridiculous enough that he let out a low, grim laugh. He was as calm as he was going to get. "Okay. Let's do this."

Sullivan eyed him for a second, then got out of the car. Tobias followed suit, and they were—wow, they were doing this.

They walked down the street, turning right at the intersection so they could get to the alley running behind Spratt's property. After a couple more minutes of walking, they could see the backyard, and Sullivan nodded. With shaking fingers, Tobias pulled down the hem of the thin polyester balaclava he was wearing so only his eyes showed, then pulled the latex gloves out of his other pocket and slid them on as well.

"Start your watch now," Sullivan said, doing the same with the one he wore on his own wrist. "Four minutes."

And then Tobias was numbly following him into the backyard. The chain-link gate creaked as Sullivan pushed it open. Tobias had to curtail the urge to flinch.

Sullivan didn't waste any time. He walked directly to the window on the right side of the door and pulled the small emergency hammer from his pocket—the kind people kept in their cars to break their windows with in case they had to get out quickly and the door was jammed. The point was steel; the glass fractured in the sill instantly and without too much noise. Sullivan knocked enough of the pane out to make room for his arm, then reached through and flipped the latch, sliding the thing open and using the hammer again—this time the end meant to slice through a stuck seat belt—to get through the screen.

Then he was sliding inside, quiet and quick, and Tobias followed, if slightly less quiet and less quick.

They paused.

The townhouse was silent; the hardwood floors and high ceilings would make for an echoing sort of place, but there was no sound at all beyond the rush of traffic leaching through the front windows. They went through the main floor first, spending seconds only, because the place was laid out roughly in a circle—a huge living space on one side of the dividing wall, an expansive kitchen and dining room on the other. There was periwinkle blue button-tufted furniture with mahogany points and an impressive entertainment system in the living room, granite counters and stainless steel appliances in the kitchen, and the place was so pathologically neat as to be sterile, leapfrogging Tobias's own compulsive neatness by miles. There wasn't a crumb on the counter, not a flipped-up corner of a rug, not a single piece of mail or scrap paper on the island.

Still, he didn't spare his surroundings more thought than that. Now that they'd determined that there was no place for Ghost to be hidden on the main floor—and they hadn't expected otherwise, but it made sense to be sure since they hadn't been able to discern the full layout of the place from outside—he focused on the stairwell tucked back beside the kitchen. Before he could do more than elbow Sullivan, they were moving again, clambering down the stairs to face a dark hallway T-junction.

Sullivan pushed Tobias to the right and they began opening doors, finding a couple of guest bedrooms— the nicer and larger of which was empty of the guest but clearly lived-in. The dim light from the barred basement window revealed keys and loose change on the nightstand, a black jacket slung across the straight-backed chair sitting in front of an elegant desk, upon which a closed laptop rested. The duvet and sheets on the bed were rumpled, like they'd been kicked off by someone getting up.

"I think—" he started, and then had to clear his throat

because the words had come out dry and cracked. "That's Ghost's computer, I think."

The closet was a walk-in without a door; other than some shirts and a pair of black lace-up boots, it was empty.

"Where is he?" Tobias asked.

"Come on," Sullivan replied, darting back out into the hallway. Tobias checked his watch—from the moment they'd entered the backyard to now, seventy seconds had gone by. As he followed Sullivan, Tobias felt the passing of every additional second in increments. Four steps to the door—three seconds. Peeking into an empty, gleaming bathroom—two seconds. Proceeding down the hallway past the stairs and opening a door to find a laundry room with neurotic lack of clutter, but for the laundry basket half-full of clothes in one corner—ten seconds.

Staring at the heavy padlock and thick, stainless steel hasp on the last door in the hallway—fifteen seconds.

Sullivan was already yanking the pack off of Tobias's shoulder, unzipping it to find the small crowbar they'd packed. He put it to the door frame, concentrating not on breaking the metal but on separating the screws from the wood. He wrenched hard, multiple times, and the wood began to splinter, but it was slow, so slow.

Thirty seconds passed. Sullivan cursed under his breath. Another twenty seconds passed, and the hasp was down to one screw, the wood clinging stubbornly but ineffectually, and finally Sullivan stepped back and kicked hard.

The door gave, and they rushed forward into a completely empty room. No furniture. No blinds on the barred window. No rugs or artwork on the wall. There was a single drowsy cobweb dangling in one corner.

"What the hell?" Sullivan said, but Tobias grabbed his arm.

"Look."

Unlike the closet in the room Ghost had been occupying, this closet had a door, and Tobias pointed at the padlock on the jamb. He yanked on the knob uselessly, but then Sullivan was there, pulling a small, silver key from a tiny hook that'd been screwed into the wall, hard to see in the shadows of the dim room. His hands weren't entirely steady as he got the padlock open. Tobias shoved the door wide and there was Ghost, naked and zip tied, a handcuff linking the tie to a D ring in the wall over his head. He was sitting on what looked like a sheepskin dog bed, leaning against the wall, and he was *gagged*. A bright red rubber ball thing was in his mouth, the black straps going around his head, saliva dripping from the corner of his mouth from how long he'd been wearing it.

And there was nothing else there—no glass of water or pail for urine, no books, no nothing.

Ghost was staring at him from above that gag, his green eyes wide and confused and perhaps even afraid, and Tobias abruptly remembered his mask. He reached up, intending to show Ghost who he was, only to jerk when Sullivan grabbed his wrist.

"Don't," he whispered, and jerked his chin upward to direct Tobias's gaze to the small camera mounted in the upper corner of the closet.

"Okay," Tobias breathed, and turned back to Ghost. "It's me, Ghost, you recognize my voice, right? You know who I—"

Ghost frowned, his head shaking once as if he didn't believe it, and then his eyes closed and his entire body sagged into the corner, boneless and small. For a second, anyway, one second before he straightened again and yanked pointedly at his wrists.

"Get clothes for him," Sullivan said, angling Tobias out of the way. Ghost tensed as Sullivan loomed over him, and Tobias wanted to say that Sullivan wouldn't hurt him, but they didn't have time, so instead he ran back to Ghost's room and scavenged a pair of jeans, a T-shirt and his boots.

By the time he was back, Sullivan was crouched beside Ghost where he knelt on the carpet, grimacing as he stretched his arms out. The gag was gone, and his lips were red and swollen, the corners cracked and bleeding.

"Here." Tobias held out the clothes and Ghost stumbled to his feet, clumsy as Bambi for a minute as his body readjusted to standing upright. He yanked his jeans on, his gaze returning to Tobias again and again as if he doubted his vision.

"Come on," Sullivan snapped, and headed out the door, turning left and starting up the stairs. Tobias thrust the shirt into Ghost's hands and followed, and he got all the way to the main floor before he realized Ghost wasn't behind him. He snagged Sullivan's arm, making him whirl and say, "What?"

"Ghost," Tobias called back softly, but there was no response.

"Where the hell is he?" Sullivan checked his watch. "We've got to go. We've got less than a minute, Tobias."

"I know." He started to head back down and Sullivan grabbed his wrist.

"Forty-nine seconds. We did our part. We don't have time to drag him out. Let's go."

"You go." Tobias gave him a nudge toward the window. "I'm serious. Go. I'll get him."

"I'm not—are you fucking insane?" Sullivan asked, and Tobias wished he could do or say anything else, because Sullivan clearly didn't understand—his face was pinched and unhappy. "Tobias. Come with me. *Please.*"

"I'm not—I can't." Tobias twisted his wrist free, shoved him in the direction of the broken window, and ran for the stairs. He called back over his shoulder, "Get out of here. I mean it."

He thundered back down the stairs cursing Ghost silently and hoping fervently that Sullivan had listened. He would have to address that hurt in Sullivan's expression later, because this wasn't a choice, not the way Sullivan seemed to have taken it. It was more that Tobias knew where his efforts were better spent, and of the two of them, Ghost was definitely the one who needed supervision. Of the two of them, Ghost would be the one to do something unpredictable and dangerous. As Tobias ricocheted off the basement wall and spun to the left, he half expected Ghost to lunge at him from a dark shadow with a gas can and a blow torch, ready to take the whole place down and he and Tobias with it.

Instead, he found Ghost in the laundry room, tearing at the tables and bins by the far wall.

"What?" Tobias asked helplessly. "We're leaving, Ghost."

"Go, then." He didn't hesitate, instead tearing madly at the small rugs that would keep the cold tile floor comfortable for bare feet. "I'm not leaving without it."

"Ghost!" Tobias grabbed at his arm. "Whatever it is isn't worth your life, now come on!"

Ghost shoved him hard enough that Tobias went flying into the wall, stumbling and going to one knee before blinking up at him in shock. For a second he thought

Ghost would kick him, but instead he upended a small cabinet so that detergent and dryer sheets came tumbling out. "I didn't go through all of this for nothing," he bit out, checking the newly cleared area for whatever it was he'd lost. "Now either help me search or get the fuck out."

Tobias got up, shaky and furious and stung, and said, "What am I looking for?"

"A USB. I threw it in here and it's—it's got to be here. He'd have said if he found it, so it must be here, it must've bounced off of something—" Ghost's words grew more panicked as he went. Tobias uselessly kicked aside the overturned laundry basket and pawed through the dirty clothes there.

He heard Sullivan call his name, his tone a rich mixture of anger and concern. Damn it. He was supposed to be gone, he was supposed to be safe by now.

Tobias went to the door and yelled back, with all the fury he could muster, "You don't need to be here. Go!"

It came out impressively commanding. A second later, footsteps echoed overhead. Something thudded loudly. Then silence.

All right.

All right. Sullivan was gone. He would be safe. He was gone. It was on Tobias now. And that was as it should be, because this was his mess, and had been since the beginning.

He glanced at Ghost, who was searching through the wreckage he'd caused with an air of utter single-mindedness. He felt suddenly certain that he'd made a tremendous mistake and was grateful that Sullivan had gone instead of following him down here into it. But there was nothing else to be done about it now—

he couldn't leave without Ghost, and he couldn't make Ghost leave without what he'd come for.

So Tobias started yanking on the washer, a black and chrome monstrosity standing on a raised dais inset in the wall in a way that would be tricky to shift. It was heavy but not immovable; it rocked when he tugged on it.

"Here," Tobias started, and Ghost's head jerked up, eyes sliding to him, narrowing on the washer when he saw what Tobias was up to.

"Yes," he said, and the two of them managed to work the washer out by several feet. It was awkward and slow, and they'd only gotten it halfway out when Tobias caught a glimpse of his watch.

00:00.

Who knew how long it'd been flashing that collection of zeroes?

"Ghost," he said, his throat tightening, but it was useless. Ghost was hoisting himself up on top of the dryer to lie flat on his belly, lurching forward so that his head and half of his torso disappeared back behind the washer, legs spread to help him keep his balance, and Tobias grabbed his ankle to provide leverage. For a second there was nothing, and then Ghost popped back up, lips pressed tight and bloodless.

"It's behind the dryer," he said. "I saw it. It's back there. Help me."

"Ghost," Tobias repeated. "We're out of time. We have to—"

Ghost didn't say a word; he only grabbed Tobias by the elbow and thrust him in the direction of the dryer, and Tobias found himself moving without thinking, found himself clutching at the dryer's corners and heaving.

"Again," Ghost gasped. "Pull."

Together they got the machine to the edge of the dais, and Ghost didn't bother waiting for Tobias this time so they could lower it together. He let it go and Tobias couldn't hold it alone; his sweaty fingertips slipped and the dryer crashed to the floor with an immense racket. Ghost was already scrambling up and over, deft as he eased his way down behind the wreckage. He vanished from sight for a second only, and then was vaulting back up, slipping over the stainless steel in his bare feet, and landing in a crouch with a small black USB clenched in his fist. He brushed past Tobias, leaving him behind without a word or glance, and as he hurried to catch up, Tobias tried to ignore the blinking zeroes on his watch. The stairwell loomed in front of him, Ghost already halfway to the first landing and then—there—the sudden sound of a door opening overhead.

Ghost froze. "Is your partner still here?" he whispered.

"I don't know," Tobias mouthed. He hoped not—the fear clogging his throat only worsened at the idea of Sullivan upstairs.

The footsteps were cautious and slow, the floorboards creaking in a vaguely circular pattern, and Tobias swallowed hard—it wasn't Sullivan. Sullivan would have no reason to work his way through the living room and kitchen like that.

"Move," Ghost said, hurrying back on silent bare feet, guiding Tobias with unkind hands into the guest room on the opposite side of the hall—the one Ghost had previously occupied. He shoved the USB into Tobias's back jeans pocket.

"Don't lose that or I'll kill you," Ghost breathed, and Tobias wasn't entirely sure he was being flippant. No, there was no— Those green eyes were colder and harder than emeralds by far, reptilian in their indifference, and a shudder ran the length of Tobias's spine. He thought, *I believe you. I believe you would kill me.* He thought, *you don't give two shits about me, do you?*

He thought, *what am I doing here?*

Ghost went to shut the door and Tobias held the knob, remembering the time he and Sullivan had hidden in Ghost's apartment. Sullivan hadn't closed the closet door all the way, mentioning that people assumed that hiders would shut doors.

He jerked his chin at Ghost—*come on*—but Ghost only shook his head and jabbed a finger hard in Tobias's direction before vanishing in the direction of the stairs.

Stay here. Of course.

As he eased out of sight from the hallway, Tobias half expected that old, dangerous itch to rear its ugly head. He expected to feel frustrated and angry, to chafe under the need to act in the face of being told to wait, but there was nothing. The recklessness had well and truly gone.

So he stayed and waited and was in perfect position to hear a crisp voice from down the hall say, "When I saw them in the closet with you, I assumed the worst. I owe you an apology for that."

Ghost, more quietly, subdued: "You don't. I almost went with them."

A pause. Then the crisp voice—Spratt, Tobias decided, placing the vaguely familiar voice as the one who'd given the speech at the civic picnic that weekend—said, "The fact that you stayed proves how much you've grown. I know what she wants you to be, what your friends on the streets want you to be. But you're so much more than that, and you've changed. Already, you've changed so much. You can be cleansed of all of that. You're better than all of that."

Tobias had been in the process of looking for a potential weapon, but Spratt's words brought him up short. Or rather, Ghost's response did.

"I'm not," Ghost said, and the words were blank, just as his body language and expression had been when Tobias had watched him through the windows from Sullivan's parked car.

"You are," Spratt replied. "Here. Come here. Wild things need order to be good. Won't you let me help you? You've taken the first step, you want to be here… I'll keep you safe from her. I'll take care of you. All you have to do is let me."

Spratt's voice made Tobias think, weirdly, of putting butter on a burn—it was a faintly greasy process, possibly soothing in the short term, but destructive in the long term. Spratt was saying other things in the same vein now, and they made Tobias's stomach roil even as he looked around the room in search of a weapon. The lamp at the bedside table wasn't heavy enough to do much damage, and it was awkwardly shaped enough that it wouldn't be easy to wield. There was a painting on the wall behind glass, but he'd never be able to get a shard without making noise, and he'd probably cut himself up in the process. There was a white vase full of silk flowers on the dresser standing a foot away. The vase was hardly sturdy, but probably his best bet. He pulled the flowers out and set them on the floor as quietly as he could before creeping over to the doorway and peeking out.

Spratt stood at the foot of the stairs in an elegant gray suit. Despite the heat outside and the rush he must've been in to get here so quickly, he looked cool and collected. His pistol was in his right hand, but it was currently lax at his side, pointed at the floor, and with his left hand, he was touching Ghost's shoulder, coaxing him forward, trying to ease Ghost closer.

Ghost complied in degrees—leaning first, a small step next, and then a second, larger step.

"You're mine," Spratt murmured. "I'll keep you safe. Help strip you of all of that virulence. All you have to do in return is talk to me, to stay here with me and be mine."

Ghost took a last step forward and pressed himself against Spratt's chest. Spratt wrapped one long arm around him and twisted his upper body, reaching behind him to set his pistol on the step so he could hold Ghost more firmly—without fear, Tobias supposed, that Ghost could reach the weapon. Ghost's face tipped in Tobias's direction, and his eyes were closed. His lips were trembling.

"I'm sorry," Ghost said.

And as Tobias watched, his vase lifted high, ready to step out and brain Spratt as soon as the opportunity presented itself, two jeans-clad legs appeared at the top of the lower flight of stairs, appeared and clambered down, suddenly giving up silence for speed, and Ghost ducked out of the way at the same time.

Sullivan hit Spratt hard in the back of the head with something that Tobias couldn't make out, but it didn't matter. The cop crumpled to the floor, ungainly in unconsciousness, face mashed against the hardwood.

"Jesus," Tobias whispered, and came out of the room.

Sullivan's eyes found him and locked on, sweeping over him from tip to toe. "You okay?"

"Yes." Tobias set the vase down. He glanced at Ghost,

who was standing over Spratt's sprawled body, emotion-
less and still. "Ghost, are you okay?"

Ghost ignored him. Instead, he bent and pushed Spratt
onto his side, tipping his head so that he would be able
to breathe more easily. His hands lingered in the air for
a moment, lost, and then he stood again and glanced up
at Sullivan. "Your timing is impeccable."

"Can we fucking leave now?" Sullivan asked Tobias,
ignoring Ghost entirely. He dropped his weapon—a
wooden rolling pin—and it clattered down the stairs to
rest against Spratt's thigh. "He might've called Tidwell
or my client as backup."

"Yes, let's go," Tobias said, and brushed past Ghost.
He followed Sullivan up the stairs, catching the soft pad
of Ghost's bare feet behind him, and they got to the window and out into the backyard without trouble. They hurried across the yard and back into the alley.

There were no sirens. No one yelling. No neighbors
lurking at fences that he could see.

A couple houses down, they paused, getting shoes
and a hat out for Ghost, who put them on while Sullivan
and Tobias removed their balaclavas, windbreakers, and
gloves and shoved them into the pack. Sullivan slid his
ball cap back into place and by that time Ghost was ready.

Gravel crunched under their feet until they reached
the end of the alley and turned right. It was hot out. Birds
were calling. Afternoon traffic was beginning to pick up.
A man in a suit barking into a cell phone passed them
going the opposite direction, pausing before crossing
the street. The walk to the car might've been downright
pleasant if not for the clammy sweat dampening Tobias's
temples and back, if not for the way his heart thundered
and he had to subdue the urge to run or look back. A per-

fectly normal day, all things considered. A normal day where Tobias had broken in to a cop's house and Sullivan had hit that cop over the head with a rolling pin like a furious housewife.

Ghost's skin was sickly pale, his eyes fever bright. Tobias almost couldn't bear to look at him. It hurt to be angry at something so fragile.

They made it to the car. There was still no sound of sirens.

## Chapter Twenty-Two

Sullivan wasn't sure what he'd expected from Tobias's friend, but it wasn't this nervy, sharp-dull kid with the hollow, canny green eyes. The guy had some sort of split-personality at work in his body language—one second his limbs appeared too heavy to move, the next he was whip-ready to strike, the next he shifted into a sly, slinky sort of invitation. And then the cycle started over, with minute variations, an endless byplay of characters and moods and manipulations. Like a chameleon trying on colors.

Sullivan instantly, profoundly disliked him.

Ghost hadn't said a word since Sullivan had keeled Spratt over. His fingers clenched in sense memory at the recollection, feeling again the weight of the wood in his hand, the meaty thud of the strike, the way his stomach had revolted. He'd thought, at the time, that he might be sick. But Tobias had come out of the shadows, big-eyed and so fucking relieved, like Sullivan had done something heroic instead of violent, like all he wanted to see in the whole world was Sullivan, and he'd wanted to say something cruel to that relief. Something along the lines of *you chose him, don't you dare look at me like that*.

Now they were seated at the table in Sullivan's dining

room. Well, Ghost and Sullivan were; Tobias was bringing Ghost a sandwich and a glass of water, asking in a
low voice if Ghost needed a doctor.

It was kind of pissing Sullivan off.

"I'm fine," Ghost told Tobias. He'd settled on subdued, apparently. His head dipped toward his plate, his
shoulders rounded, and Tobias's expression went tight
and pained, for fuck's sake.

"What did you go back to get?" Sullivan asked Ghost,
and Tobias fumbled the roll of paper towels he was carrying.

"Do we have to talk about this now?" Ghost asked in
a low voice aimed at Tobias.

"Maybe we—" Tobias started.

At the same time, Sullivan said, "Yes. We can't be sure
they won't come after him," trying to keep his voice even
as he watched Tobias flinch. "We can't be sure that we
didn't miss anything. We need to do this now." He went
back to staring at Ghost. "What did you go back for that
was worth putting Tobias at risk?"

"I don't—it wasn't anything important, I promise,"
Ghost muttered. "I've got a headache. Can I lie down?"

"Ghost, you heard Sullivan, we—"

"Just for twenty minutes? I'm so tired."

Tobias sighed and gave Sullivan a helpless, *what am
I supposed to do* sort of look. "All right."

"Will you come with me?" Ghost grabbed on to Tobias's T-shirt, his fingers low on Tobias's hip.

"Of course I will."

"Make sure you choose a room without any windows,"
Sullivan said, annoyed beyond the telling, and Tobias
looked startled, like it hadn't occurred to him that Ghost
might try to run. *You can't be falling for this*, Sullivan

thought, although Tobias's blind spot for Ghost had so far proved to be the size of the sun—and every bit as capable of burning him.

But Tobias glanced down at his own hip, where Ghost's fingers were resting inches from his jeans pocket, and something about that made it all click for Tobias, a click so tangibly permanent and real that it was written on his face bright as neon. He eased back a step, swallowing hard, the curve of his lips going tense and unfriendly, and stupid, selfish hope rose in Sullivan's chest.

"Well, that was nice while it lasted," Ghost said, and in a heartbeat he'd shifted from traumatized crime victim to languid hustler. He slumped back in his chair and gave Sullivan a sideways grin.

"What'd you take?" Sullivan asked him.

"Nothing," Ghost said. "What was your name again, handsome?"

Tobias gave Ghost a dirty look—far dirtier than Sullivan would've guessed he had in him. "His name is Sullivan Tate," he told Ghost, before glancing at Sullivan and adding, "We went back for a USB."

"It's like that, is it?" Ghost asked lazily, stretching his arms over his head.

"Yes, it is."

"Is he a good kisser? His mouth is a little mean, but sometimes that makes for the best kissing."

"He's not mean," Tobias snapped. "He helped me rescue you. Leave him alone."

"What's on the USB?" Sullivan asked.

"Nudie pictures," Ghost replied. "If you like sky-blue seventies silk, brother, they're right up your alley."

Everything about him was lackadaisical and smug; all that was missing were a couple finger guns. The effect was outrageously unpleasant, and Sullivan caught himself wondering how anyone ever got anything done where Ghost was concerned, if it was always this shifting facade that made it impossible to keep your feet. And that—that made sense actually. It was to Ghost's benefit to keep the people around him off balance.

"I'll pass." Sullivan searched Ghost's face carefully, looking for signs of trauma, for any evidence that he was reading this wrong, that he should take a different tack, but all he got was insolence. The victim was well and truly gone, and kindness would wash off the guy's back like water off a duck.

Tobias set the paper towels on the table with more force than necessary. "You can talk to him. You can talk to me. We're on your side."

"I'm good." Ghost slid the top piece of bread off the sandwich, raked his finger through the mayo, and slurped it up. "Full fat. Nice."

"Ghost," Tobias said, sounding completely bewildered.

Sullivan cleared his throat. "Tobias, why don't you go grab some fresh sheets out of my room? We'll get Ghost set up on the couch."

Tobias wasn't stupid; he knew exactly what Sullivan was doing. The real question was whether Tobias trusted him enough to go along with it. For a long moment he hesitated. He glanced at Ghost.

"I'm not scared of your boyfriend," Ghost said, patting him reassuringly on the ass, which—come the fuck on. "The hair gives him a certain toughness about the face, but if he's falling for you, he's got to be pure mush on the inside."

Tobias didn't seem to know if that was an insult or a

compliment, so he only gave Ghost a conflicted frown and reluctantly left the room.

Sullivan wasn't stupid either; he figured Tobias was probably eavesdropping, but it wasn't Tobias that Sullivan was trying to manipulate, so he didn't give a shit.

"All alone," Ghost said. "Whatever shall we do with the time?"

"First order of business. If you get him hurt, I'll give you to Spratt so fast it'll make your head spin."

Ghost blinked a couple of times. "I'm not sure you mean that. I wonder if you think you mean it."

Oh, he meant it. He could be pissed off at Tobias, he could know exactly where he ranked in Tobias's estimation, but that didn't change the fact that Tobias mattered to him, deeply and—he suspected—irrevocably. "I don't care if you believe it. I'm not trying to scare you; I'm being honest about the cause and effect here. He's my first priority. If you get him hurt, I will make you pay. Bear it in mind."

"Duly noted. Do you like fucking him?"

"Immeasurably. He's surprisingly filthy in bed," Sullivan said conversationally, enjoying the temporary pleasure of seeing a spark of annoyance in all the wry amusement. "Let's be clear, one bullshitter to another. You're only here in my house because I care about Tobias. Once I'm satisfied that nothing about this is going to bite him or me in the ass, you're free to fuck off. In fact, I'd prefer it. We both know you're going to drag him down with you."

"Are you warning me off?" Ghost asked, seemingly tickled by it.

"No. He's a big boy; if he wants you in his life, he's welcome to you. But if you're worth half the effort he's put into finding you, you'll do everything you can to keep him in the clear."

Ghost kicked his boots off and swung his legs up, putting his bare, dirty feet on the table.

"Seriously?" Sullivan shook his head as if disappointed. "I hate to think I've already broken you down to petty rebellion. Surely you have something more substantial up your sleeve."

Ghost checked his nails. There was chipped black varnish on his right hand. "You're not a cop."

"No."

"A bodyguard?"

"No."

Ghost sent a sly glance around the room, settling on the Mark III on the steamer trunk. "A PI? Did Tobias hire you to find me?" His eyebrows skyrocketed and he clasped his hands together in front of his heart. "And then you fell in love! Oh, my inner teenage girl is shrieking in happiness right now."

Sullivan tipped his head. "What's on the USB?"

Ghost smiled. "I wish you two crazy kids all the best."

"I figure it's something Mama will want," Sullivan said thoughtfully, watching that smile pick up some frigid undertones. "She sent you there to get blackmail material, and she doesn't seem the type to forgive failure. So that's your first priority, I'm guessing. Get the USB to Mama, and go from there. Which means it's evidence of Spratt up to bad shit. Drugs? Hookers? Violence?"

Ghost sat there and looked at him, every muscle in his body as relaxed and chill as the day is long—except for the muscle in his jaw, which was pulsing beneath that stiff smile. Hell of a tell.

"Explains why you're so determined to put Tobias

off his game, too," Sullivan continued. "He's a pushover about some things, but he's a good man. A deeply moral man at his core, and he won't want you giving a member of organized crime blackmail material for the top cop in the city. He'll fight you on this. You can't risk Tobias finding out what you've got. Am I on the right track?"

"And what about you, handsome? What would you do with that USB?"

"Depends what's on it. If it's enough to put Spratt behind bars? That's one thing. If it's only going to embarrass him or piss him off, that's something else. But as long as that USB exists, he'll come after you, won't he?"

"He doesn't know about it."

"Are you sure about that?"

"Yes."

"And when he goes through your laptop?"

The laptop they'd left behind, he meant, in the room that had been Ghost's before he'd gotten himself thrown into that closet. Ghost's brow tightened almost imperceptibly.

"You've got surveillance programs on your hard drive, don't you?" Sullivan asked. "I do this shit for a living, pal. If you've got a wireless camera somewhere in Spratt's house, it needs a receiver, and that means a program on your computer. He won't know what you've been filming, but he'll suspect you've got something. It doesn't matter what you do have; he'll think of the worst possible thing you could have, and that's what he'll be aiming to stop. Is he going to come after you?"

Ghost looked away.

"That's a yes. Do you actually have the worst possible thing?"

Ghost still didn't speak.

Also a yes, Sullivan decided. "You can't give the USB to Mama."

"The fuck I can't."

"She'll kill you."

"If it saves me from this conversation, it'll be worthwhile."

"She's already planning it. It's been part of the plan all along."

"Wow, Tobias didn't tell me you were psychic!"

Sullivan was sort of tempted to smile at that one, but he managed to corral it. "In 1992, a woman named Margaret Trudeau was killed. She was a live-in housekeeper for a man who was involved in local crime."

"Lovely, it's story time." Ghost rolled his eyes.

Sullivan ignored that. "Spratt and his boys worked that case. Knowing what I do about them, I'm thinking they weren't there to bring peace to the neighborhood. Hell, for all I know, they killed him themselves to get control of some aspect of his business, then used their subsequent investigation to cover it up. That part's conjecture, but what I am certain about is that Mama wasn't happy about those deaths."

"Whoop-de-fucking-do."

"The local crime guy? Mama's husband. The dead housekeeper? Mama's very good friend."

Ghost's gaze flickered. Bingo.

"You following where I'm going with this?" Sullivan sat back in his chair. "More than two decades after Spratt works that case, Mama's still got an eye on him? She plays a long game, huh? Plenty of time to figure out how to get back at the corrupt cop who took someone you loved. I figure she found out that Spratt had a weakness for you—not sure how on that one, but judging from the

way he was talking to you at his place, it's not a reach to
call it a fatal flaw. She offered you a spot on her team,
which you probably turned down…"

He trailed off, waiting for confirmation, and after a
beat Ghost gave a tiny nod.

"And maybe that seemed like the end of it. But…long
game. And when everything went down with your buddy
and the Krayevs eight months ago, suddenly she had one
over on you. All she wanted was a favor, right? That's
machinations, Ghost. That's not a woman who leaves
loose ends. Say you give her the USB. What does she do
next? You think she's going to promote you?"

"She keeps her word," Ghost said, flat and final, and
Sullivan realized that Ghost believed it. It might be the
first entirely honest thing he'd said.

"Did she say she would let you live?"

Ghost didn't say anything.

"Did she say she'd protect you when Spratt realizes
what you've done? Did she promise to let you walk away?
And even if she did, you're not idiot enough to believe
that the matriarch of a crime family has never told a lie.
You don't believe that any more than I do."

"Don't tell me what I know."

"Fine. I'll tell you what *I* know. Giving the USB to
Mama won't keep you safe. All it'll do is move your
death up."

"So I'll mail it to her and run."

"You can't run anywhere in the States—you get picked
up for speeding in bum-fuck Alaska and they'll find out
about any outstanding warrants. And there *will* be warrants. Spratt's got more connections than he'd need.
You'll have every cop in the country looking for you."

"Canada's nice this time of year."

"For now. But again, all it takes is one Mountie to pull you over and realize you're in the country illegally, and you're fucked. Canada extradites."

"Mexico doesn't."

"Not in practice, usually, no, except for in cases of murder," Sullivan agreed. "Nothing to stop Spratt from arranging one in your name. But that's a more complicated route than he'll need. After all, you don't have any skills or education. You don't have friends or family there, I'm guessing, to help you get set up right so you can live clean. That puts you back on a street corner. If you think any number of guys wouldn't take some US dollars to hit a hooker with no family or contacts to do something about it, you're fooling yourself."

Sullivan leaned forward. He could see the wild flutter of Ghost's pulse in his wrist from where he was sitting. "You're fucked," he said quietly. "I'm sorry, but he's the rock and she's the hard place."

For a long minute, neither of them said anything. Finally, Ghost cleared his throat. "I assume you have a counteroffer in mind?"

"There's nothing you can do that'll take down both of them. You don't have the clout. But you can at least take down Spratt. Make his crimes public and he'll be fired pretty quickly. Prison time will hopefully follow, but even if it doesn't, he's not going to be able to rumble law enforcement after you anymore. That makes running an option again. It's not a good option, but it's there."

"So I mail the USB to the *Denver Post* and take off? Is that what you're advocating?"

"I have a friend who knows a very reliable retired cop who can get things going on the legal side, make sure it stays with the right people. The press is always an option too. As long as he gets fired, you're in the clear on that side. The wider the truth spreads, the safer you'll be, but there's nothing we can do about Mama. At this point it's just minimizing the fallout. She was always going to kill you, Ghost."

The real question wasn't what to do with the USB; Tobias had it. They didn't need Ghost to stick around to turn the drive over to someone who could really use it. But the whole thing would be easier—especially for Ghost—if he stuck around. Sullivan considered the irony at the idea that Ghost's paperwork might come across his desk as a subpoena he'd have to serve.

"I need to think about this. I'm tired." Ghost pushed to his feet.

"Wait. Do you recognize the name Nathalie Trudeau?"

Ghost shook his head. "No. Who is she?"

"Margaret's daughter. Mama might've taken her in when she was a girl." Sullivan went to his file cabinet, flipping through the case folder until he found the picture. His fingers clenched too tightly.

"Name doesn't sound familiar."

"Just look, please." Back at the table, Sullivan held the picture out and Ghost frowned. He leaned closer, eyes tracing over the lines of Nathalie's face.

"And you think Mama raised her?"

"Maybe."

"That explains a lot," Ghost said.

"Does it?"

"Yeah. She goes by Kellen now."

"Kellen…you mean Mama's henchman Kellen?"

"The very same."

"Oh. I assumed Kellen was a man."

"Most do until they meet her." Ghost's lips twisted

into a tired, unhappy smile. "There are benefits to being other than what people expect. I'd steer clear, though. The duckling has definitely imprinted on her foster mother. She does most of Mama's wet work."

Sullivan sat back down, his whole body heavy. He'd thought—shit. He didn't know what he'd thought. Tobias had infected him with the hope that Nathalie was alive, that she could be saved, and that'd kept him motivated even once his client had shown his dirty underpinnings. But he hadn't expected this. Dead or alive, he'd been working on the presumption of innocence.

He should've known better. Jesus, you'd think he'd stop letting himself get blindsided by shit going badly.

"Is she K? In your phone? The person asking you for updates?"

"Yes."

All this time, if Sullivan had just pressed the call button, she'd have answered. Nathalie would've been right there on the other end of the line. Anticipating someone to kill, perhaps. Jesus.

Ghost cocked his head toward the stairs. "You got a room I can sleep in?"

"You can take mine for a while." He took another few seconds to get his legs under him, before rising to show Ghost where to go. "Don't ask Tobias for the USB back, by the way. He won't give it to you."

"Well, not now," Ghost muttered, and Sullivan glanced up to find Tobias lurking in the hallway behind them. "Let's tip a glass to the deeply moral eavesdropper in question."

"You couldn't have said all of that to me?" Tobias asked quietly. As he spoke, he went past Sullivan into the dining room and grabbed one of the straight-backed chairs. He carried it to Ghost and held it out. "You couldn't have been honest with me?" He laughed grimly. "I'm stupid to be surprised."

Ghost's jaw tightened. He accepted the chair with slow hands, fingers clamping on the wood until the knuckles turned white. In a low voice, he said, "I missed you, too."

# Chapter Twenty-Three

Earlier in the car, Ghost had stared out the window with a stunned hunger, as if he'd never anticipated escaping that closet and seeing something as plain as traffic again. He'd looked so underweight and hollow-eyed and young that Tobias's anger and doubt over Ghost's behavior in the laundry room had softened. How could it not? After what Ghost had been through, anyone's behavior would be questionable. They'd only need to convince him he was safe, and Ghost would be better, he'd let Tobias be kind to him and take care of him, and he'd be grateful.

Tobias stifled a grim laugh as he turned the coffee-maker on. He'd actually thought Ghost would be grateful.

He was an idiot.

First, because Ghost didn't let anyone take care of him; Tobias should know better. Second, because even Ghost's most convincing vulnerabilities usually turned out to be lies, and third, because it was incredibly narcissistic to save someone's life because you wanted them to appreciate you. But there it was. Tobias was hurt and angry because he'd thought—stupidly—that saving Ghost would be the thing that finally made Ghost trust him. Respect him. Keep him. That was not only the wrong reason to help someone, it was unfair to Ghost, whose responses

to being hurt shouldn't have a single damn thing to do
with Tobias's expectations.

He knew all of that. It stung anyway.

"What was the thing with the chair?" Sullivan asked,
coming back downstairs.

"He can't sleep in an unlocked room." It might not be
a thorough explanation, but Tobias decided to leave it
at that. Back at Woodbury, Ghost had stacked things in
front of their door at night—jars of pencils, plastic action figures he'd stolen from younger boys, one of the
ancient small radios that staff let them check out as re-
wards for good behavior—anything that would clatter
if the door was opened and the pile tipped over. Tobias
couldn't tell anyone about that, though. It felt too much
like telling a secret.

Sullivan didn't ask for more anyway. For a professional snoop, Sullivan was very respectful of boundaries.
Just one of the million things that made Tobias love him.

Okay, that sentence had gone to—well, not an unexpected place, but certainly a bold one, because he wasn't
going to take it back. Tobias did love him.

Sullivan, who'd accepted him just as he was, mess and
all, and who had been kind when no one in their right
mind could expect him to be. Sullivan, who'd followed
Tobias into a dirty cop's house to rescue someone he'd
never met out of loyalty to Tobias and because it was
right. Sullivan, who'd asked Tobias to get clean sheets,
when he could've thrown those three rules around.

*You don't have to obey,* he'd meant. *You don't have to
step aside. You don't have to leave and wait for me to
handle this. You don't have to give me the privacy I'm
asking for. But I have my reasons, please trust me.*

Sullivan hadn't wanted Tobias to be kept in the dark;

he'd wanted Ghost to feel free. Sullivan had known Tobias's absence would unlock something in Ghost—Sullivan had an uncanny grasp on the way Ghost's mind worked, despite knowing him for all of half an hour, a talent Tobias couldn't help being jealous of.

So he'd waited in the hallway and listened. And he'd known he'd not only had the freedom to choose, but that he'd done exactly what Sullivan had expected, had intended, when he'd come around the corner and found Ghost's face shocked and Sullivan's completely unsurprised.

"You all right?"

Tobias realized he'd been staring at the coffeemaker for long, silent minutes. He'd made coffee without thinking about it. "Considering that I went to enormous trouble and expense to help a friend who could tell a complete stranger more than he could tell me? I'm great."

Sullivan leaned against the counter. "It's not that he doesn't trust you. It's not that he doesn't care. You get that, don't you?"

Tobias let out a low laugh. "I'm not sure how else you could interpret it." He got out a mug for himself and shook a second one in the air in a silent question.

Sullivan nodded, then added, "And he said those things to me for the same reason you could be honest with me in the beginning. It's because he doesn't care what I think. He *does* care what you think."

Tobias slowly poured coffee. That possibility hadn't occurred to him. "I don't know."

"Okay."

Tobias passed Sullivan's mug over. "Thank you. For helping me. For helping my friend. For not leaving us. That was brave. And decent. So thank you."

He was quiet a moment, and the air shifted between them, thickened in a way that made Tobias slightly uneasy. "Are you all right?" he asked.

Sullivan seemed on the verge of saying something, then hesitated. Finally, he said, "I didn't want to hurt anyone."

"I know. I'm sorry it came to that." If any part of this sat poorly with Tobias it was that Sullivan had been forced into that position, but he didn't buy that this was the only source of the problem. Tobias studied his profile—the ordinary slope of his nose, the bony ridges of his brow and cheekbones and jaw, his strong chin and thick eyelashes. He looked tired and a little unhappy. "Is that the only thing that's bothering you?"

Sullivan scrubbed a hand over his forehead. "No. I don't know."

Tobias licked his lips. "Do you want to talk about it?"

"Not remotely." Sullivan accepted a mug and took a paper towel from the roll, wiping at spilled sugar, no doubt using the excuse of the chore to avoid eye contact. It was so unlike him—what Tobias knew of him, anyway—that a shiver of unease crept down his spine.

"All right." He wanted to push, but it wasn't like Sullivan had been unclear, and the least Tobias could do was respect his wishes. "You think we got away with it?"

"I think if they knew who we are, we'd be dead already."

"That's a small comfort, at least."

"Yeah."

Tobias went to the sink and washed the stirring spoon. "You did good with him. He's difficult. I never know what to do with him when he's like that, but you didn't have any trouble."

"He doesn't speak your language," Sullivan said, not unkindly. He jerked a shoulder. "The two of you have fundamentally different ways of looking at the world. It doesn't translate, that's all."

Sullivan had been right; Tobias didn't like it. Part of him wanted to argue, but it would be bull, so he took a breath instead and changed the subject.

"What do you think is on that USB drive?"

Sullivan chucked the paper towel into the plastic grocery sack Tobias had set out for trash. "Let's find out."

It turned out that Sullivan's laptop—outfitted with what he called the PI's computer toolbox, a collection of programs likely to come in handy over the course of a career of using different surveillance equipment—already had a media viewer that allowed them to open the files on the USB.

There was more than one—most were short, simple things, and they were all taken from the same vantage point. Tobias tried to picture the living room, and realized the camera must've been on the top shelf of the bookshelves inset in the wall. He couldn't precisely recall what else had stood on the shelf. Photographs, maybe. Or fancy pottery.

"How did Ghost hide a video camera there?" he asked.

"Some of the newer ones are the size of your pinky fingernail," Sullivan explained. "The camera would transmit the footage to Ghost's laptop, where he would be able to cut out any extraneous material and copy whatever he wanted to any other disks. I can't imagine Mama sparing any expense. All Ghost would need is a shadowed area out of a frequent sight line."

"But why all this cloak-and-dagger stuff? He could've emailed it to someone anytime." As soon as the words were out of his mouth, he shook his head. "Yeah, like Ghost would trust anyone enough to send them this. Still. He could've emailed it to himself. Or Mama. Then he wouldn't need the USB."

"Maybe he was interrupted," Sullivan mused. "Or maybe he was afraid to use his email. I wouldn't be surprised if Spratt forced him to give up his email password. But I don't think Mama has these files yet, or Ghost wouldn't have been so determined to get the USB. Plus, something must've happened to get him moved from a nice, comfortable bedroom to being handcuffed in a closet."

The image quality was surprisingly good, but there was no sound, so the first five vids were just a collection of people standing around silently flapping their mouths—Spratt talking to the balding man, Spratt talking to Tidwell, Spratt talking to a handful of other people, some in patrol uniforms, some not.

"How in the world would this be useful?" Tobias asked.

"How many times have you gone to your boss's house for legitimate work conversations? I can't imagine cops do it all that often. If nothing else, it puts a variety of cops in potential collusion. A DA could subpoena all of these people. Some of them would turn State's Evidence if they knew about criminal activities and wanted to save their own asses."

"You're thinking like a good cop," Tobias pointed out. "What would Mama get out of it?"

"Yeah, I'm the good guy." Sullivan huffed a sour laugh.

Tobias sat up straight. "Sullivan. Hey."

"Forget it. It's fine," he said wearily, and started a new

video, this one of Spratt and four other men having yet another conversation. "And Mama gets the same thing. Knowing who can be targeted, either because of blackmail or profit…"

"I really think we should talk," Tobias started, but Sullivan wasn't paying attention. He was leaning forward to peer at his laptop so intently that Tobias followed his gaze.

Onscreen, Spratt waved a hand and three of the men converged on the fourth. The fourth man talked furiously, yanking on his arms, his manner a mixture of anger and pleading. Spratt didn't seem to care; as the three other men held the fourth steady, Spratt walked up to him and punched him in the throat, hard. The man went rigid and was allowed to fall. He clawed at his throat, kicking uselessly, and Spratt left the field of view. The three men watched the fourth struggle to breathe, his panic growing by leaps and bounds, until Spratt returned with two large black heavy-duty trash bags. The men worked together to get their victim onto the plastic, leaning on his thrashing limbs to keep him in place and—and Tobias couldn't watch this.

He focused on a knot in the floorboard beneath his feet. He didn't—he couldn't—his peripheral vision caught another blur of movement, and he clenched his eyes shut.

"Holy shit," Sullivan said hoarsely.

Tobias was breathing too fast. He couldn't see the screen but he thought he could feel the light emanating from it anyway, sinking into his flesh, invisible and insidious, like radiation seeping through the air. He felt filthy. "That can't be real, can it?"

Sullivan sounded choked. "I think it must be."

Tobias stumbled to his feet and rushed upstairs, pounding on the bedroom door until Ghost yanked the chair out of the way and let him in, startled and hazy with sleep. Tobias flew past him to the bathroom, barely making it in time. He heaved into the toilet with enough force that tears squeezed from his eyes. The room was far too hot. He went to his knees on the tile, legs weak.

The images were imprinted on the backs of his eyelids—the fourth man's mouth gaping open as he strained for air that couldn't reach his lungs through his broken larynx, his eyes bulging, his struggles panicked and wild, the way the others—his fellow cops, men who had sworn to protect people, had held him down, blank faced, and the way Spratt had looked so regretful, as if he were sorry to have to take such an extreme measure, but nonetheless found it necessary, and the calm way he'd thought to get plastic to avoid making a mess. The whole thing reeked of the banal, and it wasn't—Tobias couldn't bear it.

At some point he became aware of a cold cloth against the back of his neck, and low voices in the doorway. He couldn't make out what they were saying over the roar of his own pulse in his ears, but he didn't think it mattered, really. There was only one possible response.

"We can't let Mama have this." Tobias's voice broke, and he felt young and ridiculous, but it had to be said. "We can't let her use this to manipulate him. Who knows what she'll be able to make him do? It won't stop, Sullivan. This can't be what it's like. We can't let this be what it's like."

"I know. We won't." Sullivan rubbed a hand over his back. He couldn't be too mad at Tobias if he was trying to comfort him, which was reassuring, but everything was still so hot. Tobias had sweat pouring down his temples and he was trying so hard not to think.

Dimly he heard Ghost say, "Here," and then Sullivan pressed a cup of cold water into Tobias's hand. Tobias took it with weak fingers and sipped, desperate to get the foul taste out of his mouth.

"You shouldn't have let him watch it," Ghost said. "You couldn't guess what it was?"

"He's not a fucking child." Sullivan sounded tired rather than angry. Tobias put the cup on the tile near his feet and took Sullivan's hand, squeezing gratefully. He didn't want this in his head, he wished he'd never seen it, but he wasn't sorry he'd watched it, if that made sense. This was part of being the one in control of his life—the ugliness and the darkness belonged to him too. Sullivan could help him recover from it, but he couldn't make the choice for him. He wouldn't even try.

"I'm sorry," Tobias managed.

"Don't be." Sullivan squeezed his hand in return. "Don't apologize for being compassionate, for Christ's sake."

"So soft," Ghost murmured, and his tone was a mixture of scorn and affection. That was the tone Tobias had always liked most from Ghost—when it was clear that Ghost didn't understand him but liked him anyway.

Tobias said to him, "We can't let this be what it's like."

Ghost's face did something complicated that Tobias couldn't parse. "The world's already like this."

"Not my world. And not yours either, if you'd only fight it."

Ghost just stared at him, impossible to read.

Eventually Tobias found his feet, and the others gave him a minute in the bathroom to clean up. He brushed his teeth and took a cold shower, staying in until his skin was goose-pimpled and blue and numb. He got out, toweled off, and brushed his teeth again before padding into the bedroom to find clothes.

Ghost was on the bed, sitting cross-legged, hands clasped loosely together. "Better?"

"No. Yes. I don't know." He pawed through his bag.

"Where's Sullivan?"

"Downstairs. He said something about making a call."

To his friend or his boss probably. About the vid, most likely, and Tobias wasn't ready to think about that yet. "Talk to me about something else, will you? Anything else?"

"Are you living here?"

"Sort of." Tobias tipped his head toward the bed without a frame or box spring, at the milk crate being used as a night table. "Not sure you could say Sullivan lives here, actually. He's sort of a nomad when it comes to living spaces. But whatever it is we're doing, we're both here for it." For now, anyway. Given Sullivan's recent unhappiness with the events Tobias had brought into his life, he might have some work to do there.

"You care about him."

"Yes."

"You love him?"

"Yes."

"Fast," Ghost said idly. "Too fast to know if it's the real thing, maybe. Or so people say."

"Maybe. I'm not really up for a semantic debate about the point where infatuation becomes love. I've never felt anything like it, I know that much." He pushed his bag aside. "*Love* might not be the right word, but it's the closest one in my vocabulary. Do you care or are you just curious?"

Ghost shrugged. "The second one, probably. It's interesting."

"How so?"

"I've never been in love." Ghost played with a pilled fuzzy on the duvet. "I don't think I'm capable of it."

Tobias went still. They didn't talk like this; he'd never heard Ghost say such a plain thing. He wasn't sure how honest it was, but he couldn't imagine a reason why Ghost would say something like that if it weren't true. Not that Ghost needed a reason to lie.

"You mean romantic love?" Tobias hesitated about dropping his towel. While Ghost had seen him naked a million times before—modesty didn't survive being roommates in a treatment facility—he didn't think Sullivan would be comfortable with Tobias getting naked in front of another guy. Tobias sure wouldn't like it if the shoe was on the other foot. He compromised by slipping into the bathroom to get dressed, leaving the door partially open so he could still talk. "Or familial love?"

"Any of it." Ghost stared at the blanket in apparent fascination. "I think I loved my mother. But it was a long time ago, and I'm not sure. And I'm different now."

Sometimes Tobias forgot how young Ghost was. He seemed ancient in some ways, but he was only twenty, and on some aspects of life, the four years between them might as well be a canyon.

"It's terrifying," Tobias said, coming back into the bedroom. "Falling in love. Knowing that anything that happens to them happens to you. You can't love someone with your whole heart without being terrified by what it means."

"It's a stupid thing to do, then."

"With some people, you can't *not* love them." Tobias gave him a small smile. "All you can choose is what you do once it happens."

"How do you know if you love someone?"

"Trust me, Ghost. You can't miss it. It'll take you out at the knees."

"I thought—" He paused, staring thoughtfully into the distance. "I thought there was a possibility. When I first got there, he said… I thought—"

"Thought what?"

"He's bailed me out a few times over the last few years. He caught Vasily Krayev trying to recruit me, and he kept an eye on me after that, and he always…he told me I was—but what's the good opinion of a killer worth?"

Spratt. "How did that whole thing happen?"

"She told me to get in his life. I got in his life." He leaned back and studied the ceiling. "I called him. I've had his number for ages. I told him a sob story about getting away from somebody who wanted to pimp me, and an hour later, Tidwell was at my front fucking door. When I was younger, if Spratt busted me, he'd dump me in Woodbury, but this time I said…" Ghost put on his most innocent, vulnerable mien—like everything Ghost put effort into, it was convincing. "I want to stay with you. I always mess up when I try to do it alone. Can't I stay with you?"

"He bought it?" Tobias always felt weird watching Ghost's little performances. He did them so frequently and so well that Tobias wasn't sure which face to believe. Sometimes he wondered if Ghost ever forgot which one was real.

The act fell away, and Ghost looked like himself

again—young, tired, worn. "I thought it would finally happen."

"What do you mean?"

Ghost scoffed. "What the fuck do you think? You think he did all those things to help me? You think it was because he was decent? There are people who want to use you and people who don't and—" He broke off and his whole body sagged. He pulled his feet up onto the bed, huddling like he was cold.

Quietly, Tobias asked, "Did he hurt you?"

Suddenly weary, Ghost said, "He knew. Almost the moment I walked in there, he figured it out. He's not stupid. But he gave me a chance anyway. Gave me just enough rope to hang myself, but if I hadn't tried to sneak out with the USB, if I'd just stayed—who knows what—"

It was by far the most honest conversation they'd ever had, and Tobias wasn't any less confused than he usually was when they talked. "Ghost?"

It took ages before Ghost murmured, "He didn't do anything." He blinked, staring off into space, and repeated, faintly bewildered, "He didn't do *anything*."

"He tied you up in a closet."

Ghost's eyes flew to Tobias as if he'd forgotten he was there. Blankly, he said, "Yeah, but who hasn't done that a time or two?" He cleared his throat, his gaze focusing further. "You're a clingy thing today. Get out, would you? If I don't get some sleep I'm going to punch the next person who expects me to do something decent."

And that was apparently the end of that. Tobias stood. "Do you want your key to the condo back, by the way? I've got it on my ring."

"No. Keep it. Recycle it. I don't care." He waved a

hand of dismissal that wasn't quite as carefree as he'd probably planned.

Tobias nodded. "You okay?"

Ghost gave him a blindingly attractive, entirely false smile. "Same as I ever was."

## Chapter Twenty-Four

After an awkward dinner, they got Ghost set up on the couch, and Tobias supposed they would simply have to trust that Ghost wanted the USB too much to take off without it. That video was the sole security he had in the world—short of life-threatening violence, Tobias didn't think Ghost was going anywhere.

There was nothing else to do then but go upstairs to bed with Sullivan, and with every step, the tension seemed to grow. Sullivan wasn't visibly angry or anything. It wasn't anything Tobias could point to, but the air had gotten thick in a way it never had with Sullivan before. It made Tobias's stomach feel like a bottomless pit.

Tobias shut the door and opened his mouth and was promptly interrupted.

"I don't want to talk," Sullivan said.

For a second, Tobias almost accepted it. He almost lied: *good, I don't either.* He almost told himself that if he just gave Sullivan the silence he so obviously wanted, things would be better. Tobias might feel horrible, but Sullivan would be happier, and then Sullivan would stay.

And that was everything he'd been trying to stop doing. It was everything he'd never had to do with Sullivan and damn it, he wasn't going back to that.

"Tough," he bit out. "You're not the only person in this relationship, and you're the one who told me that communication was key anyway, so we're going to talk."

"Communication is key when we fuck." Sullivan whipped his T-shirt off for a clean one, then tugged sleeping pants out of his Rubbermaid drawers. "Since we're not fucking, it's not an issue."

"It is an issue because I can tell you're mad."

"I'm not mad."

"Please don't make me say 'are too' like we're in first grade."

Sullivan shut the drawer a little too hard. "I'm not mad at you."

"But you are mad. Is it because of what you had to do to Spratt? Or is it me? Did I do something?"

"Can we go to sleep?" Sullivan asked through his teeth. "I don't want to do this."

"Will you tell me what I did wrong?" Tobias held his breath for a second, intending to wait for Sullivan's honest answer, but almost instantly lost his nerve. "I'll apologize. Whatever it was that I did, I'm sorry. You know that, right?"

"It's not anything you did." Sullivan sighed and corrected himself with, "It's not anything specific. I'm not happy with where I am at this point in time, that's all. It's…it's shitty. I want a lot of things to be different, and none of them likely will be, and talking won't change anything, so what's the point?"

"But if the problem is me, maybe if we talk about it—"

Sullivan was already shaking his head. "I don't think that's going to help."

"This isn't fair. You don't get to decide for both of

us," Tobias said, and Sullivan's jaw worked. He stared unblinkingly at the floor, then abruptly stood up.

"Fine, you want to do this? Let's do it. Get your bag. I'll drive you right now."

"My bag," Tobias repeated, his head filling with a kind of electric, painful buzzing. "I need my bag because you're—"

"I'm taking you back to the motel."

"But—"

"Hey, you're the one who wanted this."

"I want to *talk*," Tobias said, bewildered as Sullivan shoved his sockless feet back into his shoes. "This is the opposite of what I want."

"We both know where this is going. We'll talk, probably for an exhausting hour and you'll say how grateful you are for my help, and that you're sorry I was put in an awkward position and that you really care about me but that you have a lot on your plate right now, and that'll be it, it'll be over—for now, you'll say—but that's still over, and I'll take you and Ghost to your motel and you'll kiss me on the cheek and you might even mean it when you say we should get together after this whole thing is resolved, but we both know where your energy's going to be, and phone calls rescheduling dinner will turn into text messages rescheduling coffee, and it'll be pretty damn clear what your choice is, and I'd really like to skip to the fucking end right now if we could."

Sullivan was out of breath when that long, ridiculous sentence finally ended, but it didn't stop him from grabbing his wallet and his keys from his jeans. He looked dopey in his fuzzy sleeping pants and ancient running shoes and faded orange T-shirt promoting a Mexican restaurant, his brown eyes hard, his bony, handsome face tight with temper and misery, and Tobias's heart thumped hard enough that it had to be audible.

"No wonder you didn't want to have that conversation, that's an awful conversation—" Tobias began, but Sullivan apparently wasn't done steamrolling over him.

"Come on, get your things together."

"I'm not—"

"We still have to wake up Ghost, so—"

*"Ban m zòrèy mwen!"* And Tobias officially sounded like Manman when she got fed up with her children.

Sullivan stalled out, confused, and Tobias made a mental note—*Kreyòl* might be an effective way to interrupt Sullivan's doom-and-gloom spirals in the future, too, especially since the equivalent of "be quiet" in English wasn't likely to make much of an impact.

"Not to be rude, but for a generally cheerful sort of guy, you can be really pessimistic," Tobias pointed out. "I suppose that's from years of detective novels and tracking down child support evaders. Your dirtbags are in your head, Sullivan. You've let them make you cynical. Maybe you speak that language, and maybe it's good for you to have that ability at work, but you're right, it's not the language I speak and it can't be the one we speak together. So that whole horrible conversation you were describing? That's not the one we're going to have. I'm not leaving, either. I love you."

Sullivan's words dried up before he could make a sound, and he stood there with his mouth open like a fish for a good three seconds before he snapped it closed.

"That's better," Tobias said, pointing out Sullivan's stunned-stupid expression. "This is already a big improvement on the awful talk you had lined up for us."

Sullivan sank slowly onto the bed.

"It's fast, I know." Tobias rubbed his hands on his jeans—his palms were sweaty. He wished he had time to think of better words, but he didn't think it would be long before Sullivan's brain came back online, and it might come back online full of doubt, so he hurried to add, "A few weeks isn't much time, but I've been thinking about this, and given the situation we've been in and how much time we've spent together each day, we've actually been together a lot longer than two and a half weeks. A date's maybe three to four hours long, right? We've been spending every minute together for days, so that's got to jump us ahead on the relationship continuum. And you know how dog years take into account how much stuff happens in a time frame? We've got that too. There's been some really stressful stuff. We've had to work through conflict and support each other through difficult times—that's stuff that you don't usually hit until you've moved past counting how many dates you've been on, you know? And if you look at it like that, we're up to months, easy. Maybe even a year. So maybe it's fast, but that doesn't make it unreliable. Everything's in there, no matter how much—or how little—time it took to show up."

Sullivan blinked. "But you chose Ghost."

Tobias frowned, searching for anything that might've happened that could've possibly sent Sullivan that message, but nothing sprang to mind. "When?"

"At Spratt's." Sullivan tipped his face away. "You told me to go, and you went back down to him. I know what that means. I'm not an idiot."

*Oh.* And then he said apologetically, "You kind of are. But so am I, because I assumed you understood. I wanted you out of the house so you'd be safe, and that's it. I went downstairs, yeah, but that wasn't me choosing

him, Sullivan. That was faith in you. I knew that whatever happened while we were separated, whatever you
did would be for the right reasons and to achieve the right
thing. I didn't stay with him because you mattered less.
It was because I trusted you more. You get that, right?"

Sullivan's lips parted, and he looked almost fragile.
Like any sudden movement might have him flinching.
It reminded Tobias of the uncharacteristic uncertainty
Sullivan had displayed that first night when they'd tried
spanking. Like Sullivan wanted so desperately to believe him, but was afraid of how much it would hurt to
be wrong.

"You said you weren't sure," Sullivan murmured. "In
the car the other day, you said you couldn't promise how
you would feel. That—"

"I'm promising now," Tobias interrupted. "I know
what I said, and it was because I didn't trust myself, not
because I didn't trust you. But I know I won't screw this
up now. You're too important. So if you'll let me stay, I'm
not going anywhere. Let me stay." He paused. "I mean
you don't have to let me move in right away, although that
would be nice. I understand if you need some space or
time. But you're going to be a lot happier with me here,
so you should probably say yes now."

Sullivan's lips started to curl up at the corners. "You
think so, huh?"

Tobias smiled back helplessly. "Yup."

"You're going to be one of those demanding, bratty
subs who always gets what he wants, aren't you?"

"Absolutely. And it's too late for you to back out now."

"Don't want to anyway."

Tobias took Sullivan's hand in his and pressed it

against the base of his throat. "I'm not really sure how this works. Is there a collar thing?"

Sullivan's eyes darkened. "If you want one. I mean, I'm assuming you won't want to wear it all the time, like, around your parents or at work, but when we're at home…"

Tobias shivered. "At home, we can do whatever we want."

Sullivan squeezed, not hard enough to cut off Tobias's air, but enough that he couldn't ignore the weight of his hand. It was soothing and arousing at the same time, that weight, and Tobias tipped his head back.

He stared dazedly at the ceiling, his blood thrumming through his body, as Sullivan kissed and licked the skin under his ear, a tantalizing, tempting scrape of teeth coming every few seconds, an infuriating tease.

"We're going to have so much fun," Tobias said, letting himself slump in Sullivan's arms, knowing Sullivan wouldn't let him fall.

"Fuck yeah, we are," Sullivan said against the damp skin of his throat, and bit down.

Later, as their heartbeats slowed, Sullivan pressed a kiss to the top of his head. "I love you too, by the way. Since we've been together for months in dog years or whatever, I'm guessing you don't think that's too forward?"

Tobias laughed. "I put that together from your panicked desperation to avoid the breakup conversation. But thanks for saying it. It's really nice to hear, even if you're making fun of my completely nonscientific theory in the process."

"Sure. Hey, that thing you said earlier that wasn't English? I'm assuming that was you telling me to shut up?"

Tobias made a noncommittal humming sound.

"Yeah, I thought so," Sullivan said dryly. "That wasn't French, was it?"

"No, it was *Kreyòl*."

"You're fluent?"

"Yeah."

Sullivan hesitated a second. "Will you teach me?"

Tobias pressed his face against Sullivan's shoulder, inhaled the scent of his skin, and whispered, "Try and stop me."

Sullivan felt like he'd only just drifted off when his phone rang, but out the window the morning was blue as a bruise already. It was Lisbeth.

Sullivan shook Tobias enough to wake him and sat up, the sheets puddling in his lap. Coherence, he told himself, though it was a high expectation for five-thirty. He gave her a quick and dirty rundown of everything that'd happened.

"What's she saying?" Tobias asked, knuckling sleep out of his eyes like a little kid, and Sullivan wished he had enough dignity not to find it adorable, but such was his lot in life. The guy was cute, and Sullivan was stuck stupid on him.

Fortunately, Tobias had a similar problem.

"Let the grownups talk," Sullivan told him, ignoring the vengeful finger that poked him in the stomach as Lisbeth filled him in on her news.

Her friend's name was Walter Wathers, and he'd turned toward home before his daughter had managed to pass Lisbeth's message on. Something to do with spark plugs and a questionable mechanic, Sullivan gathered, and that meant that instead of a week they had to wait only two hours—Wathers had called Lisbeth from a pay phone in Laramie not five minutes ago, and he was on his way to Sullivan's. As Lisbeth was, to facilitate the introductions.

"You'll only do smart things until I get there, won't you, Sullivan?" Lisbeth asked as the conversation wrapped up.

"The smartest," he agreed.

Tobias poked him again. "What's she saying?"

Sullivan batted at his hand and tried to muffle the phone's speaker against his shoulder so he could hiss, "She's giving me the recipe to life everlasting. And if you keep poking me—ow—I'm not going to share it with you."

Tobias was grinning, and after a second, when he heard Lisbeth cough pointedly in his ear, Sullivan realized he was sitting there silently grinning back. They were just two half-asleep idiots grinning at each other in bed.

"That would be the college boy stealing your attention, I'm assuming?" Lisbeth asked dryly.

"It would."

"Is this a nice development?"

Sullivan watched Tobias lift an eyebrow and kick the sheet down a few inches, the filthy tease, and all Sullivan could think was that it was so clean. So happy, so pure. Nothing perverted about him, about them, no matter how dirty they played together. "The nicest."

"Good. I'll tell Caty you're bringing him over for dinner in a few days. I'll be there in half an hour."

"Hey, now—" Sullivan started, but she'd already hung up. He wasn't grinning anymore, unfortunately, because he had a mental picture of Caty tugging Tobias away to teach him all about "the ways of the sub," which Sullivan knew all too well was just a collection of tips and tricks meant to annoy the shit out of Doms. Though he had to admit, a bratty Tobias wasn't an unattractive one.

"What was she saying?" Tobias asked.

"We have two hours before this ex-cop guy gets here and half an hour before Lisbeth does," Sullivan said, and tugged at the sheet, thinking that teasing was a crime definitely worthy of punishment. Blow job punishment. Sounded fair. He slid down the bed and added, "Plenty of time."

"Wait, what?" Tobias sat upright, yanking the sheet back up to his navel. "Two hours? I can't convince Ghost to give the USB to a cop in two hours."

"You don't have to," Sullivan said, rather reasonably in his opinion, considering that Tobias was now doing the opposite of having sex with him. "We have the USB. We can give it to the ex-cop without Ghost's permission. Ghost can make up his own mind about whether he sticks around to testify or get deposed, but either way, you know we can't trust him to give the USB up on his own."

"You made a good argument yesterday," Tobias pointed out. "He might agree. He might do the right thing of his own volition."

"I don't know." Sullivan thought of Tobias running downstairs in Spratt's house, and reminded himself of Tobias explaining last night that it'd been about trust, not love.

"I've had a lot of important choices that I didn't fight to make for myself," Tobias said, taking his hand. "I want to give him that option. He's going to have to live with the consequences; he should at least get a say."

"Do you really think he'll do the right thing?"

Tobias dropped his gaze.

"More to the point," Sullivan said gently, "Can you live with yourself if you're wrong?"

"Let me talk to him." Tobias spoke more to Sullivan's belly than his face. "Don't do anything until I do that much, okay? Maybe I can convince him to go along with this."

Sullivan sighed and rolled to his back. "This isn't you choosing him, right? This is you trusting me to do the right thing even if you're not babysitting me, right?"

*"Yes,"* Tobias said fiercely, and threw himself on Sullivan to kiss him, hard, and Sullivan kissed him back, morning breath bedamned. They'd been together for years now anyway, apparently. They were well past worrying about that sort of thing. And the idea that Tobias trusted him was getting easier to believe with every passing second.

"All right." Sullivan brushed a hand over Tobias's shoulder. "You've got two hours, sweetheart. Do your worst."

Ghost was already awake when Tobias went downstairs. He was watching the news with the volume turned low, his skin faintly lavender in the glow of the screen. The morning anchorwoman from Channel 7 was making her way through a story on a bus accident. Tobias hoped there'd been no children involved.

"Anything about us or Spratt?" he asked.

"Not so far."

"Good sign."

Ghost lifted an eyebrow a tiny bit as if to say *take it how you like, but I know better*, and Tobias remembered Sullivan saying *you don't speak the same language*.

No, they didn't, but that didn't mean they couldn't work out a translation.

He also remembered Sullivan saying *he cares what you think*.

Tobias slipped the remote off the arm of the sofa and turned the TV off, then sat on the steamer trunk, a position that forced Ghost to move his legs.

"Look at you," Ghost mused. "It's way too early for fight face, Tobias."

"You're up," Tobias pointed out.

"Spratt keeps intolerable hours. I'll adjust back to my natural rhythms soon enough."

"Tell me how you got the USB."

"It's like your boyfriend said—I had a camera and a laptop and later I made a copy."

"Why didn't you send it to Mama right then?"

"Because two seconds after I saved it, Spratt was pounding on my door."

"Why?"

"For the sex," Ghost said, batting his eyes. "I've been told I'm irresistible to a certain type."

"You weren't sleeping together."

Ghost paused, a bare hiccup of time that made Tobias want to smile. Ghost wasn't used to having to be on his toes with him. "And you know that because Boyfriend is a professional busybody, I suppose."

"I'm pretty good at peeking in windows myself these days, too."

"You make a lovely couple," Ghost said earnestly. "But back then we *were* fucking. It wasn't until I proved unreliable that he stopped—"

"You said yesterday that he didn't do anything," Tobias interrupted, and Ghost's eyebrows narrowed for a second. "You were talking to yourself, I think, but forgetting I exist doesn't mean I actually cease to, you know."

"Fine, we weren't fucking," Ghost said carelessly.

"So why didn't you email the video to Mama?"

"There was no point. I was on my way out the door anyway. I planned to give it to her in person."

"You made the USB, tried to leave, and Spratt stopped you. And…you threw the USB in the laundry room to conceal it?"

"Ding, ding, ding." Ghost reached out and bopped Tobias on the nose with one finger. "You're very clever these days, Tobias."

Tobias rolled his eyes. "Thanks, but I still don't buy it. Maybe Spratt stopped you from leaving, but that's not why you didn't email it. If you'd sent it to her then, you wouldn't have needed the USB at all. It would've been faster if you had. Safer, too, because it meant you couldn't be caught with it by Spratt."

"Oh, God," Ghost groaned. "This is the heart of gold part, isn't it? I didn't send it to Mama because deep inside I don't want to contribute to an unjust world, right? Because deep down, you know I just want to be good. Your psychology degree's arriving in the mail any day now, isn't it?"

Tobias shifted tacks instantly. He did believe that Ghost's motivation for hesitating had been worry about what Mama would do, but saying so would only get him laughed at. "You know Sullivan's right, don't you? Sooner or later he's going to go through your laptop, and when he sees that program, he's going to assume the murder is what you've recorded. As long as that USB exists and you're the only one with access to it, Spratt's going to have strong motivation to kill you."

Ghost said nothing.

Tobias said, "You have to blow it wide open. That's the only way you'll ever be safe."

"Turning him in won't save me from Mama."

"I know." Tobias was reasonably sure they'd convinced Ghost to at least stick around long enough to meet Lisbeth's good cop. But Mama was something else. Tobias had to try to convince Ghost to do the right thing there, as well. He doubted it would work, but he had to try. "About Mama…"

"I'm not testifying against her," Ghost said flatly. "There's no fucking way in hell."

"You're going to let her get away with trying to blackmail a cop—"

"Damn straight. She's welcome to him. She can own the entire government for all I care."

*His language*, Tobias reminded himself, even if he was ninety-nine percent sure that Ghost was lying about being unbothered. Tobias wasn't going to get anywhere with moral arguments about self-sacrifice. Survival. That was the only way.

"So imagine this. It's four years from now. You've given up hustling. You're taking an online class in something. Maybe you're working in a diner like Church. And you're actually thinking about putting down roots. Staying still. But you can't, because you know it's only a matter of time before she tracks you down."

"Putting down roots? *Moi?* Don't let's be silly, dear."

"Okay, it's been three months in the same town and you're back at it—looking at a map, figuring out which new city is big enough that you can get lost, but not so big that the Krayevs will have interested partners nearby. And it's going to keep being like that, you know. A series of bland, pointless jobs and—and dicks to suck for extra cash, and long, boring bus rides before the whole thing starts all over again. And the whole time, you're wondering if this is the diner or street corner or blank, empty room where Kellen or one of the Krayevs finally catches up with you."

Tobias took a breath, then said something that was very much Ghost's language, and absolutely nothing of his own. "Aren't you tired of waiting for someone to come through your door in the night?"

Ghost might've appeared fragile and childlike in his too-large clothes, but in that moment, as his gaze snapped to Tobias's, he looked nothing short of feral—every spare mannerism and tic of guilelessness vanished, every soft curve of cheek, every tender line of lip, all of it was gone in a finger snap. Tobias swallowed hard, wondering if Ghost was about to hurt him, if it would be like that night in Woodbury when that boy had tried to touch Ghost under the dinner table and Ghost had lost it, everything human about him disappearing, all sense of sanity evaporating until only pure, vicious destruction was left.

Tobias braced himself, but Ghost didn't move. He didn't move or speak for long minutes, only sat there staring at Tobias, little flashes of rage and emptiness crossing his features for brief seconds before flickering out again.

And finally, ages later, Ghost cleared his throat. "What do you want?"

"I want you to talk to this ex-cop. I want you to let someone help you. I want you to do the scary thing now so you can have peace later. He's going to be here in—" He checked the clock. "An hour and a half. I want you to still be here."

"In a city overflowing with dirty cops—a city like any other, I suppose, but the point stands—you want me to put my life in the hands of a cop?"

"Yes."

They watched each other for another long beat, a silence that was only broken by Sullivan coming downstairs, damp and pink-cheeked from his shower. He passed behind the couch, close enough that Tobias caught a whiff of the scent of his soap, and gave Tobias a questioning glance over Ghost's shoulder.

Tobias put his hand up to the base of his throat, a reminder, he hoped of the bond between them. *Trust me*, he meant. *I'm yours*, he meant. Sullivan's expression softened, and then Ghost let out a tiny noise.

Tobias refocused on him, saw Ghost staring not at his face but at his wrist and—oh, shit, the bruises Sullivan had left there last night when he'd held Tobias down while they had sex, where he'd pushed Tobias so deeply into the mattress, gripped so cruelly, and the sight of them was enough to have his pulse quickening, but Ghost couldn't know that. All he knew was the sight of bruises, and Tobias put it together a split second too late, because Ghost was already up and over the back of the couch, launching himself at Sullivan, taking him by surprise with his speed.

Tobias scrambled up and over the couch too, more clumsily, more slowly, and Sullivan had, fortunately, been facing them, so he had a half-second to react, and that was probably what saved his life—because Ghost was swinging a knife—where the hell had he gotten a knife?—and Tobias was going to be too late, he was going to be too *late*…

Tobias heard Sullivan's grunt of pain a split second

before Tobias's body collided with Ghost's, taking them both to the floor. He tried to go for Ghost's knife hand, but he wasn't good at fighting, and he probably missed, but Ghost wasn't struggling anyway. Tobias had a vague impression that he'd taken Ghost down with enough force to knock the wind out of him, or maybe he hit his head, but either way, he lay under Tobias still and skinny, uncomfortable as a bag of sticks, his chest heaving, eyes dazed and Tobias realized he was saying, "I asked him to, I like it, I want it, they're mine, I asked him to."

He trailed off, thinking *Sullivan*, and wondering if he dared get up without restarting Ghost's violence. He'd gotten lucky, he knew that much. It had never occurred to Ghost that Tobias would have the nerve to intervene, but if Ghost knew to anticipate Tobias's interference, Tobias wouldn't get lucky again.

So he repeated, "I asked him to."

"Because he brainwashed you," Ghost said, staring up at him with something old and conflicted and weary in his face. "He made you think this is what you should want, but you don't…you don't like this. You can't."

"I'm not you," Tobias whispered. "I like different things. I like how it feels. All your time doing what you do, and you've never known someone who likes it? Stay down, please. Let me go to him."

"No, you're good. You don't want this."

Tobias flinched. On some level he knew this was more about Ghost's issues than his own, but it still cut deep. "If it makes me bad—and it doesn't, but if it did—it would still be my choice."

"I can't let you—"

"I'm not asking for permission," Tobias said, and he was so tired of all of it, tired of not having his footing,

not having his wishes respected, and he shook Ghost a
little, making those green eyes widen. "You don't have
to understand it, Ghost, but this isn't your call, and it's
not your business. I'm the only one who gets to decide
what I do in bed. Stay *down*."

And after a long second, Ghost nodded.

Tentatively, Tobias got up. He nudged the bloody
knife—God, that was way too much blood—away from
Ghost's hand with one careful foot before edging his way
over to Sullivan. He never turned his back on Ghost, but
it didn't turn out to be necessary. Ghost stayed slumped
on the floor, watching them.

Tobias's first glance at Sullivan was half-panicked,
and the blood took him the rest of the way there. Sullivan had it all over his upper body and his thighs, his
hand clamped over the wound in his forearm that he
couldn't quite cover.

"I find your buddy's shovel talk crude but effective,"
Sullivan said.

*"Mwen bezwen yon bagay pi blese sa a."* Tobias fell
to his knees at Sullivan's side.

"English," Sullivan reminded him.

"I—I need a thing for the cut." He tore his shirt off and
wrapped it tightly around the wound, then pushed that
arm up over Sullivan's head to let gravity lend a hand.
He put all of his weight on the injury, using direct pressure to stop the bleeding and making Sullivan bite out a
curse. "Hold still. Where are your keys?"

"Upstairs. Why?" Sullivan said blankly.

"I'm taking you to the emergency room."

"No, you're not."

"You're bleeding!"

"I know, but hospitals have to report criminal conduct. If they even suspect this is a knife wound, they'll call the cops."

"They're not going to know. We'll…we'll tell them it's from glass. You broke a glass. They'll buy it."

"Maybe. Maybe not. We don't know for sure, so we can't go."

"You need stitches." Tobias could feel his throat closing.

"Yup." Sullivan took Tobias's hand with his good one. "But even if I don't get them, I'll still be fine. I'm not going to bleed to death. Stop biting a hole in your lip, sweetheart."

"I'm not." Tobias totally was. He felt vaguely nauseated and lightheaded, but there was one other option. He glanced over at where Ghost still lay on the floor, watching them closely. "I need you to go upstairs and get my keys and my phone."

"But if you go to the emergency room, who's going to babysit me to make sure I'm not committing acts of evil?" Ghost asked snidely, even as he got to his feet.

"I will," came a female voice from the direction of the front door, and Tobias turned his head to see a tall golden-skinned woman in a stunning navy suit was standing there.

"Hi, Raina," Sullivan said, sounding tired. "Fancy meeting you here."

"Did you really think you I wouldn't show up after that voicemail you left me yesterday?"

"I think you should give back my house key."

"But I'm in the nick of time." Raina perched on the arm of the sofa. "It certainly looks like you could use my help." She surveyed Ghost from tip to toe where he stood at the foot of the stairs. "This would be the Ghost in question, I assume."

Ghost studied her in turn. Raina was intimidating, from her regal posture to the arrogant tilt of her chin to the keen, dark eyes that were intelligent and worthy of being studied. But Tobias didn't have time.

"Ghost," Tobias said, making him jump. "Keys and phone, please. On the dresser. And a shirt."

"We're not going to the emergency room," Sullivan said.

"No, we're going to see my parents."

Sullivan frowned, but Tobias wasn't compromising on stitches, and if they couldn't go to the ER, there were only so many other options. His papa might be angry at him, but he wouldn't turn away a patient. In this, at least, Tobias trusted him wholeheartedly.

"Ghost, please," Tobias repeated, and Ghost turned and went up the stairs.

"The USB," Sullivan said, a little thickly. "We hid it in a baggie in the toilet's reserve tank. If he gets it…"

"I'll tag along," Raina said.

"Be careful." Tobias felt disloyal even as he said it, but Sullivan broke into strained laughter.

"He's sweet," Raina called over her shoulder as she swept up the stairs after Ghost.

"You think she'll be able to stop Ghost from taking the USB if he finds it?"

"I dunno," Sullivan said. "But if anyone could, it'd be her. I wouldn't be surprised to get back and find that one of them has killed the other." He shifted uncomfortably. "Or they'll be best friends. I'm not sure which scenario is scarier, to be honest."

"Hold still." Tobias kissed Sullivan's forehead. "You called her?"

"Yesterday. I wanted to make sure that my client

couldn't use her as leverage against us if he figured out who we were."

"Wait. You explained this whole thing and told her to watch out for a bad guy client by voicemail?"

"I said it was urgent!"

Tobias snorted a laugh despite himself. "She got here safely, at least. Will you be in much trouble?"

"Probably. She's not a forgiving person. I wasn't as communicative as I should've been, and sleeping with a client won't go over well. I think I can kiss that promotion good-bye, but if I'm slick, maybe she won't fire me. I did solve an unsolvable case. Well, *we* did. Sort of."

Ghost and Raina walked back downstairs in tandem at that point, Ghost holding their things, Raina with the baggie holding the USB.

"Thank you." Tobias shrugged hastily into the shirt, which was long-sleeved and covered his bruises, a thoughtful choice that was as much of an apology as he or Sullivan was likely to get from Ghost. "We'll be back as soon as we can."

"Call me if you need me," Sullivan said to Raina, who lifted an imperious eyebrow.

"It's unlikely."

"I know," he replied. "But still. The cop's name is… fuck, I forget, but Lisbeth will be here any minute, and—"

"Sullivan?" A woman pushed the French doors open and stuck her head through. She was in her mid- to late-thirties and wore a demure blue blouse and dark slacks. She glanced around the room, zeroing in on Sullivan where he sat against the wall. "I'm assuming someone called an ambulance?"

"Long story, but no," Sullivan said. "We've got someone to help, though. Tobias, this is Lisbeth. Lisbeth, this is the college student, Raina, and Ghost."

Lisbeth turned quiet blue eyes on Ghost. "So you're the one all the fuss is about." She gestured to Sullivan's arm. "Is this your handiwork?"

"It was a misunderstanding," Ghost said.

"We're leaving." Tobias hauled Sullivan to his feet. He was shaky but capable, standing on his own, which was a comfort.

"Do you need a ride?" Lisbeth asked.

Sullivan shook his head. "Stay here for your guy. Raina can fill you in."

"As best as I can, on a two-minute explanation," Raina said, not entirely friendly about it.

"Come on," Tobias demanded, tugging on Sullivan, who resisted.

Sullivan pointed at Ghost with his good hand. "Don't trust him. Not for a second."

"For fuck's sake," Ghost muttered.

Raina gestured to Lisbeth's feet. "The pumps—Dolce? Last year?"

Lisbeth smiled. "Good eye. I fell hard for the laminated Dauphine leather."

"God save me," Sullivan said, and finally let Tobias haul him out the door.

# Chapter Twenty-Five

Tobias let them in with his key. The house was still and shadowed, and he got Sullivan propped up in the kitchen with a whispered admonishment to keep the pressure on the wound before heading upstairs.

As he worked his way through the hall, he tried to shake off the feeling of being an intruder. It had been a matter of weeks only that he'd been gone, but in that time the familiar had become somehow alien. Everything was the same—family photographs on the wall, furniture in the right places, same knickknacks on the shelves—but there was something in the air he couldn't shake. He half expected to find dust everywhere, but there wasn't a speck anywhere.

He dodged the creaking floorboard and knocked softly on his parents' door to avoid waking his brothers and sisters. Papa answered a moment later in his fuzzy brown robe, his sleepy expression vanishing when he took in Tobias and the blood on his hands and shirt.

"I'm fine," Tobias murmured quickly. "I'm not hurt. It's a friend. I need your help, Papa."

Tobias never would've described his papa as a hesitant man. His manman was no more tentative; years as physicians had taught them both that there would be time for conversation post-crisis. So it was no surprise to have them both following him down the hall a moment later, medical kits in hand, without argument.

In the kitchen, they found Sullivan standing over the sink instead of on the wooden stool where Tobias had left him, his bloody shirt dripping onto the stainless steel.

"Hi, I'm Sullivan." He gave a small wave with his good arm. "Sorry for making a mess out of your kitchen."

His parents flew into action; in moments there was a tray for tools and gauze and a bowl filled with water. Tobias was pressed into service getting towels. His parents murmured in *Kreyòl* to each other as they worked together to get the wound numbed, cleaned, and stitched up. If Tobias had doubted his own unsuitability for the profession, this would've confirmed it—he couldn't bear to look at the wound. He spent the time distracting himself by alternately planning the heavily edited story he would tell his parents and watching Sullivan look around the kitchen.

He wondered what their home looked like to Sullivan— the bright, sequined *drapo* hanging in the corner, Manman's spare rosary beads dangling over the edge of the handwoven basket on the counter, the black-and-white photograph of Vodouists dancing in a service to the *loa* on the wall. Would he think of black magic and ignorant peasants, like so many friends and neighbors had over the years?

No, Sullivan studied these parts of Tobias's life with the same open, honest interest that he aimed at any number of unfamiliar things. There was curiosity in the intelligent planes of his face, but also empathy and warmth. He would ask questions, and better still, he would *learn*.

Tobias took Sullivan's good hand in his, and Sullivan gave him a tiny smile. His parents both cast quick glances at their interlaced fingers, but neither said anything. He'd never held hands with a man in front of them; his homosexuality had been a theoretical thing to them until this point, but Sullivan was in his life for good, or at least Tobias wanted him to be, and everyone would simply need to adjust. He had no intention of hiding what he felt. He'd risked too much by hiding such things in the past.

When Sullivan's arm had been bandaged and the mess cleared away, Tobias found him a clean shirt to wear from his bedroom. Then they all sat in an awkward square for a moment, no one quite sure where to begin.

Finally, Papa said, "An explanation is in order, I think."

Somehow, they managed a non-panic-inducing version of the story. Tobias didn't outright lie at any point, but he did downplay the risks involved at times. He felt no need for his parents to know that Spratt had come back to his house during the home invasion they'd committed. He disliked having to monitor his words so carefully, but his parents' questions were cautiously phrased in return, and it struck him that they were trying hard to meet him halfway. They were frustrated, yes, and worried, but determined to do as Manman had claimed they would do in her voicemail—listen.

Once they'd wrapped up the stitching and the explanation, Sullivan checked his phone. "Lisbeth says Ghost is going with Walter."

Tobias sank back in his chair. "Oh. They're—"

"They're leaving now. I guess whatever you said to him worked." He nudged Tobias's knee with his own. "It's good news."

"It is," Tobias agreed. And he did feel a massive sense

of relief. He'd just wanted more time before Ghost disappeared again, that was all.

"Your friend is all right, though?" Manman asked.

"Sounds like." Tobias took a breath and refocused. Her velvet-brown eyes were tired behind her glasses. Since they had no reason to rush, perhaps it was a good time to clear the air. "About what happened before, with the letter…"

Both of his parents glanced at Sullivan instantly, warily. Tobias had anticipated this; personal subjects weren't often shared with friends or acquaintances. "We can discuss that later," Manman began, smiling at Sullivan, but Tobias cleared his throat.

"No, Manman. He's family to me. He knows everything anyway. And I think this will be easier with him here. I'd really prefer talking about this with him here."

His parents exchanged a look, but Manman finally nodded.

Tobias took a deep breath and reminded himself that a strong relationship moving forward was as much on him as it was on them. "I was hurt that you didn't share the letter with me. And angry. I don't blame you for not telling me the truth when I was a child about how my birth mother abandoned me. Tante Esther's version was hard to hear, but I understand why you lied."

He hesitated, then asked a question that'd haunted him ever since he'd found out. "You told me once that you let me keep Ashley Benton's name as a reminder of the woman who'd loved me so much but had been forced to give me up. If that's not true, why didn't you give me your name? Didn't you want me to—"

"It's not because you weren't mine," Manman said fiercely, reaching across the table to take his hand hard in hers. Her fingers were cold and strong. "You were always mine. From the first time I held you. You'd been in an incubator because you were so sick, with tubes everywhere, and you had a bulky cast on your leg, and for a long time, no one could hold you. But the second I did, I knew. You were such a silent baby, Tobias, did I ever tell you? You'd lie so still in my arms, even after you were healthy, like you were afraid I'd put you down if you made a peep. All I could think was that you'd spent a whole night in that Dumpster in pain, crying for help, and no one came, not for hours, and it made my heart bleed. You were so vulnerable, so frighteningly vulnerable, and I promised myself I would never let that woman hurt you again. That kind of promise doesn't end when your children are adults."

Tobias jolted at the sight of her tears; Manman did not cry easily. He squeezed her hand, reassured despite the upsetting elements of the story.

She swiped at her face with a napkin Papa gave her and cleared her throat. "We spoke to Tante Esther last week. She left some things out of the version she told you. She didn't know that your birth mother didn't sign away her rights to you immediately. Ashley Benton." She spat the name, her disgust palpable. "She was in jail for what she'd done to you when I went to see her. I brought her the pictures of you in the hospital and explained that I'd taken care of you and that I loved you and that I would continue to love you and take care of you until my last breath if she would only let me. She looked at the pictures and she said—"

Here Manman broke off, her mouth working until she could continue. "This will hurt you, but I promised not to lie to you anymore, so I won't. She said 'I didn't think about whether he would feel it.' She said that to me, can you believe it? I wanted to reach past that glass and slap her face, but I couldn't. Even if I'd been physically able to, I needed her to sign the papers."

Sullivan's knee knocked his under the table again and Tobias sucked in a breath. He could feel Sullivan watching him and didn't want to make him worry, but he needed a second. He couldn't wrap his mind around the idea of someone blind to the idea of an infant feeling pain. As Sullivan would've said, it didn't translate into a language he could understand. Finally he nudged Sullivan back and nodded, only then realizing that Manman had paused to give him a moment.

"I'm all right," he said. "Go on."

Manman continued, "So I pretended that I understood her selfishness, and eventually she agreed to give you up, but only on two conditions—that you keep the name she'd given you, and that we keep her updated with our current address so she could contact you in the future if she chose to. We've kept our word about those things, but we made no promises about passing her letters along, and so we haven't. But you're right. We were wrong to do as we did, even if we meant no harm. If you want to see her, we will—"

"I don't want to see her," Tobias interrupted, startled. "I've never wanted to, not since Tante Esther told me. I know you think I'm too weak to say no—"

"Too kind," Papa interjected. "Too willing to give. Not too weak."

"Oh." Tobias's cheeks grew hot. "Thank you. But it was never about that. I wanted the choice. Not her." He frowned, wondering how they'd managed to miss each other so completely for so long. It had never occurred to him that she might also be afraid of being left behind. "You're my Manman."

She made a soft gasping noise and came around the table to his side, pulling him into her arms and sniffling. When she let him go, he gave Sullivan an embarrassed smile, only to find those brown eyes tender as he pressed a napkin into Tobias's hand. He wiped his face self-consciously.

Papa said, "I also thought…a son should be proud of his family. I never wanted you to feel as we did, that we came from badness."

Tobias frowned. "What do you mean?"

In slow, careful words that grew more confident as he went on, he explained about their emigration from Haiti. Tobias knew bits and parts, but he'd never gotten the full story of the way Nadège and Andre Alcide had traveled to the States during the breakdown of the Baby Doc Duvalier regime, sent to the States by their upper-class parents, who had benefitted from the worst of that regime. There had been two classes back then, he said, and their family belonged to the one that had money and power— well, as much power as you could have when your success hinged on the good favor of a dictator. Their parents had turned a blind eye to the abuses of the man who'd set up a system that afforded them a comfortable life, and they had spoken out publicly only when the horrors became impossible to ignore, only when it seemed that the tides of the country would turn on them too. Tobias's parents had barely entered adulthood at that time, and were sheltered by their privilege, but they'd learned the nature of their upbringing when the protests and violence began. Particularly once they came to the States and were exposed to immigrants from poorer families and witnessed the devastation.

"It is important to take care of your community," Papa said. "That is part of what it means to be Haitian, you know this. But our parents did not think this way, and they did things that were very hard to respect. I have tried to be better than my own papa, but it is a heavy burden and I have felt very ashamed of my family at times. I did not want you to wonder if that blindness to the suffering of others could run in your veins. I hope you can understand, Tobias, or at least forgive."

"Of course I forgive you," Tobias said, a little bewildered, because that wasn't even a question. He already had. "You weren't wrong to think I might make a choice that was bad for me. Sullivan made a good point when we were talking about it before—I haven't always been honest with you about what I need and what I can handle. So it's partially my fault that you thought it was the right thing to do. I want to be more honest with you. I should've told you I didn't want to be a doctor, but I... I wanted you to be proud of me."

"I can be proud of you no matter what you do," his papa said. "It is about the kind of man you are, not the job you do. And I have never wondered about the goodness in your heart, Tobias. Lost you might have been, but never bad."

"This is good," Manman said, and pulled him back in. "We will do better, all of us."

He pressed his face against her shoulder and breathed, catching the scent of her rose cream and closing his eyes.

When they heard the stirrings upstairs of Tobias's siblings getting up for school, Manman glanced at the clock and climbed to her feet. "With that solved, it's time to get on with things, I suppose. You'll stay for breakfast, Sullivan." Talking to herself about what to prepare, she vanished into the kitchen. On school mornings they rarely got fancy, but Tobias strongly doubted his mother would allow a guest to eat Cheerios.

"And you'll eat every single bite she gives you, even if you don't like it," Tobias added under his breath, because you did not disrespect a Haitian woman's table and live to tell the tale.

"Why wouldn't I like it?" Sullivan whispered back, looking alarmed, and Tobias couldn't help teasing him by giving him an apologetic look, like they might be about to feed him insects or something, when Manman was probably making oatmeal.

Papa said, a bit tentatively, "So, have you given any thought to what you'd like to study?"

"A bit," Tobias hedged. Then, with studied casualness, he added, "Sullivan already made me look through the school's course catalog to see what I might be interested in. He doesn't waste time."

And that did exactly what he'd thought it would—his papa looked at Sullivan with new respect.

Parents could be so predictable.

Sullivan's house was quiet when they got back; only Raina remained, and she was reading an issue of *W* that she must've brought with her, because Tobias didn't remember seeing it before. She lowered the magazine and fixed Sullivan with a baleful stare.

"Not going to die?"

"Would it keep you from yelling at me if I was?" Sullivan asked hopefully.

"No."

He deflated and threw himself on the couch.

Tobias patted his uninjured shoulder sympathetically and asked Raina, "Ghost's gone then?"

"Left with your lawyer friend's retired old man, who now has the USB and says we're all to forget we saw it. There's a note for you."

"Oh, thank you." On the table, Tobias found an old utility bill still in its envelope. On the back of the envelope was a sketch of a stick figure stabbing another stick figure—this one with a mohawk drawn in jagged black lines—while a third figure with a backpack stood nearby, a speech bubble over its head that proclaimed *I AM A FILTHY HARLOT!*

Tobias grinned, the last of his tension dissipating. He left the bill on the table and took the envelope upstairs, the irritated drone of Raina's voice—going on about professional decorum and cost and profit or something—becoming wordless as he went. As far as good-bye notes went, Ghost's was hardly loquacious, but Tobias got the gist.

Shovel talk, indeed.

In Sullivan's room, Tobias took out his biochemistry textbook. The cover picture of a double helix against a blue background seemed both alien and innocuous to him now that he would never have to force himself to read another word within it. He reached behind it and pulled out the letter from his birth mother.

He stared at the two pieces of paper for a long time— two messages to him from difficult, potentially toxic people who nonetheless seemed intent on reaching out. Eventually he shrugged. The answer was the same it had always been; some things about him had changed, but others had not. The textbook went into the milk crate on

Sullivan's side of the bed in case he'd been serious about wanting to read it. Ghost's sketch went into Tobias's bag. The letter from his birth mother went into the trash can in the bathroom.

It had never been her that he wanted. Only the right to choose for himself.

He got out his phone and sent a thorough update to Church, letting him know that Ghost was off with the ex-cop and safe and sound for the time being. They texted for a while, catching up, and then Sullivan came in and sprawled on the bed.

"Ghost left a note?" Sullivan asked.

"Mmm-hmm. He says hi."

"I bet."

"How are you feeling?"

"Tired. My arm hurts. That stuff your dad gave me is wearing off, I think. Or maybe it was never enough in the first place. Either way, this sucks. Your friend is mean."

Tobias kicked his shoes off, wondering if he could coax Sullivan into taking a nap. "I'll pass the message along. Speaking of mean friends, Raina's gone?"

"Yes."

"She left you in one piece, at least. What's the verdict?"

"I'm back on subpoenas for lying and sleeping with a client, but I'm not fired because I solved an unsolvable case."

Tobias squinted, thinking it over. "Sounds fair. Could be worse."

"Really could be."

Tobias's phone buzzed, and he opened the text message from Church: I gotta go too, customers. But you're okay?

Tobias glanced at Sullivan, whose eyes were closed,

the muscles in his brow and jaw already beginning to slacken into sleep. Tobias smiled, feeling stupidly fond, and sent back: Yeah. I'm good.

# Epilogue

*Fourteen months later*

Tobias let himself in through the back door with his key and went through what he privately thought of as his home again process. He took off his shoes and undressed, opening the small cabinet so he could put his dirty clothes in the laundry basket and pull out a pair of black sweats that he kept on a shelf. Lastly, he buckled the black leather collar around his neck.

As he did, that small spot in his head that was always worrying, always wondering, always working, settled.

*Oh*, he'd thought, the first time he'd put it on. No words existed for that feeling, no description could suffice. It was just…*oh*.

He made his way toward the kitchen, careful about any debris that might stab him in his bare foot, but it seemed like the first floor could officially be termed done. It wouldn't be much longer, he knew, before Sullivan started to get that antsy look that meant he was chafing at the enclosed walls. A matter of weeks probably, before they started bugging Sullivan's sister Therese about a new place to live.

Church had asked him about it last time, suggesting that maybe Tobias should put his foot down if he was bothered by all the moving—three times in the past year—but it truly didn't bother him. Yes, they were forced to keep their belongings sparse so that moves wouldn't be stressful, but Tobias's anxiety about keeping his things neat tended to do better when he kept the clutter to a minimum anyway. Plus, when Therese had fully renovated the house Tobias had first stayed in with Sullivan—and which he still thought of as the Firetrap— he'd been surprisingly affected.

The house that had been in such ruins had been rebuilt, beauty and strength had been restored, and a family was set to be installed. It didn't feel like chaos so much as growing pains.

There was hope in that. He liked being a part of it.

"Hello," he called.

"Back here!"

Tobias wound through the family room and down the hall to the cramped kitchen and dining room, where Sullivan was sitting at the scarred table, laptop open in front of him. He lifted his head when Tobias walked in, eyes going, as always, to the collar first.

"I'm wondering," Sullivan said thoughtfully, "how you feel about romance in big moments."

Tobias's stomach rumbled and he turned toward the fridge. "Am I reiterating or is there a new development? Because if it's the first, the magic words are *Valentine's Day*. That should be enough reason to never do anything romantic for a big moment again."

That was an understatement. Tobias gave Sullivan a lot of points for trying, but the grease fire-catfish incident had ended in a two-hour wait at a nearby restaurant while they got increasingly snippy with each other because they were hangry. When they'd finally gotten some food in their bellies, they'd decided that pizza and a movie was a valid romantic strategy. They'd employed it countless times since then, and they never had to make a reservation.

Win-win.

"Valentine's Day is not a big moment." Sullivan sounded mystified by Tobias's example. "Valentine's Day is an illusion of grandiosity. I mean real moments."

"What moments?" Tobias shuffled some things in the fridge. He'd been planning to try out this new white wine sauce he'd seen in a magazine—

"The sort that come in boxes."

"Huh?" Tobias opened the crisper and pulled out mushrooms, only to turn and bump into Sullivan, who took the mushrooms out of his hands and put them back in the fridge. "What are you doing?"

"Pizza. It's already ordered. And I picked a movie. The one with the talking tree-thing you keep saying I should see. It's all set up."

"What did you do?"

"Well, this is an outrage," Sullivan said conversationally, mouth quirked with humor. "I've been very well-behaved. Not even a misdemeanor. Can't a young, innocent soul do something nice for his boyfriend?"

"Show me a young, innocent soul and I'll ask him." Tobias eyed Sullivan suspiciously. "Did you break something?"

"No."

"Oh! Did your loan come through?"

"Not yet, but the finance guy says it will, so I've started to think about some of the other important details in the meantime."

"Like?"

"Like I think I'm gonna call it Sullivan's Super-Legit Detective Agency.'"

Tobias snorted even as Sullivan grabbed him by his bare shoulders and turned him back toward the dining room. He stopped Tobias just inside the room, and dropped a kiss on the curve where his throat became his shoulder. "But this isn't about work. I wanted to talk to you about a thought I had."

Tobias's stomach abruptly filled with butterflies. It didn't get better when Sullivan nudged his jaw, directing his attention to a brown box on the table. It was a bit bigger than a men's watch box, and yeah, Tobias's whole body was vibrating with the whole nervous tension thing.

"A few weeks ago, you said something about hating leaving in the mornings, remember?" Sullivan asked, sounding a little like he was struggling with some nervous tension too. "You said it was about your collar."

The memory snapped into place. The comment had been the outcome of a truly horrendous series of events the day before. It'd been his first class session after being out with the flu and he'd been exhausted. He'd showed up for class to find that while he finished his half of a group project from his sickbed, his perfectly healthy partner hadn't.

Tobias was studying Human Services now, concentrating in nonprofit studies, planning to eventually use his skills to help smaller nonprofits that didn't have a lot of money figure out how to make their noble intentions self-sustaining. There was a lot of grant writing in his future. And he loved it, loved the classes and his work-study and his internship, but he'd spent the rest of that day not only catching up but helping his ass of a partner so they could get a passing grade.

Coughing, frustrated, and woozy, he'd come out of the library that night to find a voicemail from Sullivan that started with "Don't panic, because I'm fine," and ended with, "So the car is completely fucked but I'm really fine."

He'd held on long enough to rush home, where he found Sullivan bruised but cracking jokes about teenage drivers, and promptly lost his shit. There'd been kisses and cuddling and ice cream and *The Great British Baking Show*—Tobias was convinced that nothing bad could happen in the world while someone, somewhere, was watching that show—and sweet, easy sex that was mindful of Sullivan's incredibly minor injuries, and by the time he woke up in the morning, he'd been much more together.

Until it was time to leave the house and he needed to take his collar off.

His fingers had trembled and his stomach had been sick, and he'd almost been in tears at the idea of it, and Sullivan had had to unbuckle it for him. As soon as Sullivan had set it back on its shelf, all the fragilities from the day before had seemed to reawaken and he'd found himself turning to bury his face in Sullivan's shoulder.

"I'm okay," Sullivan had whispered over and over. "I'm not going anywhere."

Anyone was bound to be shaky when the person they loved most in the whole world had a near-miss like that, but Tobias knew it was counterproductive to his sanity to dwell, so he'd forced himself to put aside the close call. After a while, he forgot about it entirely.

Except for the ten seconds every morning when he removed his collar and hid it in a box.

"I remember," Tobias said now, and every muscle in his body went taut.

"I've been thinking," Sullivan said. As he spoke, his nimble fingers were working at the clasp at the back of Tobias's neck.

He was undoing Tobias's collar. It never came off when he was at home, never, not even in the shower—they had a special oil they put on it to keep the leather supple for that very reason, so it would never come off and now Sullivan was *removing* it, and Tobias clamped his hands down on the buckle, probably crushing Sullivan's fingers, and blurted, "Red."

Sullivan instantly stepped back, his hands pulling loose and falling away, eyes closing for a second in sudden understanding. "Shit, sorry, that's—this one's on me. Oh, fuck, I did this all wrong." Sullivan winced. "Can I touch you?"

Tobias nodded and Sullivan tugged him close. "I'm sorry," Sullivan murmured. "I'm not leaving, you're not leaving, we're good."

Tobias began to feel downright stupid around that point, because he knew that Sullivan wasn't leaving, he knew it in his bones, but his collar was just, it was *sacred*, okay—Sullivan said, "Let me show you what I got for you. Then you can tell me I'm an idiot and we can forget this happened and have pizza and guardians of the tree-things."

Sullivan held the box out to him, his eyes were questioning and hopeful, his teeth digging into his bottom lip.

"Open it."

Tobias took a breath and did, not sure what to expect. The box was too big for a ring, and Sullivan wasn't a ring person anyway, and while it might be the size of a man's watch, Tobias couldn't understand why a watch would mean he would need to take off his collar, so—

It was neither a ring nor a watch.

It was a wrist cuff.

The same expensive, plain black leather that his collar was made of, roughly three inches wide, with two small silver buckles that would hold it closed. There was nothing else to it—no skulls or rivets or elaborate engravings. It wasn't jewelry or decoration. It was a symbol of ownership. He couldn't breathe. It was perfect.

"This way you can take us with you wherever you go." Sullivan shifted his weight, his gaze flying back and forth between the cuff and Tobias's face, gauging his reaction. "Lots of guys wear these, so no one will think anything of it. You can wear it to school and work and you won't have to take it off when you leave the house. So I thought, instead of your collar—"

Tobias threw himself into Sullivan's arms, and Sullivan laughed against his cheek. Sullivan buckled it on, and they both studied it for a second, dark against the pale skin of Tobias's wrist. The constriction felt strange, bulky and obvious, but his collar had been like that at first too, and now it was as natural to him as a limb. This would be too, eventually, and in the meantime, the strange, palpable weight was glorious.

Sullivan bent his head and kissed the meaty pad of muscle at the base of his thumb. "It looks gorgeous on you."

"Thank you," Tobias said. "I love it."

"That's the idea." Sullivan lifted his eyebrows. "Is that...are we green?"

"Can I still wear my collar when we play?"

"You can wear it whenever you want. It doesn't have

to be one or the other, I guess. I just wanted you to have something you could take with you."

"Then we're green," Tobias agreed, and pressed up on both toes to kiss him.

A second later, the doorbell rang.

"Shit, hold that thought," Sullivan said. "Gotta get that before the pizza boy thinks he's being Punk'd."

Tobias looked down at the cuff, so innocuous in design. His family wouldn't second-guess it; neither would Sullivan's. Church and Ghost would suspect what it meant, but Tobias didn't mind that. Church didn't care about whatever Tobias got up to as long as he was happy, and these days Ghost was more likely to raise his eyebrow judgmentally than stab Sullivan. While Tobias couldn't guess whether that aversion to violence was the result of everything Ghost had been through in the past year or a slow-growing tolerance of Sullivan, either way, he wouldn't complain.

When Sullivan came back, it was with a large pie and a 2-liter of soda, and they settled on the couch to eat and watch the movie. Twenty minutes later, with the pizza cold and the movie completely forgotten, they'd moved to the bedroom, Sullivan was slicking his cock with lube, and Tobias was half-wrecked beneath him from trying not to come.

"You're in rough shape," Sullivan noted, amused, and Tobias didn't have the wherewithal to argue. Some days it was harder to hold on than others.

"Still better not come," Sullivan warned him, sliding between his thighs.

"Not gonna."

"You sure?"

Tobias shook his head, swallowing hard, his stomach clenching pleasantly at the low chuckle Sullivan gave.

"Better figure it out. If you come before I give you permission, I'll take a belt to your ass until you can't think."

For a split second Tobias craved the sharp, impossible fire of the belt, lusted for the crack of it against his skin. There were days when the idea of pain was unattractive to the point of being a turnoff, but there were other days, days like today when he wanted the pain more than he wanted the pleasure. He wanted it badly enough that he debated coming early just so Sullivan would do it.

He felt an instant flush of shame and guilt that he'd considered it, that he'd almost subverted the trust between them with manipulation to get what he wanted, and he glanced up, mouth opening to beg forgiveness and do as he should've done in the first place—explained what he felt.

But Sullivan's eyes were narrowed and keen, and Tobias didn't have to say anything after all.

"Later, if you want me to, I'll cane you until you beg me to stop," Sullivan said quietly. "You don't have to disobey to get what you need, sweetheart."

Tobias exhaled, both relieved and terrified, because the cane was so much better and worse than the belt, and he closed his eyes, nodding furiously. This, this was why he could give everything, could put Sullivan's needs first. Because Sullivan gave back, and so much more fittingly than Tobias could've dreamed was possible.

"Don't come until I say or I won't let you get off for a month," Sullivan warned, a far more effective threat of punishment, and sank into him.

Tobias threw his head back and held on for dear life.

\* \* \*

Later, as promised, Sullivan cuffed Tobias's wrists and ankles, and caned lines of agony into his skin and muscles until Tobias begged, and then he came with furious, painful jerks of his hips at a single stroke of Sullivan's hand. And later still, Sullivan rubbed lotion into the marks on Tobias's ass and thighs, soothing the burn with light, tender touches and soft, devoted kisses along the curve of his spine.

"That's my good boy," Sullivan whispered and Tobias smiled dozily at his leather cuff and felt hugely, impossibly loved. "You're so sweet for me. How's the pain?"

"Perfect," he murmured.

He surfaced slowly over the next hour, rolling so that he could slide a thigh over Sullivan's hip, and he was both wonderfully, delightfully sore, and thunderously, ridiculously content. They talked about school and work and the arcane, ordinary details of grocery shopping and laundry that made up a shared life, and gradually the conversation tapered toward sleep.

On Tobias's side, at least. Turned out Sullivan wasn't sleepy at all, because Tobias felt Sullivan take a deep breath before he murmured, *"Eske ou ta vle marye avèk mwen?"*

Tobias's head jerked up so fast it almost hurt.

Sullivan was pale, but his eyes were as steady as ever. He meant it. Not that Sullivan would ask Tobias *that* and not mean it, but it was…*Bondye*, this was really happening. There'd been a few dropped hints from Sullivan over the past six months that this might be their eventual destination, but Tobias hadn't given it too much thought. He knew where they stood, he knew how they loved. The collar and cuff told him everything he needed to know.

Turned out he'd been cavalier about how grateful he would feel when they got here.

"In *Kreyòl* no less," he managed.

Sullivan's lips twisted up into a self-conscious smile. "Mirlande helped me with my pronunciation."

"Remind me to thank her."

"Sure thing." Sullivan chuckled, laughing at Tobias probably, but he didn't care. He was dumbstruck, and when his brain stopped working, it fell back on the default, and as far as defaults went, manners wasn't a bad one. But it also meant that once he'd gotten the polite thing out of the way, he could only stare at this beautiful, whip-smart, sly man who was staring back with growing expectation.

Finally, Sullivan said, "Seriously? You're killing me here."

Tobias laughed, low and—he could be honest—a little damply. Right. It hadn't occurred to him that he would need to say the word—sometimes it felt like Sullivan was in his brain with him, like he knew what Tobias was thinking almost before he thought it—but for some things, words were priceless. "Yes."

Sullivan's grin was slow and wide and so very warm. "Yeah? You're saying yes?"

"Yes," Tobias whispered. "Of course, yes." He pushed Sullivan on his back and sprawled over him so they could kiss. Tobias couldn't breathe, couldn't imagine how this could possibly be his life. He kissed Sullivan again and again, eager, bruising kisses because he'd lost all semblance of propriety and all he could think was that this man was his, his to kiss and talk to and touch and laugh with and *have*, forever.

"You want a ring?" Sullivan asked.

"What do I need a ring for? I have a cuff."

"What am I supposed to wear?" Sullivan's grin was audible.

"We'll get you a cuff too."

"Oh, really?"

"You belong to me as much as I belong to you." Tobias twisted in Sullivan's arms so he could peer at his face. "Don't you?"

Sullivan's expression softened. "Oh, yeah, sweetheart. I'm all yours. Do with me as you will."

Tobias smiled and sank back down into his arms. "I think I'll start with making you the happiest man alive."

"Too late," Sullivan whispered, nosing at his ear. "Been that for a long while now."

"Can't be. I am."

Sullivan snorted. "We're so fucking sappy. It's embarrassing. I'm profoundly embarrassed on behalf of both of us. But I guess that's how engagement goes, yeah? Like, if you can't get sappy when you make a promise like this, when can you? Hey, you know what I read the other day? Apparently in the sixteenth and seventeenth centuries there were these interlocking engagement rings called Gimmal rings, and they would be worn separately during the engagement and then linked during the wedding. Kinda romantic, huh? And Gimmal rings likely led to the development of puzzle rings, which are cool, you'd like 'em…"

Sullivan rambled on, segueing from betrothal rings to diamond rings to the four Cs of diamond shopping, and Tobias closed his eyes and held on tightly, unwilling to miss a single word.

\* \* \* \* \*

*To purchase and read more books by Sidney Bell,
please visit Sidney's website here or at
www.sidneybell.com/read*

*Keep reading for an excerpt from
BAD JUDGMENT by Sidney Bell,
now available at all participating e-retailers.*

## *Author Note*

There's a long, problematic history of linking BDSM and trauma in popular culture. Dominants especially are often portrayed as aggressive, violent alpha-types who've had traumatic childhoods, which is frequently used to romanticize and excuse abusive behavior in the scene. For that reason, it was very important to me that Sullivan be a positive, healthy example of a dominant, someone who needs kink to be sexually fulfilled, but is also a decent, healthy, and normal guy who cares deeply about the well-being of his partner. Hopefully this last point is obvious, but when practiced correctly, BDSM is neither a cause nor a cure for trauma, and it should never be used to disguise manipulation, coercion, or abuse.

# *Acknowledgments*

Oh, boy. Lots of folks to thank. First, my primary beta readers—to Connie Peckman for being the person who disliked Tobias in my first, deeply flawed draft and said so, repeatedly and fervently, so I knew things needed to change. And to Sasha Gore, who liked this book even in its first, deeply flawed draft and said so, repeatedly and fervently, so I knew there was something worth salvaging. To my other betas as well, of course: Damon Talabock, Dylan Perkins, and Jill Robinson. You guys never fail to point out all the ways I'm sucking, and that's the best thing ever, really, no matter how it sounds.

Secondly, a massive thank-you to Shirleen Robinson, who not only made the book better, but also gave me excellent materials that'll help me make future books with characters of color stronger. Particularly amazing was that article by Roxane Gay about ambition in the African-American community, because it led me to *Hunger*, and that book is the best thing I've read this year. Also, Writing in the Margins is amazing, and anyone who wants to write about marginalized characters should know about that website. Finally, while they don't know I exist, the lovely, wonderful, excellent people who run the Tumblr blog Writing with Color helped my life enormously. They do important, incredibly beneficial work.

Special thanks to Dave Macrae for crucial security research yet again, because Ghost wasn't in nearly enough trouble until we talked, and a big finish can never have too much trouble. And super mondo thanks to Deborah Nemeth, Anne Scott, and Carina Press, because without you guys, this book seriously would've been a hot mess of ick, and it definitely would've had less dirty talk.

*Now Available from Carina Press and Sidney Bell*

*Embry was sure nothing but vengeance would
satisfy him—until Brogan offers him something
far more tempting.*

*Read on for an excerpt from
BAD JUDGMENT*

## Chapter One

"There are men you wouldn't mind dying for, Brogan," Timmerson said, his gaze distant, as if he were daydreaming about one of the good presidents. Lincoln, maybe. "Then there are men like Joel Henniton."

Brogan Smith sighed. He'd been working for Security Division for three years now and this was the first time he'd heard his boss—polite, reserved Pete Timmerson—willing to bad-mouth a client.

"By that you mean..."

Timmerson reluctantly admitted, "He's a dick."

"And I've worked with dicks before," Brogan said, resigning himself to another detail of annoying client behavior. Then he realized exactly what he'd said and added, "That's not how I should have phrased that. Sorry."

Timmerson's lips twitched. He was tall and dark-skinned, with ears that stuck out and a low, soothing voice that he put to good use calming down people on the verge of violence. He could make joining the circus seem rational, which might be why Brogan kept showing up for work even though he spent most of his time following around assholes. Predictably, Timmerson was using that voice now.

"Joel Henniton is the COO here at Touring Industries." Timmerson gestured to the room—and the building—at large. They were sitting in one of the tastefully appointed offices that Touring had set aside for Security Division's temporary use—large windows, expensive mahogany furniture, fresh-cut roses in a glass vase resting on top of the low bookcase that housed thick tomes of classic literature that no one would ever read. Beyond the closed door, Brogan could hear the bustle of his colleagues in the big conference room they used as a base of operations.

Timmerson continued, "Henniton's responsible for the day to day operation of the entire company, which manufactures armament. Mostly light arms for the military, until recently. Touring's trying to grow their customer base, but they're competing with defense contractors that've been around for decades and have way more money."

"So they're playing rough to catch up," Brogan inferred, and Timmerson nodded.

"Henniton's made some enemies in the process, and a few months ago, he received some death threats. That's when Oriole Touring—the CEO—contacted me. Technically, the company is the client, but the threats target Henniton alone, so he's the only one getting protection for now."

"Sounds straightforward," Brogan said, frowning. "On the surface, anyway."

"The problem is that Henniton's made very few concessions with his schedule and he refuses to call the cops."

Brogan's eyebrows flew up. "No cops? Oh, that's not suspicious at all."

"I've been told that they're working on a project that's

vulnerable to industrial espionage and they're unwilling to take the risk of leaks. We're a precautionary measure only, and Touring Industries expects this situation to resolve itself as the project progresses."

"I can't decide if that's naive or shady."

Timmerson's exhale seemed equally unsure. "Henniton's given me next to no information, so I can't even have my own investigators look into who's behind the threats. Henniton hit the roof when he realized I was having the standard background research done into the employees here to find likely suspects, so that got nipped in the bud. He wants to be safe *and* he wants his secrecy, which is making my life hell, as you can probably imagine."

"What about the CEO—Touring? He's going along with this?" Brogan asked, shifting to sit up straight without thinking about it.

"So far. There's been no violence and no signs that Henniton's being followed, which leaves me without a leg to stand on. So right now we're remaining vigilant while respecting his wishes. But that could change at any time, and I don't expect that Henniton will handle the shift with any aplomb."

"Ah. That's where I come in," Brogan said. "Okay."

"I trust your judgment, Brogan." Timmerson leaned forward, adding some heavy eye contact to his weighty tone of voice. Touring was a big client for Timmerson's company—there was a lot of money at stake, in addition to the lives of the men and women on the detail. "I know you won't let Henniton bully you into taking unnecessary risks. The fact that you won't punch him in the face for trying is also a plus."

Which explained why Brogan had been transferred from his post in Portland down to Salem.

The shift in location wasn't an inconvenience—since Security Division had offices in both cities, Brogan had bought a house in Woodburn, roughly halfway in between. He liked Salem more, anyway.

That didn't mean he was looking forward to the assignment. While the confidence his boss had in him was nice, Brogan couldn't help thinking it might be time to start throwing some tantrums just to get an easy case for once.

Without any intention of doing so, Brogan had gotten a reputation for being drama-free and hard to rattle. A deserved reputation, if he was honest—after the way he'd been raised and six years of military service, petty concerns about clients rolling their eyes at him or who drank the last of the coffee seemed awfully…well, petty. However, that usually stuck Brogan with the nightmarish clients. His boss really needed a better reward system.

"If they want everything done their way," Brogan asked, "why don't they have us train their current security staff in personal protection techniques? I mean, I saw plenty of armed guys on the drive in, and they aren't amateurs."

"I suggested that. Mr. Touring repeated that this situation is temporary. He doesn't feel it's necessary for the company to develop a permanent protection department."

"So…money."

"Money," Timmerson agreed.

"Makes sense, assuming he's right about that whole 'temporary' thing." Brogan lifted his eyebrows. "Is he right?"

"God, I hope so," Timmerson said heavily. "Henniton's only part of my headache. Ford's…well, he's his own brand of challenging."

"Who?"

"Henniton's executive assistant. I kind of like the guy, actually—he's exacting, and he's extremely good at his job. But Ford's also very sharp-tongued and he doesn't suffer fools. There have already been several altercations with Ark."

Brogan made a face. George Ark was not his favorite coworker—the guy was eighty percent ego, and a raving homophobe to boot. "What happened?"

Timmerson smirked—it wasn't an expression Brogan had ever seen him make before. "Let's just say Ford has a deft hand when it comes to criticism."

"Made Ark see stars, did he?" Brogan asked, trying not to sound like he wished he could've been there to see it.

Timmerson would never talk shit about employees, but he couldn't hide the twinkle in his eye as he said, "Ark will be taking over your old post in Portland."

Timmerson rummaged through a drawer. "Look, Henniton's going to treat you like furniture unless you annoy him. Ford, on the other hand, will notice every single thing you do. Neither one of them is easily appeased. Watch your step and don't take anything personally."

"Sure," Brogan said, resigned. Laid-back or not, he suspected he'd be spending the next few months trying not to punch people. Hell of a way to kick off the new year.

"I've got you scheduled as backup escort for this first week so you can get used to everything without having to take lead. You'll be shadowing Mario today, but this afternoon I want you to familiarize yourself with the layouts of both of Henniton's properties."

Timmerson handed Brogan a ring of keys and a thick sheaf of paper held together with a large binder clip. "Client packet. It's got the usual—addresses, floor plans, and what little info on Henniton's staff, family, friends, competitors, and suspects I was able to scrape together before he shut that down. The Touring NDA is a bit draconian—I'll give you a few minutes to read and sign it. Join us in the morning briefing next door when you're done. You can leave the form on the desk."

"Okay," Brogan said. Timmerson clapped a hand on his shoulder as he headed out, and then Brogan was alone. He took a minute to halfheartedly consider the pros and cons of getting a job at Best Buy or something, but as much as Brogan disliked drama, he loved his job—and the all-important feeling of being needed that he got when he did it well. He resigned himself to a few shitty months, and flipped back the cover of the packet to find a series of photographs of the client.

Joel Henniton was in his mid-forties, fit and good-looking in a slick, capped sort of way, but in most of the photos he was either glaring or wearing a sharp-toothed smile. With his golden tan, confrontational blue eyes, and red-blond hair, he looked like one of those pompous rich guys who lounged around country clubs playing tennis and bullying the wait staff. Not that Brogan had ever been to a country club.

Brogan turned the page and began reading about all the awful things Touring would do to him if he shared company secrets. It didn't faze him. Non-disclosure agreements were very common. Bodyguards saw a lot of shit that clients wouldn't want shared, and whether it was personal, embarrassing, or downright illegal, if it was covered by the NDA, it was one hundred percent confidential. Brogan signed it without thinking twice.

It was part of the job.

When the morning meeting broke, Brogan headed for the equipment cage. He swapped his personal firearm—a Colt 1911 A1, a .45 that he had a permit to carry concealed—for an M9 Beretta registered to Security Division. He preferred his own weapon, but if he had to shoot someone, it would make his life a lot easier if he was using one of Timmerson's. He knew the M9 from his time in the army, so it was no hardship. He grabbed an earpiece and radio, too. There was a button on the cord that could be toggled to activate the mic clipped to his lapel, allowing for constant hands free use, or so it only picked up what he said while he was pressing the switch.

He depressed the switch. "*Buenos dias*, Mario," he said, which was officially all the Spanish he knew.

"You're supposed to say 'testing,' idiot," Mario said into his own mic from across the room. Brogan was unconcerned by Mario's complaints. Their conversations often had an air of Mario playing the exasperated older brother, even though Brogan was only a year younger— something he rubbed in with pleasure now that Mario had hit thirty—but Brogan liked it. Brogan had spent his childhood raising his younger siblings, so it was nice having someone boss *him* around for a change.

Mario was a mixed bag of genetics. He said that if you went back far enough he had a relative from every country in Europe and more than a few in South America as well. He wasn't exactly handsome—his chin and cheeks were a little too round—but women loved him anyway.

Mario said it was because the blood of a thousand sexy conquistadors thundered through his veins. Brogan said it was because he looked like a chump.

They met at the elevator to head upstairs, bullshitting as they went. They'd been friends since his first day at Security Division, and they worked well together. Once on the twenty-first floor, they entered Henniton's personal reception area, a large alcove lined with small couches and low tables that gleamed from the attentions of some devoted janitor. Financial magazines were posed on a wooden rack in the corner, and an older woman sat typing behind a big desk. The night shift guys filled them in then took off, and Mario entered Henniton's office quietly.

With Mario inside, Brogan took up his position at the door. The basic gist of their protocol was that the primary—Mario today—would shadow Henniton. As backup, Brogan's duty was to ensure that nothing interfered with Mario's ability to keep bullets away from the client. He made sure the car wasn't tampered with, that their route was safe, that points of egress remained open, and he reviewed anyone who wanted access to Henniton in order to weed out trouble.

When the elevator dinged again, Brogan got ready to clear whoever stepped out, only to freeze in place when the doors opened.

The man who emerged was absolutely, excruciatingly *exquisite*.

For three entire seconds, Brogan couldn't breathe. If the stranger had pulled a weapon, he'd have had the hit no problem because Brogan was standing there staring like a complete fucking idiot, barely able to keep his mouth from dropping open in full advertisement of his own stupidity.

The stranger was in his early to mid-twenties, whippet-lean and graceful in a brutally tailored dark blue suit with a sharp vest and nearly obscene trousers that made his legs look ten miles long. Night-dark hair had been slicked into a conservative style and provided sharp contrast against pale, creamy skin. He had aristocratic features—high cheekbones, a slim, straight nose, a hard jaw and slashing brows that give him a somber, intent air—but his mouth, by contrast, was sweet, almost delicate.

Brogan's brain finally woke up, and he took a second glance at the stranger, this time searching for signs that he was a threat. He carried a brown leather briefcase in one hand, staring down while he thumbed the buttons on a smartphone with the other. There were no bulges in his clothing to suggest he was carrying, and there was nothing overtly menacing about him.

The receptionist paused in her typing to say, "Good morning, Mr. Ford."

"Suze," he said politely, looking up.

His eyes were big, black, and shrewd.

His gaze traveled to Brogan, cool to the point of disdain, and then he walked past him without hesitating.

Brogan fumbled to find his tongue. "Sir, if you could wait a moment."

"I'm on the list," Ford said without stopping.

"Yeah," Brogan said, turning to follow gracelessly. He recognized the name from the conversation with Timmerson, and the fact that the receptionist knew him was verification of his identity, although Brogan still needed to give Mario a heads up. He was just a few seconds behind, though, and those trousers were as perfectly cut in the rear as they were in the front. Frankly, Ford had an ass that made Brogan's mouth go dry all over again, because *fuck*—

Ford entered Henniton's office without knocking.

And Brogan stood there like a stupid bastard and let him.

"Everything clear?" Mario's voice sounded through his earpiece, the question vague enough, fortunately, that support wouldn't realize that Brogan fucked up.

"Uh, clear," he said, activating his mic.

"Copy."

It took him a good five seconds to recover.

"He *is* on the list, if that makes you feel better," the receptionist—Suze, apparently—said, hints of a smile curving her lips. "He's Mr. Henniton's executive assistant."

"Yeah," Brogan managed. He gave her a flustered shrug. "He's not gonna try to shoot Henniton, then."

"Less likely than most," she replied, the hint of a smile becoming a full grin. "And don't be too embarrassed. More than a few of the women have had that same reaction."

"Great," he said, shaking his head. Now he'd broken protocol and outed himself in the same thirty seconds. An auspicious start to the day.

Brogan sat back down and Suze resumed her typing, the *click-click* of her fingers on the keyboard disappearing into the background. He studied the hall, determined not to mess up again, angry with himself for mishandling a simple thing. Verifying identity and telling Mario that Ford was here, that was all he'd had to do.

Brogan had never been *that* guy. He didn't think with his cock, didn't let himself get distracted. He wasn't married to the rules or anything—he could improvise with the best of them, even preferred it at times—but he was a professional, for crying out loud. His brain had never stopped functioning just because something gorgeous walked by, and he'd be damned if he'd let it now.

Another issue was that Brogan wasn't out at work. His family and a couple friends, Mario included, knew he was gay, and he didn't live in the closet. He pulled at gay bars when he wanted to and he didn't do a damn thing to conceal who he was beyond keeping his mouth shut on the topic around his colleagues. It was one of the few things that Brogan actively disliked about his job—a hyper-masculine field like security wasn't even close to abandoning old-school bigotries about orientation, and while he doubted he'd be in danger if he were outed, he really didn't want the hassle.

All in all, he wasn't pleased with himself for how he'd reacted.

He had his game face on by the time lunch rolled around and he got his first look at Joel Henniton in person. The guy was six and a half feet of brawn with shoulders that could put a freight train in its place, and hands like mallets. He made Brogan feel small—something he wasn't used to—and towered over Ford, who was, unfortunately, every bit as impossibly beautiful as he'd been the first time he walked past.

As Timmerson had predicted, Henniton didn't deign to notice Brogan.

Brogan held the elevator doors for the others, ensuring that he and Mario stood in front for the ride down, and he ignored the quick once-over of concern that Mario threw his way.

Henniton said, "I don't like Neeley for this. He's disloyal. He'll turn on us as quickly as he'll turn on them."

"It'll be free market information in less than six hours," Ford replied. "If we don't go with Neeley, we'll lose our head start while we search for another source."

Brogan listened with half an ear. Most of his attention was on his radio, where he'd hear about any trouble that might meet them beyond the elevator doors when they got to the lobby. Henniton considered Ford's words then said, "Okay. Call him."

"All right. Now, about facilities management. We need a new director. I'm not working with that idiot anymore." Ford's voice was pleasantly deep—not that Brogan cared—but his words were astringent.

"You put up with him for longer than I expected," Henniton said. Given what he'd heard about Henniton, Brogan half expected fireworks. The tone didn't seem to offend the man, though. If anything, he sounded amused. "Fire him, then. Although I'd like to point out that I'm supposed to be the cutthroat one, Embry."

"Thank you," Ford said.

The elevator stopped on the fourteenth floor, but Mario told the woman waiting there to catch the next one.

When they were on their way again, Ford said, "We should promote Kensing to the position."

"Which one is he?"

"*She* is the one who argued for the new plumbing system in buildings ten through sixteen last year."

"That cost a fortune, didn't it?" Henniton mused.

"$26,755." Ford rattled off the figure like recalling numbers from a year ago was nothing.

"Too much," Henniton said.

"Not compared to the fortune it would have cost us if we hadn't done it. The great flood of last winter, remember?"

"Oh, that. God, what a nightmare," Henniton said. He heaved a melodramatic sigh.

"She's my choice, and she'll leave if we try an outside hire. Promote her."

"Fine," Henniton said.

Ford made a satisfied noise and typed something into his smartphone.

It appeared Joel Henniton allowed his executive assistant—someone who didn't look old enough to rent a car—to dictate a surprising number of his business decisions. At least Ford seemed viciously competent so far.

The elevator doors opened on the ground floor and Brogan and Mario exited into the busy lobby first, surveying the area as Henniton stepped out behind them. The atrium rose several stories high and people on upper floors could look over the railings all the way to the lobby. The south wall, where the main doors were set, was entirely glass-fronted, letting plenty of gray January overcast in, and the lush greenery, mahogany reception desk and leather couches extended a quiet elegance to visitors.

Gorgeous, but a security nightmare. Too many lines of sight, too much space and cover. Brogan's skin crawled.

"I'll be back at one," Henniton told Ford. "And don't forget, we've got the evening meeting tonight."

Brogan, in the midst of sweeping his gaze around the lobby, caught the quiet nod Ford gave Henniton.

Then Henniton was striding away, Mario at his side, and Brogan only got one last glimpse of dark, cool eyes and a lovely, unsmiling mouth before Ford vanished into the crush of people bustling through the lobby.

*Stop looking at him, asshole*, Brogan told himself. *And get focused before you get yourself killed.*

*Don't miss*
*BAD JUDGMENT by Sidney Bell.*
*Available now wherever*
*Carina Press ebooks are sold.*
*www.CarinaPress.com*
*www.sidneybell.com*

Copyright © 2016 by Sidney Bell

## *About the Author*

Sidney Bell lives in scraggly Southern Colorado with her amazingly supportive husband. She received her MFA degree in Creative Writing, considered aiming for the Great American Novel, and then promptly started writing fanfiction instead. More realistic grownups eventually convinced her to try writing something more fiscally responsible, though, which is how we ended up here. When she's not writing, she's playing violent video games, yelling at the television during hockey games, or supporting her local library by turning books in late. Visit her online at www.sidneybell.com.